the ways of the dead

neely tucker

penguin books

PENGUIN BOOKS
Published by the Penguin Group
Penguin Group (USA) LLC
375 Hudson Street
New York, New York 10014

USA | Canada | UK | Ireland | Australia | New Zealand | India | South Africa | China
penguin.com
A Penguin Random House Company

First published in the United States of America by Viking Penguin,
a member of Penguin Group (USA) LLC, 2014
Published in Penguin Books 2015

THE LIBRARY OF CONGRESS HAS CATALOGED THE HARDCOVER EDITION AS FOLLOWS:
Tucker, Neely.
The ways of the dead : a novel / Neely Tucker.
pages cm
ISBN 978-0-670-01658-7 (hc.)
ISBN 978-0-14-312734-5 (pbk.)
1. Journalists—Washington (DC)—Fiction. 2. Teenagers—Crimes against—Fiction. 3. African American youth—Washington (D.C.)—Fiction. 4. Murder—Investigation—Fiction. 5. Washington (DC)—Fiction. I. Title.
PS3620.U318W39 2014
813'.6—dc23 2013047847

Printed in the United States of America
10 9 8 7 6 5 4 3 2 1

Praise for *The Ways of the Dead*

"An utterly thrilling mystery set in Washington, D.C., in the late 1990s, just before the Internet and the rise of smartphones changed the landscape of print journalism. . . . Meticulously plotted, fast-paced . . . Every character is fully fleshed out and the dialogue is pitch perfect. . . . For mystery and crime fiction lovers, particularly fans of Elmore Leonard, to whom Tucker dedicates his book, this is a must-read." —Associated Press

"Tucker may be a first-time novelist, but as a career writer, he is well ahead of many of his peers, and this book is worthy of Elmore Leonard's legacy. . . . With equal ear for newsroom patter and street slang, Tucker has presented an exciting first novel that echoes the best writing of Pete Hamill and George Pelecanos, mixed with a bit of *The Wire* and *True Detective*."
—*The Miami Herald*

"Gritty and masterful . . . A mystery that will leave readers waiting for the next in the series." —*Washingtonian*

"Setting his tale in the 1990s . . . gives Tucker the chance to show how much newspapers have changed. The twenty-four-hour Internet news cycle hasn't yet taken root, tomorrow's front page is still more important than getting the story online immediately, and good reporters are dependent on door knocks, land lines, and library research rather than e-mail, cellphones, and Google. Tucker pulls off a neat, double-twist ending. . . . There's a lot to like in Tucker's storytelling." —*The Washington Post*

"A tense and gripping crime novel of race and power, but its true magic lies in the dialogue, which is textured and nuanced in the manner of Elmore Leonard, James Crumley, or George Pelecanos. This is a very fine debut indeed, and one that begs for sequel after sequel." —*BookPage*

"With a very powerful beginning and very shocking end, this debut novel is a great read that shows suspense/thriller lovers that they do, most definitely, have a new series to fall in love with." —*Suspense Magazine*

"Tucker creates a story that brings in race and economic advantage and disadvantage. . . . His unusual and obviously informed take on journalism makes this an interesting and compelling read." —*Mystery Scene*

"Tucker . . . weaves observations on race, class, crime, and the declining fortunes of newspapers into a novel that has won praise from Michael Connelly and John Sanford." —*The Cleveland Plain Dealer*

"With a well-crafted plot marked by twists, turns, and surprises, Tucker, a *Washington Post* reporter, sets his murder mystery in the grittier precincts of the nation's capital in the late 1990s." —*Washington City Paper*

"Tucker, a writer of power and grace, gives great life to the newspaper milieu and he's just as resourceful in shaping the story of an apparent serial killer in inner city Washington. It's done up in a plot full of curve balls, shocks and surprises that we readers never see coming." —*Toronto Star*

"Crisp, crafty, and sharply observed . . . Rich yet taut description, edgy storytelling, rock-and-rolling dialogue, and a deeply flawed but compelling hero add up to a luminous first novel." —*Kirkus Reviews* (starred review)

"Journalist-novelist Tucker has crafted an addictive, twisty, debut, proving that crimes involving politics and sex can still surprise and thrill us. The slightly detached and cynical air will resonate with George Pelecanos readers and yet there's a whiff of Elmore Leonard, too."

—*Library Journal* (starred review)

"With the emphasis on gritty urban life in a city rife with racism and blight, [*The Ways of the Dead*] evokes the Washington, D.C., of George Pelecanos. This riveting debut novel should spawn a terrific series."

—*Booklist* (starred review)

"[An] exciting fiction debut . . . The brisk plot is punctuated by an insightful view of journalism and manipulative editors, shady politicians, and apathetic cops, while also showing residents working to create a better neighborhood. Readers will be pleased that Tucker leaves room for a sequel." —*Publishers Weekly*

"*The Ways of the Dead* is a great read. Deep characters, pitch perfect dialogue, and a plot with as many curves as the Rock Creek Parkway as it moves through the side of Washington, D.C., far away from the Smithsonian. Neely Tucker takes this novel up an even further notch with a story framed around the hot-button issues of our time, including race, justice, and the media. If this is Tucker's first novel, I can't wait for what's coming next."
—Michael Connelly, # 1 *New York Times* bestselling author of *The Gods of Guilt*

"From the powerful opening to the shocking finale, *The Ways of the Dead* delivers the very best in gritty, hard-edged suspense. Complex characters, taut dialogue, and a riveting plot all add up to one extremely excellent novel."
—Lisa Gardner, # 1 *New York Times* bestselling author of *Fear Nothing*

"Tough, exciting, always intelligent, Neely Tucker's *The Ways of the Dead* captures the multilayered corruption and cynicism—and the edge-of-the-ledge danger—of a hard-nosed former war reporter digging out a serial killer in the backstreets of Washington, D.C."
—John Sandford, # 1 *New York Times* bestselling author of *Field of Prey*

"In a textured, wholly believable Washington, D.C., simultaneously near and far from the corridors of power, Neely Tucker, in his accomplished mystery debut, has created a gripping tale of secrets and lies, malice and mayhem . . . and very dead young women."
—Otto Penzler, coeditor of *The Best American Noir of the Century*

"*The Ways of the Dead* has everything you'd want from a book noir—enveloping atmosphere, flavorful characters, evocative writing, and a serpentine plot which seems to make the pages turn themselves. Neely Tucker is an impressive new talent."
—Richard North Patterson, # 1 *New York Times* bestselling author of *Loss of Innocence*

ABOUT THE AUTHOR

Neely Tucker is the author of two Sully Carter novels, *Murder D.C.* and *The Ways of the Dead*, and the memoir *Love in the Driest Season*, which was named one of the Best 25 Books of the Year by *Publishers Weekly*. Currently a staff writer at *The Washington Post* Sunday magazine, Tucker lives with his family in Maryland.

pour joséphine

laisse les bons temps rouler, chèr.

and

for elmore leonard,

the best there ever was.

The evil that men do lives after them.

—William Shakespeare, *Julius Caesar*

The women that were up there, they were living in the margins of life, they were with multiple people, they weren't really missed right away, even by their own loved ones.

—D.C. homicide detective Danny Whalen,
lead investigator on the Princeton Place murders

the ways of the dead

one

The first long shadows were falling across Georgia Avenue when Sarah Reese trotted down the steps to the lobby after her dance class, a big, loose jacket pulled over her tights. She didn't have long. Her mother was always a few minutes late, always dragging out happy hour drinks with her girlfriends downtown, but it wasn't as if she had an hour to burn.

She stepped onto the sidewalk outside the studio and felt the light breeze ruffle her hair. She looked both ways across the four lanes of traffic, making sure she didn't see her mother's green Land Rover idling or approaching. She bit the inside of her lower lip, felt the small roll of bills in her left hand, and then jogged across the street at an angle.

It was the first day of October, three months before the end of the twentieth century. The leaves were turning their flaming colors of yellow and amber and red and burnt orange. The colors were lush at this early stage of fall, and the air through the trees, just off the Chesapeake, carried the traces of an autumn chill. Sarah felt it as a quickening coolness, the sweat drying against her spine, her thighs, turning her forearms to gooseflesh. It was Friday night, the sky arching from black in the east to indigo blue overhead to a blaze of orange and pink on the western horizon. She would meet Michael later, after her parents had gone to bed. She shivered at the thought of it—she couldn't help it, her eyes sparkled—and she crossed the last lane of the street into the tiny parking lot of Doyle's Market. It was an old brick building with peeling blue paint and a sagging roof. The little silver bells at the top of the glass front door *cling-cling*ed when she pushed it open.

The interior was dim. She had to slow down to let her eyes adjust, turning right down the first aisle, toward the refrigerated units at the back of the store. The aisles were narrow and creepy. The place was no bigger than a little row house, which it had once been. The shelves were overstuffed with paper towels and canned vegetables and little sausages in cans and things too nasty to touch. It reminded her of a haunted house, the dim pallor, the yellowed linoleum floors, the smell of stale cigarette smoke and unwashed laundry and spilled beer and, on top of it all, a smear of disinfectant. The older girls had told her about Doyle's after class last spring, when she'd first started at Regina's studio, how the little old lady with the big hair behind the counter would sell you cigarettes or a beer and never ask a "motherfucking thing," as Letitia put it. The excursion made Sarah feel older than fifteen. It revved her up to do something her parents didn't know about.

She got a bottle of vitamin water. Then she turned and navigated down the middle aisle to get gum. She would get the Virginia Slims and the condoms at the counter. The older girls had been right. Granny would sell you crank if it came with a price tag.

Sarah was bent down looking for the gum—mint, sugarless—when she heard the door open and the little bells *cling-cling* again. Loud male voices, laughter, profanity, bursting with accents that telegraphed into her ear as *danger bad ghetto black*. She looked up. Three boys coming down her aisle, wifebeater T-shirts untucked. One dribbling a basketball, *baddabaddabapbap*. The one in front, a wide, expressive face, his hair cropped close to the scalp, stopped.

"Whoo y'all lookit. Miss Dance America." He looked Sarah in the eye and pushed backward two steps, the boys behind him peeping over his shoulder. His jeans were slung low on narrow hips. Boxer shorts bunched above the waistline. She froze, her eyes locked on his. Then she lowered her gaze and bolted past them. She could smell the sweat, the beer, the energy, a tang at the tip of her nose.

She went to the counter and realized she had not gotten the gum. The boys were walking up behind her, loud, dribbling, dribbling, dripping fat ugly drops of testosterone onto the linoleum—she could all but smell that, too. She didn't turn around. Screw the gum and fuck the smokes. Michael could wrap his own rascal. She wanted out of there. She pulled out her wallet and got two ones, pushing them across the counter for the water, jamming the wallet back in her jacket.

Dolly Parton made change and handed it back to her. As Sarah reached for the coins, one of the boys jostled her. He bumped against her butt. Her hand sprang open from the surprise of it and her change fell out, bounced on the counter, and spilled to the floor. More laughter. A quarter spun around like a top on the linoleum.

"Blondie tossing cash, y'all." This from the boy who had bumped her behind.

"Check that ass," a different one, a whisper. "White girl got a little something." *Sumpen.*

"She gonna bend over."

"I'ma smack it." Snickering.

"Smack that booty?"

"And the booty go smack."

Low fives, they were killing each other.

Sarah considered running out the door but stopped herself. Three obnoxious boys. *Boys.* She wasn't going to act like a scared little rabbit.

She let out a breath, trying to slow down. She felt her weight shift backward and she went down in a single motion, bending her right leg back and down, keeping her arms near her sides until her right toe bent back and her right knee glided to a stop on the floor. The quarter she picked up with her left hand. Her right picked up one dime by the bottom rack. She found the other dime a few inches out in the aisle. They were both heads up. She was noticing everything. Then she pressed back on her right toe and down on her left foot and felt her body rise in a straight line. As she rose, she failed to notice that her wallet was so far out of her jacket pocket that the boy behind her, the one who had talked nasty, reached forward and gently pulled it out in a smooth, single motion.

"You got all your change, honey?"

Sarah looked up and it was Dolly Parton behind the counter, sounding like a train whistle in the dark. Her soft face was smudged with mascara and lipstick. There was a twinkle of fear behind her reading glasses. Sarah saw it, a spiky glimmer in the beady little pupils that was not supposed to be there. She wondered if Dolly could call 911.

"Got all of it?" Dolly repeated, sounding as if she were hooting from the outhouse, looking down at her, and now her potato face seemed to smile and Sarah wasn't so sure if she saw the fear there or not.

Sarah nodded quickly, yes yes yes, ponytail bouncing, and she turned to the left to leave, her hair snapping sideways. She heard the boy behind her mutter, "Out front. Get the bitch when she out front." One of the boys moved to the front door ahead of her, and there was a burst of noise, an exclamation from the other one, but she was too frightened to hear what it was. She took a half step toward the front of the store, mute, going numb, but then she looked to the rear of the store.

There were double metal doors marked EXIT.

She all but sprinted for them, pushing both doors open, ready to start running, but she was in a dark storage room and there was yet another door with an exit sign tacked to it. There was another tattered sign that read ALARM WILL SOUND.

She stopped. Fuckfuckfuck. She blinked. The storage room was dark and narrow and there were rows of boxes stacked nearly to the ceiling, left and right. She turned around and could see the front part of the store through the swinging double doors she had just pushed through.

Options, a nice word, came to the front of her mind. She could go out the exit door behind her and see where that went, but the alarm would sound and the police would come and she wasn't going to do that. She could march back out front, past the boy who had bumped against her, and see what they had planned on the street out front.

That wasn't going to happen, either.

No, she'd just call her mom from right here. Mom would be pissed and there would be a scene but she would know what to do. Sarah reached in her jacket for the Nokia and there was nothing. Her eyes flew open and she looked down, digging in the pockets, trying to turn the fabric inside out—nothing, no phone and no wallet. She patted her thighs, checking the pockets there, but she was wearing tights and there were no pockets. It dawned on her, in an ugly flash of memory, that she'd left the phone in her backpack at the studio. She smacked her thighs, twice and then three times, trying to make the pocket and the phone appear. She felt her shoulders start to shake and snot begin to bubble out of her nose.

The exit door behind her swung open, but the alarm didn't sound. She turned, the shadows deepened, and then Sarah Reese dropped her change again.

two

Sully Carter, on his third Basil Hayden's (on the rocks, water back), felt the October air blow into the bar through an open window near his booth. He closed his eyes for a second, it felt that good, like a kiss from home.

His white linen shirt, freshly pressed at the beginning of the day, was wrinkled and untucked from his jeans. The sleeves were rolled up at the cuffs and he had not bothered with the razor, it being a Friday. He was sitting in the back corner of Stoney's, the Ducati racing jacket slung over the seat on the booth, the helmet beneath it. He felt good enough to punch somebody.

He rattled the ice in his glass, sipped, and felt the slight and lovely sting of bourbon on the tip of the tongue. Sneaking another glance at the bar, he caught a glimpse of Dusty, still working, taking orders next to Dmitri, the other bartender, the guy from the Ukraine. She didn't see him look this time, but she had earlier, so maybe that could count as flirting or foreplay or something.

Lean as a light pole, Sully spoke in a slight rasp, a trace of a Louisiana accent, more centered on the Irish-German sections of Nawlins, but it took an ear. He was taller than most people, but because he tended to lean back on his left leg it wasn't always apparent. The shrapnel blast he had taken while covering the Bosnian war, the hot metal that had eaten up his right knee, broken three ribs, and sliced open his left cheek—that bitch had tattooed its signature across his face and torso, too.

There were horizontal scars down his cheek, with tiny little welts around both eyes. There was a long, horizontal scar at the top of his forehead, but it was mostly concealed by the shock of black hair that fell slightly over it. He had twin scars that ran down his right side like a short set of railroad tracks, and the skin on his right knee looked like it had been put together by Dalí during a hangover.

The unusual gait, the scars, the posture, the distant manner—it all combined to create a menacing air of someone who cared less about his future than the people around him cared about theirs.

Stoney's, his favorite dive, sat four blocks from the courthouse, three from the Metropolitan Police Department headquarters, and five from the U.S. Attorney's Office. It catered to cops and prosecutors and assorted stiffs of the downtown proletarian set. It had worn hardwood floors, a mirror behind the bar that had lost most of its silvering, and an air that the smart set drank somewhere else.

Now he looked back across the booth at his dinner partner, Eva Harris, in Homicide for eight years, fifteen in the Agency.

"So why didn't the—the jury—I mean, why didn't they convict him for killing Fat Chucky?" he said.

"Self-defense," she said.

"Self-defense from what?"

"Self-defense from Fat Chucky. Fat Chucky went six-one and three-twenty. Mr. Hastings testified that Chucky wanted to make him be 'sexually submissive.'"

"At ten in the morning? On the general compound of D.C. jail?"

"That was the testimony."

"How did Mr. Hastings defend himself?"

"With a ten-pound barbell from the weight-lifting thing."

"Beat Chucky to death?"

"Beat him to death."

"Mr. Hastings," Sully said, "must not like to be sexually submissive."

"Submissive, my ass. Chucky owed money. Sly Hastings beat the man's skull open in front of a hundred and twenty-five witnesses and walked because everybody on the general compound knows better than to testify against him."

"And how did Sly Hastings come to be in D.C. jail?"

"Weapons charge. This is, what, five, six years ago? He was awaiting trial."

"And?"

"Beat that, too."

"I'm detecting a pattern, counselor."

"Yeah. There is. Mr. Hastings offs people and gets away with it," Eva said, a little heat now. "He looks like a bookworm. Wears those little round John Lennon glasses, did you know that? Read Jean Toomer during the last trial. *Cane*. Fucker made notes in the margins."

"You denying the man an interest in the Harlem Renaissance?"

"Your neighborhood don doesn't usually have literary tastes more sophisticated than *Penthouse Letters*."

"You sure this is his occupation? Because, what are we talking here—three trials, two hung juries, one acquittal? I don't want to go wading in on a piece about a Teflon defendant if the dude is, what do I want to say, small time."

"Then don't."

"But you—you think he's a badass."

"I don't *think* anything. I'm *telling* you. Sly Hastings runs things. He runs things because he gets rid of people who get in the way of him running things, and then he skates on it."

"You got hard feelings on the Fat Chucky thing," he said.

She put a hand to her short dreadlocks pulled back into a ponytail, touched her wineglass, and then set her hand back on the table. Eva, she would look at you for five seconds before saying anything, and then burst out, *rat-a-tat-tat*. She had grown up in West Virginia, went to Georgetown Law, and had no accent from anywhere unless she wanted to. When she did want to, it leaned more to city than country, Sully thought, her saying things like "he left out the house" and "my decedent."

Sully ate a French fry. He liked Eva. She was one of the few people in the courthouse he allowed himself to address by first name. He had done so since shortly after he came back, blown up and fucked up, from Bosnia. He looked at her now, sitting back in her booth, that saddle of freckles across the bridge of her nose. She was looking to the front of the bar, as if she recognized a cop coming in. On the plate in front of her was half a grilled cheese she had not touched in fifteen minutes.

He reached across the table, picked it up, took a bite, and there was a buzzing noise. Eva looked down at her right hip, lifted her pager, and said, "It's not me."

Sully rolled his eyes, still chewing, and opened his backpack. He pulled out the chunky little cellphone. The screen was illuminated and the unit vibrated. He looked at the numbers that came up on the screen and his eyebrows furrowed. "They give me this thing this summer," he said. "It's supposed to be like a perk. What it is? It's like one of those electronic tether anklets they put on parolees. It's a way for the bosses to find you."

He extended a finger and punched the little green handset sign to open the line, then put it to his ear.

"R.J., brother. It's Friday night. What?"

The low baritone burst into his ear, aural shrapnel that made him tilt his head away from the phone.

"Waitwaitwaitwait. Just wait. Is—is Chris sure? I mean, come *on*. That don't even make—" Sully looked down at his watch. It was nearly eight. "You want Chris to write it, why are we talking?" He motioned to Eva for a pen, a fetching motion with the fingers of his left hand. She pulled one from her purse and Sully scribbled an address on a cocktail napkin. He said yes and yes and then fuck and clicked it off.

He set the phone down on the table and gave Eva her pen and drained the whiskey. He put his fist against his mouth to stifle a cough. He pulled three twenties from his wallet and dropped them on the table.

"Somebody just killed David Reese's daughter," he said, coughing now. "Tossed the body, a dumpster up on Georgia." He looked at his napkin. "The 3700? Right around the intersection with, what's that gonna be, New Jersey?"

Eva blinked once but did not otherwise move, the same inscrutable expression he'd seen her use in court, the judge allows an objection, her face, the mouth in a line, she'd just say to the air, to God, to the witness, *So then you just didn't see anything after the gun went off* . . .

"I thought Reese lived out to McLean," she said.

"He does. Maybe the girl—" He looked down at the napkin. "Sarah, it's Sarah, was just dumped there. If this shit ain't right and Chris is, what, peeing in his pants and getting R.J. worked up—I mean, you piss off the brass and—"

The cell buzzed again and he looked down. "Goddammit. He's outside already. Chris. R.J. sent him over here to pick me up. Said he figures my blood alcohol is over the limit for the bike but not to file."

"Isn't R.J. your editor?"

"At last report."

"And he doesn't care if you're half lit?"

"Anybody who can't file drunk," Sully said, "oughta turn in their fucking press card."

He grabbed his cycle gear and pushed himself out of the booth, Eva following. Sully pushed through the light crowd, the drinkers at the bar, making for the front door, Eva a step behind. The light seemed to him uneven, the voices too loud, the energy he felt a few moments ago dissipating, switching gears. He did not see Dusty behind the bar, just Dmitri, and then they were outside, the sky giving up the last bit of light. He felt the cool evening air as a tactile sensation, as if a butterfly landed on his forearm and sat there, wings beating.

"What kind of death wish do you have to have," he asked Eva, giving her a distracted peck on the cheek before walking to Chris Hunter's car idling at the curb, "to kill the daughter of the chief judge of the federal court at the foot of Capitol Hill?"

three

Sully flung open the passenger door of Chris's beater, a nine-year-old Honda CRX, shoving notebooks and a camera and a stack of newspapers from the seat onto the floorboard. He slung the jacket and the helmet to the back and tumbled into the front seat.

Chris, pudgy faced, fat little fingers on the steering wheel, pulled out hard, jerking Sully backward into the seat and, by force of forward motion, slamming the door shut behind him.

"She's already dead, bubba," Sully said, wondering whether the vowels were slurred.

"Dead*line,*" Chris shot back, shifting into third. "Reese is supposed to be the next nominee to the Supreme Court. This is *monster.*"

Sully stifled a snort. The youth, the enthusiasm. He looked down and there were wrappers of fast-food sandwiches and paper cups. He burped. The backseat had three cardboard boxes and a mound of clothes on the floor.

"I see you've started your sophomore year," he said.

"Just moved to a new place," the younger man said, not taking his eyes off the road but sensing the look-around.

"When was that?"

"June."

Chris took them up through the few ragged blocks of Chinatown on Seventh, crossed Massachusetts Avenue, and headed north on Georgia. The austere beauty of Federal Washington faded into a charmless strip of storefronts and row houses with window units sagging out of their upstairs windows. Black iron bars covered the street-front doors and plate-glass windows. Men stood or sat by open doorways, beer cans and cigarettes in their hands, the fresh evening drawing them out. Sully let his window down and let the air rush in.

After a while, he said, "It's October, ace."

Chris, leaning forward, ignoring the jibe, both hands on the wheel, was going on about the way he'd gotten the call from a beat cop almost an hour earlier. He seemed impressed the officer had thought to call him, an honest-to-god tip on something big. He was talking rapidly and his eyes were darting back and forth. Sully kept his mouth zipped.

A few minutes later, traffic stalled. Sully leaned out the window. Georgia was blocked off up ahead, the revolving lights of the police squad cars and fire trucks marking the edge of the crime scene barricade.

Chris cut the wheel hard to the left to make the turn onto Park Road, three blocks short of their destination. He went up to an alley, turned right, and then pulled into the parking lot of a bank and Giant Liquors, the letters on the sign in banana-yellow neon. He was turning off the ignition when his cell rang.

"Hey, man. I'm here, parking. Where are you? Yeah. The where? I can go with that?" He listened again. "Okay. Yeah, yeah, right. Just as a basis of knowledge. Not attributing to you."

He hung up after a moment.

"Sorry. My buddy. Gives us official confirmation on one Sarah Emily Reese, DOB February 14, 1984. Parents notified and are here. In the chief's car at the moment, inside the cordon. FBI is here, so are the U.S. Marshals. Secret Service. D.C. cops. The mayor. It's a cluster-fuck. The kid was at a dance class or something. My guy says it's on the west side of Georgia. Apparently Sarah went to get a soda at the store catty-corner across the street. Ran out the back. Found in the dumpster in an alley behind the store. Body's already been removed."

Sully wrote it all down.

"Why was she taking classes here and not in some tony studio out in Potomac?"

"The owner, what, Regina something or other, used to be a dancer in Alvin Ailey in New York."

"Why'd she run out the back?"

"I don't know."

"That would seem to be the question we would want to know."

They got out of the car and walked down to the commercial strip of Georgia, then up the sidewalk, Sully twisting his shoulders to get through the mass of bodies, the crowd stalling and spreading out against the yellow tape.

Three squad cars were blocking off Georgia northbound at the intersection of Otis Place. Sully could see a knot of uniformed officers outside a building on the west side of Georgia, which he presumed to be the dance studio. There was another knot on the far side of the street, in front of Doyle's Market.

They were on the south side of the scene and the police barricade was keeping the crowd a block away from the store where the girl had been killed. Sully guessed they would also be blocking the north approach from the same distance. If the east and west approaches were also blocked off like that, the perimeter would be four city blocks. He wrote that down in his notebook, too. The wide swath of roped-off real estate told him MPD was clueless and was casting a wide net.

He inhaled deeply, trying to get a read on the scene, trying to figure if Dusty would be pissed about his unannounced departure, trying to shake the whiskey out of his head.

He looked to his right, up the slight incline onto Otis, and could see the Park View Recreation Center at the end of the block. The name Lana Escobar floated into his mind. That was last summer, the last time he'd written about the neighborhood. She was a working girl whose body had been found on the outfield grass of the complex's baseball field. The police had scarcely bothered to block off the outfield. There had been no gawking crowd. It had been raining and the police tape had sagged to the ground. The mud beneath his feet, the techs lifting her into the body bag, the sound of the rain spattering on the hard plastic, Jesus.

"So how are we doing this?"

It was Chris at his elbow, the kid looping a lanyard with his photo ID badge around his neck. He had his mini-recorder and a small notebook in one hand. He looked like a fat puppy, ready to chase a tennis ball. Chris was beginning to annoy the shit out of him, and when he was annoyed and drunk he tended to be unpleasant. So the people in the Employee Assistance Program had told him. The little fuckers.

"You want to do the street, since you know people up here," Chris panted, "and I'll do the cops?"

Sully patted his pockets. He had his ID. Fabulous. And gum. Gum was useful, particularly to take the smell of bourbon off your breath. People had been known to misunderstand. He put the side of the notebook in his mouth and used both hands to tuck his shirttails back in. He pulled the notebook from between his teeth and popped a stick of Juicy Fruit in his mouth.

"You do that, champ," he said. "I'll do the vox pop."

He looked ahead at the mosh pit of reporters clustered at the far side of the street, the television antennas rising like metal saplings. Dave Roberts was over there, setting up for a live feed, the hometown hero. Played high school ball at DeMatha before Maryland and the NFL and was now the local television reporter everyone loved.

"Here's a thought," Sully said to Chris. "Don't ask it up there in that scrum. Just nudge the cops that maybe this is random. Everybody else is going to be playing up the aspect that it's got something to do with Reese. See if there's any intel that maybe it's not."

Chris looked up at him and shifted his weight from his right foot to his left. He didn't like the idea, Sully could tell. He was looking for an inside tip on something big—a local gang member, a Colombian drug lord, or maybe one of those anti-government Idaho nut jobs—striking at the federal bench. It would be days and days of 1-A stories, the kind of boost that would shoot him up from the dredges of Metro to the exalted wonders of National.

Chris shrugged. "I'll ask." He started to turn into the crowd, then leaned back. "You need a ride back? Should we meet up?"

Sully shook his head. "I'll get the cycle stuff later."

Overhead, far above the streetlights, two police helicopters swept back and forth, shining spotlights onto roofs, alleys, backyards. Sully felt the first touch of fall place a finger at the nape of his neck, the warning note of winter about to descend. There was still the bourbon buzz tingling through his bones, and now the electric murmur of *murder* on people's lips, the morbid milling around, blood on the asphalt, the dark thrill of a Friday night being turned into something big, something mean, something to talk about. The television trucks, the networks and cable news channels, they were pouring into a neighborhood they usually never noticed, beaming a bit of neighborhood D.C. into living rooms in Seattle and Chicago and Tucson. *I was just coming out the store, you know, and then all these police cars come flying up, cops with guns out and shit . . .*

He checked his watch. Fifty-seven minutes until deadline. A shell burst of adrenaline ran up his spine.

Edging through the gawkers, he could see Dave outside the television van, wrestling a tie around his neck. His cameraman was setting up a shot with the dance studio across the street in the background. Sully could see the "Big Apple" sign across the second floor. The stems of the "A" were shaped like a pair of dancer's legs; the top of the letter was an inverted, heart-shaped ass.

Sully pushed to the front row behind the police tape, now holding his press badge up as if it were a police department shield, people giving him a little room. He caught Dave's eye with a wave. The older man, dark skinned, broad shouldered, still looking like he could bust your ass at outside linebacker, waved him inside the tape.

"Gloamin' of the evenin'," Sully said, waving a hand at the falling dark, then catching himself. Put the "G" on the goddamned end, this wasn't back home.

"I was on my way to the movies with the missus," Dave said.

"She pissed?"

"Twenty-two years of marriage says I'm not getting any when I get home."

"Tell her I said hello, if she's speaking to you when you get there. Christ almighty, I think I see everybody but the *East Jesus Gazette* out there. D.C.'s finest coughing up anything?"

Dave saw the rearview mirror on the van, a revelation, a place to check the knot in the tie. "Just got it from a brother over in 4-D. There's a BOLO for three black guys, teenagers, who were in the store. They're going for them hard but keeping it low-key. You know, they can't just say, 'Niggas killing white girls! Whoo! Hide your women!' But that's what's up. Owner of the market there told the cops there was some sort of scene between them and the girl."

"Here we go."

"No no no, I'm not opening up all that shit."

"You calling the suspects black?"

"On air? Not unless there's better ID."

"This business," Sully said.

There were people on porches, men with arms folded. Horns honking at the stalled traffic. A cluster of people forming along the yellow tape a dozen yards away, forming a circle around someone. He nodded to Dave and moved quickly, forcing his way back into the crowd and pressing to the outer edge of the cluster. In the center was a young woman, thin, long boned, wearing a too-big T-shirt, BIG APPLE DANCE across the front in that split-legged logo.

"—so I's telling Gina the girls had been doing that. Sneaking over there. Something to eat, I don't know."

Someone asked something that Sully couldn't hear.

"Momma calls the cops, they come running and I went upstairs. Then there's all these sirens and I looked out the window and all them go running to Doyle's, around to the back. Momma sees that, takes off running. Flat-out *screaming*."

A lady next to Sully: "Been my baby, Jesus."

The young woman in the circle started talking to someone next to her and the crowd shifted, losing interest. Sully pushed forward to the woman.

"Ma'am? My name's Sully Carter. I'm—"

"I know you," she said evenly, eyes dancing over his scars, starting to walk away. "You came around asking questions after that Spanish girl got killed last summer."

"Did I talk to you?" he cocked his head, falling in step alongside her, handing her his business card.

She shook her head. "You just stopped in the studio." She remembered the scars, the limp. Everybody did.

"You knew Lana?"

She had taken the card, that was good, she was looking down at it now, slowing, giving in. "Yeah, no, I don't know. To talk to. Maybe I saw her around."

"So you saw Sarah Reese go across the street? About what time?"

She looked at her watch, then up at him, deciding to stand for it for a moment. "After her class let out. A little after seven."

He pulled out the notebook, started scribbling. "Went over there by herself?"

"Like I said."

"The girls, the students, they tend to do that after class?"

A nod.

"How much later were the sirens?"

She folded her arms across her chest and grimaced. "The first cops, they didn't come with any sirens. They may have been what, Secret Service? Who is it the judges call? The cops, the sirens, the ones that went over to Doyle's? That was right at eight."

"Marshals," he said. "Judges are protected by U.S. Marshals. Why do you remember the time so well?"

"'Cause I was closing up. Eight thirty, we're all done."

"Anybody from the studio go over there, to Doyle's, before the cops, to, what, look for her?"

"Probably. Maybe. I don't know. Once Momma got here. I mean, look—their lessons were over, okay? They're supposed to wait in the lobby. I saw Sarah go over there and I had another class. We didn't know she was missing until Momma came in."

"Had problems with Sarah before?"

"She was alright. Maybe a little scared of the sisters, you know."

"How did she come to be taking lessons down here?"

"Maybe she heard Gina'd been in Alvin Ailey, I don't know. Gina gets girls from all over, the serious ones."

"Did Dad bring her to class, or was it Mom?"

"Mostly Momma, from what I know. But I've seen Daddy in there on Saturdays dropping her off. Handsome, like."

"How many lessons did Sarah take a week?"

"What is this, two million questions?" Arms unfolding. Sully caught it from the corner of his eye. He looked up. You had to have eye contact or they got pissed.

"Sorry. Hey, look—I'm not an ass, I just play one on TV. You're helping me out here. So. About how many classes?"

"I think it was two. Friday night, Saturday morning, lots of girls do that. Gina'd know for sure."

"Okay. Sarah ever come with a boyfriend, anybody like that?"

"Not that I saw."

"Any pervs hanging out? Strange calls to the studio?"

"I don't answer the phone, mister."

"Don't imagine you do. We got started talking, I didn't even ask your name."

"You going to put it in the paper?"

"Only if you say I can. I don't know your name right now. If you don't tell me," and here he looked up again, smiling, trying to muster some charm, "I don't have any way of doing that."

"Why you got to put me in there? Police'll tell you all that."

"Hard as it is to believe, ma'am, we get accused of making the shit up."

"I see a little white girl run off to get killed and you want to tell everybody where to find me?"

"How about first name only?"

"Gee, that'll help."

"So, okay, look—if you gave me your middle name I wouldn't know the difference. And nobody would recognize it. And I wouldn't have to make you an anonymous source."

"Anonymous. I like anonymous. Make me anonymous."

"They won't use it. Which would be bad, because I think you're telling the truth."

"Why would I lie?"

"Because everybody does."

She eyeballed him.

"I been doing this twenty-something years," he said.

"My middle—okay, it's Victoria? You can put that in there. Make it

'Vicky.' But don't put I work at the studio. Gina'll fire my ass, talking to you."

"Deal, Miss Vicky." He reached out and tapped the card she was holding. "You remember something else? Call your old friend Sully. You work here most every day?"

"Yeah."

"I might stop by."

She nodded, walking away, looking at the card. He waited for her to toss it in the grass, but she didn't, and he had a little hope.

He looked at his watch. He had forty-fucking-three minutes.

He started walking away, pushing back through the crowd. He turned left on Otis, hustled past the recreation center to Warder Street, then turned left for a block until he got back to Princeton Place. He turned left again, having made the block, and now came down the street behind Doyle's Market.

Halfway down, a cruiser blocked off the street and yellow tape stretched all the way across both sidewalks. Sully walked down the middle of the street until the yellow tape stopped him. This was a block of old houses, duplexes, at least half a dozen of them boarded up. Most of the streetlights were out. A cop in the cruiser was talking on his radio and stood up out of the car to eyeball him. Sully stopped and held up his press ID and gave the cop a half wave. The cop nodded and went on transmitting, still eyeing him.

He was maybe seventy yards from the intersection, fifty from the alley in back of the store where Sarah's body had been found. Houses and trees blocked the view, but it was easy to see squad cars, a forensics van, unmarked vehicles. He walked over to a light pole just off the sidewalk and leaned against it, taking the weight off his knee.

He had thirty-one minutes to file.

The child's killer or killers had left the scene three hours before, maybe two and a half, and had vanished into the breeze. Nobody on the street knew a goddamned thing. Right at this minute, local cops and the feds were crushing perp lists, sex offender files, credible threats to the judge, Sarah Reese's lists of schoolmates . . . and he had dick.

Sweet fuckall. He didn't have any more time to work a source, to play an angle.

But because of the paper's reputation, if not his own, the story in tomorrow's paper would be regarded as a cornerstone document in shaping the narrative of the murder of Sarah Reese in the national imagination. He was going to dictate a large chunk of that narrative while tired, not exactly sober, and knowing little more than any sad son of a bitch on the sidewalk.

He spat. Nothing like starting in last place.

four

"**Sully, my boy.** You are calling in poetry, I know it. But I got to ask you something first."

Tony Rubin's cigarette-scarred voice blared down the line, followed by his smoker's cough and the flurry of keyboard tapping in the background. Tony had the abrupt nature of a man who'd spent the past twenty-one years switching subjects on deadline and the attaboy patter of a Little League third-base coach, coaxing writers past the freezing point on deadline, the fate of the late-night man on the rewrite desk. He'd gotten divorced, for the third time, two years earlier and spent the following four months living in the newsroom, mostly without detection, as he showered in the old pressmen's locker room and slept in the deserted warrens of the Sunday Magazine. Sully had come across him there one morning, dozing and sweaty, a jacket for a pillow, curled beneath a copy editor's desk, dreaming of anarchy and knifing his third wife's boyfriend.

"Yeah?" Sully said. "What?"

"Sunday, the Skins? Four-point line against Carolina. At home. Too much chalk? Talk to me." The patter, nervous, finishing up a previous feed, stalling him until he was ready for the dictation.

"I'm a Saints man. I don't really—"

"You're a gambling man."

"Only games I know something about. But off the top of my head—look, we beat Carolina and we suck. Skins are scoring like crazy, so at home I'll say they cover. You see the Giants game? Fifty points, I mean—"

"Got it," Tony said and then, finally, the flurry of typing stopped. "Okay. I'm clear. Go go go go."

"You got the BOLO on the three black suspects?"

"Yeah."

"Not from Chris, though, am I right?"

"Nope."

"Boy couldn't find his dick with a flashlight. Okay. I got the BOLO, too, secondhand, coming out of 4-D, but from a hack I trust."

"Jamie has it from the feds, the FBI."

"Good."

Dictation, then: He narrated Victoria's view of Sarah crossing the street, omitting that her perspective came from the dance studio. In this telling, she was simply a happenstance witness—accurate, not entirely forthcoming, but not exactly misleading. He said she withheld her last name for fear of possible retaliation. He knocked off the rest on the fly:

"'Prosecutors have said that this fear of retribution is common across high-crime areas of the city, as witnesses are loath to put themselves at risk of further violence. While the Park View neighborhood is not among the most violent, it does have problems with street crime and robberies. At least one woman on Princeton Place, Lana Escobar, has been killed in the past eighteen months. Escobar was strangled to death on the outfield grass of the Park View Recreation Center, less than one hundred yards from where Sarah Reese's body was found. No arrest was made in that case. It is unclear tonight—' Tony, make that '*was* unclear *last* night—' Um . . . 'was unclear whether the incident involving Reese was part of the street violence common to the area or was an unconnected tragedy.' Wait. Make it '*random* street violence or whether she was a targeted victim.' There we go."

He then described the scene on the street, the helicopters overhead, the crowd and its resentful energy, the television antennas, the failing light of day, the horns of stalled motorists in the distance.

He looked at his watch. They were past deadline for the suburban.

"What does that alley look like?" Rubin asked.

"It's seven minutes after ten."

"I moved an early version. The alley?"

"The center of police activity. I'm calling it narrow, wide enough for one car at a time. I remember walking through there once or twice before, when I was doing the Escobar thing. It's pretty nondescript. Alley, dumpsters, needles, condoms, beer cans. It's the back of all the stores that face Georgia."

"How far is it off the street?"

"I haven't stepped it off, but sixty, maybe seventy feet? Doyle's is a little weird—it has four or five parking spaces in front of it between it and Georgia, this little parking lot."

"Are the dumpsters right behind the market's door?"

"Unknown. But they couldn't be far. The alley bends, okay? It doesn't go straight across. It bends backward, away from Georgia to accommodate an office building, the one with the restaurant, the Hunger Stopper, on the first floor, and then it comes out onto Otis. Shit. Look up whether that's Otis Place or Street. The dumpsters couldn't be in the turn, so, yeah, the dumpster is within twenty or thirty feet of the back door of the market."

"She was found in the alley between Princeton Place and Otis Place? That's accurate?"

"Yes. I mean, no—yeah, Otis. I don't know if it's street or terrace or whatever."

"I'm looking at a street map. Princeton Place, Otis Place. Princeton runs east and west. It's only two and half blocks long."

"What, it picks up at the golf course and dead-ends into Georgia? The other side of the golf course, that's whatsit, Catholic University? So yeah, it wouldn't pick up again over there."

"Alley is pavement? Not brick?"

"Ah, affirmative."

"And you're sure about that location for the alley? It's not shown on my street map."

"I'm looking at it."

"What's the population back there right now?"

"In the alley? I'm counting two squad cars, three unmarkeds, and a tech van. The van is just outside the alley. What's Chris telling you about the investigation?"

"Cops are mostly shutting him down. A statement coming at ten thirty from the chief, then the mayor. They're going to do a stand-up in front of the store."

"Suspects?"

"Well, the BOLO, if you want to count that. Cops are calling them persons of interest, asking witnesses to come forward. Particularly any who may have been in Doyle's."

"How many hacks feeding you?"

"I got Jamie on the FBI and Main Justice. The obit desk, which has the bio stuff on Reese. Got a feed from National. Something about judges being targets of crimes, and another about him being the presumptive next nominee to the Supremes. Research is putting together a list of his recent decisions. Metro has the kid going to the Hazelwood School. That's like twenty grand a year, you know. Looks like we're getting a picture of young Miss Sarah from the yearbook. Metro also has somebody out there in the neighborhood, trying for friends and family. We'll add in the police and the feds when they go on at ten thirty. And there's you and Chris. How many was that?"

"Like about twenty people who don't know fuckall."

"Well, it's what we do best."

Sully clicked off the cell and dropped it in his pocket. The rotating lights of the police and emergency vehicles bounced off the houses, scattered through the leaves of the trees overhead. The breeze came back up. The last of the bourbon pulsed at his temples. He tapped his pen against his notebook and his foot against the pavement. Something about the neighborhood was bouncing just beyond the reach of his memory.

The press conference was going to be in front of the dance studio, well inside the perimeter—Chris would cover that—and somewhere offscreen there would be the parental misery of David and Tori Reese, a wound that would never heal. He could give a fuck about Reese himself, Washington parasite that he was, but he felt a twinge in his chest for Tori, the well of sorrow she was falling into, a blackness he knew well enough.

"Keening," he said out loud to nobody.

And Sarah. He would rather not think about the child's last minutes, but that was the job. He looked at the moths circling above and found himself wondering why a girl—white, rich—would run into an alley in a neighborhood like this. Had somebody lured her back there, and if so, with what? She had crossed the street for a soda from the store—fine, he could believe that. But why did she leave from the back entrance? A drug buy? Weed?

Drugs, that was the smart money. Sarah, what, goes out back to buy some weed—maybe that was the point of the whole foray from the dance studio—and pulls out too much cash? Maybe that's what the three black guys in the store were doing, a little dealing. Hey, white girl, you want some quality endo? Y'all come on out back. She goes, pulls out her money, dude grabs it, she bucks, gets the knife, and that's the end. Or, maybe: She pays and they try to get a little what-what with the transaction. She bucks, the knife, the same.

Maybe a rapist who had spotted her before—she would have been in the same place, same time each week—and finally made a play? He blew out his lips. Possible, but less likely.

Then there was the Big Idea story that his colleagues would love most: Daddy was the target, she was the message. This struck him as the most likely to be bullshit, but if it was true, the killing would almost certainly be a professional hit, designed to be quick, clean, and most likely done efficiently with a firearm. Or maybe the killer liked the knife because, if he was sure of his physical control of the situation, it offered the benefits of silence and no left-behind ballistics.

Of course none of this really mattered—the initial BOLO would fix the narrative on television, radio, newspapers, the national consciousness. Three young black guys, one dead white girl. This was how shit got started.

He looked up and saw three people walk out of the alley. The low yellow light was not good but he recognized the police chief's short, rotund outline. The other figure, a tall, broad-shouldered dude in a suit, he didn't know. He guessed FBI. They both turned and went away from him, toward the lights on Georgia Avenue.

The third figure, who started walking his way, was a woman. She passed under a streetlight, crossed the street, passed the cop in the cruiser, and pulled out her car keys. Sully smiled.

"Counselor," he called out.

Eva turned, startled, but did not relax her shoulders when she recognized him. She crossed the street, walking to where he sat.

"Thought you guys dug out information. Not come to a crime scene and sit."

"Odd for you to be out on a scene, isn't it?" he said.

"No," she said, a little too quickly. "We don't always wait to get suspects to file indictments."

"A grand jury original?"

"'s what they call it."

"This'll be your case."

"It might, but you can't print that. It's not settled." She turned and looked toward the alley. "They got more people down there than the state fair. FBI, Marshals, ATF. Surprised I didn't run into LAPD."

"Who are the guys in the store just before she died?"

"Listening to the BOLOs, are we? Three young men we want to talk to. We don't have names, so don't ask. There'll be a bulletin in a few with a general description."

"Are they suspects?"

"I believe the term is 'persons of interest.'"

"So arc they suspects?"

"If you were one of them, and half the local and federal police agencies in the nation's capital were hunting your ass, what would you feel like?"

"Thought so. Where's the girl? Sarah?"

"She *was* in a dumpster back there. She *is* at the morgue. I imagine they'll be reflecting the scalp in a bit. You know what that is? Reflecting the scalp?"

"I've heard."

"I've seen. It's something that shouldn't happen to fifteen-year-olds at dance class."

"What happened to her in the alley?"

"Can't say."

"Can't or won't?"

"Either. Both. Pick."

"Cause of death? Proximate cause of death? We got word this was a stabbing."

"You're looking for attribution or confirmation?"

"Either. Both. Pick."

"No attribution to me or my office. But I will confirm, as a law enforcement official familiar with the investigation, the stabbing."

"Multiple? Or a one-shot thing that hit an artery?"

"Usually when you cut someone's throat you get the artery."

"Multiple wounds or just the one?"

"Only one apparent."

"Sex crime?"

"Sully. The parents. I'm not saying. Forensics will bear that out anyway, one way or the other."

"Is there any evidence it's targeted? Her being Reese's kid?"

"Will neither confirm nor deny."

"So what was her condition in the dumpster?"

"Wrapped in a big black trash bag, like the ones contractors use. But it's not clear if she was wrapped in that by whoever killed her or by the uniform who found her."

"I didn't hear that right."

"The cop who found her. Canvassing the alley—her mother was screaming and everybody knew who she was—officer looks in, sees a body, facedown. Jumps in and rolls her over to, I don't know, try to save her. Then he sees the cut. She'd bled out onto this black trash bag that was under her. He pulled that back over her body, now that she was faceup, until other units got here."

"That wasn't good."

"Hey, no shit. Now we don't know if she was wrapped up before she got thrown in or if it was already there and she gets thrown in on top of it."

"Ah."

"And when I say thrown in, let me be clear. This is a tall, big, heavy dumpster, about five feet high. She was down inside there on top of a couple of feet of garbage."

"Blood on the pavement outside the dumpster? Side of it?"

"Some."

"A puddle, a lake, a drop?"

"More than the last, less than the middle."

"Eva, for Christ's sake."

"It's not clear if she was dragged there or killed on the spot if that's what you're asking."

"Blood nearby?"

Sully saw her look down at him. The light was muted, from overhead. He could see the beginning of crow's feet, the full lips, the strong, high cheekbones. It struck him, her age, and by extension, his.

"Scene is still being worked," she said, finally.

"Alright."

"You look like you're half asleep," she said.

"You look fried."

"If I'm not, I'm going to be." She nodded good night in parting, turned, and walked to her Jeep Cherokee. She pulled out and was gone.

Sully called Tony, affirming the manhunt for the three black men in the store and giving the details of the throat slashing. He was careful with the description of the blood's amount and location, to make it less likely he'd get burned if Eva's initial description was less than exact. He decided to omit the bit about the black garbage bag; it was just too complicated to get into.

Tony took the information and cut the line, no bullshitting this time.

He blew out his lips and cursed softly.

Eva was dripping out intel to her benefit, handing out the leak on the throat slashing like it was nothing, then holding back on the rest. Fine. Nothing personal. But his job, and his problem, was that he had to get ahead of her and the detectives and the federal agents swarming over this, putting their stamp of What Happened Here on it all.

Trusting the police—particularly as fucked up as D.C.'s—had never been on his list of smart things to do, and he wasn't going to start now.

He limped up Princeton away from the crime scene, and slowly, as he thought, purpose came into his step. The pace picked up. He knew where he was going and what he was going to do. There was risk attached, yeah, but if he'd learned anything from eleven years in the worst hellholes on earth, it was that reporting without risk was an oxymoron.

five

The night was cooling by degrees and he was thinking maybe he should have kept the cycle jacket. A left turn on Warder, crossing Quebec—the neighborhood, Park View, row houses and semi-detached homes, had been an immigrant niche even before World War II. It had been Jews and Greeks and Italians then, waiters and carpenters and dockworkers and owners of shoe stores and merchants of hats and olives and corner markets.

Now the immigrants were Jamaicans and Hondurans and Ethiopians and Nicaraguans and Nigerians and Algerians and a handful of Lebanese, taxi drivers and custodians and hotel doormen and lawn maintenance workers. The founding generation of this black and brown group—here for twenty, thirty, forty years, keeping their lawns looking as if they were trimmed with scissors, the azaleas fertilized—were seventy years old and stuck living alongside the drug dealers and the prostitutes and the alcoholics, a slow-motion spiral of decline of the second and third generation.

He turned onto Rock Creek Church Road, passing three young men standing against the side of a house on a corner. They watched him walking and he watched them back and he nodded and they did not nod back. The trees were old and stout and cast great shadows beneath the streetlights. The yards were raised from the sidewalk, with low stone walls as borders, and the houses had porches populated by cheap folding chairs or old couches and lime-green outdoor carpeting.

At a house in the middle of the block, Sully opened the metal gate, rusting on its hinges. He limped up the five concrete steps, two of them with chipped and broken chunks, and onto the front porch. There was an overstuffed couch, with several rips and exposed stuffing, and a wooden swing with peeling paint. Before he reached through the security gate to knock on the door, he heard the dog growling inside.

The wooden door swung open on a dark hallway. The Rottweiler barked twice, his ears up and alert.

Sly Hastings materialized from the darkness. He was wearing a white pullover, black basketball shorts, white socks with black flip-flops, and small, wire-framed glasses.

"Donnell, hush up," he said to the dog. He unlocked the door and pushed it open. "I hope you know more than what's on TV, brother, 'cause they don't know shit."

six

The steel door leading to the basement was open and Sully turned right, took a step down to the landing, and then went down the steps. The house, a ramshackle shell above, turned into a well-appointed apartment below, one of the bases of Sly's growing business enterprise.

Downstairs, the overhead lighting was muted, and a large television was against a wall. The kitchen was at the far side. Sully went to the refrigerator, pulled out a Miller, and returned to the couch. He held the cold can against his right temple.

"Damn," he said. It felt that good.

Sly returned to his seat on a bar stool at the counter, where a newspaper was folded into a quarter panel. He picked up a pen and looked down at the paper. The television was turned to a twenty-four-hour news channel broadcasting from the crime scene but the sound was off. The dog flopped down on the kitchen floor. Sully closed his eyes and let himself sink back into the comforts of the couch. Sly was, in the context of his life, in the context of working in Bosnia and Rwanda and Liberia and Lebanon and the taxi wars of South Africa, a warlord, and sort of a minor one at that. He would kill you graveyard dead—sure, they'd all do that—but most warlords, the ones who would tolerate your presence at all, would not fuck with you if you did not fuck with them. If you had the nerve to walk past the guns and the machetes to get to their front door, and did not jump the first time a flunky put a gun in your face and told you they were going to blow your fucking brains across the street, then they'd talk to you, give you their misshapen view of the world. Sly, operating in the United States, who didn't even have a machete, was not, actually, one of the most frightening people he'd ever met, and probably was not in the top ten. He was deadly, yeah, and he killed people, but the United States had such a limited understanding of the uses of homicidal violence, and really none at all since the Deep South terrorism of the early 1960s . . . After a minute, Sully looked up. Sly was peering at the paper, writing on it occasionally, barely looking up at the television. Sully said, "I thought you'd be more bothered."

"By?"

Sully nodded toward the screen. "The recent unpleasantness."

Sly did not look up. "Didn't say I wasn't."

"You don't appear concerned."

"I don't appear to be a lot of things."

Sully said, raising his chin, gesturing at the paper, "You been working that all day? It's damn near eleven."

"It's the Friday," Sly said, still looking down. "You can't fucking do the Wednesday."

Sully popped the beer tab, slurped, looked at the television. "They catch the bad guys yet?"

Sly looked up. The news channel had cut to a stand-up shot on Georgia Avenue, the dance studio in the background. Klieg lights blasted the scene, the shadows deep off to the side. The police chief and a cadre of others were standing at a bank of microphones. Sly pointed a remote at the television, bringing up the audio.

"The search in this case is intensely focused in this neighborhood," the chief was saying, "but it is national in scope. This is not a D.C. homicide investigation. This is a national security issue. The task force we are putting together, that is already acting, reflects that. There are federal agents from more than half a dozen agencies already at work on this, and they will continue to be until it is resolved."

Shouted questions, brief mayhem.

"There are three men in the store we want to talk to, yes. Suspects, I don't know about that, but they are persons we are interested in talking to, obviously."

Sly snorted. "Them three." The hand came up again with the remote, and the volume retreated to zero.

Sully looked at the scene unfolding a few blocks away. The chief was still talking, taking questions.

"Them three?" he said.

"Hell yeah, them three. In the store."

"Who are they?"

Sly did not take his eyes off the television, but his tone was amiable. "You don't need to know everything."

"But you know."

"Oh, yeah."

"And they won't be turning themselves in?"

Sly looked over his glasses at him.

"Do they need to?" Sully asked.

"Carter. Nobody in this neighborhood is stupid enough to kill the first white girl to come through here since God was a baby."

"So it's outsiders after the Honorable Judge Reese?"

"I didn't say that."

"This wasn't a Sly Hastings operation?"

"You really don't want to come in somebody's house and talk that kind of shit."

"So who should local law enforcement be looking for?"

Sly looked at the television, then down at the crossword puzzle in front of him. He sipped his coffee. "I been thinking on that. I don't know."

"That's remarkable, Sly," he said, slurping the beer. "I thought it was your job to know."

Sly tapped the pen on the paper. He did not look up. "I said I did not know. I did not say I *will* not know."

"Bets?"

"The habit of fools and drunks. The wise man follows the evidence at hand."

Sully kicked off his shoes. "Police get to have *evidence*, Sly. I'm a step back, if not two. They're going to be all over shit until they lock somebody up and, you know, they're gonna come looking for you and an alibi."

"It had never dawned on me, helpful white man."

"I'm saying this is one of those incidents where you and I can work together. Mutual benefit and all."

"Maybe."

"So where might I find them three for a dramatic interview?"

"Nowhere. It ain't time yet. Me and Lionel, we only started looking into this. Them three need to stay incognito. I got investments tying me up just now."

"The apartments? I thought your sis was running them for you."

"Nikki is my half sis and she can't do every goddamn thing. She been distracted, got the day job at D.C. Housing. We're up to three buildings now, twenty-eight units, I tell you that? But that ain't on my mind right now. What's on my mind right now, you were supposed to have dinner with my girlfriend tonight. What's she saying?"

"About what?"

"Me."

"About what I told you she would. That you're an asshole who needs to be locked up, a menace, blah blah. Also, they took that Chucky thing personal."

"Chucky? Fucking *Chucky*? That's where they're at?" He paused a minute, looking at the television, and then laughed. "Good. I like that. That's good."

"I got the idea he was a cooperating witness."

"He was."

"They know you're in Park View but they don't really know what you're into."

"She didn't sniff you out?"

"I said I'm looking at writing about a motherfucker who's got juice. She brought you up."

Sly dropped his pen on the newspaper, folding his arms and swiveling in his chair. "Well. That's almost a compliment. That's good. Who else did she mention, power-broker-wise?"

"We were interrupted by the passing of Miss Reese. But I didn't sense she had anybody else in mind. Well. Rayful Edmond. She gave me Rayful as a history case. She was trying to sell me on a story about you. I guess to see if maybe it'd make you jump."

"If that's what they down to."

"I think they're down to seeing who cut Sarah Reese's throat. So—so come on. You wanted me to see if they had anything on you they'd spill, so I did. Now. If it ain't them three, who out there has got a dick problem? A little-white-girl problem? Who works with a knife?"

"You just said her throat got cut."

"I did."

"They ain't saying that on the TV."

Sully smiled. "Tomorrow's news today, amigo. You ain't the only one who knows shit."

"Who said?"

"You don't need to know everything. So. Who works with a knife?"

Sly got up and went to the refrigerator, stepping over Donnell, irritated now, his phrasing being tossed back at him. "You trying to get to the end of the game without going around the board. Something this bad, there's going to be all sorts of shit that pops out in the next twenty-four to forty-eight and almost all of it is going to be nothing. It's going to be all about them three. White girl dead, police looking for three scary black dudes. Well, they going the wrong motherfucking way. That's what I know that nobody else does. That's what's going to open things up for me to look elsewhere."

"How come you sure it ain't them?"

Sly stepped back over Donnell coming out of the kitchen, pissed off now, maybe a little rattled.

"Because I am. Because I fucking well am. You don't trust me, go ahead with your cops. They don't know shit. Her throat cut? So? They gave you a lollipop. That's a what, not a who. But you *do* happen to be talking to the one person who is ahead on this. You know why I'm ahead? Because while the rest of the world is looking for them three in the store, I already talked to them. We had a conversation. Yeah. So I know that. I also know that somebody just started some shit on my turf without prior fucking approval, and that shit is not going to stand. I know that, too."

He paused, seeming to catch himself. He was three feet from the couch.

"Now. I can't just go shut this down. It's too far above the waterline. What I need is for local law enforcement to take care of this, pronto. I don't need a—a swarm of FBI and CIA and DEA paratroopers pounding the street out there for weeks on end, rattling brothers on warrants, on child support, on whatever. Some shit is going to pop out, they do that, and I ain't in the shit-popping-out business. So I'll ask around, keep you in the loop—yeah, alright, okay, I can use a story in the newspaper with the true facts in it, put a little heat on the feds to play straight. You, now, you're going to let me know what you hear about them getting anywhere close to me."

They looked at each other, the place quiet. Sly knew far more about the killing of Sarah Reese than he was saying, Sully knew that. His was the best intel on the street, possibly better than any law enforcement agency had. But there was no way to know exactly what it was, who it helped or hurt, or how Sly would play it out. But there was the same lesson from the war zones he'd covered until he got blown up applied here: If you want to know what the bad guys were doing, stick to the guys with the guns. They know the shit.

"Deal," Sully said.

"Good enough." Sly clicked the remote and the television died. "You can go home now."

"I ain't got the bike. Gimme me a ride?"

Sly snorted. "You can walk up to Georgia and try to get a cab or you can flop out on the couch. You not calling somebody to get you here."

"I'll flop."

Sly shook his head, heading for his bedroom at the back, still tense, still worked up. "I'd stay on the couch, I was you," he said, flicking off the lights. "Donnell ain't partial to drunks walking around in the dark."

Sully felt around on the back of the couch until he found a throw, laid back, and pulled it over him. He put one of the couch pillows under his throbbing knee and another under his head, then fished his cell out of his pocket, the thing bulky and awkward. He punched in Dusty's home number. It went straight to voice mail.

"Look at the news," he whispered. "I didn't just cut out."

seven

Breakfast was an important start to the day, so Sully had another Miller and scrambled eggs. Sly, sitting on a bar stool at the kitchen counter, skipped the eggs and was sipping coffee, reading the A section, open to an inside page. It was just after eight and it was misting rain. He had taken Donnell out for a morning walk and was dressed in a black tracksuit that zipped up the front with white piping down the sides and sleeves.

"Says here Reese is a Republican," Sly said.

"From Texas."

"I got that he was one of those Southern crackers from the accent, the time I heard him in court."

"He's an asshole but he's not a cracker."

Sly did not look up. "Say that again."

"Texans aren't crackers."

Sly grunted.

Sully doused his eggs with hot sauce. "I done told you. Dipshits from Georgia, north Florida, the Carolinas, *those* are crackers. West Virginia, Kentucky, Tennessee, Arkansas? Hillbillies. Hicks from Mississippi, Alabama, and north Louisiana—and just up in that western part of Tennessee and just across the river in the Arkansas delta? Those are your rednecks. South Louisiana? Cajuns. Not even God can help you with them."

"Y'all all look the same to me."

"I can't help you with your prejudices."

"Which ones are the poor white trash?"

"The ones who'll shoot your ass somewhere between you calling them 'white' and 'trash.'"

"Which one are you?"

"The river is sort of neutral ground. Mostly we stayed on the Louisiana side."

"You got Creole to you?"

"Not so much as I know."

"So what are Texans? You never said."

"Texans. They fucking think the sun rises in Beaumont and sets in El Paso."

Sly went back to the paper. "You people."

There was jazz on the stereo, a sax on the lead, but Sully couldn't place it and wasn't going to give Sly the satisfaction. He drained the beer. "So what are we saying about yonder judge and his dearly departed?"

"That he's next in line for the Supreme Court."

"As long as the Republicans win next November, which is a done deal, you ask me."

"Y'all ought to be easier on brother Bill."

"Brother Bill ought to stop getting blown by interns."

"Look here. Y'all saying that there's a 'massive manhunt' for them three. A federal agent, name withheld here, says so. Police chief sticks to that 'persons of interest' bullshit, but says, yeah, it's on. Got a whole article here about his cases, like you trying to say somebody he sentenced got involved. They're talking about the Junior Simpson trial last year. That crew he was running over in Trinidad, behind Gallaudet? Judge popped Junior to twenty-five to life. Junior said something at the end of sentencing"—he peered closer at the paper, through his glasses—"'I'll see you again.' That's what he said to the judge. Lawyer said Junior was talking about an appeal."

"What's he say now?"

"'Declines comment.'"

"I guess the fuck so."

"Judge also dealt out life without parole to some dude y'all call a terrorist. From Libya. Made bombs."

Sully was putting his dishes in the sink. "This is all busywork, ass covering, you-never-know stuff. Surely we put the token in there."

"Them dishes don't wash themselves, brother."

Sully turned back around, took the dishes out of the sink, and put them in the dishwasher.

"Thank you. I got an ant problem up in here." Sly went back to the paper and, a moment later, rattled it approvingly. "Token white boy, right here. Well. Italian. Does that count? 'The rest of Judge Reese's calendar has mostly been white-collar corruption cases, court records show, but three years ago he presided over a racketeering case involving Joseph Fiori, an alleged member of the New York crime syndicate. Justice Department sources said they were skeptical of Mafia involvement in Sarah Reese's slaying.' Shit. That wasn't hard."

"You don't like the mob for this?"

"Nobody from a professional organization would pull this. Even Junior knows better. Not that I'm calling his outfit professional."

Sully came and looked over his shoulder at the paper.

The story he and Chris had written anchored the right side of the front page, the traditional spot for the lead news story of the day. The picture dominating the middle of the page was of the crime scene, the yellow police tape across the front of Doyle's Market, two young white girls weeping and embracing just inside the tape. The headline: "Chief Judge's Daughter Slain."

"Massive Manhunt for Three 'Persons of Interest'" was the deck head.

Tony had put the throat slitting in the third graf.

The related stories inside took an entire page and a half. There was the story Sly had been reading from, the judge's bio and his recent cases, and another story about Sarah, quoting friends and schoolmates. Christ, Sully thought, they must have been finding the kids on deadline. Hello, Mrs. Wealthy White Lady, may I please talk to your son Brandon? Hey, Brandon, I'm a reporter and I'm sorry to tell you your buddy Sarah is dead, yeah really, it's terrible, I can't even imagine what you must be going through, so . . . what was she like in class?

He went to the coffee table and pulled his shoes out from underneath and sat down to put them on.

"Should I be looking for them three today?"

"If you want to waste your time."

"Jesus. Okay. So, then, who works with a knife?"

"People who ain't got a gun."

"We're behind on this, brother."

"I know it."

"Then let's move. You got somebody who can run me down to Stoney's?"

"Lionel's at the end of the block. Tell him to get on back."

Sully walked out of the basement door and heard Sly bolt it behind him. He came to the top of the steps, the mist chilling his skin. Down at the corner of Rock Creek Church and Warder he saw Sly's 1982 Camaro, black over gold. When he got within thirty feet of it, Lionel materialized, coming out of the corner market, head down, face obscured by a White Sox hat. The car alarm *beep-beep*ed and Sully opened the door and sat down, heavy, in the passenger seat.

Lionel talked like he had to pay by the word, and Sully wasn't in the mood this morning himself.

They passed a couple of miles in silence, the easy rhythm of Saturday morning traffic going by, making good time.

"This's going to be some shit," Lionel said finally.

"He seems pissed," Sully agreed.

"When he's like that? Nothing good happens."

"I'll keep it in mind."

Lionel pulled into the narrow street and stopped in front of Stoney's. The bike, a 1993 Ducati 916, sat alone, rear tire at the curb. He'd bought it, cash, through some highly creative expense reports during the war. It was known as filing for overtime.

There had been a million ways to do it, the easiest of which was telling your employer that the bureau car in Sarajevo had been stolen, backed up with a police report. In reality, Sully and half the foreign press corps had kicked $500 per report to a compliant officer, who would complete the form—amazing, the bureaucracy that kept functioning—and then you sold your car, at an exorbitant price, through your interpreter (another $500 tip) to an aid agency or the UN or the highest bidder. You'd pocket $18,000 to $25,000 and change.

When he straddled the bike and cranked it, the engine rumbled into life. The seat was still soaking wet and cold, a clammy hand grasping his crotch. He let out on the clutch, twisted the throttle, leaned over the gas tank, and lifted both feet off the ground. The rear wheel spun on the wet pavement and found traction, the bitch hitting seventy before the first light.

His place was small, narrow, a brick kiln in the summer, a 107-year-old row house on Capitol Hill, on Sixth Street. It was spare and decorated with pictures and carpets and paintings and things from his overseas postings. Persian rugs he'd bought in Beirut and a teak dining room table that had been made from railroad sleeper cars in what had been Rhodesia. The dishes and plates all came from a tiny ceramic studio in Warsaw. He'd bought the entire set on a freezing winter morning just after the fall of the Wall in Berlin. He'd thought, at the time, it might help domesticate him. There were post-impressionistic paintings from the Netherlands in a narrow hallway, and two framed pieces of mud cloth he'd bought at a market in Nigeria.

Nadia's photograph, a portrait he'd taken of her on a snowy morning in Sarajevo, was the only thing that passed for a picture of family or a friend. The black hair, long and only partly pulled back out of her eyes, no makeup, her prominent nose, the full lips. She was wearing jeans and one of his Chart Room T-shirts, from the bar where he'd worked in New Orleans. He had been leaving Sarajevo that morning for a reporting trek in the countryside and she'd walked him down the steps from her third-floor flat. She'd tugged on the clothes after their hurried predawn roll in the hay, he scrambling to meet the other reporters at the Holiday Inn before they left, and when the door swung open she had stepped into the snow and crossed her arms, shivering. When he'd brought the camera up, she'd playfully put her index finger to her pursed lips, making the sign to hush, don't tell, don't let anyone know . . . It was in a teak frame beneath the lamp by the couch.

This morning, he grabbed a Corona from the fridge, stripped off, got in the shower, and thought of what to tell his bosses he was doing today—particularly before they called him with some bullshit assignment. The water beating down on his back, his skull, he decided that he believed Sly that the three suspects were bogus, and he did not want to get sucked into that if it was going to be a dead end later on. He'd let Chris and Jamie run with that. The long money? That was on nailing the actual killer. For that, he was going to need street intel, and for that, he needed to be hoofing it around Princeton Place, keeping Sly close, kicking over rocks, looking for a man with a knife. So until you had that, stall.

He got out of the shower and called R.J. at home. "I'm going to write you a moody neighborhood profile," Sully said. "Swing sets in the rain, poverty, meanness."

"Bukowski," R.J. said, not missing a beat. "Pure Bukowski." Sully pictured R.J. in his living room, coffee in hand, up since dawn and his morning hike through Rock Creek Park already finished. He could hear Elwood, his partner for a quarter century, noodling on their baby grand, but he couldn't place the tune. "I love it," he continued, after a sip on the coffee. "But don't you want in on the manhunt?"

"Nah," Sully said, going with Sly's word on the three suspects being a dead end, but not coughing that up just yet. He'd take the high road. "Not my turf. Don't like bigfooting."

"We may pull you into it later. But we could use the neighborhood scene for atmosphere. Think 1-A here. We've got to own this one. For tomorrow, yes?"

"Yes."

"I'll let the desk and photo know. Go, boy, go."

Sully wolfed down a turkey and cheese sandwich standing up in the kitchen, in front of the sink, looking out at his postage stamp of a backyard. The cherry tree—he'd planted it when he bought the place, before his first foreign posting—was shimmering in the mist, leaves wet and dripping, spreading over the lawn. Three weeks every spring, it was a pink cloud. He went to the bedroom and pulled a light sweater over his head and stepped into black slip-on shoes. He got a slender backpack and put a notebook, a camera, a recorder, and a couple of pens inside. There was a moment of hesitation; then he went to the closet, the top shelf, a small box. He pulled out the Tokarev M57, the Zastava, ancient but accurate, that the commander had given him after the night on the mountain, him blown to shit. He checked the clip, then got his backup cycle jacket, the one for bad weather, and tucked the pistol into the right interior pocket. Because if he'd had a pistol when that night started instead of when it ended he wouldn't look or walk like he did now.

The bike took him up Massachusetts Avenue to North Capitol, then left on the four-lane expanse of Irving Street NW, and he was back in the Park View neighborhood. The row houses sprang up on each side of the road, their porches coming to within a few feet of the sidewalks, their rusting iron gates and railings hard on the edge of the concrete.

He parked the bike on the top half of Princeton Place, looking at the row of weathered houses, picking one in the middle of the block. When he got to the front door, he pressed the doorbell, looking down, hands clasped in front of him, notebook tucked under an arm, trying to look as non-threatening as possible. An elderly, diminutive black woman opened the door a crack. She was wearing a pink house robe and did not take the business card he held out.

"Hi, ma'am, I'm sorry to disturb you this early, but my name is Sully Carter and I'm a reporter for the paper? I'm working on a story about this incident down to Doyle's last night? I was—"

The woman blinked, her brown eyes steady, and gently closed the door in his face.

eight

You never stopped moving. That was the thing. You just kept pushing, driving, asking, sticking your nose in people's faces, taking the shit, the insults, fighting back the depression and the sense of hopelessness and then, out of the void, sometimes somebody told you something.

The basketball court at the rec center, where the three suspects had been playing the night before, was roped off with police tape, the afternoon game moving to an adjacent alley, the netless hoop nailed to a telephone pole. He was three steps in the alley and the players were taunting him.

"Hey, paleface, the fuck you doin'?"

"'less you got a warrant, keep walking, bitch."

"Whyn't you walk right?"

He went a block up. There were two houses, crack squats, a small cluster of zombies out front, guys with hands in their pockets, eyeing him, seeing if he was trolling for a dime bag, a nickel rock . . . A woman sitting on the front step of an abandoned house—flabby, ashy knees, bloodshot eyes—offered to blow him for twenty bucks. When he turned to say something to that, she said, "Ah, you know the price, yeah? Gimme ten."

Roll-down steel gates shuttered the entrance to the Big Apple. The gates were at half-staff at Doyle's, lab techs ducking their way in and out. He remembered that Doyle lived somewhere near the store but he didn't have an address. Directory assistance said there was no such person listed. He should have thought to have news research run property records last night.

The strip joint up the block was the Show Bar. It hadn't changed since he'd stopped in while working on the Lana Escobar story. Six customers, one woman on the pole, a bartender with a light thumb, a queasy reddish light to the interior. Les Samuels, the manager in the jumbled office in the back, not telling him anything he didn't already know.

By three in the afternoon, Sully had knocked on fifteen doors, talked to half a dozen store owners, heard nothing about the three suspects, and was getting the distinct idea that nobody in or around Princeton Place gave a good goddamn about Sarah Emily Reese.

A beer delivery man got out of a truck in front of the Hunger Stopper, the vehicle burping exhaust from the tailpipe. Sully, half jogging up the street now, deadline looming, flagged him down with an "Excuse me." Getting a dolly out of the back, the man eyed Sully, the grayness of the day reflected in his expression.

"Not to be any sort of way about it," he said when Sully said what he was doing and why, "but you a little late to the party, aren't you, brother?" He broke eye contact to look at the scars, then back at Sully directly. "Park View's been beat to shit for years. That Hispanic girl, she got killed last year. Noel went missing? I didn't read nothing 'bout *that* in the *news*paper."

He kept going, white girl gets it, lookit the TV cameras, white girl gets it, lookit the papers . . . But the name blossomed over Sully—Noel. Noel Pittman. That was the incident he'd been trying to remember the night before. Howard student, party girl. Disappeared after leaving a club last year. She'd been living on Princeton Place.

Sully leaned back on his good leg, letting the man talk but working his way into the monologue. "Lana, Lana, I remember Lana," he finally elbowed in. "I wrote a little something on her. But you're right, it wasn't much. Back of Metro." A shrug. "Her dad was a federal judge, I imagine we would have done more."

"Daddy was a federal judge," the man said, "it would have gotten solved."

Sully smiled. "Sounds like you knew the other one? Noel?"

"Don't I wish. To say hello. You'd see her at the clubs. She was one of the dancers out at Halo, on the elevated platforms? Then one day I'm making the rounds and see her face on a 'Missing' poster."

"And that was it? She was just gone? No loco boyfriend?"

The man leaned on the dolly, reaching a hand out, shaking it, as if flicking water from his fingertips. "You heard neighborhood talk, flapping gums." He stepped inside the truck and opened the glove compartment. He sifted through a stack of papers, then unfolded a sheet, eleven by fourteen, that had holes in the top and bottom where it had once been stapled to a telephone pole.

The picture showed a young woman smiling at the camera, brown eyes, brown skin, radiant complexion. Bold-faced lettering spelled out her name at the top, above the picture. Below, it read, "Last seen—April 24, 1998." There was a phone number underneath.

"Mind if I hang on to this?" Sully asked. "I'm sorry, I didn't ask your name." He leaned forward to shake his hand. White guys in this town, you didn't really do this with, lean forward, shake, make the eye contact. Black men, you damn well better.

"Rodney," the man said, taking his hand in a solid grip. "Rodney Wilson. Grew up over on Warder. Keep the poster, put her name out there, hunh?" The man looked at him, taunting: "Do a little something for the block, other than just feed off it?"

Sully nodded, letting it slide. A couple of television crews were doing stand-ups in front of Doyle's Market. The rain had started misting again. He pulled out his cell and called the number at the bottom of the Pittman flyer. A recorded woman's voice said to leave a message if the caller had information about Noel, no questions asked. There was a beep and Sully explained himself and asked for a call back.

The watch on his wrist read 4:17.

The sixth floor of the newsroom was vast and unpopulated, nobody around on a Saturday afternoon except the sports staff, televisions hanging from the ceiling, ablaze with college games.

He walked through the low cubicles spread across the expanse of the room, checking to see if the top staff were in their glass offices on the south wall. Edward Winters was in his executive editor's office—always always—but Sully didn't see anyone else. In the main newsroom, a handful of weekend editors were seeing the Sunday edition into print. Over on National, there were a hardful of reporters. It was quiet and most of the overhead fluorescents were dark.

His desk was tucked into the far left corner, around a small nook, in the no-man's-land between Investigative and Metro. Chris had draped his jacket over the chair and set his helmet on the desk. There was a spent brass mortar shell, carved in intricate patterns, that he had bought from refugees in Bosnia. There were a dozen or so prayer beads he'd collected, more as tourist keepsakes than religious talismans, draped over it, along with purple and yellow and green Mardi Gras beads.

But the main feature of his space was the hand-sketched homicide map of the city, his pride and possibly his joy. It was a poster-sized grid, thirty-six inches wide and fifty inches tall, marked off by the seven police districts with a few major roads indicated, and it was his oracle of Washington. It was his manner of understanding the living, by studying the ways of the dead, a habit so natural to him after years of covering war and conflict that it was no longer a conscious thought. If you wanted to understand any animal, he would tell college classes when they asked him to give talks, then you have to understand the behavior that made them unique, and what made human beings unique among animals were the prefrontal cortex, the opposing thumb, the well-developed voice box, and the propensity to torture and kill other members of their species. When students sometimes objected to this as morbid, or sought to invoke deities and religious perspectives, he would say that he had yet to see evidence of deity, but any textbook offered three thousand years or so of recorded history to back up his thoughts on humanity.

"Even if you believe the Bible is literally true," he would say, "when the population of the planet was four, Cain killed Abel, reducing it to three. Homicide is not an aberration. It is the norm. It is part of who we are."

On his map, each killing of the current year was marked with a pushpin, a tiny cross, and a number. The pins were color coded to the race of the victim. The crosses denoted case status: black for closed, red for open. The tiny numbers taped to the pins denoted the chronological order of the killings in each year. These numbers correlated to a database Sully kept that had the victim's name, date of the crime, suspects (if any), relatives' names (if any), and the name of the lead detective. Each killing then had a manila folder of its own, complete with photographs of the crime scene, the victim, the killer, and so on.

A half dozen years earlier, at the height of the crack cocaine epidemic, there would have been more than four hundred crosses each year. There were about two hundred so far this year, nearly all of them clustered in the city's poorest quadrants: east of the Anacostia, then a spine up through the neighborhoods of eastern Capitol Hill, Trinidad, and on into Brookland. The most violent housing projects—Benning Terrace, Barry Farms, Potomac Gardens, Sursum Corda—were a thick red smear of crosses.

Rock Creek Park, its eastern edge reaching as far as Sixteenth Street, split the city, both in geography and homicide. Nearly all the slayings were to the east and south. West of the park—west of the park's jogging trails and rising hills and tumbling streams—the city got wealthy and mostly white, and the few red murder crosses there appeared as droplets of blood.

He was looking for a pin and a red cross for Sarah.

"Sullivan, God, I'm glad to see you," a voice called out, startling him. Melissa Baird, the Metro editor, was smiling, closing on him like a fast hawk on a slow rabbit. "R.J. tells me you've got a beautiful piece on this neighborhood, just really beautiful."

She was wearing her shoulder-length brown hair pulled back in a ponytail, and her pressed jeans and an open-collared shirt—her idea of a casual Saturday—had an air that all but screamed Master's in Fucking Journalism from Columbia, born on third base in Westchester. Social climber, vertical blur at a paper that idolized the Ivy League and East Coast wankerdom. He swiveled in the chair, eyes darting to a clock posted on a beam behind her. It was nearly five. Front-page meeting starting in fifteen.

"Thank God you've got something so eloquent," she was saying. "Nothing happened on the investigation, other than they're still looking for those three guys in the store." She came into his cubicle and made a slight hop to sit on the edge of the desk, her newsroom trademark. Legs crossed at the ankles, back straight, hands on the desk beside her.

"Hunter's sources on cops zipped up tight," she continued. Sully itched, wondering how long this would go on. Pert. She was just so damn *pert*. "The feds aren't even returning calls. Reese family is sequestered at home in McLean. We'll put the investigation story on the front page—we've got to, right?—but we're looking pretty thin. Your piece is saving us. The art's already in. Have you seen it? Early-morning mist in an alley, looking across Georgia at the store where the girl was murdered, a couple of storefronts, a guy in ragged pants and shirt walking across the street, stepping in a puddle. R.J. saw it and said it was just the kind of atmosphere you've got."

"R.J. is a kind man."

"He said something about Charles Bukowski poetry."

Sully recognized the drill, and he recognized Melissa's skill at it. She was pumping him up while letting him know the pressure she, and by extension he, was under. And, he recognized, without telling him what to write, she was telling him *exactly* what to write.

"Well, a piece like this," he said, thinking of something to bullshit her with, "I think we just tell people what it feels like on the block down there. We tell them what the beer delivery guy is talking about while he's loading up a dolly and what song is thumping out of a car stopped at the light. We tell them what the bathroom in the strip club just down the street smells like. We tell them about the elementary school, swing sets in the rain and needles in the playground grass from the Friday night junkies, and that the people who live here, the people in left-behind America, they, they're the people least interested in the murder story that, you know, is horrifying the rest of the nation's capital."

Melissa, beaming, smiling, leaning back on the desk, holding up her hands. "Perfect! That's just golden. Never mind a lead for the five o'clock, but go ahead and write in a public basket so we can peek in, okay? Helps the headline guys. Move a final by seven?"

Sully nodded, sure sure, yeah.

Melissa popped her hands together and got off the desk, starting to back away, pep talk done. "That bit about the people there being the least interested in the murder that's fascinating the rest of the city? Perfect. But you can make it the rest of the country. Slow weekend. This thing is all over the networks, the cable channels. The Beeb just did eight minutes."

She nodded, as if that were information he really needed right now, turned and walked away, everything but a spring in her step. He put his pen in his mouth and typed in a slug for the story—PRINCETONPLACE—and not twenty seconds later felt the bulbs of sweat start pushing through the pores in the small of his back, under his arms, on his palms. Why couldn't you drink in the newsroom anymore? What was wrong with that?

Someone dumped the body of Sarah Emily Reese into a garbage dumpster less than 200 feet from the intersection of Georgia Avenue Northwest and Princeton Place NW in this scruffy corner of the District on Friday evening, a crime that has fascinated, if not horrified, the nation. But there were no memorials of teddy bears, flowers and hand-scrawled posters at the scene yesterday, the typical signs of neighborhood mourning in this part of the city.

Instead, neighbors and residents here may be the people in America least interested in the brutal slaying of the child of a prominent D.C. jurist in their midst. Neighborhood bars kept their televisions tuned to sports stations yesterday, not the blanket coverage of the killing carried by cable news channels. Pedestrians sidestepped the yellow police tape around Doyle's Market and ducked into the Hunger Stopper restaurant for breakfasts of waffles and fried chicken. Speculation wasn't on the menu. The Show Bar, a strip club two blocks from the murder scene, did a brisk afternoon trade in the regular bump and grind . . .

Sully had this in the system and heard Melissa hoot from across the room. "Sullivan *Carter*! 'Speculation was not on the menu.' You're killing me here!"

"Un-hunh," he called back, without looking up.

The dwindling clock, the fact that half a dozen editors were looking at his copy as he was writing, that the copy desk was already composing a headline, that any mistake in spelling or a mistyped digit in an address or a failure of memory about facts would result in a credibility-dinging correction and sour faces from the brass . . .

He stopped to look up a few clips of old crime stories and did a database search for Lana and Noel. That led to a few perfunctory grafs of background about the Honorable Judge Reese and the probability of his future with the Supreme Court. Then onto Regina Blocker's dance studio, the neighborhood demographics, what the traffic was like in that segment of Georgia on a Friday night. The keyboard strokes came in bursts:

The Park View neighborhood has fast-food chicken places and two liquor stores and a couple of corner stores and a Chinese carryout and a used-car lot. The people who live on Princeton Place and adjacent streets tend to be bus drivers and nurses and Metro mechanics and check-out clerks and employees in the city's parks and recreation department and secretaries in other city agencies. Some people still own. Most rent. Violence, drug deals and prostitution are not unusual.

Lana Escobar, 25, was found dead in outfield grass at the Park View Recreation Center's baseball field last July 14. She had been strangled. Her slaying remains unsolved, but police say Escobar was involved in prostitution and believe the killing was related to that trade.

Another young woman, Noel Pittman, a part-time student at Howard University, disappeared April 24 of last year. A call to the telephone number listed on a flier asking for help finding her was not returned yesterday . . .

Sully looked at the clock: 7:15. A kicker and he was home. Flipping through his notes, he remembered he hadn't said anything else about the strip club, after mentioning it in the lede. If he came back to it now at the end, it would appear as if he'd intended that all along.

Les Samuels, who runs the strip club, said residents and neighbors were not indifferent to the Reese slaying. He was in his office in the back of the club yesterday afternoon, filling out paperwork for the array of city and law enforcement agencies that license his establishment.

"What people don't want," he said, "is trouble they ain't already got.

People got plenty of trouble all by themselves. A rich white girl gets killed up the street? That's a fresh lot of trouble. That's something you want to stay about a million miles away from."

"Sullivan!"

He hit the send button. "Yours!"

The bathroom, a place to walk to. Water ran from the tap in a cold torrent, and lowering his face to the sink, he cupped his hands to catch it, splashing it over his face. A damp hand through the hair and he looked up to the mirror. The scars were there, like bones melted by fire, by electricity. He thought of his house and its silences, awaiting him like an entombing crypt, and he did not want to go there, did not want to be left alone with his thoughts.

Back at the desk, he read through his notes for fact-checking, checked the names to be sure, and then Melissa was waving, beckoning him. She had made a few tightening and clarification changes. She called the story up in layout, so they could see the front page and how it was displayed.

There was no one else nearby, but she lowered her voice anyway, part of that bullshit hey-I'm-doing-you-a-favor air of familiarity she liked to convey. "Fabulous work today, Sullivan. It saved us. Now. Look. Really need you at the Reese house tomorrow. They're making some sort of statement at one."

He blinked. She needed to whisper to hand him a lame-ass assignment like that?

"Chris—let's let him get that," he said. "Lemme push the investigative side, something related to the manhunt but not precisely on it."

She looked away from the screen and at him, not pleased with the push-back. "Thanks, but cops are Chris's beat. Jamie is working the feds. I need a real pro out there with the family. This statement, or whatever it is, isn't going to be much, but I know you can do something with it. We'll box it on the front."

"A statement? You're serious?" He was whispering back, as if they were trading stock tips. "You're sending me out to McLean to take *dictation*? Send a shooter and an intern."

"No," she said firmly, holding his gaze now. "I need a scene setter.

It's a Sunday. Nothing else is going to develop on a Sunday. I need you to do just what you did today: Write the story onto the front page. The family statement, you know, pathos, the eternal grief of parents of murdered children."

"Reese and I have a certain history—"

"Which nobody cares about," she said. "You two are both professionals. Surely a tiff several years ago will not affect either of you when it comes to the murder of his child."

"A *tiff*?" It burst out of him, loud and hot, before he could stifle it. "He tried to get me fucking *fired*. He leaked me intel and then tried to say it—"

"So you always said," she shot back.

"Screw you," he said, standing up. "Just fuck that—"

"Sullivan," Edward Winters cut in, looking like he was pulling the leash on a poorly trained dog. Starched striped shirt, tie, hair swept back in a perfect coif, he seemed to materalize at the right of the copyediting desk, prim lips pursed. Sully walked over, this little summoning to the principal's office. Copy editors, leaning back in their chairs, trying to glance over without looking like they were glancing over.

"What's it about?" Edward's voice a harsh whisper, the blue eyes hard, that whole Princeton and Martha's Vineyard thing. In his sixties, lifetime of privilege. Twits like this running things, nothing you could do.

"Reese. The Judge Foy thing. You remember. You suspended me a week."

"What's that got to do with this?"

"Melissa wants me to babysit his presser tomorrow in his front yard."

"So do it."

"It's wasting my time," and here was where he should play his ace. "I'm working something, Eddie. The three suspects? They're not connected. It's a wrong turn."

"How do you know that?"

"From a source. It's developing. I need—"

"No, what *you* need? *You* need to realize you're not still working in a war zone. *You* cover that presser at one. This is the next Supreme Court justice we're talking about. We *need* to own this story, and you—you *need* to get over your beef with Reese. You fucked up. There were repercussions. End of story."

Sully held his gaze for a beat, then two.

"Sure thing, boss."

He went back over to Melissa, who was running with it now. She was leaning forward, elbows on the desk, eyebrows pulling down and together.

"Let's get this straight," she said. "I am. Your boss. I. Am. Your. Boss's. Boss. You pop off like that to me again? I'll slap a memo to HR. You'll be covering high school soccer until you quit. That bit Eddie just told you about the war being over, that's exactly—"

"What war are we talking about? I remember about six. Depending on your definition of open conflict."

"Then all of them, Sullivan. You're back home. Look at a map. The rules are different here."

He kept his face flat, but felt the fury boiling from his throat into his head, the humiliation. Times like this, since the shell, maybe before, his mental wires crossed. The doctors, they had talked to him about the rage and how to contain it, and all that was washed away in a flood.

"Just you try busting me," he said, leaning closer to her, whispering back, smiling, pure malice now. "Go the fuck ahead. Walk into *your* boss's office, good old Eddie back there, and explain assigning your best reporter to babysit a presser 'cause you thought it brilliant to have a twenty-seven-year-old newbie on the cop beat get bitchslapped by the *New York Times*."

She broke her gaze and leaned back, to defuse at least the appearance of a scene. "Okay, Sully. Look, it's late. Everybody's tired. Let's just cool off and—"

"You'll get your presser," he cut in, his voice ragged. "And in the next twenty-four to forty-eight? You'll be eating this. Be a sweetheart when you do."

He managed to make his feet turn and walk, the walls seemed to vibrate, and the thundering in his ears was so loud that he had to blink it back.

When he got to the hallway and reached for the elevator button, his thumb was trembling.

nine

When he blew in the door, Dusty had called, and that was just fucking great. He listened to the voice mail—*Call me, it's been too long, what's the deal?*—and decided to ignore it. The blackness, the bile—she wouldn't understand and he couldn't explain. He poured Basil's over ice, skipped the splash, and opened the Dutch door to the backyard, sitting on the steps.

He blinked and looked at the cherry tree, trying to slow his breathing the way the doctors had taught him: Focus, focus on something small. The tree, the tree. It would be shedding leaves in a matter of weeks. The chill in the air would stay. The ghosts in his head would leave. Winter would descend. He listened to the traffic passing on Constitution and his chest slowed. He held out his hand. The tremors were almost gone.

He went back inside, got the bottle and went upstairs. The shelf in the closet held the box, the kind of storage box law firms used to use for case files. He took it to the bed, unwrapped the silk drawstrings, turned it upside down, shaking it out onto the top of the sheets.

Pictures, old passports, documents in foreign languages, wrinkled currencies in faint shades of blue. Nadia's scarf. He climbed on the bed, propping the bourbon against a pillow. There were several sets of pictures from Bosnia, bound together with a green rubber band, and he sorted through them until he found the packet he was looking for. He pulled the rubber band off and the pictures spilled out. They were taken at the school and they were poorly lit and Nadia wasn't the subject of most of them because he did not know her then.

The story had been about an elementary school that was functioning in the basement of an apartment building during that first winter of the war, populated by children of parents who'd stayed behind by choice or necessity now that the routes into and out of Sarajevo were blocked. The siege had a surreal quality to it. The drudgery of the war, the intermittent shelling, the bread lines, the snipers, gasoline at a hundred dollars per gallon, twenty-five dollars for a bar of chocolate, had not yet settled in.

The school was composed of fifty-six children from six grades, being taught—if that was the verb—by three teachers. It seemed to Sully more like a lesson in crowd control. The children were aggressive, loud, anxious. They stood when they were supposed to sit, they ran when they were supposed to walk, they threw things. They were wildly energized by a foreign reporter dropping in, and this gave cause for more noise and frenzy. Children had never done much for him, and Sully had been of a mind to pop them upside the head and tell them to pipe down. His old man hadn't been wrong about everything.

The two other teachers were older, maybe early forties, and Nadia, a decade younger, was the quiet one who didn't say much. She taught the youngest children. He had been struck, immediately, by her genuineness and warmth (well, her eyes, too, a deep, honeyed shade of brown) and, after a few minutes of conversation, the sly wit, the rough voice (she smoked).

That first day, snow had just fallen. Where were the pictures . . . ? Here. Here she was, blue cable-knit sweater, jeans, boots. Black hair, loose, free. The kids surrounded her, excited by the camera, mugging. A kid named Sasha put his head on her shoulder as she sat at her desk. Here she was in teaching mode, writing on a whiteboard, one arm drawn across her chest to keep her coat close in the near freezing air.

A month passed before he saw her again. He took her a copy of the story, a version that had been picked up and run on the front page of the *International Herald Tribune*. By then four kids in her class were dead and they had moved the classroom twice. He saw her in the Merkale Market, too, just long enough to say hello. Two weeks later, he saw her there again. She lingered, standing outside next to a table scattered with anemic vegetables, a pale winter sun barely over the mountains, her skin white as parchment, a cigarette in her left hand. His voice nervous, he couldn't help it he said hi and hello and then just did it.

—So maybe could I take you to dinner or something sometime? I could—

—Nobody goes to dinner. Only foreign *novinari* and UNPROFOR.

—Okay. I wasn't trying to—

—You can come over if you want pasta.

—'m sorry?

—Pasta. Do you eat it?

—Yes, yes, but—

—Is English one of your languages?

—Yes.

—So you know, come over, eat pasta.

Teasing him in that Balkan accent, that world-weary Euro air, looking at him now, those eyes.

—Yes. I can. I can come over. I got two bottles of red from duty-free.

And so it had proceeded in the speeded-up hyperreality of war. Before the calendar turned to February, they were making love, on her bed, on the couch, on the carpet in front of the couch. He put her on her knees in front of the couch and neither of them lasted long like that. Pillow talk:

—You like Yugoslav girls?

—I don't know that I've sampled the lot. But this one, touching the tip of her nose with his index finger, yeah, I like this one. But I thought you guys were Bosnian now.

—I was Yugoslav when I was born. Tito said we were all Yugoslavs.

—Tito's dead. Yugoslavia's dead.

—It does not change what I am. You, you're American. From the south part?

—Louisiana.

—What do they do in Louisiana? *Loo-ee-see-anna*.

—Fight. Fuck. Play football. Fish.

Giggling, brushing her hair back from her face, propping her head on her elbow, the muslin-thin moonlight streaming across the room behind her. There were the hills in the distance, a deeper dark than the sky above it. He could see them behind her. She was a shadow, a shape, and she possibly had the most beautiful voice he had ever heard.

—Only things that start with the 'F'?

—Okay, okay. They cook. They speak English funny. They go to church, a lot of them, anyway, Catholics and Baptists, not Orthodox. They teach you to shoot before they teach you to drive. Manners. Most of them have manners, unless you're being an asshole, and then they don't. Then they really don't.

—And your parents?

—They're dead. Like Tito.

—They were Louisiana?

—Yeah.

—So you would stop being Louisiana if they called it something else?

By summer, they had progressed to the point where he'd stay with her when he was in the city. They talked of him hiring her as his interpreter and trying for a visa, issued by UN forces that were running the airport, to come with him past the siege lines. But they both knew that would not work, and the idea sank into the gloom of the apartment in the late evenings. There was nothing but candlelight and books and their conversation filling the long hours. She read Bulgakov, reread Gogol, she got him to read Ivo Andric. She read Günter Grass, she read the García Márquez and the Faulkner he'd bring. She read an Elmore Leonard book in a single evening, trying out the slang, working on her accent.

She read like this, and made love to him, he believed, because she knew she would never get out of the city as long as the war lasted. She was a Serb living with Muslims and Croats, a living anachronism, a relic of the days of Tito. She knew and he knew she would be detained on the far side of any checkpoint. The Serbs, identifying her as a traitor for staying behind in Sarajevo, would tell her they could not guarantee her safety if she proceeded into Serb territory, which was the nice way of saying they would shoot her in the back of the head if she took another fucking step.

So she stayed, parentless, without family, like him, and they talked of their lives before and maybe after. The war progressed into the next summer and the following winter.

—It won't end until we are all dead.

—Yes, it will. It will end before then.

—Your Americans, the NATO, is never coming to help us.

—Eventually they will. I think they will.

They were in a pizzeria on the eastern side of town on an August afternoon, a small stucco place in the middle of a block on a narrow street. The location was shielded from snipers and a shell would have to whizz-bang straight down to hit it from the Serb-held hills, an angle that was beyond the laws of physics. There was moderately cold beer. It cost seventeen dollars per bottle. She had eaten two slices and half of another and was still too thin, the stress, the diet pasta and almost no vegetables, her skin breaking out across her forehead.

—We will be in Paris in a couple of years, he said, and then this will only be the way it used to be.

—I don't like Paris.

—Okay. New York. We'll go to New York.

—I don't like New York.

—You've never been.

—I wouldn't like it.

—Tell me then. Tell me where.

She thought, looking at him.

—Santorini.

—Greece?

—I like olives.

—To live?

—Why not?

—It's a tiny little island. What will we do there?

—Olives. We will raise the olives. And goats. And kids.

—Baby goats are kids. You call them kids.

—We will make baby goats, she laughed, finally, her mood swinging back the other way, and she slapped the table, tipping her beer back, laughing harder. Sully and Nadia, they fuck and make the baby goats!

Sully pulled her scarf, the only thing of hers he had left, over his lap.

He did not smell it anymore because he knew the scent of her had long since faded.

In the late winter of the third year of the war, when spring was still just an idea, he flew into the city on an aid flight. He was unable to get to her apartment because of the late hour, the curfew, and the falling snow. He spent the night in the hack hotel, the Holiday Inn, and went by the hospital the next morning to talk to a doctor he knew for a story he was working on about surgeons operating without electricity or anesthesia or running water. He stopped in the morgue on his way out because the only way to count the dead in a city with no phones was to go there and count noses. There were several bodies on stretchers on the freezing concrete floor and there was Nadia, eyes closed and half her head gone, heaved in twain by shrapnel from a mortar. The rest of her body, when he had pulled back the sheet, was completely untouched.

The photograph of her in the cable-knit sweater was in his hand now but he was hearing her voice, that husky Balkan accent that would say his last name in the dark, two syllables, *Car-ter, Car-ter,* like a chant, like a prayer, when they made love, as if it were carried by the breeze that would blow in from her balcony window.

ten

The sun was streaming across the room in ribbons of light, the sound of traffic coming up from the street below. There was no clear sense of the hour. Cotton balls seemed to fill his mouth, and there was a dim throbbing at his forehead. The phone was ringing.

He blinked and sat up. He had his shirt on from the night before but had taken off his jeans and socks. The pictures were everywhere, on the bed beside him, on the floor, on the bookcase. His eyes wandered till he found the clock by the bedside lamp. Twenty after ten.

"Fuck me," he said.

The caller ID on his cell read PRIVATE NUMBER. He coughed and clicked it on. "I didn't think you did Sunday mornings," he croaked.

"I do brunch on Sundays in good weather," Sly Hastings said, sounding like he'd been up since six, gotten in a nice run and a workout at the gym. "I'm sitting here reading my paper in a reputable establishment, a place people stand in line to get to, and this story you got here, you trying to run down my property values."

"I didn't create the neighborhood, Sly, and I didn't kill anybody in it."

There was a pause. "What, you got jokes now?"

Sully, coughing some more, brushing the pictures back in the box, "No jokes, hombre. They wanted poetry of the neighborhood. You want better poetry, move to a better neighborhood. What's the reputable establishment?"

"Colorado Kitchen. Where they make real waffles and fried chicken.

Which is what I got today, thanks to you. Put me in the mind for it, me and Lionel."

"So at least I did you a favor."

"I wouldn't go so far as a favor. A suggestion. But look here. That's not what I called to tell you. I called to tell you to be ready for some news today. I think our friends in law enforcement will stumble across them three brothers they looking for."

Sully paused, then said, "You didn't."

"You damn skippy I did. MPD and the DEA and FBI and all them other goons? Out there like ugly on ape. Two detectives and a fed came and knocked on my door last night, you know it? Acting all friendly, asking if maybe I knew something about something. You know what that tells me? It tells me I ain't got no outstanding warrants, I ain't got a goddamn *parking* ticket, 'cause they will bury you with that shit if they can. So, they asking a favor? Well. That's a business proposition. So, as a responsible homeowner and taxpayer, I assisted local law enforcement. About where maybe they might could find them three."

"And what time is this to happen?"

"You know, police can't ever just go get motherfuckers. They got to call SWAT and fifteen other badasses."

"I thought it was bad form to cooperate with police."

"It is if you're in the getting-caught-at-it business. If you're in the keeping-your-ass-on-the-street-and-making-money business, which is my line of work, it is a sound decision from time to time. Particularly when you know they ain't done it. They'll be in D.C. jail for six months or something and they'll be back home. Daddy Sly'll be there for them when they walk out."

"How you know they won't get drilled?"

"This ain't the parade of the innocents, you hear me, so I wouldn't worry about these three brothers even if they do wind up catching a twenty-five-year bid. But they ain't no way they did this, and not even the U.S. Attorney's Office is going to think that."

"You tell your new friends in MPD that?"

"Oh, hell no. They out there saving white folk from crazy-ass niggers, far as they know."

Sully hung up a minute later and went downstairs to put on the coffee. When it finished, he called the desk and told them to look out for an arrest of the three suspects. Patrick Ogle, running the paper for the day, startled, asked him his source, and Sully said it was reliable and not to worry about it. Sweet as spun honey, he said he'd love to help more, but that Melissa had asked him to cover the Reese family announcement and that he had to run. Also, since he'd be on the bike? He couldn't take any calls. Sorry. Clicked off to end it before Patrick could say anything else.

He drummed his fingers on the kitchen counter and put three spoons of sugar in the coffee and sipped and looked at his tree. Picking up the cell, he punched in the numbers of MPD lieutenant John Parker, deciding to see what he could get out of him.

John was a decent sort but last year had been put in charge of the city's demoralized homicide squad, a group beaten down by years of crack wars, union infighting, and then, the coup de grâce, the chief's sudden orders to decentralize. The chief had the brilliant idea that he would spread his best detectives out to the city's seven wards. Supposedly this was getting guys out on the street, closer to the action, closer to the Fat Chuckys of the world, who would turn on bigger players like the Sly Hastingses, which would help them solve more of the sixty-five percent of the cases that were now going unsolved. It was a pathetic closure rate, Sully would grant the chief that—two out of three killers in the city were literally getting away with murder—but blowing up the department, separating your best thinkers and most experienced ballbusters was just depriving yourself of decades of institutional knowledge. And then there was the practicality of it all: John had guys twenty years on the force and suddenly their commute got bumped from twenty minutes to get to headquarters to an hour, each way, to get out to 7-D. It was a morale killer, and John was still swimming upstream in a river of shit.

This morning, his cell rang five times and went to voice mail. Sully cleared his throat, still waking up.

"Hey, John, how you living? I just need to know what time and where the raid is going down on the suspects in the Sarah Reese homicide." "I just drove by and saw your car out back of 4-D so don't even fuck with me that you ain't working this. I'll call you back every three minutes. You know I love you."

He hung up and went into the backyard.

The tree, he decided, would look better with flowers around the base. He walked out front to get the paper. Flapping it open, he saw that his story was the centerpiece. The phone rang.

"You're not half as smart as you think you are," John said.

"I'd believe that if you hadn't called me back so fast."

"You get this from our shop or the feds?"

"I'm a popular young man, John. People like talking to me. It's flattering. And this is—have I mentioned?—never seeing the light of day. I have not spoken to you."

"We're going to talk about this later."

"Un-hunh."

"The 1500 of First Street, Southwest. First and P. Three-story apartment complex. Don't even try to get on First. Stay on P."

"When?"

"I'd say just before dark. And keep your head on a swivel."

A couple of Tylenols later, Sully was dressed and taking the bike out on Constitution Avenue, past the museums and the Mall, opening up the throttle as he crossed the bridge, looking over the dark brown waters of the Potomac until he was in Virginia, peeling right on the George Washington Parkway. The rain had blown through and now the air felt so clean it seemed somebody ought to be charging for it. Far below, the yachts rested out on the Potomac, bright white dots in the sun. The doctor, the guy at Landstuhl, the one who had told him to focus his mind on something good and hold it there? He had said it was a bit of mental discipline to pull himself out of everything that had happened in the war, the things that he had lost.

By the time David Reese emerged from the front door of his house at one thirty-five, the press herd on the street out front was fifty or sixty strong, nervous, mooing in their discontent. Reese was in a black suit, white shirt, and black tie, walking briskly down the sidewalk, turning and walking up the driveway toward the street. The house was an impressive but not overbearing two-story colonial on a street filled with them, the kind of well-to-do-but-not-ostentatious place federal judges seemed genetically programmed to seek out. Manicured hedges, mulch in the flower beds, half a dozen oaks in the front yard, a canopy of green. In the back, Sully guessed, was the pool and the deck, maybe with one of those little rock waterfalls. It took him a few minutes to spot the security cameras, discreetly mounted on the balcony over the front door and next to the light over the driveway. Just once, he thought, watching Reese move up the sidewalk, he'd like to meet a federal judge who lived in a row house, drove a Civic, and vacationed at Ocean City because that's all he could afford.

Now, with Reese in plain view, the press crew bolted into action, cameramen trying to pull him into focus while he was walking—a few extra seconds of video would go a long way for background fill—with Secret Service officers or U.S. Marshals flanking him as he approached the bank of microphones. He stopped there and they kept walking toward the mob of reporters.

The taller one with dark hair said, almost in a whisper: "No questions. No questions at all. There will be no questions. Judge Reese will make a statement and that will be the end." Then he and his partner moved back, flanking Reese.

The judge stood at the microphones and looked from left to right expectantly. He was a tall man, perhaps six foot three, and weighed, Sully guessed, about two hundred. His face, usually tanned, was ashen. He seemed to blink in slow motion. Valium? Handful of Ativan? Sully glanced to the house to see whether anyone was looking out a window, but not a curtain stirred.

"On Friday evening, October first, our daughter, Sarah Emily, was killed after her dance class in Washington, D.C.," Reese began. His voice was full and assured. He leaned down slightly to talk into the microphones. The act of talking seemed to lend his eyes focus, but it was as if the skin were not animated. The man looked like a talking mannequin. Sully, standing at the edge of the scrum of reporters, turned on his recorder and held it out. "We would like to thank all branches of law enforcement for their full support and professional work, which is ongoing. We would like to thank the White House, the President and First Lady, the House and Senate leaders for their remarkable support and personal offers of condolences and sympathy. And we would like to thank the thousands of Americans who, across this country of ours, have reached out to Tori and me to express their empathy, their concern, and their prayers. It is stirring.

"It is equally stirring to us that we have had to look out our windows each day, all day, at a street full of reporters and cameramen and photographers who have expressed no sense of grief but whose job apparently is to document our sorrow by pressing on the boundaries of our privacy. We ask the employers of these workers to release them from these morbid obligations and leave us to our grief. The memorial and funeral service for Sarah will be private. There will be no further announcements or statements from the family at any time on this—this *subject*."

He paused, and rocked back slightly on his heels. His hands had been folded in front of him, and now he pulled them behind him, clasping them behind his back. He was beginning to sweat, the beads starting to form high on the forehead. Sully thought he was ready to launch into another phase of the speech. Instead, he simply gave a curt nod.

"Thank you for coming," he said. "Now, if you would please leave. Thank you."

He turned and began to walk back down the driveway.

No one said anything for a moment until, as the lights began to turn off, a cameraman said softly, "And the godless, blood-sucking vultures of the American media thank *you*."

There was low murmuring and chortling behind that, and Sully saw Dave Roberts emerge from the herd. "I'd say he loves us," Dave said, slapping Sully's shoulder and moving past him with a cackle, headed for the truck. Sully followed. "That was perfect—you got to give the man his props," Dave said. "Give it an hour and watch. They'll scatter like crows."

Sully nodded and stepped aside to call in a couple of paragraphs on the scene. Patrick said yeah, yeah, typing it in, but hang on, Eddie wants to talk to you.

Edward came on the line. "So what's this about the manhunt, the suspects?"

"What I told Patrick earlier. I got a heads-up it might go down today."

"Chris says he hasn't heard anything."

"That surprises you?"

"Take the high road, Sullivan. Can you work it some more?"

"I can try. No promises. You want any more on this out here?"

"No. I was watching. Reese was very effective. We write a scene-setter on a bereaved father asking to be left alone, we look like cock-suckers."

"So—so you want me going on the suspects now?"

"Yes. I don't have to tell you how important this is."

He clicked off, and be damned if some of the reporters were not already drifting back to their cars, pulling out. Television trucks were striking tripods, loading up. Dave's crew was dragging, but they were wrapping up, too. Dave was sitting in the passenger seat of the truck, wrestling the tie off his neck.

"Hey," he said, looking up at Sully. "There's an honest-to-Christ seafood place about two miles up. They got a bar. Want in? We're killing time till the six o'clock stand-up."

"Maybe I'll catch you up down there."

"The Chesapeake. Two miles west, on the right."

Sully nodded and walked back to the bike, sitting astride it in the shade. He sat, thinking about it, watching the trucks pull out. After twenty minutes, when it was deserted, he went limping back toward the house, turning down the driveway like he owned the place.

An officer stepped out of his patrol car, stringy, incredulous. A U.S. Marshal came out of the garage and the pair began walking rapidly toward him. Sully kept walking, his hands up and away from his body, a business card between two fingers of his left hand.

"Please give this to the judge," he said, looking at the officer, extending the card, "and tell him he wants to talk to me for a few minutes. But right now. He needs to talk to me right now."

"You know my orders are to arrest the first reporter who tries some shit like this?" the cop said, almost chest-bumping him, sweating in a bulletproof vest.

"'s why I said please."

The cop took the card, looked down at it, and motioned to the marshal. The man took it and walked back into the house. He reemerged a few minutes later, flicked his finger at Sully, and escorted him into the foyer. It was high ceilinged, spacious with stone floors, a mirror in a heavy frame on the wall and a small credenza. Thick carpet started in each room off the foyer, and the staircase was just ahead. It was oppressively quiet.

"You are in a world of shit," the marshal whispered to him. He was a tall, chubby man, his black suit coat buttoned, his brown eyes bright and harsh. He stood about nine inches from Sully's face, leaning in from the waist. It was the stance and position of men in authority, and Sully resented it as much as he recognized it.

He pursed his lips as if to kiss the agent on the lips, and the man recoiled, stepping back.

"Thought so, tough guy."

The agent glared and motioned him to follow down the carpeted hallway. At the end, he knocked softly on a door, swung it open, and motioned for Sully to enter. It was the judge's home office. David Reese sat behind a heavy desk. His tie was still knotted at his throat and his jacket was still on. There were framed diplomas on the wall. The place had the air of a funeral parlor.

"I honestly cannot believe your temerity," Reese said, as soon as the agent closed the door. "I cannot believe you would send some sort of cryptic note to my family at this hour. The only reason I allowed you in was so I could document your behavior to your employers, who will be informed of this, at the highest level, within the hour. I can assure you that my graciousness will not be so profound this time."

"The last time we had dealings, David, you lied about what you told me, then tried to get me fired, so let's cut the foreplay," Sully said, sitting down, uninvited. "I am truly sorry about your daughter. Honest to Christ. Now. If you're going to call my bosses and tell them I'm the only hack who got into your house today by handing a cop a business card and telling him it was important, they're going to be more impressed than pissed. But go ahead. Eddie Winters'll take your call. I just talked to him. The phone's right there."

They looked at each other.

"Go ahead," Sully said. "I'n wait."

"There is some point to this," Reese said.

"Yeah. There is. It's an off-the-record visit. I'm not reporting anything about coming to your house or what it looks or sounds like in here. I'll report what you said in the driveway and that's it. I came to tell you that apparently at some point today, or perhaps early tomorrow, police are going to arrest the three men or boys who were in Doyle's Market when Sarah was there."

The man rocketed to his feet, knocking his chair back. "How do you know that? No one has told me any such thing."

"It's going to happen very soon. But that's not the point. The point is that, as a matter of decency, I did not want your family to put much faith in those arrests. They're not going to stand. You're a prick, David, but I thought it was the decent thing to do, for your wife if nobody else, to let her know to condition her expectations."

"How could you even know about the arrests, much less if they'll stand?"

"It's a long story."

Reese shook his head. "I don't trust a goddamn thing you're saying."

Sully stood up and nodded. "Doubt I would if I was you, either. But I wanted to let you know. It seemed right to me. Do with it what you want. I am sorry for your wife. I mean that."

He backed out of the room, opened the door, and was escorted to the edge of the property by the marshal.

"Soon, and very soon," the agent said.

"Blow it out your ass," Sully said.

eleven

Sully took the bike back downtown, feeling the energy, the adrenaline coming up now. By the time he peeled off 395 and onto South Capitol, the building itself in his rearview, he was where he needed to be, ready for the shit to start.

He turned right onto O Street SW, one block short of his destination, maybe a mile from the waterfront docks and clubs and restaurants, and a good cannon shot from tourist country. He passed Half Street and then turned south on First, approaching the intersection John had given him. Two white Chevy Caprice Classics, parked illegally, four men in each, screamed that he was in the right place. He went back up to the McDonald's on East Capitol, got a Coke and called John Parker again, getting the answering machine.

A blue Olds Cutlass sat in the parking lot, the engine running. He would have sworn he'd seen it in his rearview on the GW Parkway. "You got to be kidding," he said out loud.

After twenty minutes without a call back from John, the blue Olds still in the parking lot, he went back outside. He went to his bike, helmet in hand, then turned and walked rapidly to the Olds. There were two men inside, both white, jeans and sweatshirts. In this part of town.

"Hey," he said, rapping on the passenger-side window, leaning in.

The window came partway down, the guy not saying anything.

"You should try the burgers," he said. "I think this place, it's gonna catch on."

The window went back up.

• • •

A few minutes later, he ripped the bike back onto South Cap, giving it full throttle, up to ninety in less than two hundred yards, no way anything on four wheels could keep up, and then he braked and leaned hard to make the right onto M, took two other turns, blowing the stop signs and, less than three minutes later, was on P, the tail gone.

Parts of the job he liked: This.

Midway down the block one more time, he popped it into neutral, then hit the kill switch. The engine coughed and died. He made a show of pushing his visor up, looking down over the motor, to the left and right. He let the bike coast about fifty feet, distracting attention from his right hand, which he was squeezing ever so slightly, to apply the front brake and stop the bike before he passed an alley to the south.

The three-story brick building John had described was in a direct line of sight. Pulling off the helmet, he spit on the street, acting disgusted. He unlocked the seat, pulling the tool kit from the underside niche, and, taking a knee and pulling out a wrench, he loosened and tightened the screws of the frame that held the battery in place.

It didn't take long. A car rolled up behind him, unnaturally close. He half turned and saw it was one of the white Caprices.

"'s the problem, Evel?" A low baritone.

Sully turned back to the bike and reached for a wrench. "'s it to you, ace?"

"Hey," the voice said. Sully ignored it.

"*Hey*," the voice said, and he heard a door open and it slapped into his back, knocking him into the bike.

He stood up and wheeled around, acting shocked, acting pissed, selling it hard. The cop, one of the SWAT team members sitting in the car, bulletproof vests under sweatshirts, held a badge up beside his face, but not outside the car.

"Get your broke-ass bike off the street," the man said, nodding toward the badge.

Sully took a half step to look at the badge, peered at it, still with the dumb thing. "Well, Christ, dude, how was I supposed to know? Want me to push it over there?" He indicated P Street with a nod of the head.

"Further down," the man said, motioning down First.

Sully figured he had about fifty yards to give and still be in eyesight of the apartment building. He heard a chopper overhead, somewhere in the distance.

"Let me get my tools up and I'll push off."

The cop flicked cigarette ash off his chest. "Put them on the fuckin' bike and *move.*" He backed up until he got back in the car. They rolled off, went down the street, and made a left. Circling, Sully thought, back to their original spot.

He pushed the bike down First, watching the building from his peripheral vision, then stopped, pulling the wrench back. He kneeled behind the bike.

A few minutes later, a white cargo truck parked across the street in front of him. There was a pause, and then a heavy van with blackened windows rolled past him, wheeled hard onto P, and slammed to a stop. Four, five, six SWAT team members leaped out, running to the front of the apartment building, the first one carrying a Plexiglas shield, two behind him with assault rifles. At the same time, the back door of the cargo van rolled up and a jumble of agents leaped out, sprinting across a neighbor's yard, leaping over a small boundary fence.

Percussive booms ran up the street and a puff of smoke emerged from the apartment building. Yelling. A window shattered. Two and then three flat pops. The overhead *thump-thump-thump* intensified, the helicopter directly overhead now. Sully ran to the street now, pretense gone. A cop turned, briefly put a gun on him, Sully stopped, hands up, and the cop turned back.

Officers boiled out of the narrow doorway of the apartment building, a handcuffed man between them, head down, pushing and pulling, yelling, swearing, an awkward run to the black van parked in the street. Another knot of officers at the apartment doorway, a plume of smoke trailing them, and a second man emerged, again in handcuffs, again force-marched to the van. Seconds later, a third man, feet dragging. He did not appear to be conscious.

Sirens hit full force, the vans and squad cars roaring out. Sully whipped out his cell and called Patrick on the desk.

"Suspects just got popped," he said, giving the address and a few more grafs to get the story started.

"I'm coming with the rest," he said, looking over his shoulder. Cops on the perimeter were looking at him, talking into their fingers, starting to move toward him.

He cursed, rushing to put the tools back, hearing a siren start *whoop-whoop-whoop*ing, and saw a patrol car start to make a U-turn. He cranked the bike, and it roared into life, and then he had the helmet on, leaning over the gas tank as he hit the throttle to keep the front end of the bike from rearing into the air as he shot forward, leaving the patrol car behind.

A block down, blowing the stop sign, the bike flying past sixty, now to seventy, he saw the blue Olds parked at the curb, waiting, not bothering to give chase.

Five hours later he was sitting at the mahogany bar in Stoney's at the back end of the long L-shaped fixture, the Sazerac in front of him, the glass chilled, the lemon peel at the bottom like a little pickled fish.

"Wait," the guy at the other end of the bar was saying. "Turn it back up. They saying something."

Sully looked up in time to see Dmitri, working the bar, trying to clean up and close down, reach above the mirrored glass and turn the sound on the television up.

"—and have just released the names of the three suspects apprehended today. They are Reginald Jackson, seventeen, of the District of Columbia; D'onte Highsmith, eighteen, also of the District; and Jerome Deland, twenty-two, of Prince George's County." The man was looking down at a sheet of paper reading. "According to a police spokesman, all three have criminal records. Deland has four arrests, for assault, battery, unlicensed use of a vehicle—that's the District's charge for car theft—and possession of marijuana with intent to distribute. Court records show he was on, ah, parole. Highsmith has two arrests, both on drug possession charges, and had been released five weeks ago to await trial.

Police say Jackson was at Oak Hill, the city's juvenile detention facility, and escaped two weeks ago. They were apparently at a neighborhood basketball court just before the Sarah Reese killing, and then again minutes later, and were found to have an item of Sarah's in their possession when arrested earlier today at—"

"What is 'item'?" Dmitri said. "Why don't they just say?"

"'Cause the police didn't tell them," Sully said. "They didn't tell me, either. Why bother? It'll come out in court. What they want—what the police want right now—is for people to go to bed thinking it's all over."

Dmitri turned the sound down. "You want another?" *Vant.* Sully tapped the top of his glass in response. Dmitri raised his eyebrows at the man three seats down, who shook his head no. Dmitri made another Sazerac and told him that would be the last one. Sully said sure and then his phone buzzed.

"How did you know?" Melissa.

"Lucky guess."

"Look, if you're just going to be an ass—"

"So glad I was out at the Reese house taking dictation while your boy was killing it on the investigation."

There was fifteen seconds of silence. Then, "I *said* you were right, okay, but—"

"I wouldn't get real excited about these arrests, either," he said, jumping ahead to keep her off balance. "They look screwy."

"Screwy? Eddie said you were on about this. These morons were just out of jail when this went down. Something happened in that store and they—"

"I'm sure you'll tell me about it tomorrow," he said, and clicked off the phone.

A bartender had materialized from the back room, walking the length of the bar, turning the sound down on the television, sliding around Dmitri in the narrow space, her shoulder-length brown hair swinging as she did so. She walked up to Sully and put one hand, then two, on the bar between them. She took his whiskey glass and took a pull of the Sazerac.

"Dusty," he said, "as I goddamn live and breathe."

twelve

She was in the shower, talking behind the curtain, the door to the bathroom closed, the mirrors steamed over. He had already gotten out of the shower and was sitting on the closed toilet seat, a towel wrapped around his waist. Two bourbons, ice melting in the glasses, were sitting on the top of the toilet tank.

"So you're saying, if I'm following this, the person who killed the judge's kid is still out there? And Sly rigged it that way?"

"More or less." He liked her being in the shower. He liked listening to her voice and the water and the sound of the spray hitting the soft plastic of the curtain. It wasn't often there was a voice in the house besides his, and hers, in its softer inflections and higher pitches, in its laughter and warmth, made the place seem better than it was.

"So why? Why would he do that?"

"Needed the cops off the street, or so he says. He knew where the suspects were, so he threw 'em to the cops."

"Sounds like a setup."

He was examining his toenails and wondered where the clippers were. "That's what I just said."

"No. I mean to cover his own tracks."

"*His* tracks? You're saying Sly Hastings killed David Reese's daughter?"

The shower water turned off. She pulled the curtain back and reached for her drink. She took a long draw on it, then set it back down and reached for a towel.

"How should I know? He had time and opportunity, didn't he? Did you ask him where he was? All that's missing," she said, stepping out of the shower, standing in front of him, her breasts at the height of his eyes, smiling playfully down at him, "is motive. Which you tell me no one ever really knows."

He uncrossed his legs and swept the towel to the side, trying to be, what was the word, present. There was him, a chasm, and then everyone else. When that had come to be, he could no longer say, but he had first noticed it after Nadia's death. Then, after the shell that had blown him up, it had become a yawning gulf, a canyon, a thing so broad that the other side was out of sight. The assumption he'd made was that this was the new normal and it would never change. But hope was a stubborn thing, and in the eight or nine months he'd been dating Dusty (sort of steadily), there had been times like this when he could feel it closing—the gap. When he was a child, his father had taught him to swim in the Mississippi and told him classes were over when he finally swam from side to side, Louisiana to Mississippi, more than a mile, the old man beside him in a johnboat with an outboard and a shotgun for the cottonmouths. Since then, Sully tended to believe that vast distances could be crossed if you only had the grit for it.

Dusty stepped forward and straddled his lap, sitting across him. He put his hands around her back, at the curve of her buttocks, and pulled her farther up on him. She leaned her head back, leaning into his grip, and used the towel to dry her hair. Then she leaned forward, draping the towel around her shoulders. She gently pressed her breasts into his face, wrapping her arms around his shoulders. "I missed you, I think," she whispered into the top of his head.

He nodded, turning his head sideways, his eyes closed. She was warm, the space between her legs and the back of her thighs still damp. The shower dripped.

"I don't see the percentage in Sly killing the kid," he said. "Very high risk, for what reward? He's got no beef with Reese."

"Can we talk about something else?"

"Not right now."

"Why does it matter so much?" Her hands in his hair.

"Because it's my job."

"You're off the clock."

"Because it's me."

She held him, swaying the tiniest bit.

"Okay," she said, settling her shoulders. She was trying to work him through it, he could tell. "So—so somebody who does have a beef with the judge hired him? He's setting up the guys in the store to take the fall for him?"

"Well, one, people don't hire Sly Hastings. He hires people. And, two, if he's setting them up to take a fall, why tell me they didn't do it? I don't see the angle. He was mad Friday night. Somebody did something on his turf he didn't want done, and he was pissed."

"So the real killer is out there walking around?"

"I think so. I think Sly wants to find out who it is before the police do. I think he's using me to help him do that."

"'Cause he's going to wipe them out himself? He wants you to help him figure out who to get rid of?"

"Not if I can help it. And I'd rather not think of it that way."

She coughed, stifling a laugh, he thought. Then she said, "Is this supposed to be foreplay?"

He pulled his head back and smiled up at her, the spell the case had over him broken. "You Miami girls. So impatient."

"Fort Lauderdale, you moron," she said lightly. "It's not the same place. Well? Is it?"

"Only if it's working."

"You got to be kidding."

She stood up, pulling the towel around her body. She started out of the room. "Bring that massage oil, mister. You owe me for running out the other night. And bring my drink, too."

"You think you're giving orders?"

"Every day," she said, voice disappearing down the hall to the bedroom.

He turned out the light and got the drinks. He took three steps before he remembered the oil. "You always talk that smack," he said, "until I tie you up."

He heard her getting in the bed in the darkness, saw her lying across the sheets in the slats of light coming in from the streetlights. She lay on her stomach, hair falling across her shoulders, her olive skin, her long, slender legs. She crossed her arms in front of her and lay her head across them.

"Louisiana boys," she said, "talk too much."

thirteen

Dusty stirred. The black silk band Sully had used as a blindfold was pulled down around her neck. He slipped out of bed, looking at the clock—Christ, what was with the early goddamned phone calls?—and picked up the cell before it could buzz again. He didn't recognize the number. He walked out in the hallway and down the steps, grabbing a pair of basketball shorts as he went.

"This better be spectacular," he said into the phone.

"Good morning to you, sunshine, and yes, it is."

"John? Lieutenant Parker? Is that you? What number is this?"

"Borrowed a line. Look. You need to get your skinny ass up to Princeton Place. And hey, nice to see you on the front page. I didn't think you actually worked there anymore."

"Princeton Place? Can't a man have company over every now and then without this shit?"

"It's a free country for white people, Sully. Stay in bed and bonk like a bunny rabbit, you want. I'd get my ass to Princeton Place, but that's just me."

"What am I going to see there?"

"Me, brother."

The line disconnected.

He swore, standing there shirtless, thinking about it. Then he went back upstairs and found jeans and a shirt. He tiptoed to the bed, leaned over, and kissed Dusty between her shoulder blades. He left his mouth there. The taste of her skin was like peaches, that soft little down brushing against his lips.

"Got to go. Something about this Reese thing."

"Umm-hmm."

"Can you stay?"

"Nnnhh. Work in Baltimore tonight." She was half asleep.

"I'll call."

"Mmmm."

He walked out to the bike, parked on the street, and turned to look at the upstairs window, the smell of her still on him. It was open, the curtain twisting, flitting over the frame, and Dusty asleep a few feet away, unseen in the shadows.

The yellow police tape that had been blocking off the street during the Sarah Reese investigation was back, but this time one light pole farther up the block. Another squad car was parked diagonally across the street, in almost exactly the same spot as before. There were other squad cars down the street. Sully approached an unmarked car with the door open. A hand emerged from the window, waving him closer.

He limped down the middle of the street, ducking under the yellow tape.

"You showed," John Parker said, sunglasses propped on his shaved head. He was wearing a light brown suit, a dark brown tie over a starched white shirt, sitting in the front seat.

"You promised spectacular."

"I did. And I'll deliver. Right after you tell me how you learned about that little takedown yesterday." He got out of the car, his suit coat falling just so, the broad tie knotted perfectly at the neck. Sully always meant to ask him how he got the knot like that.

"Come on, man."

"Was it from us?"

"What, you worried I'm dating someone else?"

"Fun is fun and leaks are leaks, Sully, but that was in a different category. I'm trying to get control of this group, the squad. You know how bad we are right now? And that leak, brother, was high level."

"You know I can't say."

"Was it from us?"

Sully paused, let out a breath for the theater of it. "No."

"Alright," John nodding, eyeing him, seeing if he believed it. "Alright, then. I'll settle for it. I find out different, I'm not going to be amused, at you or your snitch. But you watch your ass, you hear? This is big-boy shit."

"Noted. Hey. You got any guys working out of a blue Olds? Beefy white boys, plainclothes?"

"Not out of our shop. Somebody bothering you?"

"Not yet."

"Also," John said, touching his fingertips to his temples, bringing them back down, "before I forget. The beach house. Already booked for Christmas and New Year's."

"Super Bowl?"

"I can check. Mrs. Parker handles all that. Summer is still mostly open."

"Never liked the beach in the summer. Winter is terrific. It's deserted." He nodded and lifted his chin to point farther down the street at the squad cars. Officers and lab techs were walking out of the house at the end of the block. "So what's the attraction?"

John let out a sigh. "Noel Pittman. What's left of her, anyhow."

Sully coughed, the late night, the whiskey. It wasn't what he was expecting.

"The girl from Howard?"

"Found her late yesterday, ID'd her this morning through the dentals. She was in the basement. It's packed dirt with a wood floorboard over it, like big plywood panels with carpet over them? She was in this tight little space down there, covered up with a lot of trash and junk."

"You guys had a cadaver dog in there?"

John blew out his lips in a raspberry, leaning on the car door. Twenty-three years on the force, started on the street, it was all white guys running Homicide, the big cases, and now here he was, the lieutenant, trying to get the homicide unit off its dysfunctional ass, kicking the shit with a reporter on a Monday morning, the rotting body his problem now.

"Fat fucking chance. Uniform just out the academy is doing a recanvass, seeing if somebody remembers something they forgot the other night about Sarah Reese. Him and a partner. Mr. Gung Ho goes to the abandoned house, 788, knocks, and, instead of saying it's just empty, does a walk-through. Goes down to the basement. Sees a pile of old chairs, some lumber, stacked up odd in the middle of the floor. Pokes around, sees bones."

"Goddamn."

"Goddamn."

"That was impressive."

"I may make him chief of detectives."

"Any connection to Sarah Reese?"

"Just the geography, apparently. Pittman lived right up there. That house, 742, at the end of the block."

"So who owns this place?"

"The bank. Foreclosed on two years ago, some guy out of Delaware buying houses, trying to flip them."

"What about—?" He was going to ask about Lana Escobar getting it on the baseball field, but skipped it. "What about—where—I mean, Pittman's body's been there the whole time?"

"I'd suppose but I don't know."

"Didn't, ah, didn't you guys search the hood after she went missing?"

"Some, it turns out, but not much. She was last seen pulling out of the club, not back here. We never found her car. And look, hey—this was a missing persons case, okay, not homicide. We have a hard enough time with our own."

"Wouldn't there have been a smell, though?"

"You may have noticed the crack squats on this block? The ones everybody's scattered from this morning?"

"I have."

"They all sorta smell."

"Jesus H."

"Yeah. You ever see the pictures of Pittman?"

"Nah. I mean, yeah, the one on the flier."

"No, I mean *the* pictures. Girl was a model. Naughty model. Posed nude. They got around the department when she went missing. She'd done a test shoot, I think it was for *Playboy*. Girl-on-girl stuff."

"I'm just a polite boy from a small town on the big river, John."

"You won't be after you see these."

"Could you assist in a viewing of same?"

"Probably."

Sully thought for a minute, the beer truck guy, Rodney Wilson, the bitterness, the black and brown girls, no word in the papers.

"I'm gonna write about this one, I think, Lieutenant Parker. You show me the naughty pictures? It'll count as research." He looked over the hood of the car, down toward the row house on the left side of the street, with squad cars out front and two officers standing on the front porch. "Anybody down there to talk to?"

John half turned in his seat, then turned back to Sully. "Just the techs scraping the place. Chief came and went. Mayor, too, since there was a TV camera."

"This broke this morning?"

"While you were at your love-in. Saw your colleague up here earlier. Who was it, that fat one?"

"Chris. I'm surprised the desk didn't—" And he thought of his call with Melissa the night before. She'd just paid him back. Well well well. This was getting better by the goddamned hour.

fourteen

Twenty-five minutes later, he was walking into the newsroom, past the rows of cubicles, moving at a clip. His backpack was slung over a shoulder, and he'd stopped at the cafeteria downstairs for a soda, needing the caffeine. R.J. must have seen him getting off the elevator because here he was, already out of his chair, a tall, meaty blur moving toward him, heading him off before he got close to Melissa's desk. R.J. shook a fist, bluff and hearty, booming out congratulations on the arrest story from last night.

"No one else was even *there*," he said. "Not even television. They're crediting your story on the networks with the narrative of how it went down. Brand X didn't have *anything*."

He guffawed, but Sully could see it in his eyes, the searching, seeing if he knew about the Noel Pittman discovery, testing the waters to see how angry he was, to see if he had the breath of bourbon on him.

Sully played it low-key. "So, hey, I was out at Princeton Place just now? Turns out I was the last one to the Noel Pittman party. Hear Chris was out there two hours back."

R.J. peered at him over his bifocals, the bow tie at his neck, the beefy frame, the still-black hair oiled, the close-cropped beard. He had Norman Mailer bluster when he wanted, or he could sit and cross his legs, the dapper newspaperman, professorial, discussing not his first Pulitzer, but the second, still keeping himself between Sully and Melissa, who was somewhere back there in Metro.

"Pittman is a sideshow. A stale story for Chris, something to keep the youngster busy. This—this, now, is your chance to take over the Reese story. You see it now? The play here? The suspects are going to have their initial appearance in court this afternoon. We can have you there, overseeing, and moving on to takeouts on—"

"The C-10 is a presentation," Sully said. "There's no bail in the District. It's just flight risk and danger to the community. They're not going anywhere. Keith covers the courts. Give it to him."

"Yes, but we're going to need to know everything about these men, teenagers, whatever, so yes, Keith can handle the hearing. But we need you out in the neighborhood, the old pro, going for the families, the relatives, the neighbors."

"Lemme guess. I'd dig up a fucked-up home life, discipline problems in school, a mom who says her baby just wouldn't do this, and a father who—"

"Did you have a point in mind, Sullivan?"

"Yes. I did. I do. We're going to advance this story through the *killings* on Princeton Place, not the kill*ing*. That's what I was trying to say yesterday, and Melissa and Eddie didn't want to hear it. Three women have been killed within 150 yards of one another, none of the cases solved. The Reese kid is just the latest. It's—"

"Wait wait wait. Sarah Reese, Noel Pittman. Who's the third?"

"Lana Escobar. Prostitute. Got killed up at the baseball field at the top of the block, last summer. Lana, Noel, Sarah. Three."

"A prostitute? Well, Christ, Sullivan, take off your tutu and come back from the ball. I just don't think so. They just got the bad guys on the Reese killing, or did I misread your story on the front page? Now, this morning, we got the body of some young woman, perhaps more fond of cocaine than a fixed address, discovered in a basement a few doors down the block. No arrests on that one, probably never will be. And a street hooker. You put this in what blender to get a story?"

"The blender of 'Who's killing all these women?'"

"You're pouting. You didn't get the call this morning. It doesn't suit you."

"The three suspects on the Reese thing, R.J.? They're not going to stand. We don't want to follow this too hard. We'll get burned."

"Your own story is bullshit?"

"Three men were arrested in a dramatic raid and the police say they killed Sarah Reese. That's what I reported, and that's not bullshit. The arrests aren't going to stand. Also no bullshit."

"And who says that?"

Sully tried to let his shoulders loosen. He had a knot in the middle of his upper back. His bowels felt cramped. The office, the office—who the fuck ever came up with the idea of working in an office?

"Okay. Okay. Part of that, what I know? I can't tell you because it's a confidential source and—"

"Whose name and position is?"

"Can't say."

"You can't hide sources from your editors, you know that. Confidentiality means we don't put it in the paper—"

"I don't need the primer—"

"—and that eventually, you might go to jail rather than reveal it to a judge or to the public. But editors know the reporter's source if need be. And I'm saying there's a need."

"Then we'll just have to discount that part of it, because there is no way I'm giving up the source on this."

R.J. blinked and looked at him, wrinkling his nose, making the bifocals twitch. He did not otherwise move. "You do remember your suspension. You went with a confidential source about Judge Foy—"

"My source was David Reese."

"He says not. Edward agreed with him."

A deep breath.

"Okay, think about this, R.J. Give it the smell test. These three guys? They're shooting hoops on Friday evening, early, drinking beer, talking shit, a couple of blocks off Georgia. They go to the store, they bump into some white chick—and what, they drag her in an alley and slit her throat?"

"The police say they found the girl's wallet on them."

"That's what the 'item' was?"

"Chris got it from a detective this morning while he was at the Noel Pittman thing. It'll be mentioned in the hearing this afternoon."

"Okay. Okay. So she drops it in the store, they pick it up. Maybe they stole it. That I can believe. I can't believe they somehow got her in the alley and killed her just *boom boom* like that."

It seemed as if all the air was going out of R.J. The man looked as if somebody had pulled a little plastic plug out of his chest and now he was a deflating balloon. He looked like he was wondering what Sully would blow on a Breathalyzer right about now.

"Do you have an aversion to the smart money, Sullivan? You have a clear path to the number one story in the paper, if not the nation, and you're begging to take a back-road detour. This is called self-negation in psychiatric circles."

They had made it to Sully's desk and he plunked down in his chair, glad to have the weight off his knee. He motioned R.J. to pull up another. He needed this man for an ally, R.J. well placed to play the Ivy League mind-fuck games that the paper required—hustles that, Sully damn well knew, he lacked the formal education, tact, and patience to tolerate. R.J., on the other hand, after a turbulent and moneyed youth in Boston, and after being drummed out of the U.S. Army during Vietnam (sodomy, insubordination), had blossomed into a high-brow journalist and intellectual of the type that Washington society, and New York publishing, adored. Four-time Pulitzer finalist, two wins. He and his partner, the artist Elwood Douglas, were big in the D.C. arts and museum circles. Their house was filled with art, mainly with Elwood's canvas works, but also, on the mantel, sat one of Capote's hand-decorated snakebite kits, this a sign of R.J.'s whimsy, his easy wealth, and his sincere, if slightly patronizing, ideas about Southern art and madness.

Behind R.J., the homicide map loomed on the cubicle wall.

"Okay. So look—just look at the map, R.J. It's behind you. No—lean up—yes. There. The pin dots are homicides. Black pins, black male murder victims. White pins, white men. Yellow pins, Asian. Orange, Hispanic."

"This is quite racist, you know."

"Pink pins, women victims of any race."

"Have you had a talk with HR on sensitivity training?"

Sully knew, without counting, that there were two hundred and six pins of all colors so far this year. One hundred and seventy-one pins were black. Eleven were orange. Four were white. One was yellow.

"There are only nineteen pink pins, R.J. See how they're spread out, but mostly east of the Anacostia?"

"All of them are mostly east of the Anacostia."

"Yeah. Well. Watch this." He reached into the top sliding drawer of his desk and pulled out three pink pins. He rolled the chair over to the cubicle wall. He found the intersection of Georgia and Princeton Place, then traced a finger slightly to the right to get to the rec center. He pushed all three pins in—marking the deaths of Sarah, Noel, and Lana. Then he pushed his chair back, rolling until he stopped alongside R.J.'s chair.

The map documented, in ways that economists and social scientists spent oceans of time and expense duplicating, the diamond-shaped city's fault lines between race and class. To the west of the green expanse of Rock Creek Park, there were only three pins, two white and one black. To the right of the park, to the east and south, there were more than 190, almost all of them black.

Right in the middle, apart from any other pins, were the three pins Sully had just inserted. They formed a tiny pink cluster, a raised welt.

"Twenty, twenty-one, and twenty-two," Sully said. "Right on top of one another. That includes the only white child of either gender, the only Latina woman, and one of about fifteen black women. All within two hundred yards of one another, all within eighteen months."

R.J. shook his head.

"Before we start debating statistical analysis, which neither of us can spell, the Reese murder is, at least officially, explained and off the map. Now. You've got a prostitute killed up the block and a body dumped in a basement. That's not what—"

"Give me three days, R.J.," Sully said quietly, leaning forward so the man could hear him. "Give me three days and let me see what I get."

"To what end? Look, we've got Jamie and two others on the National doing the federal investigation, and Keith handling the issues on the bench. But this story on the suspects! It's the one that's going to drive our coverage! It's yours! And you want a three-day holiday to jerk off on a piece about misbegotten girls of the night? You can't possibly try to tie all that to Sarah Reese. There's no connective tissue."

"Like I said—we're not doing the death of Sarah Reese. We're doing the dead and missing women of Princeton Place. If nothing else, I'll write a bio of Pittman and Escobar, you know, young lives lost in a rough neighborhood."

"That sounds like what you did the other day."

"That was the *block*. These are the *victims*. Come on, R.J. A cluster of killings like that? Tell me it's chance."

R.J. let out another sigh and stood up. He hitched his pants up slightly and his fingers found his slim golden belt buckle and fussed with it until it was perfectly in between the first and last loops of his slacks and directly beneath the point of his tie. He crossed his left arm across his chest and propped his right elbow against his left hand, holding the arm upright so that the fingers on his right hand could stroke his chin.

"Jesus. Okay. We'll play it your way for now. I'll keep Chris on the Reese investigation. Keith will handle the courts; Jamie, the feds. You go out there in the demimonde, you go dig and claw around in the world of prostitutes, johns, and the party world where good-looking young women get buried in the basements of abandoned buildings, and you come back and tell us all about it. You'll start right now, giving Chris fill for the story tomorrow on the discovery of Pittman's body. We'll bump it from fifteen inches to twenty-five."

"You got it."

R.J. leaned forward and whispered, mocking the way Sully had spoken to him.

"Got a minute, hero boy?"

"Just that."

"Everybody knows you're drinking again. You haven't noticed Edward tippy-toeing around this story? Asking you a bunch of dick-holding questions? It's not the old days when holding one's liquor was a job description. Now look me in the eye and tell me I don't have to worry."

"You don't got to worry."

The old man stood. He rapped Sully on the shoulder, more of a punch than a pat, his face scowling behind the white beard. The skin was flushed, reddish. "When this is done, you'll take your ass back to rehab."

A spin on the heel and he was gone. Sully looked after him, settling the papers on his desk. He looked up at the homicide map and then back across the newsroom. He took a long pull on his soda, in a Styrofoam cup, the plastic lid keeping in the sweet and lovely scent of his afternoon bourbon and Coke.

fifteen

By midafternoon, Sully was slumped back in his chair, feet up on his desk, going through the clips that had been written about the disappearance of Noel Pittman.

Noel had gone to school in the city, Coolidge High, enrolled at Howard part-time, made decent but not spectacular grades, and was known on the black party circuit that thrived on the eastern side of the city—as opposed to the polo-playing Georgetown trust fund set who'd reliably turn up in the glossy society mags, beaming at the camera. Nobody from Noel's set got invited to those parties.

And almost no one, including his own paper, had written about Noel at all. About the only notice of her disappearance was from Howard's campus paper, the *Hilltop*, in which a student staffer wrote a short piece about her disappearance in March of the previous year. They described her as a Jamaican immigrant.

There was a picture of her, smiling, hair up, dangling earrings, light brown skin and dark brown eyes. She was laughing in the photograph, a warmth that seemed to bubble up out of her. Sully reached out and, without realizing it, touched the photograph.

She was last seen leaving her weekend gig as a featured dancer at Halo, the high-end club on New York Avenue, at about two a.m. after arriving to work four hours earlier. It put her disappearance two hours into April 25. She had never been seen again. She drove her car out of the club's parking lot and into the void. Her apartment on Princeton Place was a house that had been divided into two units—the basement to itself, the top floors another—and she had lived on the top floors. The basement apartment had been empty at the time of her disappearance.

There was nothing in the clips about a *Playboy* shoot, and a database search of court records with her name did not turn up any hits. He'd been out to Halo once or twice, enough to know that "featured dancers" were the girls who danced on elevated platforms above the dance floor on the penthouse level. The dancers wore G-strings, heels, and a miniscule lingerie top.

He tapped the keyboard to move into the paper's copyediting system to read Chris's story. It was being laid out to run on the lower right-hand corner of the Metro front. It was the basic "missing woman found dead" story. It noted the proximity of the Sarah Reese case as a coincidence that police were checking for any possible connection. The police chief was quoted as saying it was unlikely but could not be ruled out immediately. The photograph of her being printed was the same as the one on the flier. That reminded him to try the number on the flier again. He picked up the phone, dialed, and after five rings got the same voice mail message.

To get a live voice in the story, he called the home phone of a professor of criminal justice at Georgetown. The professor confirmed what was obvious—three women being killed, *if* Noel was killed, within two hundred yards of one another was extremely unusual and pushed at the boundaries of circumstance. That went into the file he was writing up for Chris.

"We're nervous," said David Belham, the Ward 1 city councilman, whose district included the area, Sully getting him at his home. "Whether these are connected or not, it's too many. It feels wrong."

John Parker, when he finally picked up, had nothing to add on the investigation, but did say that he had Noel Pittman's pictures. Sully arranged to meet him at eleven the next morning.

Looking up at the clock, deadline was on him. He typed quickly now, information from the clips, filler stats, things he knew without having to think.

The series of unsolved deaths in such a concentrated area makes criminologists wary of a coincidental explanation . . .

After a few more paragraphs like this, he hit the send button and bounced an internal instant message to Chris, letting him know the file was available. He thought about it for a minute, then got up and walked over to Chris's desk, the newsroom mostly empty. The place always smelled vaguely of—of—what was it? Takeout Chinese?

He leaned over the cubicle. Chubface did not look up and did not remove his hands from the keyboard. "You got it," Sully said.

"Un-hunh. Thanks." Not even looking up.

Bitchy, bitchy, bitchy.

Back at his desk, the whiskey was gone in two long slurps on the straw. He looked around and then took the ice-laden cup to another reporter's desk and dropped it in the trash can.

The cycle boots were under the desk, and he reached down and pulled them out, thinking about a burger at Stoney's, wondering if Eva would pick up the phone if he called her, Dusty up in Baltimore at her weekday bar. There was a cough and a soft "Hey, man."

Chris again, hands on the chest-high divider of Sully's cubicle, leaning forward on it, a piece of paper in one hand.

"Yeah?" Sully said. "You filed? What happened with the guys in court?"

"No surprises. No guilty plea, held until trial. Keith did it."

He extended his fingers, pushing a slip of paper at Sully. "This woman left two messages on the Metro main answering machine yesterday, asking for you. Said she was returning your call. The news aide delivered it to me today, I guess because I was working the story."

Sully took the slip of paper, which had a 301 area code, Maryland. The name was Lorena Bradford. The name was a blank.

"She say what it was about?"

"Yeah. She said you called her Saturday, before the body was found. She's Noel Pittman's sister."

John Parker was already sitting at a four-top, coffee in front of him, when Sully walked in the next morning, nursing a modest hangover. He got a Coke and sat down.

"You checked your messages?" John asked.

"At the office? Should I?"

"That story you and the fat kid did today? Whole neighborhood is jumping. We got forty, forty-five calls asking if there's a serial killer on the loose."

"I didn't say anything about a serial killer."

"You didn't spell the words. But 'unsolved deaths'? 'Concentrated area'? Don't pussyfoot. You know how the game goes. So does Belham. He's setting up a community meeting tonight, calling in the chief, everybody."

"Well. I didn't think he'd do that. But you don't buy the cluster?"

John shrugged. "No. Not for homicide. Know what you get when you get a lot of crackheads in a small area? Lot of deaths of people too young to die. I see how you get there for a newspaper story, but coincidence doesn't make much of a homicide investigation." He slid a manila envelope across the tabletop, the pictures of Noel Pittman. "Adult audiences only," he said. "Someone sent them to you in the mail."

Sully peeked inside, thumbing through the eight-by-tens without pulling any of the explicit pictures into public view. "Wow."

"Yeah."

"So what was the story on these?" He got out a notebook.

"Based on the file I looked at, which didn't have all that much, it was straight missing persons. This was last April. A family member starts pushing us on it, so a couple of uniforms looked around. Like I told you, decedent lived on the top end of the 700 block of Princeton. Ten, twelve houses up from where she was found."

"What'd the place look like?"

"Not tossed, if that's what you mean. I don't have anything other than that. Report says the guys went through it. Nothing unusual about the calls on the voice mail, stuff on the computer. Her car never turned up. So it was pretty flat until this photographer guy calls us. He got wind we were making calls, thought we were snooping him. Runs a studio up there in Petworth."

"She was a client?"

"Man said Pittman told him that she wanted the stills to send to lingerie magazines, upscale men's magazines, like that, a portfolio. She came in for shoots in his studio, the results of which you're looking at. First day just her, second day the girl-on-girl stuff. This about two months before she went missing."

"What about the shooter? You scope him out?"

"Yeah, look, he's a sleazeball, you ask me, but we didn't find anything we could hit him for. Makes a lot of money on what they tell me is boudoir photography."

"Housewives in the buff?"

"Something like it. Girlfriends, whatever. He shoots a lot of advertising, fashion, like that. He checked out."

"So who's girl number two?" Sully asked, peering into the envelope.

"Our mystery guest. Photog didn't have a record of her name. So that was about it. File says a uniform went out to Halo. You been?"

"Once or twice. She was one of the platform girls out there."

"So we looked at that. Report says the uniform talked to bouncers, bartenders, the guys in the kitchen. Got nothing. Well. She was scoring a little coke out there, but nothing to make any to-do over. We kept an eye on one or two of the bouncers for a while. No crazy ex-boyfriends or ex-girlfriends or whoever. She also worked part-time, a lingerie-like shop, over to Union Station. And college at Howard. Marketing major."

"What about her car?"

"Older black Acura, two-door. From what we were told, ripped front seat, a dent in the right fender. Put out tracers. No hits."

"Get much on her background, finances, all that?"

"Nah. Jamaican, came here when she was eight or nine. Not much family around, just a sister. She was the one pushing us to do more."

"She did coke; she owe anybody money?"

"Not so far as I could tell from looking at the report. Look, you got to remember, this was never a criminal investigation. Missing persons only. You know how many of those come in? Pisses family members off, they want us to do more, but there's only so much we can do if there's nothing suggesting foul play. She owed a couple grand on the car, maybe about that on a credit card. I'm saying I don't think the coke was a habit."

Sully pulled out a few of the photographs.

They were black-and-white glossies. These were not hammy boudoir shots; this was art photography. He was impressed. Placing them on his lap between his chest and the table, where he could see them without anyone else doing so, he went through them slowly. There were perhaps two dozen.

Noel Pittman had honey-brown skin, shoulder-length straightened black hair, lips that formed a natural pout, full breasts, nice hips, and long legs. She seemed, in her regard for the camera, to have a sense of style, of presence. The photographs, her tousled hair, her eyes glittering. He wondered what her voice had been like. The nude photographs—lying across the bed on her stomach, looking back at the camera over her shoulder, wearing a necklace and a thong, leaning against a shower wall.

"Suspects?"

"We just got the body, partner. But no, none. At least we know now she's not doing three-ways for a billionaire in Buenos Aires."

"Who's got lead on it?"

"Jensen. Good luck. We don't call him Dick for nothing. He's liaison to the Reese investigation, as due diligence, but this—look, this is cold-case material. We'll look at the coroner's report and if something comes up it'll be followed."

"Spot me Jensen's cell?"

"You didn't get it from me." Parker consulted his phone and scribbled a series of numbers on a napkin.

"Who's the lead on Sarah?"

"Bill, Billy Hairston. But look, I'm not kidding—not even a phone call to him, you hear? Man is overwhelmed. Can't take a crap without the bureau guys going in the stall with him."

Sully stood up. "Thanks for the glossies."

"Perks up the day, doesn't it?"

Sully walked outside, called Richard Jensen's number, got the answering machine, and left a message. He rated his odds for a call back as zero. Jensen was two years from retirement but mentally had a foot out the door. He wasn't going to do anything to jeopardize his pension, being quoted by some hack at a newspaper.

sixteen

The Office of the Chief Medical Examiner of the District of Columbia sat in a gray concrete lump at the back end of Capitol Hill. It was adjacent to the jail, at the bottom of a small hill that backed down to the Anacostia. The grass lots were filled with knee-high weeds.

Sully parked in front of the morgue, Building 27, and sat astride the bike while he called into his office voice mail. Thirty-two new messages. John hadn't been kidding. He clicked it off without listening to them. He didn't need the hate that people called in to vent, and, actually, if anybody ever bothered to ask him, he would be happy to tell them he had never given a flying fuck what readers thought. He wasn't running a goddamn wine bar. It was better when he was on one continent, sending stories back to his newspaper on a different one. That was swell.

A few steps took him to the front glass doors, their surfaces reflecting his image, wobbling in a funhouse effect. Once inside, the faint, cloying smell of formaldehyde and chemical compounds permeated his nose, his clothes, his skin, and his mind suddenly flashed a picture of Noel, the brain matter, the sticky sheet . . .

The receptionist looked up at him with a flat stare.

"Hey, now," he said, reaching out to the counter to steady himself, the image fading now. "Is the man himself in?"

She said, "Haven't seen you around here since you got rid of the last man himself."

"I think it was the city council that did that."

"After that thing you wrote. Jason's back there, you want to talk to him. You still riding that motorcycle?"

Sully looked down. He had the helmet in his right hand. "Every day," he said.

"Be seeing you in here soon enough," she said. Then she spoke into the phone. "Dr. Reitman? Your reporter friend is down here." There was a pause. "The one with the motorcycle."

Jason appeared a few moments later, loose limbed, lanky, goofy grin, pushing open a steel door and holding it open for Sully to enter.

"Let me guess. Sarah Reese," he said.

"Noel Pittman," Sully said, limping down the hallway. Jason fell in step, his white lab coat over a dress shirt and tie, walking heel to toe, rising off the toe on each step.

"Pittman? You get demoted? Nobody's talking about Pittman. Everybody is all over the Reese thing."

"I'll let them run with it. Let me guess, though: no signs of sexual trauma on young Miss Reese?"

Jason looked straight ahead, still walking, tapping his clipboard on his hip, that rolling gait. "The office has no comment on any pending case, particularly not any case currently the subject of an intense media circus. So I couldn't possibly comment on your completely unfounded but totally correct assertion."

"Didn't think so. Nasty, though, the throat slitting."

"In the mood for news on that?"

"Could be."

"Like before? I trusted you before and you were straight up. I don't know any of these other guys, and I'm not about to go sticking my neck out. But it's weird, dude, really weird."

"Not for attribution," Sully said. "Possibly to a 'law enforcement official with knowledge of the matter.'"

Jason considered. "There've been so many suits through here that will probably stand up. But I'd rather you get someone else to confirm it."

"Alright already."

They had reached Jason's narrow office and turned in. Jason plunked in his chair, swiveling side to side.

"The throat slitting?" he said. "It was postmortem."

Sully frowned. "Somebody slit her throat *after* they killed her? What was the cause of death?"

"Asphyxiation. Somebody suffocated her. Looks like they shoved something in her mouth—there are fiber matches to something like a tennis ball—and then put their hand or a pillow over her face. The hyoid was broken, too."

"So they suffocated her and then cut her throat?"

Jason nodded. "Very little bleeding, at least for that kind of cut. Usually you'd have buckets, spray, splatter, the works."

"Why would they do that?"

"You're asking me? A thrill. They liked the sight. Wanted to send a message. She died too soon. Anything."

"But she wasn't raped?"

"Not for publication or attribution, no. No bruising, no tearing. Panties in place. She did appear to be experienced in this area, though. She wasn't a virgin . . . but you didn't come to hear about that."

Sully paused. "Actually I didn't. I came to see if you could not comment on Noel Pittman."

"I could not comment very well on Miss Pittman, as I did the autopsy, such as it was, yesterday."

"That quick?"

"I actually had some time. Old cases are more interesting, besides. Autopsies of twenty-three-year-old men with an extra hole in their heads are not, what do I want to say, professionally challenging."

"So what can you not say?"

"Alas, Yorick, I did not know her well. Decomposition is an unpleasant fact of afterlife. Insects and rodents and bugs, you know, all God's creatures have to eat. Some of the skin had—you'd call it mummified, but there was very little flesh left."

"Could you get a cause of death?"

"Not from the cut. She didn't have any broken bones. Nobody shot her in the head, I can tell you that."

"OD'd?"

"Toxicology not possible."

"Strangled? Throat cut?"

"What, you're thinking she and Sarah went out the same way? Yeah, well, no—no way to tell. Flesh from that area was all gone. You really want to picture a skeleton in some rotted clothes."

"What were the clothes?"

"Appeared to be jeans, a belt—there was a metal buckle—maybe some sort of jacket or coat."

"Was she killed there? In that basement?"

"Ask MPD. Nothing I saw on her suggested anything one way or another. And back up just a second, while I'm not saying anything. Based on the material we have, you can't say someone killed her."

Sully blinked. "You're saying being stuffed in a hole in a basement isn't a sign of a violent and unnatural end?"

"It's a sign of a violent and unnatural *burial*. But we're about what happens to people *before* they die. For all you or I know, she overdosed and her coke buddies wanted to keep using the house, so they arranged for a private burial. That violates city code, I'm sure, and probably some sort of misdemeanor about death notification, but that would be about it."

"This sounds like bullshit, Jason. You guys are always pulling this. Dead body turns up and an 'undetermined' cause of death. The torso found in the dumpster by the waterfront, what, last year? You guys called it 'undetermined.' A torso in a dumpster, and nobody says 'homicide.' It keeps the murder rate down. I'm not blaming you, I mean, I know the politics of—"

"Nope. That was the old administration. Peter pulled that stuff all the time, in addition to the embezzling you wrote about. He was a real piece of work. I'm happy to label it homicide if there's evidence. On this one, you can say the autopsy was inconclusive as to a cause of death, but that we described it as suspicious."

"You think that's what happened?"

"What happened?"

"OD'd and a friend panicked."

"Are you writing about this? Or we just girl-talking?"

"Wanting to write about it. Bosses are less than thrilled. You're still off the record, if that's what you're asking. I'm just looking for direction."

Jason made a face.

"You look constipated, Jason. Look. I'm interested in your irresponsible speculation. It's better than mine."

Jason leaned back in his chair and folded his arms across his chest. He swiveled back and forth for a moment.

"I don't. I don't think she overdosed. If you're interested in unfounded speculation, I think it's highly likely someone raped her and killed her and hid the body. She was young, gorgeous, known to take liberties with portraying herself as a sex object, and was apparently known to do drugs. So you take anyone with that background and stuff them in a hole in the basement of an abandoned house in a crappy neighborhood, my first instinct is that she ran into Ted fucking Bundy. But I don't know that, and there's nothing in the autopsy to point to it as a forensic standard of proof."

"What if you'd examined the body the day after she was buried?"

"Fibers, signs of bruises, cuts, bleeding—all that would have been available. Whoever buried her, or stuffed her beneath that trash pile or whatever, did a good job. Well, I should say buried her the first time. She's being reburied today."

Sully sat up. The funeral—pathos, symbols, a lead anecdote to the story. This he needed, what with the heat R.J. was putting on him. He needed something he didn't have, which was family, which was emotion. You want emotion, you go to a funeral.

"Today? The funeral's *today*?"

"Funeral home claimed the body as soon as we were finished. And I don't think this is so much a funeral as a burial."

"They—they just found her yesterday morning," Sully said.

Jason shrugged. "Jews, we bury them quick. She's not a member of the tribe, but maybe there was a family rush."

Family. Her sister would be there, the one who'd put out the flyer, who had called him.

"Got the name of the funeral home, Jason? For a carrion-feeding media vulture?"

seventeen

The rain started falling.

It had started slowly, before he got to the cemetery, a cold and desultory spattering. It fogged the visor; it dripped off the back of the helmet and landed on his neck and coursed down his back. He could feel the tires spinning the water up from the road onto his thighs.

By the time he reached Everlasting Cemetery—it was a good four miles outside the Beltway, way the hell out New Hampshire Ave., the northern edge of the burbs—it had picked up to a steady downfall and he was soaked to the bone. The graveyard was off to his right, at the crest of a long, slow hill. He downshifted into first, kept the bike as quiet as possible, eased toward the back of the place, and there it was. Two cars and a hearse pulled to a stop near a green awning, a hole yawning beneath. The casket, white, was raised on the bier.

A woman in a black dress and a stylish black hat and two men in suits were getting out of the cars. They were all beneath umbrellas. Sully pulled to the roadside and switched off the engine. He pulled his feet up onto the pegs and folded his hands across the gas tank.

The woman and the two men in suits went beneath the green awning. There were only the three of them. Until he saw one of the men produce a Bible, open it, and apparently begin to read, he didn't realize the dynamic. There was a pastor and there was a cemetery official and there was Noel's sister and there was no one else.

"Christ almighty," he said. It was too goddamn sad to look at.

They all stood beneath the awning for a while. Then the woman and one of the men sat in the plastic lawn chairs the cemetery had provided. The other man in the suit, who did not sit, approached the casket and apparently pressed or pulled something. The casket slowly lowered into the ground, disappearing into the red dirt. The woman dropped long-stemmed roses into the hole after it. The pastor rose and held both of her hands, facing her. They prayed for several minutes. Then their hands released. The woman sat down again. The two men remained standing.

After a while, the woman stood. The trio stepped out from under the awning and raised their umbrellas and started back toward the road and their cars.

Sully took a deep breath, cursed, and cranked the bike. He rolled downhill slowly, until he was several yards behind the last car, and stopped the bike and killed the engine. Dismounting, he took off his gloves and then his helmet and put the gloves inside the helmet and then set it down on the roadway. He unzipped his jacket and walked forward and pulled a hand back over his hair, brushing it out of his face. The rain was coming down harder now. He hated himself for being here, for intruding in this way. He made eye contact with the men first, giving them a slight nod, and then he looked at the woman in the hat.

That it was Noel Pittman's sister was beyond question. She was tall and had the same honey-brown skin. She had high cheekbones and straightened hair and deep brown eyes. She was looking at him.

"Pardon me, everyone," he said, taking them all in with a glance, but then looking back at her. "Ma'am? My name is Sully Carter. I'm a reporter. I've been trying to reach Noel Pittman's sister. If that's you, Ms. Bradford, I apologize for just showing up, but I believe we exchanged phone messages."

The trio stopped, the men looking at him and then, almost at the same time, back at the woman. She regarded him blankly. One of the men started walking toward him, a serious expression crossing his face. His eyes stayed on Sully but then his focal point shifted, a small tic, the scars, always the scars.

Sully did not back up. He returned his gaze to the woman.

"I recently called the number on a flier about Noel Pittman's disappearance. A woman called back to my newspaper, but there was some confusion, and she wound up leaving a message with a different reporter. There was a number and I called back but didn't get an answer. I left a message. Again, if that was you, Ms. Bradford, I would like—"

The man in the dark blue suit stepped directly in front of him, no more than a foot from his nose, breaking his eye contact with the woman. He had a good seventy-five pounds and two inches on Sully; the man had girth. "This is a private service," he said in a hushed tone. "You're going to need to get out."

"Cemetery gates were open, and I'm not talking to you, mister," Sully whispered back, meeting his gaze. "If the lady doesn't want to—"

"What does he want, Mr. Robinson?" the woman called out. She was beneath her umbrella, and she had stopped walking. The man did not take his eyes off Sully, but moved his head slightly to the right. "He says he's a reporter. He says he called you."

She was still standing in the grass of the cemetery, not yet on the roadway. Her heels were sinking in the mud. She looked down at her feet, then at the pastor, and then back at Sully and Mr. Robinson.

"You the one who wrote the story in today's paper?" she said. "About how she was found? Serial killer and all that?"

"I don't think I said—well, yes. Yes, ma'am. I wrote most of that story."

The pastor took her elbow and helped her onto the roadway. The rain fell harder. She walked over to him, beneath her umbrella, and looked up into his eyes. Her eyes dilated slightly, he noticed, the black expanding, the brown iris turning into a thin band, and he was about to register the depth of them when she spat into his face. He said nothing, only blinked the phlegm out of his eyes. He did not wipe his face. She glared, a foot away, and then she turned and started walking back to the limousine.

Mr. Robinson reached out with his right hand, formed a point with two fingers and, smiling, tapped Sully twice on the chest. His face was a smirk, a mixture of menace and contempt, and then he turned and left.

eighteen

The light changed, a couple of cars passed, and he turned left onto Princeton Place. He toyed with parking in the alley behind Doyle's, but went up a couple of houses, parked between two cars, lifted his helmet from his head, and walked back, his feet heavy on the pavement.

The thing he should do was follow up on Jason's tip and try to find someone to corroborate that Sarah's throat had been cut after she was dead, to keep the heat off Jason if there was flak about it. It put the slaying in a different light and made it, in his estimation, far less likely that the three teenagers were the killers. They might have cut her throat in a moment of panic, or loathing, or brutality, but to tack it on after she was dead seemed calculated and impersonal.

And then he leaned forward and spat in the alley before turning the corner. Chris could get his own damn scoops. What he was going to do was push this story on the trio of killings, and Lorena Bradford and her spit could drop fucking dead. She was insulted her sister might have been the victim of a serial killer? Didn't like reading about her dancing, her nude pictures? It amazed him, what people in this country thought was insulting or intimidating or humiliating or whatever.

So now he needed to know what Doyle Goodwin had seen the night Sarah was killed, or, actually, on any others. *If* the actual killer was still out there—and the killings *were* related—then the killer had been in or around his store, probably often. Psychopaths were creatures of habit, not impulse.

He pulled open the right side of the glass double doors, the little silver bells ringing at the top as he did so. The television blared and there was Doyle's cousin Bettie, ringing up chips and soda for a teenager. He had almost forgotten what a pain in the ass she was, the beehive hairdo from the 1960s, the shrill voice, the soap operas blaring on the television behind the counter.

Making an excuse to kill time while the lone customer left, Sully walked up and down a couple of aisles, picked up a bag of M&Ms and a ginger ale, dawdling by the magazine rack, then came up front when the store was empty, nearly having to turn his shoulders to get down the narrow aisle.

"Hey, Bettie," he said, smiling. "Sully Carter, from the paper? From last year, remember? Good seeing you again."

Her plump face squinched together for a moment, and she peered at him through her glasses. "Well, hi, shug," she said. "Did somebody drop you in a swimming pool?"

"No ma'am. It's pouring. Got caught on it on the bike."

"Well, bless your heart, you need to run right on home and get a hot shower and a good supper."

"That's right where I'm headed, but I was on the way home coming down Georgia there, and saw y'all were back open, and thought I'd stop in to talk to Doyle about it for a hot second."

"Lord have mercy, did you know I was right here when all that happened? Maybe the last person on this earth to talk to that gal?"

"That's what—"

"Why, it was just awful. Awful. And them three Negro boys running around in here the whole time. The police, now they saying they did it, and now everybody around here thinks I told on them. But I didn't! I didn't say anything like that! I don't even know their names! They just run out the front door, that's all I told the police because that's all I know. But now nobody wants to come in 'cause they think we told on 'em!"

Sully put his items on the counter along with a ten-dollar bill, forcing a concerned look to his face, slumping his shoulders for emphasis. "That's terrible!"

She made change, the talk never slowing, her eyes lighting up now.

"Doyle's back there, you want to try to talk to him, but he's not going to say anything, not at all. He's just been so upset. The police, just banging in here, keeping us down there at the station all night asking questions."

"I guess they wanted the video of that afternoon," Sully said, leaning against the counter and nodding toward the small surveillance camera suspended from the ceiling behind the register.

Bettie looked straight up, without turning her head.

"Oh, hon, those things haven't worked since Jesus wore short pants. The repairman came and wanted all sort of money to fix it. It was the second time it had busted and Doyle figured—Doyle, c'mon out here, hon! That boy from the paper is out here again!—and Doyle, he figured they were just using us for a steady account, I guess to pay for their new golf cart at they country club."

"So you just kept the cameras?"

"That's right. That's just exactly right. To make these little robbers and bad people think we're watching everything on tape. It helps, I guess. We ain't had a problem worse than shoplifting in years. People think it's dangerous, a store like this in a neighborhood like this, but the people like us just fine, you ask me, they just—"

"Bettie."

They both turned to the baritone coming from the back. Doyle Goodwin stood just inside the swinging metal doors to the back room. He was wearing khakis and a starched blue oxford-cloth button-down shirt, the sleeves rolled with precision to the elbows. He had a narrow, weather-beaten face, his salt-and-pepper hair cut short and brushed neatly to the side, looking like the navy man he had been. What had been his rank? Something like storekeeper? He had taken off his glasses and was cleaning them with a small bit of cloth.

"Hey there, Sully," he said, softly. "I guess Bettie's been catching you up on our little excitement."

Sully nodded toward Bettie and walked over to Doyle, reaching out to shake his hand, to say hello. He had forgotten that the man was only about five foot seven. His chest and shoulders filled out the shirt, though, testament to some straight-up time in the gym, that military discipline.

"She has," Sully said. "And I'm really sorry about everything. The minute I saw where it was, the store, I remembered coming up here and talking to you."

"Appreciate that, Sully. I do. It's been a terrible time. A terrible thing for that family, that little girl."

"You mind if I just ask you a question or two about it?"

Doyle paused, then nodded his head to the back. "Come on."

He pushed open the door and retreated into the storage room. Sully followed him, past the sign on the door that read EMPLOYEES ONLY. The overhead lights were off. Wooden shelves closed in from both sides, stacked floor to ceiling with boxes of canned goods and a pallet of soft drinks and paper towels and paper plates and toilet paper. There was a narrow toilet off to the right, the light on. Doyle's office was at the back. It had a little sign that read OFFICE.

Doyle pushed the door in and took two steps and sat down behind an old steel desk, the thing looking like it weighed as much as an aircraft carrier. It had an old computer and a monitor on top of it. There were clutters of paper and what looked to be a scattering of receipts and a stack of thin black accounting ledgers. Boxes of merchandise, holding individual units of macaroni or cans of soup or packs of gum.

Sully sat down in a yellow-and-brown chair that was almost touching the front of the desk.

"You got wet," Doyle said.

"Got caught in it when I went up to Everlasting Cemetery, out in Colesville or some damn place," Sully said, peeling off his jacket. "Ran up there for the Noel Pittman funeral."

Doyle settled himself in the chair and touched some papers on his desk. He gave a slight shake of the head. "God and sonny Jesus. I guess we're in a little bit of shock. I mean, thirteen years here and nothing serious and then this. Had a drunk pull a gun one night in the store, but he was just drunk. Then we get—we get these two things in the space of a few days."

"Bettie was saying things are really slow since you opened back up."

"About fifty, sixty percent off, I'd say. God-awful."

Sully paused. This was always the tricky part of interviews like this. He tried to make them conversations, but the fact was that he was extracting information, like pulling a tooth. The touch was to do it while keeping people from feeling like that was what you were doing. "So you didn't see Sarah Reese that day, I take it?"

"Well, now wait. Are we talking to put in the newspaper? Because, I don't mind telling you, I don't want to spend another night at MPD going over the same damn things with detectives fifty-eight times and looking at photo arrays until three in the morning. It was the one time I regretted bringing Bettie up here."

"Why so?"

"Well, look, she's my aunt, you know. Lost her job at the nursing home back home—we're from just outside of Newport News—had to be five years ago now. Some cousins called me and put me up to offering her a job. She's been fine, if you can get past the soap operas, but she was a damned embarrassment in the police station. Screaming and hollering and crying."

"I imagine she was pretty scared."

"She's thinking those guys in the store, or their friends, are going to come in and shoot us to pieces."

"It's not totally paranoid."

"No, but—" He pulled off his glasses and rubbed the bridge of his nose. Sully could see the slight bags around the eyes, testament that he wasn't sleeping well himself. "But there's a way things are done. You just don't—well. You didn't come here to listen to family woes. What is it you wanted?"

"Just to hear a little bit more about what happened. And to find out a little more about Noel Pittman, if you know anything. It's her I'm actually writing about."

"Pittman? I thought this was about Sarah Reese?"

"It's a little bit about both. And about Lana Escobar, the young woman who got killed up on the baseball field last summer."

Doyle did not look pleased.

"Okay, that was what you wrote in the paper that's got everybody so upset. Look. We're barely getting by here, and this thing is bad for us, bad for the neighborhood. I can't have the store in the paper again, not like this. Bettie might lose what's left of her mind."

"Off the record. Just for my information, so I'll have a better understanding of what's happening."

"It's not going to help you much. You already know Bettie was the last to see the little Reese girl alive, except for whoever killed her, I suppose. The girl got scared of the three black kids. She ran out the back door, Bettie said. We didn't know anything until, I don't know, half an hour later, something like that, when the police came in."

"Did she come past you here? In the office?"

"To get to the back door, she would have had to go through that walkway we just did," he said, and put his glasses back on. "But I can't tell you for sure. I was at home. I open the store in the mornings, Bettie comes in from about ten till seven or so, and I come back and work until closing. In the afternoon, I go home and take a break, a siesta, have a cold beer, something. I was down there—it's just two blocks—when I heard all sorts of sirens. I walked the first block. When I got to the top of that rise, there at Warder, I could see all the police cars were here at the store. I ran the rest of the way."

"So you didn't know Sarah Reese at all?"

"Never saw her, to the best of my knowledge, till they showed me her picture at the police station."

"What about Noel Pittman?"

He shook his head. "I read your story that said she lived here on the street, between my house and the store. But I don't remember her any which way."

"Lana Escobar?"

"You mean the prostitute? It's possible if she was working out there on Georgia that she came in here to pee or get warm for a minute in the winter. I let the girls do it. Cost of doing business. But no, I didn't know anything about her."

"Hunh. So the day Sarah Reese got killed, nothing unusual?"

"Not until the police came banging in. It got pretty unusual after that."

"Any creepy-looking guys, or maybe not so creepy, but guys that hang around a lot?"

"Not such as I'd call creepy. The neighborhood characters, you know. Why do you ask?"

"I got an idea, maybe those three guys didn't kill Sarah, but maybe the killings in the neighborhood are related, something like what I wrote about, but I'm pushing it hard now. Don't know if you saw—"

"I can't put much to that. I mean, I just don't know. We work right here every day, and we haven't seen anything like that, like somebody stalking or anything."

"Could you show me that alley back there? I don't know exactly where they found her."

Doyle looked at him, and Sully noticed a certain exasperation. "No, I'm sorry. You're welcome to look yourself. I go back there to throw out the trash, and I leave through that door during the middle of the day to go home. There's a sign that says an alarm will sound, but that's just to scare off any shoplifters who sneak back there. So that's all I know about the alley. I can tell you the police have put a new dumpster back there. They took the old one."

"That stands to reason, I suppose," Sully said, standing up. This was going nowhere.

Doyle stood with him. He ran a hand through his hair, then put his hands on his hips.

"Look, Sully, I don't mean to be abrupt. I run a business, I keep my nose clean, and I don't get into it with the city councilman or the neighborhood commissioner. I sponsor a kid's basketball team in the city rec league. I don't prosecute the shoplifting. It costs me a small fortune, but I don't. And part of that has part to do with this . . . business right here. You know this as well as I do—Bettie and me are white witnesses, or whatever, against black teenagers in a murder case involving a little white girl. We don't have a winning hand here."

"I can see that."

"Okay, so can you tell me what the police are saying? Do you think these guys' friends, associates—whatever they call them, their crew—are going to come after us?"

"No, but you're right to be careful. I bet in this case the cops must have DNA and other stuff, to have made those arrests so quickly. I bet those guys know they've got bigger problems to worry about than Bettie."

Doyle nodded. He gave a brief smile that showed, at least to Sully, that he didn't buy a bit of it. The man was, Sully thought, rattled to the bone, in a way they can't teach you about in the military, when you have a gun and authorization to use it. Civilian life didn't carry those kinds of comforts.

Outside, the rain clearing off, he leaned against the bike, making a call, getting John Parker at his desk.

"I tried Jensen three times, John. He's not calling back."

"Figured, but I can't tell him to call you."

"Yeah, so, okay—so okay—so let's go at it a different way," Sully said. "I need to look at a photo array of johns arrested in 4-D. Repeat offenders only. Their cards, it'll have the name of the girls they worked with, right?"

"I'm not sure that's—"

"It's a public record, John. You know it is."

There was a pause. "You're wanting to see if there's a guy who got busted with Escobar, and maybe Pittman. But Pittman wasn't a working girl. We already ran the cards on Escobar when she got killed. She hadn't been at it that long, didn't have any sort of steady clientele. If there was something there to see, we would have moved on it."

"But there's more to look at now. It's a bigger canvas. Maybe the guy who did Pittman, maybe he only thought she was a working girl. Maybe he's a guy been out to Halo, followed her home. Maybe there's somebody in the john cards, does prostitutes, got a separate record for working with a knife."

"You're reaching. You're back to the idea that we got the wrong guys on Sarah Reese."

"Escobar was strangled. Reese got her throat cut. Pittman is unknown. It's somebody working with their hands. It's worth looking into, at least on my clock."

"It's your time, but you're wasting it. I'll put you in the room with the array. You can look at those pricks till I'm done. How soon can you get here?"

"Gimme ten minutes."

"Come in the back."

When he clicked off the phone and started pulling on his helmet, he noticed that a car up the block, maybe five spaces, was idling, lights off. He didn't look directly, but he looked in the rearview when he pulled out. It wasn't the Olds, but it was a heavy sedan, four-door, and appeared to have two silhouettes in the front seat. He pulled out to Georgia, revved it down the block, and then came back up Otis and Warder and back down Princeton, making the block.

When he got back to the bottom of Princeton, the car was gone, an empty spot next to the sidewalk.

Jasper, James. Darden, William. Turner, Darrell. Green, Andre . . .

The names and their sorry little pictures, clicking by on the array. Johns were a sad fucking bunch on the best of days, but this was the rock bottom of the trade, guys picking up women on the street for ten dollars, or thirty dollars, or just a rock, doing them in abandoned houses, maybe getting blown in the front seat, the car parked in an alley.

Sully wrote down the names and details of Turner and Green. Both were young, tall, and heavy—men who could strangle a woman if they wanted to—and they had priors for assault, and both lived within a few blocks of Princeton Place. On their last contact with police, both were unemployed.

Jasper, a stringy white dude who appeared to have a long love affair with meth, was another possible. He lived in an apartment block on North Capitol, not far away, but neither his picture nor his record gave off vibes of fatal violence.

Darden, Sully liked him because he liked his hookers young, which might have been a draw to Sarah, an impulse crime that went wrong before he could get her panties off. Sully's eyebrows raised—one of

Darden's prior arrests was for assault with a deadly weapon—a butcher knife he'd pulled from his girlfriend's kitchen.

John came in at ten till midnight. The room was otherwise empty.

"I'm going, which means you got to, too. You see anything I need to know about? That my aces missed?"

Sully gave him the marked cards, and John ran off two copies on the machine, handing one set back to Sully. He looked at the names. "Not a cast I'm worried about. Darden, I remember that asshole. Busted him, what was it, ten years ago? Beat the shit out of his woman at the time. I was working out of 4-D. You go see him? Tell him I said I got no problems popping his ass back to lockup just on GP."

nineteen

He was lying on his bed in the dark, sleepless, still wired, mind racing in circles, going in loops. The green LED numbers on the bedside clock read 2:23 a.m. Dusty finally answered.

"You just closed up?" he asked.

"Yep."

"Want to drive down?"

"From Baltimore?"

"I'll come up. Always liked the bike late at night."

"It's closer to morning."

"Details, details."

"I guess not," she said.

He was in basketball shorts and nothing else, the window open, the October coolness flooding the room, the soft orange light of the halogen streetlights filtering through the trees, casting the bedroom in shadows that moved and shifted, ghosts in the darkness. He was throwing a tennis ball up in the air and catching it, the phone in the crook of his neck.

"So, you know, I would like to see you," he said.

"Other than at night, in bed?"

"Hey, wow, slow down. Yes. Sure. Daytime, a late lunch and a matinee. I'll play hookey."

"We tried that. You canceled on me."

"The one time you were available," he said.

"It was twice, and don't try to flip this on me. It's almost a year we've been trying to make this work. Basically I've been at your beck and call and you've been available when you want to. Nadia. Is this how you did it with Nadia?"

He caught the ball and held it.

"That's one toke over the line," he said.

"It always is, anytime someone says her name."

A deep breath. "Okay, look, maybe I'll—"

He heard an equally exasperated sigh come down the line back at him. "Okay, look. Look. Sorry. Our schedules don't exactly match. You're doing your thing, I'm doing mine. You've got irregular hours, I've got the bartending and nursing school. This isn't easy." The apology, yes, but her voice held that distant tone, the way she was when she was tired, or moody, or off, or whatever it was she was.

"Look, I voiced a desire, that's all," he said, the ball going back up, and then down. "I said I wanted to see you. Tell me again how that was wrong."

A pause. She was walking. He could hear the footsteps.

"You walking to your car?" he said.

"The apartment."

"You got home fast."

"Yep."

"Long night?"

"And I've got an early start. A nine-thirty class."

"So—"

"So lemme call you back tomorrow afternoon. When I'm in a better mood. This place I'm working now? Not the harbor tourist crowd. Mangy. Makes John Waters look like a Boy Scout."

"Can't you land at a bar down here full-time?"

"See, that's what I'm talking about. *Can't you*. Like it's up to me. I've got another year of classes up here before I get the degree."

"I know, I just—"

"It's late, Sully. Really."

"Okay, okay. We can—"

The line clicked off.

He looked at the receiver, then put the phone on the bed. Up the ball went again, back down. Higher, back down. Palmed it, a one-handed grab to end the inning. It helped to consider the opposing point of view. Their schedules were crazy, that was true. And maybe, he being the older one (seven years older? eight?), his career already established, maybe he was being the jerk and she was the patient and loving girlfriend. It could be. It might be. But he knew he wanted to hold her as he did the tennis ball, safe, strong, secure. He did. Really. But the gulf. The gap. To connect, like, really connect, it was—it was—it was a lock without a key. For the first time, he felt her slipping away through his fingers, like water, like blood, and he got the idea she had been feeling it for longer.

The clock now read 2:31. Sleep was not going to come. It was another four hours and change until daylight.

Up went the ball, down went the ball.

twenty

The morning mint julep was on the back step, just to make him feel right, something to beat back the sleep-deprivation headache, his mind turning, setting up moves on the chessboard for the day. R.J. had said three days and today was either day two, as Sully would count it, or day three, if you counted the half day when R.J. gave him the deadline, and it would be just like a fucking editor to call this the third day.

To do, to do. He punched in Eva's office number on his cell and closed his eyes when it began to ring.

"Mr. Sully." Her voice smooth.

"Screening our caller ID?"

"We have things to do."

"You doing enough to know those knuckleheads didn't kill Sarah Reese?"

There was a pause.

"We are talking on background?"

"Jesus. Everybody. Sure."

"I would say the case is very strong. There is very solid evidence for obstruction of justice, possession of stolen property, and theft."

"I didn't hear 'murder in the first.'"

"The rest of the case is developing, as they say in the courthouse."

"But murder one was included in the presentation in court the other day."

"It was, yes."

He paused. The idea of floating the postmortem throat slitting popped into his head, to show her he had something, but he held back. Instead, he said, "So what's happening is, you haven't found the weapon and none of them are talking."

"I'll neither confirm nor deny. I will observe that they are charged with murder and that we like our case."

She was at her office and being close to inscrutable. He sipped his drink.

"Okay, so does the timeline bother you? And motive?"

"You're asking me to give you a psych eval of people who kill other people? I don't really know. I don't really *have* to know. I have sent people to prison for always and forever and had no idea why they did what they did. But I would say that opportunity is a powerful motivator. And chance. And, without being indelicate, sex, or the possibility thereof."

"In the alley behind the store?"

"Did I omit stupidity?"

"But all those things could apply to something opportunistic, but stops short of murder."

There was an exhalation on the other end of the line. "You think you know something, Sully?"

"No. I would just—" He heard a voice calling his name.

Sly Hastings's head and upper body appeared above the chest-high brick wall bordering his backyard from the alley, the man wearing a white shirt and sunglasses. He looked at Sully and took off the shades, then reached for the handle that opened the metal back gate. Sully wagged a finger at him, signaling him not to come closer.

"I would just do your usual excellent job. Just look out on this one. Thanks for the time."

"If there's something you're hearing—"

"I'll call you." He hung up.

"Been knocking out front, brother," Sly said, unhooking the gate. "You really got to be more sociable. People could get the wrong idea. Come on. We got work."

• • •

Sully was sitting in the back of the Camaro, Lionel driving, Sly in the passenger seat. Lionel was taking North Capitol heading up to the neighborhood, Sly leaning sideways in the front seat, talking back to him, shades on.

"Me and Lionel, we been driving around," he said, "the past few days. We been asking people a few questions every now and then, if it looks like it might be profitable for us to do so."

"Profitable? You just said 'profitable'?"

"I did, yes, genius. Profitable. Fuck with me again—go ahead. See if it gets you where you want to go. We asking around, seeing what's profitable. I talk to this dude down there on Columbia Road, the 500 block. He starts telling me his niece ain't around no more. His niece—it's his niece, Lionel?"

"Niece. From his ex-wife."

Sully looked from Sly to Lionel and back again.

"Some dude can't find his ex-wife's niece? And this is profitable to know?"

"I said she wasn't around no more. I didn't say a thing about they can't find her. They can find her just fine. She's out to Lincoln Memorial Cemetery. Girl's name is Escobar. Lana Escobar."

He turned all the way in the seat and pulled off his glasses. "You want to talk to my boy now?"

Sully went up the steps of the narrow row house and into the front door, behind Sly and in front of Lionel. There was a small group of people, Hispanic, in the front room. Sully nodded, trying to make eye contact, and got nothing for it. They were in a hallway and then in a small kitchen, disheveled, a cabinet door open. A barrel-chested man with a mustache was sitting at a folding table. He was wearing work pants and a large white T-shirt. There was a cup of coffee in front of him. He was leaning forward on the table with his elbows and looking from Sly to Sully.

Sully couldn't interpret whether this meant he was accustomed to strangers barging into his kitchen or whether Sly had told him that was the way it was going to be.

Sly whispered to him for a minute and the man gestured for Sully to sit. He did, in a green chair on the opposite side of the table.

"*No hablo español,*" Sully said to the man, getting a smile in on the end of it. "Not much, anyhow."

The man regarded him with his still brown eyes. It occurred to Sully he resembled Gabriel García Márquez, the slight potbelly, the salt-and-pepper gray hair and mustache, the flat gaze.

"It's okay," the man said. His voice was highly pitched. It didn't match his physique, it was like Aaron Neville, that angelic voice in the bar bouncer body. "I been living in Washington fifteen years. I speak English pretty good."

"I'm Sully," reaching across the table to shake his hand.

"I'm Hector Ramos."

"I'm a reporter."

"I'm a grass mower."

"Let me ask you something," Sully said. "And it doesn't matter to me at all personally, but are you here legally?"

The man shook his head no.

"So you don't want to be quoted in my newspaper, right?"

"Never. They would deport me."

Sully looked at Sly.

"Hector, tell the man about your niece. He don't gotta know your name. Tell him what you was telling me."

Hector looked at Sully. "You want for me to tell you about Lana?"

Sully nodded, pulling out his notebook. "But, okay, look. If I write a story—*si*, if, maybe—I'm not going to name you. I'll say you're a relative who is in the country illegally. I will use what you say, but not your name. Is that okay? Is there someone else in the family who could talk and use their name?"

Hector shook his head. "Only me. And the other, so, okay. Just no name."

"*Sin nombre.*"

Hector nodded, a slight tic of the head.

"Thank you," Sully said. "What can you tell me about Lana? I don't know much. I wrote a very short story when she was found, but that was about it."

Hector's face tightened, the muscles contracted.

"So, okay, Lana, she did not run around with men for money, like you say in the paper." He held up his hand before Sully could say anything. "The police say it, but you write it. It was on the television, too. Well. Maybe she did once or twice—I cannot say for sure because I was not there. How am I to know? She was an illegal, too, but was taking some college classes, someway she and her aunt figure it out. That was my wife then, you know? Her aunt. Then her aunt and me, we divorce, and her aunt went back home, to Guatemala. Lana stayed here. We got along okay. She was going to help me with my business. She was going to answer the phone and talk to the people. Her English was very good. It was like she was born here."

"She wasn't?"

"No. We are all from Guatemala. Chimaltenango is the city. I met my ex-wife and Lana here. My ex-wife, she brought her here for her sister."

"How did you meet your ex-wife? Lana's aunt?"

"Her cousin was a friend of my cousin."

"Lana have a boyfriend?"

Hector blinked. "She was not smart with men. She took the pictures for one of the men."

"A picture."

"Without the clothes."

"Oh," Sully said. "Naked? No clothes at all?"

"Only her shoes."

"Her shoes."

"Yes. The ones I saw, she had on only shoes."

"You don't look happy about this."

The man shook his head, hard. "No, no. This is not how my family does things. We go to Mass. We work. We do not do drugs or—or things like this. It is a nasty business."

"Who was the guy taking the pictures?"

"I do not know. I never met him, and Lana, she would not say."

"How did you come across the pictures?"

"She left them in her room. On the bed. We lived a few blocks away then. Many of us. Lana had her room. Her phone was ringing and I went in to get it. The pictures were on the bed."

"Were they ever in a magazine? You know, one of the magazines with pictures of naked women?"

"I do not know. How would I know? I do not look at such things. Never if I knew it had Lana in it. I was very ashamed."

"And angry."

He nodded. "This was all just before she died. Maybe four, five months. It was in February. She left the house. I did not see her again. She was dead in July."

"She left, or you threw her out?"

Hector raised his shoulders, then lowered them and looked at the table. "It was some of each, you know what I am saying? She said I was a filthy man for looking at her pictures. I said she was a nasty girl to take the pictures." He shrugged. "She said she would go and I said okay. She found some little apartment several blocks away, on Thirteenth Street. She moved all of her things there. She did not call us. My wife—my new wife, not my old one—would call and talk to her. I did not call her."

"When did you find out she had been killed?"

"Not until the week after she was dead. My wife, Saundra, she went to file a missing persons report. She was nervous for her. She liked Lana. She thought Lana was just angry and ashamed for the pictures, you know? And that she would calm down in some months? She did not hear from her for one week, then two. She went by the apartment—"

"Sorry to interrupt, but do you remember the exact address?"

"It was Thirteenth Street, 3508? Yes, 08. The apartment, it was 36-A."

"Okay, good. So your wife went by there?"

"She goes by there and she sees the police tape across the front door, but she thought only that maybe she had not paid the rent and had been kicked out. She went to the police station. She filled out the forms for a missing person. That's when they came back and said, 'Oh, this woman is dead.'"

"But she had her ID on her when she was found, didn't she? I mean, they identified her. Didn't they call you?"

"No, no. Lana was my ex-wife's niece, not my daughter. She is Escobar. I am Ramos. Hector Ramos. She was only my ex-wife's sister's daughter, you understand? Her mother is in Guatemala. We were not on any of the same forms."

"You didn't see the story in the paper? Nobody mentioned it to you?"

"We do not read the English newspaper. If it was on one of the Spanish radios, I did not hear it. It was only to the funeral that someone brought your newspaper."

Sully wrote fast to keep up. He knew now why it had seemed Lana had been alone in the world when she'd been found. New address, nothing much there, no papers, maybe a prostitution bust when she tried to turn a few tricks to pay her new, higher rent. The little investigation that got done, she appeared to be a Hispanic prostitute in a bad neighborhood who turned tricks on playgrounds. The police never knew of any relatives until Ramos's wife went down there. By that time, no reporters, including Sully, were looking at the case.

"Do you have any nice pictures of Lana? That I could put in the paper? And did you happen to keep the naked pictures?"

Hector sat up straight, pulling his forearms off the table. "You want to look at my niece while she is naked?"

"No, no. I wanted to see if the pictures might give me a clue about who shot them, or when, or where."

Hector took a deep breath. He rubbed his hands together, then pulled them apart and put them back together finally. "We have some good pictures of Lana. Nice pictures. When she was at school. I'll ask my wife where they are." He paused. "I did not keep the nasty pictures."

"Do you have any idea of who might have wanted to hurt Lana? Bad boyfriend?"

Hector Ramos looked up at Sully. He blinked several times. There was some emotion behind the flatness; it was reserve that held him in check, not a lack of compassion. "We have asked ourselves that question many times. She was in this country with us." He stopped and held up a hand. "I think it was right for her to leave. I do not regret that. You have to have some sort of—of—a conduct. But we should have known more of where she was. We should have not let her go so far out of our sight."

He looked at Sully and did not say anything more.

twenty-one

The two eight-by-tens were from parties that Lana had been to, something like a prom, where there was someone taking pictures of couples. The pictures were sitting across his lap. Sully raised his voice to be heard above the traffic, the wind blowing in from the rolled-down windows.

"So how did you say you found Hector again?"

"I didn't," Sly said from the front seat. "I said we found him, me and Lionel. So what you think?"

"I think it was profitable."

Sly turned around and looked at him. "Hardy fucking har har, motherfucker."

"No, I mean it. Noel Pittman? Posed nude, naughty-girl pictures, for this photographer up in Petworth."

"And when were you going to tell me this?"

"I just did. I just found out yesterday."

"Gimme the name."

"Don't have it, but I can get it."

"Well, get on the motherfucking phone, man. Shit. Both these bitches take their drawers off for some dude to take pictures? And they turn up dead? Nah nah nah. This is the dude we want to go see."

"I dunno. The shots of Noel, they look professional, they're not peekaboo porn. And she apparently called the photographer, so it wasn't like he was out there trolling. Or so I hear."

"So who do you hear this from?"

"MPD."

"They ain't looking at it?"

"Not hard, the guy they got on it, he's just cold-casing it."

"Who's that?"

"Dick Jensen."

Sly laughed, a bark. "Ha! That motherfucker. I know Dick Jensen. He arrested my ass, what was it, fifteen years ago?"

"You don't sound impressed."

"Look, what I'm saying, you get busted for a felony? Pray that Jensen is the man with the cuffs."

"So you beat it at trial."

"It was an AWD, and it didn't even go to trial. Dismissed. Lawyer had a field day."

They rode for a bit, the passing traffic, Sully's mind working, not liking the flow of information going from him to Sly.

"So your girlfriend, she's prosecuting the Sarah Reese case," he said. "She seems pretty comfy thinking your three boys ain't all that innocent."

"I ain't said they was all that innocent. I said they ain't killed the Reese girl."

"And you know that for sure because?"

"Because they said they didn't."

"They wouldn't lie to you?"

"I didn't ask politely."

"Sly, dammit. What does that even mean?"

Sly turned back in his seat to look at Sully. "It means Jerome, the oldest one? It means he got a sister, fourteen, name of Jazzmine. Day after this happened, Saturday, I picked up Jazzmine from the playground, the park, whatever you call it, there at the end of her block, you know? I took her over to one of my places and I had her call him from there so she could tell him where she was. I got on the phone and said tell me where you are. I left Jazzmine there with Lionel and I went to see him. They were down in Southeast in this little apartment, scared as shit. I said I'm going to go home and fuck your sister in the ass and then I'm going to cap her in the back of her head as soon as I come.

Then I'm going to throw her ass in the Anacostia for the catfish. Unless you tell me what happened with that white girl."

Traffic went by for a few minutes.

Sully said, "That is a very profitable way of asking questions."

"I noticed that all by myself."

"So what did he tell you?"

"That they saw that girl in the store. Talked about her ass a little bit. She gets bitchy. Drops her wallet out of her jacket and runs out the back. They pick up the wallet and run out the front. It had like thirty-five dollars or some shit like that. They kept the money and threw the wallet in the trash can, the one at the basketball court, up there by the rec center. They go home, it's all on the news that the police looking for they ass."

"They're the last ones to see her and then wind up with her money, their prints."

"Seem to be."

"That's not good."

"I already told you they're going to walk. Look, this shit ain't over. Whoever it was that brought this down on all us, who done killed the little white girl, and whoever killed that fine sister and the Mexican chick, I'm thinking they can't be but one person that stupid out there. Now. There some brothers out here with a dick problem. I—"

"She wasn't Mexican."

"Who?"

"Lana Escobar. She's Guatemalan, not Mexican."

"Guatemalan, Mexican, Costa fucking Rican. She's dead."

"What is it you think happened?"

"To who?"

"Any one of them. Sarah. Noel. Lana."

Sly looked out the front window. He started to chew on a nail and stopped.

"The white girl is the biggest problem, see. I go asking around on that, you go asking around on that, we going to bump into dudes with badges, you see that? The way I got it, I find out who offed that Mexican chick, or Noel, or both, that'll tell me something I need to know."

"How you figure?"

"One, it's going to tell me who killed two bitches on my turf."

"But you didn't go looking when Lana got killed."

"She's a ho. That shit happens. Noel, college girl passing through. Far as I knew, she's in LA making look-at-my-ass porn flicks."

"But now?"

"Now the white girl changes everything. This makes three, and you and me, we know the police are all wrong on it. So we find out who killed the other two? Maybe it's nothing. Or maybe it's the same one what killed the white girl. That'd be *three*-for-one shopping right there. But I can't go around asking on the white chick. I'm taking the play that's available. Cops go left. I go right."

He half turned in his seat. "You?"

"Why you think," Sully said, "I'm taking notes on Lana Escobar?"

Sly and Lionel dropped Sully off a few minutes later. He walked stiffly to the black iron gate at the sidewalk and then up the steps. The real problem, he thought, turning the dead bolt on the front door, was that if Sly figured out who the killer was first, no one would ever know. He'd off the dude and that would be that. There would just be years of unanswered questions.

And Sly was motivated, he could see that. The nail chewing, the antsy chatter—the man was rattled by the police uptick in a neighborhood that usually got ignored, feds slapping on doors, busting guys on meaningless warrants just to get them downtown, threaten to violate them on their probation, squeeze them. Usually, these were the neighborhood cops, who knew the perps, who knew them, and everybody knew the game.

But the feds were assholes who didn't care about the day-to-day rules. Who knew what knowledge was out there that, if it changed hands, could rain down hell in another direction? That was what Sly was sweating. That was why he needed Sully's help to get Sarah's murder solved and the feds out of his neighborhood. If resolving the other two killings helped do that, fine, but there was no fooling anyone—nobody cared who killed Noel and Lana. It was all about Sarah Reese.

twenty-two

Two hours later, the woman let him in, telling him to sit down, motioning toward a worn-out couch. There was a television and an empty bag of potato chips and two beer cans on the floor beside a chair. The house, a sagging brick row house in a crappy block of Thirteenth Street NW, ten or twelve blocks away from Princeton Place. The last known address of William J. Darden, hirer of prostitutes, beater of women.

She went upstairs, was up there a minute, and Sully sat down on the couch, waiting, wanting to come out of this with something he could use, something about the grime of the trade, the whole poverty and debasement of it all, the soup they were swimming in. Footsteps came down the stairs, hard, fast, not feminine, and more than one set of them. Sully startled, spread his feet, ready to stand in a hurry, but did not get up.

William Darden was a big man—Jesus, the arrest card hadn't said the man was a fucking grizzly—and he stomped into the room, a head of steam, barreling forward. There were two men behind him, not as big, but Sully didn't have time to look.

"You—" he said, pointing at Sully, moving forward. "You are one dumb motherfucker."

Sully stood. The man was fully sleeved, the jailhouse tats running down both arms. "Mr. Darden, I was just looking to talk to friends of Lana Es—"

The pistol came out in Darden's right hand as if he'd shucked it out of a sleeve and he brought it hard and fast, head level, not even slowing down. Sully got an arm up and turned, blocking part of it, the force of it knocking him sideways, skittering by the couch but keeping his feet.

His vision blurred and one of the men behind Darden, quick as a cat, got both hands on his shoulders, shoving him into the foyer and into the wall.

The notebook went flying, his shoulders banging against the wood paneling. He kept his feet but kneeled over, out of breath, reaching into his cycle jacket. Darden was closing on him and Sully sat down backward and then he was whipping the heavy Yugoslavian pistol up and out of the jacket in both hands, flicking the safety down with his thumb and firing two rounds into the ceiling, the muzzle flashing, then pointing it back at Darden's chest.

Darden flinched backward at the shots, nearly falling over himself.

"The fuck you doin'?" he bellowed. "You can't do that!"

"Swing on me one more time and I'll put two in your goddamned brain," Sully said. He had both hands on the pistol, sitting on the floor, back against the wall, three feet from the door, his hands steady as iron. The man on his left wasn't moving. The third one had vanished back up the stairs.

"Repo men can't get a goddamned gun," Darden said, still looking shocked. "You—you can't come in here shooting."

"I'm not a goddamned repo man."

"What? She said you were here about the flat-screen."

"I could give a fuck about your big-ass TV. I—"

"You a narc? Show me—show me the badge."

"I'm a fucking reporter. At the paper. I don't give a goddamn about what you—"

"A *reporter*? With that thing? What, it was your daddy's?"

"Put the goddamn gun down," Sully said. "This is some shit. All I wanted to ask you about is a hooker."

"A what?" But the tone softening.

"Lana Escobar. A hooker. You got busted two years ago, an undercover female cop, a sting? You gave up Lana's name as one of your steadies. Girl's Hispanic, about five-two, thick. Nice ass."

Darden pointed his gun down. Sully did, too.

"Show me the ID. And keep your voice down."

The woman upstairs somewhere, listening.

The press card was on a metal-beaded lanyard around his neck. Sully pulled it off and tossed it. Darden caught it, looked at it, then tossed it back.

"Thought you came for the television. She's behind on it."

"Yeah, well, I didn't."

Darden went to the half-ass couch and sat down, still looking at him, amazed. Sully put the pistol back in his jacket pocket, then mopped the sweat from his face with his shirttail. He let out a long breath. "I don't mind telling you, Mr. Darden, that was some shit just then."

"*You* telling *me*?"

Sully almost laughed, and then he did. "Alright, Christ. Okay. Let's get this over with and get on with our happy lives. So. Lana Escobar. You gave her up in the sting."

"Man, I barely remember. I don't know nobody's name. They showed me some pictures. I picked her out. They violated me on parole. Got to, you know, give up somebody unless you want to go back."

"You take any pictures of Lana? Like, naked?"

"What, I look like a freak? And who's gonna pay for them holes in the ceiling?"

The rest of the list he checked out by dark.

Jasper had moved, and nobody knew where. Nobody answered at Green's. Darrell Turner, living on the top floor of a two-story walk-up, didn't answer. Sully knocked and could hear footsteps on the wooden floorboards inside. A shadow, blocking the light at the bottom of the door, someone just on the other side, not moving. There was no peephole. Sully knocked again, the person stood there, three inches away, not moving. Sully tensed, holding his breath, watching the shadow beneath the door. It didn't move. He backed way, not turning his back, and left.

By the time he got back home, getting ice into a plastic bag, putting the bag on his jaw, trying to lower the welt that Darden had given him with the gun, he felt it coming on. Darden, Darden had rattled him, Jesus Christ. This fucking job, the dipshits you had to deal with . . . Your nerves, man, your precious bloody nerves. When the shit was going down, he was fine, just fine, always had been. But Nadia, the shell, and now look at him. Just fucking look. The shakes. It was all over and gone and now he had the tremors, standing in his kitchen in front of the refrigerator. His left hand, held aloft in front of his eyes, vibrated all on its own, like a tuning fork. The gun had come up and out and fired as if it had its own mind. The air in his lungs getting less, his chest growing tight, the noise in his head building to a roar, like standing next to a tarmac with a jet taking off, goddammit, just goddamn. He crossed the kitchen in a rush, feeling like he was about to vomit, opening the top of the Dutch door to the backyard, some fresh air, trying not to gag or hyperventilate. Bend over, breathe. Deep breaths now. Come on. Come on. It was alright. It was alright now. It wasn't the night on the mountain. It wasn't. It was all okay. The doctor at Landstuhl, he'd told him there would be things like this, and he should have stayed on the medication, yes, he should have, but he just couldn't stand the shrink looking at him, asking him questions. He felt his breath coming back to him. The left hand, when he held it aloft, was slowing down. There was a crystal tumbler right there on the counter. Five cubes of ice and a splash of Basil's, sit on the back porch . . . and then, shit, he remembered the community meeting he'd caused, the panicked citizens of Park View, worried a serial killer was loose among them.

twenty-three

The Park View Recreation Center sat at the corner of Warder and Otis, an early 1970s American urban renewal project, its no-frills brick architecture testifying to government frugality and the utter lack of Nixon-era imagination. Thirtysomething years of use made it look sixtysomething years old, a hulking relic from another time, a mound of metal and brick filling space in a low-slung skyline.

The noise of the community meeting, being held on the basketball court, reverberated before he got into the arena itself. He checked his watch. Nearly seven. Dick Jensen was already at the microphone, trying to talk over the accusations.

"So you saying three dead girls and no arrest is nothing we need to worry about," the man at the microphone in the audience was saying. He was standing, holding the microphone with both hands even though it was on a stand, as if he had a choke hold on a python. Impossibly skinny, he looked to Sully to be Ethiopian. "I got *girls* here. I got a *wife* here. I got—"

"You got what we all got here, which is a stake in a safe place to live," Jensen cut in, louder. "Don't look at me and think because I'm white I don't give a damn or that I can't tell your son in baggy pants from a three-time loser just out of Lorton."

Jensen had surprised himself with the outburst, Sully saw, taking a seat in a folding chair at the back of the crowd. He'd also silenced the audience. The tension hung, suspended, somewhere high in the room, as if in a balloon that might pop.

"Look," Jensen said, his voice lowering. "We've been at this nearly an hour. All of you are upset. I get it. I am lead detective for MPD on the Noel—"

"And you ain't done *shit*!" a woman shouted. "Where's the lead cop on the Hispanic girl?" A roiling flush of crowd noise followed, "Whoo" and "That's it" and "Can't hear ya now" and clapping and an unfocused surge of hoo-has and catcalls and emotion that seemed to swell from the back of the room to the front, the balloon threatening to burst.

"If you'd let me *finish*," Jensen said. His voice was exasperated and tight, the words clipped. Wearing a three-piece suit, keeping the jacket on, Sully figured, to keep the sweat stains from showing under the armpits.

"*I* am the lead on the Noel Pittman case. Lead on Pittman, and liaison to the Sarah Reese case, which is being worked, in our shop, by my partner, Billy Hairston, who is seated just to my left. Billy—" He reached over, a gesture, making sure people saw a stern black face, Hairston with his shaved head, arms folded, pot-bellied, looking grumpy, looking mean.

"So I'm looking at Pittman for any ties, similarities, you see what I'm saying? I'm not going to be defensive up here. The chief, over here to my right, and Council Member Belham, over there to his right, asked us to take time out of our work to be available. If I wasn't here, I'd be working *on* the cases you care about instead of talking *about* them."

The room quieting now, people sitting back down.

"I've been working major crimes in this city since Ford was in office. I know you're worried. I know you saw the story in the paper, maybe watched some of the TV. But I want to stress this: There is nothing true today that wasn't true last month or last week. You and your children, your family? You're in no more danger than you were last Christmas, on the Fourth of July, or this morning when you woke up. The only thing that's different is a misleading newspaper story. It takes three deaths that took place in a small area and suggests a link between them based on their proximity and nothing else. It's ridiculous. Newspapers, television stations, the radio—they don't have to be right at the end of the day. They don't put people in prison. They got what they wanted here, which is a reaction. They sold some papers.

"We are the police, and *we* have to get it right. It's not as easy as publishing stories with selective facts and scaring people. Billy here did the work on the Escobar homicide. Which, as you know, took place right outside. There has never been a viable suspect. I can sit here and talk till I'm blue in the face about the work we have done on that, but one thing I can tell you is that no one, absolutely no one, has told us they saw anything. At all. Did you see something? Do you know something? Did all this prompt a memory?"

His eyes went over the room, trying to catch an eye looking a second longer at him, a head with a half nod, a shoulder sagging with the weight of responsibility. Sully couldn't see if anyone responded, but it was fully quiet for the first time since he'd entered the gym.

"Tell me later. You don't have to come say now. You know where we are." He nodded to his partner, pacing to his right, then took a step back from the microphone, looking like he'd forgotten his place in a speech, like he had overrun some mental mark and now didn't know where he was going.

He approached the microphone again, speaking while he still had the room, selling his sincerity, selling that sense of purpose, a man with a sober haircut and a gun on his hip, working to get that trust, that tip. "I can also tell you that we just discovered Noel Pittman's body, and the list of cooperating witnesses is just as long as in the Escobar killing. Zero. Nada. We're working that case as the forensics dictate. The Sarah Reese case, we got a break. Someone identified suspects. Someone told us who they were. That is the one and only reason we've made an arrest. That one is white and the other two are not is coincidental."

"So you can't arrest nobody unless you get lucky?" It was the man at the microphone. He hadn't moved.

"Pretty much," Jensen said, "if by getting lucky you're including witnesses who'll testify. People kill people and then they hide. They don't call us up and tell us about it. They don't shoot each other in front of the precinct. So they have to leave something behind. Or they have to be seen. They have to screw up. Or, as you put it, we have to get lucky."

"When you going to search the rest of the houses?"

It was a man's voice, plaintive but demanding, coming from the far side of the room.

"I'm sorry?" Jensen said.

"The rest of the houses. When you going to search them? That Pittman girl turned up under one. You know how many abandoned houses there are around here? My daughter, she's been missing a month now—"

Sully's cellphone buzzed. Shit. It was R.J. He lingered long enough to hear the man's last name, Williams, and then quick-stepped to a side door, out into a hallway.

"Sully! Lad!" the voice boomed into his ear. "So wonderful to hear your voice, particularly since we haven't seen you in the newsroom. How are your peregrinations into the demimonde of our fair city? I trust you have not contracted any communicable diseases."

"I'm at this community meeting, over on Princeton. Working the streets to—"

He paused to listen.

"I'm going to need a few more days," he said. "Escobar wasn't so much in the life like we thought. Dug up her, what is it, sort of stepfather. Nobody's talked to him before. And I found Noel Pittman's sister. Was actually out there for the funeral." Another pause. "Out in Colesville. She wasn't friendly."

R.J. spoke for a while.

"Hey, man, I know nobody cares," Sully said, pacing, his shoes clicking on the tile floor, still jittery, still wired. "We're going to make them care, okay? But you gotta give me some time. I'm up to my ass out here in hookers and illegal immigrants and, funny thing, they don't like white guys with notebooks, right? Turns out there may be some girls missing up here, too, not just dead, so tell Melissa to pipe the fuck down."

He clicked the phone off and yanked open the door to the gym. The meeting was breaking up, the stage empty.

David Belham, the Ward 1 councilman, had come in front of the podium, into the center of a cluster of people, writing things down in a datebook and looking up at each constituent. You could see the man counting the votes. There was the woman who was the advisory neighborhood commissioner—no, he wasn't going over to her, she was batshit crazy—and an MPD spokesman. The chief was somewhere in a larger knot of people. There were television cameras and lights around him. Sully looked, but didn't see the Williams man anywhere. Jensen, there *he* was, working his way toward the door. Sully loped that way.

Taller than those around him, the man looked over their heads, saw Sully, and tensed, stopping, his eyes locking on him.

"You want to talk about the *problem*?" he said, a loud stage voice, halfway to the people around him, halfway toward Sully. "Why don't you go talk to this guy? Carter here's the one who wrote the story."

The trail of people around Jensen, elderly homeowners, a young activist, four or five women who looked indignant, stopped and turned, sizing him up.

Play it straight, he told himself. He smiled, making eye contact all around.

"I would have been happy to quote Detective Jensen in that piece if he had returned any of the three calls I made to him before I wrote it."

"We don't talk to reporters, particularly about open cases," Jensen said, playing out the theater. "Everybody knows that."

"An odd position for a man who just said he needed witnesses to talk in order for him to work."

Jensen turned to the people around him. "Listen, thank all of you for coming out. If you have information about any of these cases, you got my card. Call us. We'll come to you."

He swiveled on a heel, turned, and walked. The crowd did not follow. They muttered among themselves, darting looks at Sully.

Someone bumped his right shoulder from behind, hurrying past in the crowd. Sully turned, halfway between an "Excuse me" and "Watch where you're going." He was surprised to see it was Doyle Goodwin.

"I need to see you tomorrow," Doyle whispered at his ear, and then he was past him, melting into the crowd, the knots of people still forming and re-forming, their voices bubbling, the anger and tension in the room still fluttering, like cigarette ash that had been flicked into the air.

twenty-four

Just after nine the next morning, Sully edged the Ducati around stalled traffic on C Street, wedging it into a space between cars illegally parked in the designated "Motorcycles Only" spots.

He walked past five or six cars and there was the hot dog cart at the curb in front of the Department of Motor Vehicles. A half smoke with mustard and ketchup, lord yes, he ate it sitting on the steps, washing it down with some sort of crappy iced tea they sold in a glass bottle. He'd reached Doyle on the phone earlier, making plans to meet him at the store later in the day. The man had offered no clue as to what had been on his mind the night before, or why he couldn't say what he had to say over the phone. This was annoying but it wasn't like he was being Jensen, blaming him for homicides that cops couldn't solve. Sully burped softly into his fist. Half smokes.

Just the other side of the two lanes was the U.S. District Courthouse, the federal seat of power, where the United States sued and was sued, where David Reese was the highest-ranking judge. It sat at the foot of Capitol Hill. Pennsylvania Avenue ran in front of it, America's Main Street, and in the course of a dozen blocks to the west encompassed the Department of Justice, FBI headquarters, the U.S. Treasury, and the White House.

C Street, all of two blocks long, ran just behind the court, the ass end of it, and offered nothing but a portal into the shithole of Washington. The DMV squatted on one end, the great time-waster of urban bureaucracy, and upstairs, in the headquarters of the MPD, were the cops who plowed into the city's drug deals, stolen cars, burglaries, phone scams, homicides, rapes, and beat downs, usually to little effect.

Next door, across a small park, was Superior Court, where the vast majority of defendants were no-papered the morning after their arrest, down in C-10, the same arraignment room that the Reese suspects had passed through. You could smell the depression in the room amid the piss and the plumbing and the burnt toast from the cafeteria down the hall. A tunnel ran between the court and MPD, used to shuttle defendants between the two without bringing them into daylight. If the defendants actually got charged, their plea bargains and their trials were heard in the brown-paneled courtrooms upstairs, where no one but a few family members and victims' relatives were ever likely to show up.

Sully threw his foil wrapper and the bottle into a curbside trash can and walked in the DMV entrance, taking the back entrance into police headquarters, so that any beat reporters around the front entrance would not see him enter the place. He turned left and then right and walked around the long corridor, passing through security and heading for the Youth and Preventive Services division on the third floor, the dead end of missing persons cases.

The counter, a long marble divide that ran the length of the room, was not staffed. He stood there long enough to be noticed and a thickset woman in uniform pushed up from her desk in the back of the room and came to the counter and asked him what it was he thought that he wanted.

"Looking for Rudy Jeffries," he said. "Could you tell him Sully Carter is here?"

"Why does Sully Carter want to see Rudy Jeffries?"

"Because I'd like to ask him about a missing woman. Actually, maybe two."

She put both elbows on the counter and arched an eyebrow, bored or giving every appearance of it. "Relatives?"

"No."

"Dependents?"

"Nope."

"Then why do you need to talk to Sergeant Jeffries about them?"

Sully shifted his weight. "Because I'm a reporter working on a story about them, and I think Sergeant Jeffries might be able to help. He knows me."

"I'm thrilled he does. You didn't check in with Sergeant Malone, in the media relations department, did you? 'Cause he didn't call up saying you were coming."

"I know Sergeant Malone, and no, I didn't, because I'm not looking to quote Rudy. I'm just—"

"Since you know so many people, you should know the protocol. Sergeant Malone is on the second floor. But then, hey, you know him. So you know where to find it."

She was turning her back to him when Sully rapped on the counter and leaned forward. "Nobody's trying to get around any departmental regs, okay, Officer? I got a simple question for Rudy about how something works. It's no big fucking deal."

He dropped the expletive for effect, figuring it would backfire or blast the door open a crack. It didn't really matter if it was the former, since she was shutting him down already. Malone, he'd relay the request to Rudy, yes, but in his own sweet time, and Sully would lose half the day. She was the troll at the bridge, and trolls *ran* the bridges, and trolls were a pain in the ass, but you couldn't get around them.

She sauntered back between the desks, and then into the corridor of offices. A minute later, Rudy came into view, beckoned impatiently, and disappeared back down the hall. Sully lifted the divider in the counter, smiled sweetly at the officer, who ignored him, and walked down the narrow corridor. The door was open. Rudy had his bulk crammed behind his desk. He was on the phone and motioned for Sully to sit down.

"'Cause I told him to be there," he said into the phone. "I'm not interested in stories, Leon. I don't care if it's an excuse or a reason. I don't care if his dick fell off. Tell him to pick it up and meet me at the time and place appointed."

He hung up but kept looking at the phone, keeping his hand on top of it, as if it were going to run off if it got the chance.

"Kid is seventeen about to be eighteen and he's got a dope problem, right, and he's run off from home and now his momma's looking for him, getting us involved?" he said, still looking at the phone. "Kid gets a lawyer. Didn't *hire* him, see, just talking to him, right, on the phone, getting *advice*, and the kid doesn't want to go home, and he's saying, See, if I stay gone for another month then I'll be eighteen, and the lawyer's saying, Hhhmm, and I'm trying to get the kid's ass outta wherever he's staying before he gets picked up for something else, something that's going to send his punk ass to lockup."

"Why's the lawyer care?"

"Leon. Leon King, one of your pale-faced brethren on a mission to save us from ourselves. Kid's telling him life's shit at home, momma's a crackhead, blah blah."

"Is she?"

Rudy rolled his neck, popping his vertebrae as he did so and finally looked up at Sully. "Merlie? I really don't fucking think so. We graduated Roosevelt the same time. She works at Macy's, the makeup counter. Sings alto at Metropolitan AME. So no, dipshit is *not* being raised by a crack momma. *Her* problem is she loves the little chump, which is a losing proposition, you ask me, but she called me up and got in my ear about it." He leaned forward, meaty forearms on the edge of the desk, already looking somewhere between tired and worn down. "Which is not why you're here."

"Thought I'd come by and flirt with my girlfriend. What's her name out there?"

"Sherice? Nah, Sherice don't care for your kind."

"Which 'my kind' we talking about?"

"Reporters. But now that I think about it, she probably don't care for white people too much, neither."

"Pity."

"Well."

"Noel Pittman."

"Yes."

"You ever see the pictures?"

"They are legend, brother."

"You guys chasing it as a homicide?"

"Go ask Homicide."

"It started off as a missing persons."

"Out there in 4-D, yeah."

"The homicide case did. But I'm talking about when it was just a missing persons thing. Don't y'all track missing adults, citywide, out of this office?"

"Used to. But in that reorg the chief loves so much? He moved all the missing persons cases out to each ward last year, when he transferred Homicide out of central command."

"Ah, shit."

"Yeah, baby. The way it is now? The seven wards, they're supposed to report their numbers into us but work the cases themselves. The adult cases, that is. The kids, citywide? We still do that here."

"This sounds sort of fucked up."

"It sort of is."

"So even though Pittman started out as a missing person—an adult—you guys didn't do anything with it down here out of headquarters."

"Goodness, but you're a bright boy."

"The name Lana Escobar ring a bell?"

Rudy paused. "Last year. I was still in Vice. She turned up dead, up therc at Park View."

"So she was, as they say, known to the vice squad?"

"You'd have to call over there for the Rolodex. If she got booked, there'd be a record. It wasn't a big enough name for me to know about, I can tell you that. I just remember, you did a little squib on it. Again, all this is when Chief started moving shit around. I was leaving Vice. People were leaving downtown, Homicide and Major Crimes and all that, out to the wards."

"Her family says they filed a missing persons report."

"Bully for them."

"I mean, they said that when they reported her missing, that's when they found out she was a Jane Doe down at the morgue."

"I am grieving for them still."

"It bother you that Noel Pittman, once a missing person, turns up in a basement in the 700 of Princeton Place, and Lana Escobar, once a missing person, turns up on the outfield grass at Park View Rec Center, which is also in the 700 of Princeton Place? And that they went missing within about six months of one another?"

Rudy leaned back in his chair and put his hands behind his head. The fluorescent light overhead gleamed on his shaved dome. He looked up at the ceiling. "This is your story the other day."

"Dick Jensen didn't like it."

"Dick's not all bad. A hard-ass and old-school, but there's worse. Played golf with him once. He didn't cheat."

"So you think the story was bullshit, too?"

"Well, look, you put it like you just did, the missing females? Yeah, it sounds off. But you know how many missing persons cases we get? Forty-one hundred last year. We're at three thousand and change this year. That's about ten a day, all year long, including weekends, holidays, and your religious observances. I think the homicide number last year was 260. This year, so far it's 190? Something like that. So in a city that's all of sixty-nine square miles, filled with thousands of reports of missing people, and where you get a homicide about every thirty, thirty-five hours, you're asking is it odd that you get a combination on the same block?"

He unclasped his hands from the back of his head, pulled his gaze down from the ceiling, and leaned forward in his chair, his forearms back on the edge of the desk. "So I'd say probably not. I'd say maybe. You think it's to the right of that."

"How would I check into other girls, women missing up in that area?"

"Under eighteen, right here, but we can't tell you shit because they're underage. Adults, you got to go out to 4-D. But I got to tell you, don't be looking at the files out there like they're Scripture."

"Because?"

"Well, one, I refer to my earlier statement, senator. It's kind of fucked up. Two, adults have the right to disappear. It's not a crime not to keep a fixed address, and it's not against the law to move someplace your momma and them can't find you. And I'm saying ninety-eight, ninety-nine percent of missing adults are the homeless, vagrants, the mentally ill, your hard-core methies and crackheads. They turn back up in a week or two in McPherson Square, Freedom Plaza, or living beneath an overpass in Brooklyn, or five years later in a homeless shelter in Minneapolis, or they turn up as a toe in the morgue. Not more than a handful are quote-unquote actual missing cases—kidnappings, girls who leave for work and never come home.

"Meanwhile, look at this here. You're a uniform out there in your district, pulling double shifts, busting your ass? Family calls, brother's missing, they're hysterical or they're pissed or they just feel on obligation. They know he's fucked up but they call it in because it's family and what else you gonna do? You catch the case, and this isn't—you ever see the NCIC form? It's like thirty fucking pages. Dental records, tattoos, list of surgeries. You wouldn't believe. So you sit with them, fill out the form, but it's not even a perp card, right? The guy didn't do anything. You lose ninety minutes of the only life you'll ever lead and you send it to us downtown.

"Now, five days later, the asshole turns up living beneath a tarp on Farragut Square. You find out he's had a crack problem since high school and the family knew it but didn't tell you because they knew if we knew then we wouldn't look. They'd be right but it's bullshit. So you're pissed the family hustled you, but you got to stop what you're doing, go erase him from your system, then call us and say, Hey, erase him, then we've got to have somebody actually erase him instead of just thinking about it, and if you forget or we forget then the numbers get off, and you can multiply that process by about a million. That's the files you're looking at."

"So you're saying the Old Testament is more reliable?"

"Don't get me started on the Bible. Merlie is, what do I want to say, a special friend."

twenty-five

You had to be kidding. People tell you things like this, this is the way it is, and you still just couldn't believe.

From a file drawer, the clerk at 4-D had pulled out page after printed page of official police notifications of the missing, the sheets spilling out onto the floor at one point, a sheaf of them. God.

On each sheet, a picture of the individual was centered below MISSING in bold, black type. Their name, their age, and last known location was listed at the bottom, along with an MPD phone number. There were more than a hundred, could have been two. They were in no particular order, and the database was not much more than a computerized mess. Some of the cases were closed out, with marks for "Reunited" or "Dead."

Some listed the precise date they went missing; others just read "Summer 1998." Some went back to the late 1980s. One—he took this one—had been filed the week before. Others listed an address for the missing, not the place where they were last seen. It had the surreal look and feel of a fever dream, postcards from a nightmare of America gone wrong.

He stopped at the bulletin board in the front lobby on the way out, another bastion of "Missing" posters, most of these handmade. There were pictures of smiling young women, plump-faced middle-aged men. Nearly all the faces were black, most of the rest Latino, and there were two or three white faces, old, grizzled men who did not look coherent. There were a couple of handbills that he recognized from the files he'd just gone through in the back. He went back to the copies he'd made and turned down an ear of the paper on those, to mark it as someone whose family appeared to be seriously involved.

Jogging across the street to the McDonald's, he got a Coke and some French fries, went to a booth, pulled out a flask, topped off the Coke with a lace of bourbon from his flask, and settled in.

Six or seven cases immediately appeared to be possibilities. Linda Blackwell, Kellie Meikle, Rebekah Bolin, Andrea Thompson—good god, all these in the past three years, all listing a home address within four or five blocks of Princeton Place? Was *anybody* paying attention?

He pulled out his cell and started dialing. Blackwell, Meikle, both had answering machines. On Bolin, a woman answered, listened to his spiel, and said abruptly that her daughter was dead.

"Ma'am? I'm terribly sorry to hear that. I—I am. But it would be helpful to me if you could tell me where she was found. I don't see her on a list of homicides."

"They found 'Bekah beneath a house on Princeton Place, the 600 block," she said.

Sully, who had been scribbling notes, stopped.

"Beneath a house?"

"The floorboards. The—what do they call it, the crawl space? It was abandoned."

"When was this?"

"January, this year. When they found her. She'd been there awhile."

He looked at the poster.

"It says here—the poster—that she was last seen in June the year before, like seven months prior."

"That's right."

"Was it unusual for you not to see her for that long?"

"I told you she's dead."

"Yes'm, I hear you. I'm sorry. But—it sounds like—maybe—it says here she was twenty-three, that maybe she was out a lot."

"'Bekah had been in the wind since she was seventeen."

"But—why—why didn't they call it a homicide? I don't mean to pry, it's just—"

"'Bekah had been on the streets since she dropped out. She weighed ninety-three pounds. She had been arrested I don't know how many times for drugs. She'd come home and I'd have to put her out, send her to her father's. She'd steal everything."

"There was a community meeting at the rec center last night, and the police, they didn't even mention her name as—as a case that might be—"

"They said her death was of 'undetermined causes.'"

"But she was found beneath the floorboards of an abandoned house."

"They said to me, they said, Look, she's been doing crack forever, got busted recently for heroin, likely she got a hot dose, you know, and it likely gave her a heart attack—"

"Likely?"

"—and she died from that. Yeah, likely. What else? I loved my baby. But I ain't going to sugarcoat what she was."

He waited, trying to think of something kind, something patient, to say. Nothing came to mind. The lady knew what she knew.

"Okay, like I said, I'm writing about Princeton Place, and some of the things going on up there. Can I get a picture of Rebekah to—?"

"You can use the one on the flier."

"Thank you. May I ask your name? I never—"

"Pearl. Pearl Bolin."

"And, just making sure I heard right, you were her mother?"

"I still am."

He hung up, the whiskey forgotten, his mind tumbling the numbers to a combination lock. Something was off here, something—this many women and he wasn't even looking hard yet . . . Where was it, where was it? There it was. Williams. The handbill from the police station, Michelle Williams, the dad from the night before.

He dialed the number on the flier and held his breath, looking at the picture on the handbill, a smiling young woman, plump, pretty.

The phone picked up. The baritone he'd heard last night.

"Hello? Mr. Williams? Sir, my name is Sully Carter, I'm a newspaper reporter, and I'm working on a story about missing persons in the

District? Right around Princeton Place, in fact? I was trying to reach the family of Michelle Williams. Someone mentioned her name at a community meeting last night, and I was just following up to see if—"

"This is Michelle's father. That was me. Why you calling? Has she been found?"

"No, not that I know of. I'm a reporter. I'm working on a story about missing young women. Michelle appears to be one of those. That's why I was calling."

Silence. It went on.

He looked at the phone and said into it, "To find out some more about her. I saw the flier at the police station, saw the report, and heard just a part of your question last night. It looks like she's been gone about a week."

The phone rustled. "Four. It's been four *weeks*. They finally just now put out the flier, they got the date wrong to boot. What else is it you need to know, reporter man?" The tone wasn't hostile. It was resigned, and Sully sensed an opening.

"Well, actually, a lot, Mr. Williams. The basics—the last time you saw her, places you might think she could have gone—but also something about who she is, what she likes to do, what her plans are."

"*Were*. What her plans *were*. If my baby's been gone four weeks without talking to me, she's dead. But I'm asking, what's it to you?"

Sully let out a breath. "It's . . . it's partly my job, Mr. Williams. I'm not calling you in my spare time because I have an odd interest in missing young women. I'm at work. I've been doing this twenty years and I'm serious about it. There are a couple of other girls who are missing from around this neighborhood and—I'm not going to lie to you—they've turned up as homicide victims, or drug cases. I'm writing about them, and that research led me to Michelle's name. I'd like to come see you, find out some more about your daughter, and, if it's okay with you, put her picture in the paper."

There was another raft of silence.

"Where are you," the baritone said, "right now?"

"The McDonald's on Georgia, just up from the intersection with Missouri."

"You know where Warder is?"

"I do."

"I'm at 3535. I got to be at work at four. You can come now, you hurry."

The block was mostly row houses and the Williams place was like the rest: two stories with a basement, an awning over a concrete porch (his was painted gunship gray), four steps down to a grassy yard, a brick walkway to the street. A rusting chain-link fence lined the sidewalk. Two green city-issued trash cans sat just inside the fence, their plastic shells mottled and stained. Sully turned to look up the street toward Princeton Place as he opened the gate to walk into the yard. He could make out the stone edifice of Park View Elementary two blocks down. On the far side of that, in the baseball field at Park View Rec Center, was where Lana Escobar had been killed in the outfield grass. Noel Pittman had lived in the first building behind the center field fence. Rebekah Bolin, she'd been found on the east side of the Warder intersection. Michelle Williams could have walked by all of them in less than five minutes.

When he knocked, the bolt drew on the interior door, and it swung inward to reveal a tall, broad-shouldered man, a paunch beginning to strain the front of the T-shirt that was on under his unbuttoned Amtrak uniform.

"Sully Carter," he said, opening the screen door and extending a hand.

"Curtis Williams," he said, gripping Sully's hand, backing up a step to let him inside. It was a narrow fit; Williams was a big man.

The hallway was dark, as was the front room off to the right. It was quiet save for the tick of a ceiling fan in the living room, its rotation slightly off, clicking on each circuit.

"The kitchen," Williams said, gesturing down the hall. Sully went into the room, the yellow tile, dim light overhead. There was a small rectangular wooden table pushed against the wall and two chairs. Sully pulled one out and sat down, putting a card of his on the table as he did.

"I got maybe twenty minutes before I got to go," Williams said.

"Yes, sir, listen—thanks for the time," Sully said, looking him in the eye. He had maybe sixty seconds to gain his trust. People made their minds up fast, almost on instinct. It was about a feel, a perception, and that was based on physical observations and a sense of comfort. It was about sincerity and it couldn't be taught or faked.

"You work at the Amtrak station, Mr. Williams, or you make the runs?"

"The runs, mostly. I do the ticketing, keep the books en route. Sometimes the café car when they don't have anyone else."

"You don't sound like the new guy."

Williams raised his eyebrows. "Twenty-three years," sounding out each syllable. His voice was deep, but he spoke so softly Sully had to lean forward to catch it. He took the card Sully extended and looked at it while Sully went back over the story he was writing. Thirty or forty seconds into the explanation, Williams reached over into a stack of papers on the table, and pulled out a picture of Michelle. It was a school photograph. She had her hair pulled back, a bright smile, a deep blue T-shirt, and dangling earrings. Thin eyebrows, indicating they were plucked and managed. She was a little on the heavy side. She was twenty-four, her father said.

Sully smiled, looking at it.

"You got kids?" Williams asked.

Sully shook his head no. "It wasn't good when I grew up. I got a sister who I haven't seen in six, seven years. She lives out in Phoenix. Kids appear to be something my family doesn't do well."

Williams nodded. "I hear you. My wife took off when Michelle was three. It was just me and her. I got people, but they're down in North Carolina. She'd go stay with my mother in the summers. I stopped taking overnights on the train for a long time back when the wife left, just up to New York and back, the same day. Michelle and I did okay. She went to school down there at Cardozo."

Sully wrote this in his notebook and nodded. "What's her birthday?"

"August 22, 1975."

"Could you tell me about the day she disappeared?"

The man pulled out a chair, far enough from the table that his legs did not fit under it. He sprawled as much as sat. When he went from standing to sitting, his body posture went from dominant to defensive.

"Not really," he said. "I was out on an overnight to New York. I had started back on those a few years ago. Last train up, first one back the next morning." His voice had the same resigned effect that it had over the phone. "Now, see, I didn't think it was unusual when she wasn't home when I got back after my run. She liked to stay with one of her friends over the weekend. She was grown. And, ah, she had problems with the drugs, Mr. Carter. She'd be out to all hours. She'd get one job, lose it, and go back to getting high. So it wasn't all that out of place for her to be gone a few days."

"She'd been to rehab?"

"Several times. We'd fought about it. She'd been raised right. And then—I don't know. High school, started running with the lowlifes. This neighborhood, I been here since I got out of the service, and that was just before Michelle was born. Older folks been here longer. And it just seems that a lot of our kids, they're good, but they just wound up without any . . . any ambition."

Sully leaned back in his chair, pulling up his pen from the notebook for a moment. "It's hard, with kids."

"It was a joy. For a long time. When she was four, I always said I wanted her to stay that age forever."

"What was that date, when you came back from that overnight?"

"September third. A Friday."

"Was she working anywhere when she went missing?"

"No. She'd worked at the Hunger Stopper up there on Georgia for a hot minute, worked at some place in Dupont Circle, then the drugstore over on Sixteenth. That was all in about two years. She got fired from each one. I don't think anybody wanted to hire her after that."

"So you got back that Saturday, what happened?"

"I got back about one in the afternoon. She wasn't around, and like I say, that wasn't unusual. She didn't come home that night, and that wasn't unusual, either. I tried her pager Sunday afternoon."

"She didn't call back?"

Williams shook his head and let one of his massive hands flutter off the table, a surprisingly delicate gesture. "Never again. I was home then—they let me take a paid week off to look for her, not even making me take vacation—but there was nothing. It was like she walked off the edge of the earth. I went down to the police station Tuesday, I think it was. They looked up her record—she'd been arrested once, for drugs—and I told them she had that problem. They said she hadn't been picked up, but to try the homeless shelters and then try them back."

Sully looked down at the flier he'd taken off the wall at the police station. "Hunh. This wasn't posted until October 3, a few days ago. It lists September 13 as the date last seen."

"I know. The police ain't no damn good if you haven't noticed. I went down there the first time, like I said, and they didn't do nothing. I went down there again a week later, September 13, and that's when they decided she was officially missing. It took them nearly three weeks to even produce that flier, and then they got the date wrong. That's why I went to the meeting last night, to give them what for."

"You've asked about Michelle 'round here, I take it?"

"Michelle's been in this neighborhood all her life. If she was getting high over on Thirteenth Street, somebody would see her. And they'd tell me."

"And your family, your ex, her friends, she didn't touch base with any of them?"

Williams shook his head. "No boyfriend, either, far as I know. She'd gotten to where she'd go out with a guy, just one night, I suppose, they'd get high or whatever. She used to date a guy Kevin for a while, he ain't worth shit but he wouldn't hurt nobody. He works for the city, maintains school buildings. I went to see him, and he was surprised as I was. They hadn't been seeing each other for two, three years anyhow."

"Police didn't do anything at all?"

"They checked at the morgue, here, Baltimore, Richmond. They put a note out to those kinds of places if an unidentified body turned up. Said there was no evidence of a crime. They asked me for her dental records."

Sully stopped writing and looked at her picture. Williams told him he could have it, that he had plenty. He shuffled in his chair. Sully recognized the interview was over. He looked around the kitchen. It was small and neatly kept. There were no dishes in the sink. The countertops were clean. There was a box of Ritz crackers pushed to the back of the countertop.

"Did you ever remarry, Mr. Williams?"

"No."

"Anybody—anybody at all—you know of want to do you or Michelle any harm?"

"Police asked that. No. Michelle and me, we didn't bother nobody. We went to church every now and then when she was little. She played basketball at Cardozo. Her grades were pretty good. And then she just got to thinking that cocaine was the answer to everything."

"Do you mind if I look at her room? Just so I can describe it for the story?"

Williams finally looked up from the table. "I'd rather you didn't. I don't see the purpose. I appreciate your interest in Michelle, I do. But I don't know how me letting you into her room would help anyone find her."

Sully nodded and stood up. He was looking for personal, touching detail, and the man wasn't buying. "You mind if I ask around the neighborhood about her, show her picture around? I don't want you to be startled, somebody telling you there's some guy out there asking after Michelle."

Williams shrugged. He checked his watch, walking Sully to the door. The gloom of the house seemed to close in on them in the hallway, and Sully realized only then that the kitchen light over the sink was the only one on in the house. Williams's voice was low and somber in the dimness.

"Ask around, suit yourself. I don't expect anyone to find her anymore. I think she's dead, myself. But I jump when the phone rings. When I hear a girl laugh on the train. I figure that this is just how it's going to be."

He motioned to the door. Sully turned, opened it, and stepped out. He blinked at the light, sun slotting through the clouds. There was no reason to turn around to say good-bye because the door was already closing behind him.

twenty-six

So there were not three young women killed, dead, or missing on the same street in the past eighteen months all within two hundred yards of one another.

There were five. Five that he knew about.

There could be more, of course. There was no reason to think he knew about all of them. He had dozens of fliers he hadn't gone through. Now, there was no way to say they were all homicides—sure, okay, Rebekah Bolin OD'd, maybe. It happened, like John Parker said, and it was just sad, not mysterious.

But crackheads don't crawl under floorboards to die. Rebekah and Noel Pittman, dead in the flooring of houses, a block apart? Lana, strangled in the outfield in between? Sarah, her throat slit fifty feet from where Noel's body was found? Michelle, maybe somewhere near, waiting to be found?

This could all be a combination of chance and dysfunction, yes—no reason to discount that. But he also let himself say it out loud, walking down the street, because if he couldn't, then there was no way he could sell it in the newsroom.

"There is somebody out here," he said out loud, "killing women."

Before him, the old row houses, the brownstones, sat back from the street on their sagging foundations, mute and somehow menacing in their poverty and dilapidated meanness. They were all almost identical to the Williams place. Two stories with attics and little dormer windows, basements, the concrete patio. The city had planted saplings in front of every other house in the narrow strip of ground between the sidewalk and the street. They were supposed to provide shade and greenery, a little makeup on the neighborhood's aging face. But they were so anemic, so poorly maintained, that they ended up adding to the sense of age, of breakdown.

He picked a door, went up, and knocked. Somewhere, behind one of these rotting doors, somebody knew more than they were telling.

By five, he had done better than he'd expected. Half a dozen places, people had answered the knock and had memories of Michelle. No one knew Lana, and only one or two recognized Noel.

Two of the older couples knew Curtis Williams from way back. They talked about seeing Michelle walking by since she was a kid, going to the corner store for a Push-Up in the summer, coming back from the swimming pool at the rec center. Two elderly women who talked to him through the door but gave their names and who remembered Michelle well said they had seen Noel once or twice. One young woman, who answered the door in a long shirt and apparently nothing else, said she had talked to Noel on the street, said hello, had seen her at one club or another. Sully conducted the interview in the doorway, not invited in and not inviting himself.

He ended two doors from the abandoned house where Noel was found. There was nobody home at 786, the place next door, and he came down the sidewalk and stood in front of 788. It was shabby, long since abandoned. Someone had hammered plywood over all of the downstairs windows and most of the upstairs. The yellow police tape that had surrounded the porch after the discovery of Noel's body had fallen to the ground.

You could just step over it. Sully thought about it and looked up and down the street. It was empty. He went fast. A half dozen steps covered the weed-choked walkway and he was up the steps and onto the porch. There was another yellow sticker on the door emblazoned with large letters reading DO NOT ENTER—CRIME SCENE. He tapped on the front door, tried the handle, and pushed.

It opened.

A tingle went up his back. His spine straightened and he instinctively spread his feet to the width of his shoulders, balancing himself. He put his hand in his pocket, feeling the weight of the pistol, but did not pull it out.

Using a knuckle, he pushed the door, hinges creaking, and it went back until it bounced lightly off the interior wall. It was dark inside. He could see the stairwell and peeling wallpaper. When he leaned to the side he could see a tangle of furniture, a couch and some chairs and upended buckets in one of the side rooms.

He glanced behind him and stepped inside, easing the door shut behind him. "Hello! This is the Metropolitan Police Department! We are securing this property! Come forward now!"

The words bounced up the stairwell, nothing stirring. Dust motes floated in front of his face. He looked up. The roof had been leaking, the ceiling was pitted and rotting. He waited some more. Outside, he could hear the cars and trucks on Georgia, the hum of passing traffic. He reached in his backpack and found a small vinyl pouch. There was a tiny LED flashlight inside, one of the things that came on a keychain. He clicked it on and took three more steps forward.

"Hey, asshole, this is MPD! Identify yourself at once! You are trespassing on a police crime scene!"

Weak light from the end of the day streamed in from upstairs, where there was nothing over several broken windows. Slips of light leaked in from the plywood that had been nailed up over the downstairs windows. He stood perfectly still, scarcely breathing. He counted to twenty. When there was still no sound, no rustle, he let out his breath and moved forward. If there were crack addicts inside, they would have stirred, they would have run for it. The door to the basement was just ahead, in the narrow hallway that ran beside the stairs leading to the second floor. He set his backpack down behind the front door. He didn't want it slowing him down, giving someone something to grab, if a crack zombie materialized.

He went up the stairs, intent on making sure no one came down behind him to cut him off from the front door. He put his feet at the far outside of each step, the wood gone dark with rotting and water stains, to prevent them from collapsing under his weight. He made the upstairs landing.

The bathroom was filthy, rat and pigeon droppings in the tub, the shower rail rusting, the mirror broken and pieces of glass and chipped tile on the floor. The light fixtures had been stripped out long ago, exposed wires dangling from the ceiling. Puddles of water stained the floor. There was a bed frame, with springs but no mattress, in the back bedroom. Roaches scurried in front of him.

The windows in the front bedroom had sheets of plywood nailed across them. It was dark and dank and the room was empty, save for trash in the corner, beer cans and cigarette butts and empty bags of potato chips and the unmistakable smell of urine and defecation. It was hard to believe that people had lived, slept, dreamed, and made love in this space, that there had been voices spoken and plans made, a sense of the future. There was nothing now, just squalor and decay. He turned and went back down the steps, looking into the kitchen and then pulling open the door to the basement.

A dank, fetid smell greeted him, earth and rot and a stale exhaust, the breath of a corpse. He coughed. It was black without relent. He shone the light on the landing to the steps downward. There were footprints and long, clean marks, as if something had been dragged, visible in the dust, the detritus of the police and investigators and crime scene techs. He tried to picture the night—he figured it would be night—when someone had carried Noel down into this space.

The woman he had seen in the photographs, the beautiful skin, the perfect hips, the dangling earrings, the hair spilling to the left—she was racy, she was sexy. She wasn't some down-market crackhead. Nothing but desperation would lead anyone down these steps, and he'd seen nothing to suggest Noel had been desperate. She wasn't living when she was brought into the house, he was sure of that now.

He stepped into the void and put his feet squarely on the landing, squatting down and shining the flashlight to the bottom of the steps.

The beam sliced a narrow tunnel in the darkness. There was a heap of chairs and trash bags and an old car seat and shoes and a mop and what looked to be mounds of clothes and an ancient television, turned on its side in the corner. He could see the gaping maw of the shattered plywood flooring. He took a deep breath and walked quickly to the bottom of the steps, swinging the flashlight in a ragged circle as he went. His foot caught on something and he staggered forward, catching himself at the bottom, cursing under his breath, sweat puddling in the small of his back now.

When he stood upright, he swung the light onto the grave, a few feet to his left. The flooring had been linoleum slapped down over plywood planks, as John had said. The planks had been pulled up and stacked against the brick exterior wall, and there were old metal folding chairs and part of a washing machine and ripped-open bags of garbage. Shards of it lay everywhere. Brown dirt was stacked in a heap toward the back of the room, clods of it scattered about. The hole was maybe two feet deep, no doubt dug deeper by the crime techs than the original burial. The smell of wet dirt and rot was choking. Worms moved in the dirt. The hole seemed to waver and move, a thing hungry to regain its decomposing meal of flesh and blood and viscous rot. It was open and raw and as filthy as a mass grave he'd seen once in the Bosnian war, a filled-in ditch that gave up its dead in a watery muck.

He extended the light over the hole, stepping around it, going to the jumble of material at the wall that had been moved out of the way. The chairs, the washing machine, empty cans of chili, shoes, shirts, pants, women's blouses, empty containers of canned vegetables, cigarette butts, two, three crumpled packs of Marlboros, like his old man smoked, an old metal rack for bread or something . . . He went back to the grave, following the beam in the pitch-blackness.

Kneeling down, peering at the dirt, reaching into it, letting his hands get the feel of it. The earth at the bottom was molding, crumbling, soaking.

"Noel," he said softly. This is where she had wound up, where someone had placed her. Someone working the dirt in the darkness—did they hurry?

Upstairs, the front door swung open. Footsteps directly above him. The door slammed shut.

A sparkle of fear lit at the base of his spine, sending flares up and out and now there was someone above him, someone who had him pinned down here, in the dark, in the muck. He shut off the light and worked the pistol out of the jacket pocket, thumbing the safety off.

The footsteps moved, heavy, contemplative. They went to the right, then around to the kitchen. Sully looked up the stairwell. He'd left the door to the basement open and the backpack behind the front door.

Quickly, he inverted the flashlight, pointing it straight down. He put his hand over the glass, flicked it on and let the light bleed down through his fingers, illuminating his feet. Dirt and nothing else. He took one step. No sound. Then another step and two more and he stopped.

He was beside the grave and out of the line of sight from the landing at the top of the stairs. He turned the light off. The footsteps above him did not go up the stairs to the second floor, but seemed to wander from room to room, back to the front door.

Then, without warning, they raced down the narrow hallway *baba-babam* and stopped, just as suddenly, at the basement door.

Sully ducked backward, kneeling, almost falling over. He was desperate to get out of the line of sight. All that son of a bitch had to do was lean forward with a flashlight and they'd have him pinned like a bug on an insect board.

The shadow at the top of the stairs did not step forward onto the landing. It did not move the door backward or forward. It stood there for one minute, two. Sully, his legs starting to cramp, breathed into his hands.

The door to the basement creaked forward, as if lightly pushed. It bumped against the wall, then swung back, and before it hit the jamb a darker shadow appeared.

A flash leapt from the end of the shadow, a bullet—*phhhfttt*—slamming into the dirt beside Sully, stunning him. The second shot shattered a broken piece of wood, Sully staring at it, thinking,

Silencer, the person above has a silencer, and there were two more flashes, cracking a slab of marble, ricocheting off the concrete block wall.

Sully took a step backward and his heel caught on something in the dark. He wobbled too far back, his momentum was carrying him past the point of balance, he couldn't stop it. Helpless, he raised the pistol and fired as he fell, one two three times, hitting the steps, the landing, blowing a hole in the basement door.

The blasts covered the noise of his falling in the dirt and whatever he'd tripped over. It felt like an overturned bucket. He rolled to his right and stopped, gun up.

Two rounds came back at him, one slamming into the dirt, the other shattering a chunk of porcelain. The steps above him retreated toward the front door, Sully tracking the sound with his pistol but not firing.

The front door open and slammed. Silence fell.

Sully closed his eyes and opened them, ears ringing from the blasts of his gun, the weapon still up and out, his left hand bracing his right wrist.

He stood slowly, letting the blood circulate down his stiffening legs. His right knee—God. He swung it back and forth several times. He held his left arm out and shone the flashlight at it. Six twenty-two. He shut the flashlight off and counted. When he got to one hundred and had heard nothing, he turned the flashlight back on. Six twenty-four.

The gunman was gone or waiting him out, hiding just inside the front door, the slamming a ruse to draw him out.

He shone the light over the dirt and carefully walked to the bottom of the steps.

Once there, he counted again, this time to fifty, scarcely breathing, and then took one step on the stairs, flashlight in his left hand, pistol in the right. Listening, holding his breath. Nothing. Then he rushed up the rest of the steps and yanked open the door. He stopped, just for a half beat, and then flashed a hand out into the first floor. Nothing.

Whoever it was had gone.

A breath let out of him, slow, involuntary. He put the pistol back in his jacket. A careful step took him onto the landing, then into the hallway. Nothing was any more amiss than it had been before. He was surprised to see the intruder had not taken his backpack.

Picking it up, quickening his step, he listened for sirens—had nobody else heard the gunshots?—and trotted back to the kitchen and a door that opened onto the backyard. He peered out the window; nothing but high grass and trash. The dead bolt was still in place. It turned easily. A tug on the handle and the door popped open.

The fresh air washed over him like an absolution. He breathed it in deeply, looking outside before stepping there, wiping a hand across the sweat on his forehead. He pulled the door closed behind him and walked quickly to the back of the property.

He vaulted himself over the iron fence with a grunt and a hop on his gimpy leg and found himself in a narrow walkway that ran off the alleyway behind the shops on Georgia. A few steps brought him to the curved part of the alley, his hands trembling, nerves firing. It was rough concrete with bits of gravel. To his right, the dumpster behind Doyle's sat thirty feet away. He looked to his left and the alleyway curved out of sight. Just around the bend, he knew, would be the dumpsters for the Hunger Stopper and other stores. You couldn't see them from here. The dumpster where Sarah was killed, or had been dumped, was in a blind spot.

Sully turned to his right and walked to the dumpster. It was conspicuously green, without a spot of rust. It looked new. He walked down the rest of the alley, onto Princeton Place, and turned left. A few feet later, he was walking past the tiny parking lot for Doyle's, and then onto the sidewalk of Georgia.

Lights were on in the stores, the streetlights cast an overhead glow. Cars had their headlights on, red brake lights tapping. It was rush hour. Nobody was screaming, nothing had happened. The stars were in their courses. Just after he passed the Hunger Stopper and turned onto Otis, heading back toward the bike, Doyle flashed through his mind.

Christ. He'd forgotten.

twenty-seven

Doyle was reading a magazine behind the counter. The store was empty, the light was flat. Something else was odd, and it took Sully a second to peg it—there was no television blaring.

"She's off getting her hair done," Doyle said when Sully asked.

Sully got a bag of peanuts and a Coke and headed for the counter, buying something just to be sociable, to give his hands something to do, the blood still thrumming from the shooting. Doyle, peering over his glasses, rang it up and said Bettie had taken to leaving him several days a week to mind the store on his own.

"Scared silly," he said, letting out a sigh. His khakis were pressed to a sharp crease, his blue oxford-cloth button-down shirt starched into place.

"You have other folks working for you, though, right?"

"A couple or three. But Bettie's family. I pay her a salary. Everyone else is hourly. If I call somebody else in, I'm paying her *and* them."

"Maybe you should just tell her to take a week out."

"I guess I could. Customers do love her, though, and we need to keep people reassured right now. Business is bad enough off as it is."

Sully, chewing a handful of peanuts now, took another swig of the soda to wash them down. "Which reminds me," he said. "Customers." He reached into his backpack, giving Doyle time to get comfortable to say whatever he was going to say, rustled past the notebooks, and found the pictures of the girls.

He set them out on the counter, spinning them around so they would be right side up for Doyle. "You recognize any of these three? Lana Escobar, Noel Pittman, and this one is Michelle Williams. I'm writing about the neighborhood."

"They all live right around here?" Doyle asked.

Sully took another handful of peanuts, chewing as he talked. "Yeah. A couple blocks. I'm asking around this afternoon. They come in here much? You know 'em at all?"

Doyle was looking down at them, peering through his glasses. He gave them a thoughtful looking over.

"Maybe, I don't know. Bettie does most of the register, I'm in the back. Who's this one? Think I saw her walking on Princeton. This business, it's hard to keep track of the young people. The older customers, the steadies? Those you know."

"That's Noel," Sully said, "I guess—"

"Lord, boy, you been playing in the mud? What happened to your *shoes*?"

Doyle, startled, peering over the counter. Sully looked down. The sides of the shoes, even the tops, were stained with dried mud from the basement.

"Well, hell," Sully said, looking down, stalling, debating whether to say he'd been snooping in the house next door, telling him something about the drama, the gunfire, and then went against it. "They're watering the grass up there at the rec center, out on that baseball field? I was interviewing people and cut through. You come in off the outfield into that dirt path for the bases? I took two steps in it before I realized it was a mud pit."

He went outside, stomped on the concrete, rubbed the soles and sides of the shoes against a parking barrier, and came back in.

"Sorry. I best get home and change. But hey, I was interested. What was it you wanted to tell me last night?"

"Your shirt's a mess, too." He indicated Sully's back using two fingers to tap the back of his own.

Sully looked over his right shoulder and tugged at the shirt. He could see the dirt, the grime spreading over the right shoulder blade, a large smudge. It had to irritate a man with Doyle's sense of starched order.

He tugged at his own shirt now, shaking his head, nerves flaring again. "What else? Man, you lean up against one wall, some of the houses around here. Damn."

Doyle waved a hand, coughed. "Okay. Look. I just needed to—I just need to tell you something about this Reese thing, but privately? I didn't want to do it in front of that crowd last night. I don't know if this is important or not. But it's just not right."

Sully kept brushing at the dirt, glad Doyle was finally getting to it. "Yeah? What's on your mind?"

Doyle nodded, his small, muscular shoulders rolling forward. He took his glasses off. "But you can't print this. Or you can't say that I said it. If somebody else tells it to you, fine, but there's no way in hell I want my name attached."

"I can't know what it is until you tell me, partner, but I'll agree I won't print it unless I get a second, if not a third, confirmation."

"Okay. So, here it is. I think. The judge? Sarah's father?"

"Yeah?"

"He used to come in and get a Coke or something, sometimes late on Friday just after I'd taken over for Bettie. Saturday mornings, too. I open up, stay till noon. I guess he was taking the little girl to dance rehearsal."

"Okay."

"I don't mean to be any particular way about it, but there aren't a lot of white folks in the neighborhood anymore. You notice one another, say hello. A well-dressed white man coming in the store? Not a lot of that clientele. You remember it. So this one Saturday morning I saw him at the top of Princeton Place, right by the baseball field. He was getting out of a car, a Mercedes or a BMW, something silver. Well, now. I was walking by, on my way in, and I recognized him, so I nodded, said hello. He stood there and looked at me like I hadn't said anything at all. Looked at me and then just turned back to what he was doing. Rude as you can be."

"Snotty little prick, ain't he?"

"But that's not what I'm telling you about. What I'm telling you about is that I was sort of peeved about it. I said to myself, 'You know, he thinks he's some big-shot judge and I'm a little storeowner, and he didn't even recognize me. Or doesn't think I'm worth talking to.' I'm retired navy. I served my country. I don't have an apology to make to anybody. I've been making this store work for a dozen years now, and I *knew* he recognized me. I turned around, honest to god, and I was going to go back and say, 'My name is Doyle Goodwin, and you come shop in my store down there at the bottom of the block and you damn well know who I am.'"

"Good for you, coming back at him."

"But I never got anywhere with that, because when I turned around, what did I see? He was on the front porch of that house the Pittman girl was living in. She opened the door. She kissed him on the mouth."

Sully choked, the Coke going up into his nostrils, burning his sinuses. "You said *what*?"

"She had some little nightie-something on. They went into her house there."

"They *knew* each other? Like, biblically?"

"That's what I was wanting to tell you."

Sully stood flat-footed. "I can't—I just—what did the police say?"

"Didn't tell them."

"Didn't *tell* them?"

"They interviewed me before the Pittman girl turned up dead. When they were interviewing us, I didn't see the point. The man's daughter is dead, and I'm going to go tell the police he was catting around? I wouldn't have done that in a million years. But after the Pittman girl turned up dead, it started feeling different."

"You still haven't called them?"

Doyle sat on his stool behind the counter. He rubbed a hand across his chin, his cheek. He rocked back and forth slightly.

"Thought about it. But look. Like I told you, this girl getting killed out back has really hit us. People, they think we fingered those guys to the police, they don't want to come in no more. So in the midst of this, to go wading into that police office and tell them a federal judge was fooling around with this black girl up the block? If I thought the scales were fair, maybe. But they're not, Sully, and you know it as well as I do.

All it would do is get covered up. And hey, surprise, I'd get a ton of grief from everyone from the zoning administration to the IRS. I'd get audited eighteen years in a row. I'm a little guy, Sully. He'd bury me."

"I can see your thinking. I can. I'm not trying to talk you into anything. But, Doyle, I got to tell you, this is a big goddamned deal. A federal judge involved with a young woman who turns up dead? And his daughter killed on the same block?"

Doyle slapped the counter with a flat palm, making his glasses teeter down the end of his nose. "Which is why I don't want my name on it! We're barely staying in business! You been in here ten minutes, you seen anybody? Bettie flinches every time the doors open, thinking she's gonna get shot up!"

He took a deep breath, reining himself in. He put both hands on the countertop. His voice dropped. He was working at it.

"We might be okay by Christmas. Might, this thing blows over. But not if I get crossed up with some federal judge. I. Will. Be. Dead. Meat." He popped an open palm on the counter with each word, the cords on his neck standing out, his face flush.

Sully, taken aback by the outburst, leaned against the ice-cream case, hoping to God no one came in the store. His mind was scattering, bright little shells bursting against the back of his eyes.

"Okay. So okay," he said. "Here's what I can do. Okay. I won't put your name to this, but I will tell people that I have a source who saw Reese and Pittman together, romantically involved. I won't tell them who that source is. If my bosses press me for it, I'll have to tell them, but that doesn't mean it goes into the paper. It just means they want to be sure I'm not making it up."

"Why would they think that?"

"It's not personal. It's the way it is. Things go in the paper, everybody wants to be sure. You were in the navy. Somebody says, 'I see a Russian sub!' the captain isn't gonna say, 'Sink it.' He's gonna say, 'Show me.'"

Doyle looked down, then back at Sully. His arms were folded across his chest. "So who is it you're going to be telling you've got this source? You can't tell the police."

"No, no. I'll just use it as a basis of reporting. I'll go around the neighborhood here, take Reese's picture, like I did with these three girls here, and ask if anybody recognizes him. Like I just did with you, right? I showed you the pictures, asked you if you recognized them. I didn't say anything about anybody else."

"Okay."

"Alright. So." He took a breath. "Did, did Reese keep coming in the store after Noel went missing?"

"I wasn't taking notes on it. But it's been a while since I've seen him."

"Okay. Okay. I'll ask Pittman's family about it, and tell them someone says she was involved with a guy named David and see what they say."

"The judge. Will you tell him?"

"If some other people say they saw him, or I find another way that shows he and Pittman were having an affair, then I'd have to go see him and see what he says before I could print it."

"But you're not going to use my name?"

Sully extended his hand over the counter. "I don't burn people, Doyle."

The man nodded and shook his hand. He leaned back on his stool. He cleaned his glasses with a cloth by the register, apparently a nervous tic. "I just feel better now that I told somebody," he said. He managed a dry cough, his eyes lighting up, relieved. "I felt terrible, holding on to a secret like that."

twenty-eight

Sully came out of the store, his mind aflame, and before he could think of anything else, there was the bright red light of the Big Apple Dance Studio directly across the street, like a slowing magnet.

Crossing during a lull in traffic, the cold and the dark settling in, he tugged the glass door open, the thumping music from the studio upstairs assaulting his ears. The receptionist desk was along the wall.

He asked for Regina Blocker, the owner, and the lady told him she had gone for the day. He was about to ask for Victoria, then remembered that was her middle name. He was tongue-tied until he turned and she was coming down the steps from upstairs, as if on cue.

She had on tights and running shoes and a white sweatshirt, the top collar scissored open for a deep V-neck. She had a white hair band keeping her braids back and a gym tote bag slung over one shoulder. Sully thought she looked athletic, attractive, like a small forward on a college basketball team.

"Look at you," he called out, "right on time." He jerked his head toward the door and started walking, as if they had plans.

She gave him a wary look but went outside with him. "I'm just running across the street to get something to eat," she said, gesturing toward the Hunger Stopper.

He nodded. "Then let's make it my treat."

Halfway across the street, she said, "Something going on? I don't mind helping you out, but I don't wan—"

"Nobody made you as 'Victoria,' did they?"

"No," she said, flashing him a smile. She was comfortable, opening the door to the restaurant, stepping up to the carryout window, looking up at the menu items listed overhead, on her turf. "We're good."

"I still don't know your name, you know."

"A tragedy."

Sully, itchy from the news Doyle had given him, stood beside her, waited while she ordered a roast beef on rye and coffee to go. "You eating that right before class?" he asked. "After," she said. "They close before class lets out. Get it now or go hungry." He reached into the backpack for the three pictures. He spread them out, as much as he could, on the takeout counter, glad no one was in line behind them. "So I got to ask you one more question," he said.

"That's Noel," she said.

"And I didn't even have to ask."

"She used to come in the studio. Hip-hop." She looked at the other pictures. "That's that Spanish girl you were asking about last year. Don't know the other one."

"Noel took classes?"

"Yeah. She had this gig out at Halo. She didn't want to be embarrassing herself out there."

"Was she a regular student?"

"More off and on. She just came to a group class, so far as I know."

"You saw her in there?"

"I taught the class."

"Oh." He paused. "So you can dance like that, like they do out at Halo?"

"You like that sort of thing, Mr. Newspaper Man?"

He laughed, caught. "No, no. I didn't say that exactly, I just—"

"Guys do. Don't be so shy about it. So why you showing me these pictures while I'm trying to get something to eat? I got to get on back."

"I—I was working in the neighborhood and happened to stop in. You know David Reese?"

"Sarah's dad, sure."

"He around the studio?"

"Drop off, pick up. Mainly Saturdays. Like I told you before."

"He hang out at the studio while Sarah danced?"

"Nah. Sometimes he'd be ten, fifteen minutes late picking her up."

"You remember what time those classes were?"

"Sarah's? She was in Intermediate Modern. Starts at six on weekdays, ten on Saturdays."

"Okay, so when were the lessons that *Noel* came in for?"

"Saturday mornings. First thing. Well—and, well, there was a second hip-hop class. It started at eleven. I taught that, too."

"I'm guessing the first one started at like nine."

"Aren't we the smart little cookie."

"Which means that early class of Noel's would have been breaking up right when Sarah's was starting."

"And the second one started when Sarah's finished. It bookended."

The man behind the counter brought a paper cup of coffee with a plastic lid on it and a folded brown paper bag. Before Victoria could put any money down, Sully handed him a ten-dollar bill and told him not to worry about change.

"You remember which one Noel came in for most often?"

"Why, look at you," Victoria said. "Thanks. And no. It's a ten-week group class. You sign up and pay, you can come as much or as little as you like."

She was walking then, back outside, sipping the coffee, waiting for traffic to clear so she could cross back to the studio.

"So how long did Noel take classes?" he said.

"Can't remember. You can ask Regina, but she's not going to say anything. It was maybe a year. Probably less."

"Was she coming to class right up until she disappeared?"

She shrugged, a hunch of the shoulders. "I don't know when she went missing. She just didn't come anymore. There were six or eight girls in the class. It's not like I was keeping attendance."

The traffic cleared then, and she started across the street. Sully stayed on the sidewalk. "You can tell me your name if you want to," he called after her.

She turned in the street, walking backward, smiling. "You asking for my number?"

This was unexpected. It wasn't unwelcome, it just threw him, the idea, maybe something other than Dusty . . . "Should I?"

She turned away, laughing, raising the coffee cup as a parting. "Keep me out of this shit."

"What about your number?"

"You got to do better than this," swinging the paper bag with the sandwich.

Sully stood on the sidewalk for a moment. Victoria was, if he stopped to think about it, kind of damned hot, and she was playing with him, which he kind of liked, but there was Dusty and . . . He blinked and blew out a breath. Focus. Too much shit at once.

He pulled out the cell and punched in Sly's number.

twenty-nine

Five minutes later, Sly Hastings opened the door, unlocked the gate with the steel bars. Sully followed his angular frame into the hallway and then down the steps into the basement.

There was music on—Sully recognized it as Miles Davis, that middle register—and Sly went to a bar stool and sat down. Donnell was asleep on the kitchen floor. The dog opened an eye and watched as Sully stepped over him and went to the refrigerator.

"You got to start keeping bourbon in here," he said, looking inside.

"I don't drink the shit."

Sully got a can of Miller, popped it open, and took a long swallow.

"Somebody took a shot at me," he said. "Shots."

Sly, settling on a bar stool, looking at the television, a news channel with the sound off, looked over at him. He did not seem surprised. "For real?"

"In that house on Princeton, where Noel Pittman was found."

"Why?"

"The fuck do I know? I was down in the basement poking around, seeing what there was to see. Fucker came in, put a hand in the basement door, and let loose. We didn't talk about it."

"You didn't get a look at who it was?"

"No."

"Just one shooter?"

"Near as I could tell."

"So why didn't they come down and waste you?"

"Possibly because I shot back."

Sly's eyes narrowed, and there was a pause.

"You went to this house, down into this basement thing, and you went packing?"

"Yeah."

"I didn't know you carried."

"Since somebody blew me up with a grenade."

"That was in the war, though, right?"

"I took it personal."

"I didn't think reporter types were supposed to do that, carry a gun."

"Not that I'm aware of, no, we're not."

"But you do."

"I do."

"And you tried to shoot this motherfucker over there just now?"

"What did I just tell you?"

"I'm just saying, you got two dudes shooting at each other, nobody hitting anything. Most times, you want to shoot somebody, you do."

"I'ma go to the range in the morning, work on my aim."

"What were you looking for down there?"

"Whatever there was to see. I don't know. You never know unless you go look." He looked at his hand, the tremors again. "Jesus, don't you got whiskey? At all?"

Sly ignored him, thinking. "Well. This shooter. In that house, taking potshots at somebody in the basement. The dude didn't see you? Didn't know it was you in particular?"

"Not so far as I know."

"Then this means what? That somebody out there, maybe who killed Noel, don't want anybody down there. Maybe he thinks he left something."

"The cops have already been all over it."

"Yeah, well, still. Maybe they missed something. You trespassing in a house nobody owns. Don't make any sense. Somebody'd havta be following you or watching the house—"

"Wait a minute. I had a tail, I'd swear it, a blue Olds a few days ago. Tailed me from that presser at Reeses's. Two chunky white guys, the sweatshirts, the hoodies, the whole undercover thing. I took them to be detailed to Reese's case. I went into Reese's house, we had an unpleasant conversation, so I figured they slapped me with a tail. A brushback pitch."

"What was unpleasant about the conversation with the judge?"

"I—" It dawned on Sully, almost too late, that he had used Sly's information to tell the judge the three arrests were bogus. He couldn't tell Sly that. "I would say that every conversation I have with Reese is unpleasant. He's a prick. Plus his daughter had just been killed."

"Hunh."

"But that's not what I came here to tell you, though. David Reese. I came to tell you something else about David Reese."

Sly nodded, sitting at the counter, twiddling his pencil back and forth.

"He was screwing Noel Pittman. Or at least I think he was."

Sly kept the poker face, but his pencil stopped mid-twitch. "And why do you think that?"

"Because somebody who might know just outed him to me. I'm curious if anybody else who might know told you."

Sly leaned back on his bar stool and crossed his arms. Sly working to keep his jawline steady. They regarded each other for a moment. Sly waiting to see if he'd say more. Sully didn't.

"Well, then, we got ourselves another problem," Sly said, "because nobody told me that shit at all."

His face seemed to become stronger and yet more diffuse, things working beneath the surface, a storm cloud building, lightning inside the vapor. Sly put his left hand to the top of his forehead, pulling it down his face until his hand cupped his chin. He cursed, suddenly, with a violent jerk of his head. "I don't know how I didn't think of this before."

Sully pulled another draft on the beer, eyeing him. "Think of what?"

"Come on, goddammit," Sly said, getting up. "Put that thing down. We got to talk to somebody."

He was up and out the basement door, no coat, no jacket, Sully pouring the rest of the beer down the sink, hurrying to catch up.

Sly walked them down Warder and then turned right onto Princeton Place. The baseball field was just across the street. Sly walked past the first large house, past an alley paved with brick, and then past three, four houses, the yards slightly elevated from the sidewalk, more so as the street sloped downhill. At one house, Sly turned right, went up four or five concrete steps, and, motioning Sully to follow, strode across the sidewalk and then up five or six more steps to the porch. There was a wooden swing and two iron chairs with striped cushions.

Sly rapped on the door, hard. "Open the door, Mommy. It's me. Open the door."

They stood, waiting. Sully could hear footsteps just behind the door and felt, rather than saw, someone looking through the peephole. The door slid open, chain still in place, and an elderly woman's face appeared through the slot. She peered unhappily at them both.

"I said it was me, Mommy," Sly said. "Now open the door. Come on."

The woman closed the door and the chain slid back and the door opened into darkness, with a light on in a room at the end of the hall. Sly followed her into the kitchen. Sully trailed them both. It reminded him of Curtis Williams's home, only decorated in grandmotherly fashion. There were cheap prints on the wall, of black people at an island-style open-air market, of a woman drinking from a coconut.

In the kitchen, the woman returned to the stove, stirring whatever was in the pot before her. Sully was about to guess she was from the Caribbean when she opened her mouth and removed all doubt that she was Jamaican.

"What are you wanting me for?" She said it to Sly but was looking at Sully. She was wearing jeans, a floral print top, slippers, small gold hoop earrings, and a scarf wrapped around her head. The television was blaring from the other room. Sully saw two bottles of ginger ale on the table. He wondered where the other ginger ale drinker was.

"He's a reporter dude," Sly said, nodding back at Sully. He pulled a chair out from the kitchen table and sat down without being asked. "He wants to ask you something. I wouldn't mind knowing myself." He nodded at Sully.

Sully sat down, pulled out his backpack, and laid out the pictures of the three girls.

The woman came over from the stove and said, "Oh my Jesus."

Sully looked inside the backpack again and pulled out a newspaper. He flipped to an inside page, the story of Reese's driveway press conference, a large photograph of him at the microphones, folded and quartered the paper so the picture was dominant. Spinning it around so it was in front of her, he cleared his throat and said, "My name is—"

"Skip all that old shit," Sly said, cutting him off. "She knows you're a reporter, right, Mommy?" The woman narrowed her eyes and nodded.

"My name is Sully Carter and I work at the paper," Sully said, glaring at Sly, giving his standard spiel anyway. "Okay, then. I'm working on a story about these three girls. You recognize them, I think. What I want to know is if you've seen this gentleman on the block." He tapped on the picture of Reese, smoothing the paper out as he did so.

The woman looked at Sly, who nodded. She pulled her glasses, hanging on a thin gold chain around her neck, up to her eyes, and opened them wider. She slid her feet across the floor and sat down at the table. She leaned down over it, then reached out a finger and tapped the picture.

"Long time, but I know him. He came to see she over there across the street. Saturday mornings. Sometime Fridays."

"Which she are we talking about?"

"She. The bad one. She from Manchester parish. She had the devil in her." She tapped the picture of Noel.

"When was the last time you saw her? Noel?"

She shrugged. "Not since nobody saw her no more."

"And how long before? How long was he coming over there?"

"I have no notebook," she said. "But six months. Maybe even one year."

"And you're sure? Absolutely sure?"

She nodded. "The white devils around here are few."

Sly slapped a fist onto the table. "And did you *think*, did you one goddamn time *think*, that I might want to know that information? That the goddamn chief judge of the U.S. District Court was fucking a college student in my neighborhood? Four blocks from my goddamn *house*?"

The woman took one step back to the stove and, lightning quick, snatched a knife off the countertop and stepped back, the blade toward Sly's throat. It had seemed a single motion, slippery as mercury and as quick.

"It is my house! *My* house! You black Americans have no respect! I have no fear from you!" She held the blade out, three inches from Sly's neck, the blade steady.

Sly regarded her with a glare. He spoke softly and with menace. "I pay you, Mommy."

"You didn't tell me who this one was! I told you a white man came to see a black girl on the street and you say to me, 'So what?'"

Sly blinked and sat back in the chair. He thought for a moment, his eyes still on the woman. His hands were flat on his legs. He raised one hand and then softly put it back down, tapping the leg, one two three, a gesture of recognition, of defeat. "I did," he said, finally. "You did. I was in the middle of—I did."

The woman went back to her pot and put the knife down. It was quiet.

After a minute, Sully whispered to Sly, "I can't use it if I don't have her name."

"Tell him your name, please, Mommy," Sly said. He looked like he had a migraine.

"Is it in the paper?"

"Yes."

"I don't want it so."

"I didn't ask you, woman."

She stared at him and then looked back at Sully. Her tone softened. "Marilyn Winston," she said. "You will keep me safe." This was directed at Sly. He nodded, rubbing his forehead.

"Ms. Winston, I have to ask, what is your profession? Or what was your profession if you are retired?"

"Why you need that?"

"Mommy. Jesus. Please."

"Nurse. I was a nurse at the Washington Hospital Center for twenty-five years. In the intensive care ward."

• • •

The idea floated around his mind for an hour before he screwed up the nerve to actually do it. He was sitting at Stoney's, nursing his second Basil's, the night getting late, looking up at the television behind the bar, listening to the desultory chatter around him. He pulled out his cell and looked at it.

He didn't want to make the call. He also didn't see any way of not making the call.

The 411 operator answered on the third ring, and he said in a resigned sigh, "A residential for Lorena Bradford, living in the District or maybe, I guess, in Prince George's County, Maryland." There was typing on the other end. He rattled the ice in his drink and looked at it without hope. Then she said, "Currently not showing any Lorena Bradford in the District of Columbia or surrounding counties in Maryland, but I do have five L. Bradfords."

"How many can you give me without me calling back?"

"Two."

"Let's do it."

She read the numbers and he wrote them on a cocktail napkin, then looked at his watch. A little after nine. It was late but not radically so. He pressed the numbers and wondered what hell Sly was inflicting on his network of neighborhood sources, who had failed to notice a district court judge wandering up and down Princeton Place. That wasn't going to be pretty.

The first two numbers the operator gave him both went to answering machines, with a male voice on each one. He pegged each of them to be white, and crossed them off. Noel's sister had not seemed like the interracial type.

Hers was the fourth number. She picked up and he recognized her voice immediately.

"Miss Bradford, hi, sorry to call you so late, but it's Sully Carter at the paper. I know you made it pretty—"

"You the one at the cemetery?"

"Yes. And I wouldn't—"

"I'm glad you called," she said. There was a breath and her voice shifted to a softer, more feminine tone. "I wanted to apologize for that—that scene. I lost your number and then the idea just got lost, too. I—I shouldn't have done that. Spit on you, I mean. I can't believe you came to the funeral to interview me—that was just plain wrong—but that doesn't make what I did right."

Phone crooked between his shoulder and his ear, raising his hands in front of him, good god, people, you just never knew . . .

"Don't worry about it," he said. "But—I didn't like being there myself—thank you. I am still interested in what happened to your sister, though. There has been some information that has come to my attention that I just can't avoid, about one of her relationships, and I would like to come by to talk to you about it, to see if—"

She said, "Is this about David?"

thirty

The District is a diamond-shaped city, elongated north to south, and Lorena Bradford lived in the far northern tip, at the apex of the diamond, at the top of Rock Creek Park.

The house was on the 3000 block of Chestnut, about five blocks west of the park and about the same distance south from Western Avenue, which marked the Maryland line. On the north side of Western, you were in Chevy Chase. Property values skyrocketed, the public school system catered to parents who could afford private-school tuition, and the median income was double what it was on the south side of the street, in the District.

Lorena's house, on the modest side of the divide, was a solid one-and-a-half-story redbrick bungalow, four steps up to a front patio and a dormer roof. She was at the door, opening it, already dressed for work, when he was halfway up the walk the next morning.

"What do you know about David?" he had asked, shell-shocked, the night before.

"A little," she had said. "I sat up nights going through her things after she went missing. She kept datebooks. The Week-at-a-Glance things. 'David' or 'D' was written on each Saturday morning, and sometimes Friday evenings, in the months before she disappeared. That's it. Why? Do you know who he is?"

When he told her what he thought he knew, there had been a very long pause. The invitation to her house followed.

Now, just over twelve hours later, he having barely slept, the long watch of the night filled with nightmare-filled patches of sleep and pacings of the house, sitting on the back step, wanting to call Dusty but feeling burned from the other night, the daylight never seeming to come, and now, finally, he was walking up the steps, calling out, "Not going in early, are you?" smiling, acting as if he were on top of the world, a man in control, motioning to her outfit. He was vaguely conscious of trying to make himself appear to be disarming. *Gentle,* he said to himself, *gentle. Gentle. You are gentle.* He saw her eyes flick away from his as he approached—the scars—before returning.

"No, no," she said, stepping to the side to let him enter. "Just wanted to make sure I didn't run out of time, talking to you, and have to run to work without my face on."

The interior of her house was compact and neatly presented. A few prints on the wall, grown-up furniture, runners in the hallways, polished wood floors, all speaking of maturity and sensible choices. The couch in the front parlor, the coffee table, the sitting chairs—they could have been ordered from Ethan Allen. She was the IT director at a small law firm, she told him, and the house looked like it. He couldn't help but think, *Serious big sis, wild-ass little sis.*

There were four large plastic boxes sitting by the coffee table, and she sat on the couch by them, gesturing to a parlor chair for him.

"I packed up all this in such a hurry," she said. "By that time I—this was when she was missing for three months—I knew she was dead. I was just throwing things in boxes. It's just crazy."

As she was talking, she was removing the tops from the containers. The contents looked, to Sully, incredibly well-organized. Maybe this was the difference between reporters and IT people.

He took a deep breath, still standing. She was rushing, she wasn't thinking, she appeared to have anger management issues. Might as well deal with that first.

"Look," he said. "I want us to be square. I want to thank you for having me out here today. But I want to make sure you're okay with going forward."

"You're asking if I'm going to spit on you again?"

"More or less."

She touched the palm of her hand to the tip of her nose and looked down and back at him. "No. I mean, yes. I'm sure I want to go ahead. First impressions, though, right? I don't blame you. I'm not psychotic, Mr. Carter, and neither was my sister. Noel and I were different, but we were family, and we were close. And I don't mean to jump into this right now, but I'm still not absolutely positive the 'D' in her datebook was David Reese. I mean, we talked, she told me she was taking classes at Big Apple, and she did not ever say anything about him. It could be 'D' for 'dance class.'"

"If it's him, it'll be clear soon enough. And it's Sully. Just call me Sully. You mentioned Noel's files last night. That's what's in front of me?"

"I mentioned to you how disciplined Noel was, particularly about finances? I used to tease her about being the world's only accountant in fishnets and heels. So this is all of her datebooks, her files, her paperwork that was in filing cabinets. She was bad to keep receipts stuck in jars and coffee cans at first, apparently, and then she put them into some sort of filing system."

She was pulling out yearly planners, thin black spiral things that went back three or four years. There were notebooks and file folders with tabs denoting ACURA and RENT and HOWARD U and PEPCO and BANKING and TAXES and VERIZON and HALO and SATIN AND LACE and dozens of others.

It was the dead woman's entire life, spelled out in minutiae. He finally sat down and asked whether the police had ever looked at all of this. Lorena said no.

"Not even after they discovered her body?"

She did not look up from the files. "Mr. Carter—Sully—other than a detective calling to notify me of the recovery of Noel's body, and of the autopsy nonresults? I have not heard from the police at all."

"What's 'Satin and Lace'?"

"The lingerie shop where she worked. It's at Union Station, the top level."

"Right, right," he said. "I had forgotten."

Sully pulled out the Halo folder. It had copies of her pay stubs and a work contract and an employee handbook. She had signed on in the fall of 1997, about six months before she went missing. He sat down and started to pull out the brightly colored folders and flip through them, then caught himself.

"When do you have to leave? For work?"

"I took the morning off."

"Good," he said.

The material was a sprawling mass of information, but it was gold only if he could find the vein of her disappearance and follow it through the mountain of details that Noel had kept and codified. As he sorted through the boxes, as he pulled out folders and datebooks, he recognized that Noel's mind saw the world around her and reduced it to slots and cubicles and placed things in a taxonomical order. He blinked, going through the Howard U folder. It was stuffed with class schedules and a map of the campus and student loan documentation.

What did anyone need to know about a young girl who was dead? What was useful and what was prurient? Well. The last time anyone saw her, she was pulling out of the Halo parking lot at two in the morning in April 1998. Then, in October 1999, her decomposed corpse turned up in a basement of an abandoned house a dozen houses down from the upstairs apartment in the house she was renting.

That was the puzzle. In front of him were more pieces than anyone had ever seen. He felt the drumbeat of a tension headache begin to thump just behind his eyes.

"Sure you want to help?"

"Of course."

"Then we're going to build a chronology," he said. "Let's start it on the first of April. You've got a laptop? What we want to do is create a master file on that hard drive, and then we'll copy it onto a floppy. That way we'll both have the information. Everything, no matter the source, gets entered by date."

He picked up Noel's checkbook and her datebook, opened them to the last month of her life, and glanced at the first few entries on both.

"So April 1, she pays her rent, right? The girl's a machine. April 2, her datebook says she's got a meeting at two with her marketing professor. Like that. All these sources—canceled checks, datebook entries, receipts, class schedules—go into that master file, the chronology. That will create a timeline of the last three weeks of her life."

Lorena reached into the second plastic container, pulling out an answering machine. "The police listened to the messages on this, but the only caller on it was me. I don't think that's going to help."

She then walked into the kitchen and came back. "But they didn't see this, because I didn't come across it until this morning when I was going through her things to show you. It was in the front pouch of a Howard sweatshirt, one of those things with a hood. I had her clothes in boxes. I was going through them this morning, pulled out the sweatshirt, and it fell out. I didn't know to look for it when she went missing, because I didn't know where it was. I thought it was with her."

She held up a cellphone.

"Jesus Christ," Sully said. "How did she afford a cell? The job pays for mine."

"She said all the kids at college had them. The hip ones, anyway. Fad 101."

"Does it work?"

"The service is dead, but the unit isn't. It should still have her numbers and contacts."

He held up a hand for a moment, like a traffic cop, and then pulled out the appointment books, starting with the book for 1998. He couldn't believe Jensen, the detective, had not followed up on this after Noel's body had been found. He guessed they were too busy with the Reese case, but it was shoddy any way you looked at it.

He flipped the book to April.

The first few days looked like all the rest. On April 24, the last day she went to work, there was her marketing class at Howard in the morning. There was nothing else during that day, with "Halo 10-2" written in ink for that night.

On the morning of the twenty-fifth, at ten fifteen, there was written in her elegant, spidery hand, a single, one-letter notation: "D." That night was another notation for her shift at Halo.

Turning the pages backward one week, then two, three, four, five. The same "D," at the same hour.

He reached to Lorena. "Let me see that, please," he said, taking the phone. She had already turned it on, and he tapped around on it until he found the contacts folder. There were a lot of names. And right there, plain as day, in its place alphabetically, was a single letter "D."

There was a tension in his gut as he clicked on it. Two numbers came up. One was a 202 area code with a 354 exchange, which he immediately recognized as that of the U.S. District Court for the District of Columbia. The other was a 703 area code.

"Son of a bitch," he said.

"What is it?" she asked.

He pointed it out to her. "'D.' That first number? Beginning 354? That's the courthouse. I'm giving eight to five it's David Reese. Want to make a call for me?"

She nodded.

"Wait, not the house phone. Do you have a company cell?"

"Of course. I'm on call all the time."

"Is it in your name?"

"What do you mean?"

"The phone. Would caller ID show your name, or the name of the firm?"

"The firm. It shows a switchboard number."

"Fabulous. May I?"

She got it out of her purse and he punched in the courthouse number from Noel's contact list. "Just say you've got the wrong number if there's an answer," handing the phone back to her.

She put it on speaker. After four rings, David Reese's answering machine came on. His chambers, not that of the secretary out front. Sully reached over and disconnected the call. He then rapidly dialed the 703 number, before he could change his mind. He held it up between them. Lorena leaned over, putting her ear above the phone, looking over at him as she did so.

The phone rang three, four, five times. Then it picked up. A man's voice, low, guarded, said, "Yes? Who is this?"

Sully pointed at Lorena. "Oh, I'm so sorry. Wrong number." She clicked it off and looked at him.

He leaned back against the couch and blinked. "That was David Reese."

Lorena punched buttons on Noel's cell, going into the list of recent calls.

She looked, then turned it to him. The glowing screen showed that the last call that Noel Pittman had ever made was to the 703 number they had just dialed.

It was placed on April 25, at 10:47 a.m., more than eight hours after she drove away from Halo and into the ether.

thirty-one

"So we're about to say what, exactly?"

Melissa was sitting behind her desk, looking at him as if he had a bad disease. Eddie Winters leaned up against a glass wall of her office, flanked by the deputy executive editor and the assistant managing editor for news. The national editor and the paper's top attorney were seated in chairs against the back wall. R.J. was sitting next to him, as if he were his attorney and they were in court.

She continued: "That the chief judge of the U.S. District Court in D.C. was having a personal if not intimate affair with a wannabe porn star? And that said wannabe is the young woman who turned up dead, buried in the basement of a house immediately adjacent to where the judge's teenage daughter was murdered a year later? Oh—and he's white and wealthy and fifty-three. She was black and twenty-five and an exotic dancer. Have I left out anything?"

"She called his personal cellphone eight hours after she was last seen," Sully said. "I would add that."

Her forehead wrinkled, her hands splayed out, sarcasm personified. "Thanks, yes. I'd forgotten. Did she write in her datebook how he killed her, too?"

"Let's wait a minute here," Eddie said.

His arms were folded across his chest, and the gold and steel Rolex glittered as he shook it loose from a tight grip on his left wrist. He'd been watching Sully while he gave the summation of his findings of the past several days, the missing Michelle Williams, the dead Rebekah

Bolin. He had leaned forward and nodded as Sully described how Lorena Bradford had given him access to her dead sister's files, information that law enforcement had not seen, and that she had spent several hours helping him start a timeline for that information.

"How many sources again? How many put Reese and Pittman together?"

"Four," Sully said, ticking them off on his fingers.

"One, Doyle Goodwin, who runs the market at the bottom of the street, but I can't see him going on record. Too scared, too much to lose. Two, the lady across the street, Marilyn Winston. She's on the record. Three, Pittman's datebook and her cellphone. Four, an off-the-record source at the dance studio, who confirms Noel and Sarah's lessons overlapped, and that Reese often dropped his daughter off and picked her up. But the killshot is that the numbers listed as 'D' on her cell were his personal line at his office and his cell. He answered the latter this morning when we called it, or at least I would say I recognized his voice. I checked the court directory this morning, called directory assistance, and went online. Neither of those numbers are listed."

Eddie considered. "Can we get more on the record?"

"I'll take his picture up and down the street and see what we get."

"How could they have plausibly met?"

"The dance studio. Pittman's lessons were ending when Sarah's were starting on Saturday mornings, and then there was a second class after Sarah's. He was walking in, she was walking out, something like that."

"Can we prove that? On the record?"

"I can ask the studio owner if she'll confirm, but it's solid. My source taught Noel, knew Sarah. Sarah's Saturday morning class? Ten o'clock. The time in Pittman's datebook she was to meet 'D' or 'David'? Ten fifteen."

"Does Reese have any idea we know what we do?"

"Not that I'm aware of. Lorena called his office and cell from her cell. It wouldn't trace back to us."

"Lorena?"

"Her sister. Noel's."

There was a pause. Lewis Beale, the paper's lawyer, heaved into the conversation, his great girth wobbling as he sat forward in his chair. "Tell me again how we came to be in possession of Pittman's phone and personal effects."

"The sister, Lorena. There may be more things coming. We're meeting back at her place tonight, after she gets off work, to keep going through the files. And, Lewis? Technically, we don't have possession. The sister does."

"Wait. Isn't she the one who spit on you at the funeral?" he asked, spreading his hands.

"Yes."

"Now she loves you."

"'Love' is a little strong."

"What happened?"

"Myself, I'd put odds that she wants us to put heat on MPD, to stick Noel's death as a homicide."

"So she's using you?"

"Most women do."

Guffaws around the room, everyone looking down for a minute, doodling on their notebooks, relieved.

"No. I mean, do you trust her?"

"As much as I do or don't anyone else. I have great faith in documents, though, and cellphones with David Reese's private numbers on them."

Lewis sighed and looked over at Eddie, then at Sully, then back to the boss.

"Originals, possession, if at all possible," Eddie said, taking the cue. "If we print this, it's going to have to be bulletproof. This will be litigated. With real money on the table."

"Eddie, you can't be serious," Melissa cut in. "If this were from another reporter, maybe. But Sully's had a vendetta against Reese since the Judge Foy thing. You heard how he went off when I asked him to cover the family statement—like a madman, cursing—and, if we can just name the elephant in the room, he is *drinking* on the *job*."

Eddie gave her a sharp glance. "You are wading into HR—"

"Everybody knows it! Why is it HR material? We can't trust it because of who reported it. Besides—look, let's say all of this is completely true. We still don't have Reese being guilty of anything other than an extramarital affair, poor judgment, and perhaps the victim of a gruesome coincidence."

She looked around the room, to the lawyers, the other editors. "It's bullshit. It's tabloid. The blowback will be tons of sympathy for Reese and vitriol for us. And what are we going to do *this* time when it's wrong? We can fire him, but we'll look like such parasites—"

"When did we get in the popularity business?" R.J. boomed, suddenly leaning forward in his chair, his gruff voice bursting out, people jumping.

"We don't run stories because we think they will make people *like* us. We run stories, these kinds of stories, because we are in the public accountability business. David Reese is an eminent public figure in Washington. If there is a timely change in the administration at the next election, he will almost certainly be the next Supreme Court justice, at which time he would determine the law for three hundred million Americans. His judgment isn't one thing about him, it's the *only* thing about him. Some of us in this room know that he lied to the upper management of this newspaper in an attempt to have Sully fired—don't look at me like that, I never signed off on the suspension—in the name of saving himself from an embarrassing political gaffe. This is a far more emphatic moral failing. What if, let us say, this affair with Noel Pittman and perhaps others emerge during confirmation hearings? And it becomes public that we knew of this liaison and did not publish? You haven't said one word about the actual facts of—"

"That's not—" Melissa started.

"And that isn't even quite the main focus, to my mind." He was steamrolling now. "The issue here is not, 'What does this mean for poor David Reese?' The issue is, 'What does this mean for poor Noel Pittman?' She was a child of this city, a college student, never arrested and never convicted of any crime. She disappeared after work one night. She was murdered, buried in a basement. We know from multiple sources, who have no apparent benefit in lying, that she was romantically involved with one of the most powerful men in this city, who is incidentally married to someone else. We know this man's own child was murdered less than fifty yards away. And, today, Sullivan tells us that the last call she made, eight hours after she was last seen, was to this man's cellphone."

R.J.'s voice had been slowly building, rising in tone and moral indignation. Now he was almost shouting, staring at Melissa through his bifocals. "And you're telling me that isn't a *newspaper* story? You're saying it would not merit the interest of law enforcement agencies investigating her murder?"

"There *is* no murder investigation," Melissa shot back. "Pittman's death isn't labeled as a homicide."

Sully had been chewing the inside of his lip, and then the anger burst clear of him.

"There's no murder investigation now because that's the narrative," he said, leaning forward. "'Rich, pretty, white Sarah Reese gets jumped by three bad black guys.' That's the story. It's a cautionary tale about being in the wrong place at the wrong time, it's the modern scary bedtime story. Now. 'Poor, maybe not-so-smart, black Noel Pittman gets whacked and stuffed in the floorboards of an abandoned house because crazy-ass shit like that happens in Park View.' Everybody knows that story line, too, because that's the story we tell all the time. Us, Brand X, cable television, the talks shows."

He ignored the rest of the room, glaring at Melissa. "But what if *that* narrative *this* time is inconveniently wrong? What if our first idea wasn't the right idea? What if the freight train is rolling down the wrong track?"

"Don't sit here and patronize me, either one—"

Eddie unfolded one of his arms and waved it up and down briefly, a terse cease-and-desist motion.

"Okay," he said, and all eyes moved to him. "Interesting arguments all the way around. It's good reporting work, Sullivan. Melissa and R. J. both raise considerations worth thinking about. The good news, for us, is—"

"He's a drunk with an ax to grind."

Melissa said it softly, looking at Edward. "No, Eddie. Please, no.

We cannot trust him on this. You want somebody else to verify and take—"

"I said I heard you." Eddie's tone was ice, cutting her off. He turned to the rest of the room.

"As I said, the good news is that Sullivan has put us way out front on this. We don't have to do anything right away. It is even possible that Miss Pittman's sister, Sullivan's source, might take this information to the police herself. If that happens, and they move on it, then we can report on police activity in an ongoing investigation, and not go out on a limb and report our own findings about a public figure's indiscretions. That would have us *following* an investigation, not *creating* one. A lesser story, certainly. But it has the merit, as Melissa points out, of us not being perceived as picking on the family of a murder victim."

He paused. Sully cut in.

"Not to keep moving the goalposts, Eddie, but I would add to R.J.'s thought that we seem to be forgetting our original line of investigation. It was not just Noel Pittman's death. It was also the deaths of Lana Escobar and, now we know, of Rebekah Bolin and the missing and likely dead Michelle Williams. All this within a three- to four-block radius. Is the Reese murder an outlier or part of some bizarre thread? That's the story line I was working."

Eddie nodded, still skeptical, but bending a little now.

"And it may be the one we publish. Now. On another point. Have you gotten anything—anything at all—that suggests a link between Judge Reese and the three young men in the store—the ones charged with killing his daughter? Would they want to, in some way, retaliate against him?"

"No, I haven't been through his case history, but every reporter in town, and I'm sure law enforcement, has been. Nobody's made a match. It appears random."

"Okay. Maybe they're looking in the wrong place. Maybe it's a tie between *Pittman* and those young men, and *she's* the link back to the judge. I don't know. Just look at that."

Eddie took two steps forward. "Other than that, dig through everything you can get your hands on about Pittman's personal history. Do it with an eye toward Reese. We want to document what happened to her, but we absolutely must know how Reese was involved. I don't see how we can publish a story about her disappearance without mentioning the affair prominently. If it turns out that it's all too muddy, just a big mess of glop that we can't put in context, then the answer may be not to publish anything at all. We hold on to lots of secrets about Washington. This may turn out to be another one of them."

He looked at Melissa, pointedly. She had decided to bide her time, Sully saw; she was sitting back for now.

"But whatever else you find, I want you to go to Reese's office when you're finished reporting and confront him with this. We want that interview on the record. We owe him a fair standard of publication and a regard for his privacy. We don't owe him a free ride."

Someone opened the door, and Melissa half spun in her chair, back to her desk. The meeting began to break up. Sully was about to lean over and say something to R.J. when Eddie stopped in front of him.

"Sullivan, the suspension. The Judge Foy matter. Reese doesn't like you, and if what he said to us in a sworn deposition was true I don't blame him. I also can't imagine, one way or another, that you hold him dear."

"You believed him, you didn't believe me, Eddie. He lied, in my humble opinion."

"Fair enough. So. I'm not going to pull you off this. You've done all the work. But remember that every bit of this reporting has to be above reproach. The interview must be recorded. I would imagine he'll record it himself. Keep in mind that he's going to release anything on that recording about you that might not be flattering. So keep your temper. Watch your language. Remember that anything you say might turn up on the evening news, excerpted by other news organizations who would be delighted to have us showing some sort of bias, some sort of personal vendetta. Agreed?"

Sully nodded. "Yeah. Agreed."

"When do you think you'll go talk to him?"

"Not for a day or two. I want to hit the neighborhood with his picture. Go to Halo, see if anybody recognizes him from the VIP room or whatever they call it out there, just to check. Go back through Noel's things. See if I can find a note from him, a picture, anything that would lock that relationship down or spell out more clearly what it was. All the due diligence. Then—then I'd go see him."

"Good," Eddie said, patting him on the arm, hard. "But, Sully? If you're wrong on this? On a fraction, on a day, a date, an hour, on a decimal? If I get one more report of bourbon at your desk? Or of you drinking on assignment? I'll fire your ass all the way back to Bumfuck, Louisiana."

thirty-two

On April third, Noel had breakfast at the Hunger Stopper for $4.37 (she'd noted a two-dollar cash tip) and went to work at Satin and Lace, parking at Union Station's garage for six hours, punching out at 5:19 p. m. She bought groceries at the neighborhood Giant, apparently on the way home, the $38.15 receipt time-stamped at 6:43.

She had been frugal, and she had to be. The lingerie store was paying her about nine dollars per hour, and Halo was two hundred dollars per night plus tips, but she was paying her way through school, paying for her own place, her own car, the works.

Sully and Lorena had been back at the files, building the chronology for hours. The evening was getting on, the delivery pizza demolished, nothing left but bits of crust on the cardboard. Lorena was still in her work outfit, the two of them plowing through datebooks, receipts, everything Noel had left behind. Lorena had run out to a copy shop, and now there was a blown-up street map of the city leaning against the couch. The map's center, like a bull's-eye target, was Noel's apartment on Princeton Place. There were red, blue, yellow, and green pins stuck into the map, with tiny bits of paper flagged to each one, tagging her movements based on receipts that had a time/date stamp. Blue was for the first week of April, yellow the second, green the third, and red for the last week, up until the twenty-fifth, when she disappeared.

"I went by Satin and Lace right after you left this morning," Lorena said.

"I thought you were going into work."

"I called in. I wanted to work on this. You're the first person who's shown any interest."

"Okay. What'd they say?"

"I walked in and talked to the girl on the floor, got fifteen seconds into saying something about Noel turning up dead and she used to work there and this girl cuts me off. Said she started six months ago and didn't know anything. So I asked for the manager. She says, 'What for?' You know, with some lip to it. I said, 'To ask about my sister.' She goes in the back, comes back out. Says the manager'll be right with me. Ten minutes later, this redhead with her hair in a bun comes out, said she's called corporate and says she can't say anything. I said, 'This is my sister I'm talking about.' She puts her hand on mine—bitch put her *hand* on me—and says, in this whisper, personnel laws, privacy, she was sure I'd understand. I said I sure as fuck did *not* understand that somebody murdered Noel, her employee, and all she could say was not a fucking thing."

"I don't think that—"

"She called security."

"Ah."

"I was asked to leave."

"You can apply for your press card now."

"I went two steps outside the door and called Detective Jensen, left a message that Satin and Lace had information about Noel's disappearance and they were concealing it. *Real* loud. They were standing there staring at me, I was standing there staring at them. Three women in heels, looking like we were ready to take it outside."

"So what did Jensen do?"

"Called me back fifteen minutes later and asked if I was alright."

"Were you?"

"I was sitting in my car in the parking garage shaking."

He looked at her, staring off into space, her face tight, clenched.

"Then I was going to go out to Halo," she said. "Playing Nancy Drew. Like somebody's going to tell me something. They'll see I'm her sister, tell me everything."

"Maybe," he said. "But they're more likely to be more nervous around you for all the same reasons. Why don't you let me head out to Halo, see how it goes."

"You think they're going to talk to *you*?" *Yooouuuu*. The sarcasm.

"I have been known to be persuasive."

She hunched her shoulders, as close as he was going to get to an agreement.

"Well," he said. "Sometimes I'm persuasive. I got Regina Blocker, owner of the dance studio, on the phone? Our conversation was shorter than yours at Satin and Lace. But I think you should let me go to Halo."

"Well," she said, "if you're making the rounds." She was looking in her purse, her bag, then pulling out and tucking a business card into his palm. It was for the Eric Simmons Photography Studio. It took him a second: the man who shot the nudes.

"Thanks," he said, putting it into his back pocket. That he had already seen the pictures, leaked to him by a police executive, seemed to be something that might be good to forget to mention.

Now he looked down at the chronology. "I'm not seeing anything for the last few days before she disappeared."

She looked down at the paperwork, reached out and touched it, like she was trying to jog a memory. "I was trying to—to stick to doing it sequentially, and I haven't gotten that far yet. And besides—" She was sitting on the couch, but her spine had curled and now she was hunched over.

"Too much in one day?"

"Confronting her death? Like this, following her around, her old jobs? It's morbid. If this is what you do for a living . . ." She blinked, went in another direction. "My mother, she had to leave us in Jamaica when she first came here. My dad was off working in Kingston, then he followed her here when she could sponsor him. We got left in Maidstone, our village, with Mrs. Bailey, who lived down the road. This is up in the hills. *Way* up in the hills. We went to Nazareth All-Age School. It was one building, yellow and blue, concrete block, with a courtyard. The boys could play and get dusty and dirty, but the girls couldn't. In the mornings, you had to clean the floors, which were also concrete, and in the afternoons, the teachers would open the windows and there was this breeze, I guess coming up from the ocean, and it was just the best thing you've ever felt in your life. We were there two years, maybe three, with Mrs. Bailey. There were phone calls from Mommy twice a month, on Saturday mornings. I wound up more like Noel's mom than her big sister. Mommy finally flew back to get us when they could afford to rent a big enough place for all of us here."

She got up, went to a stand by the window that was filled with family pictures and small houseplants. The picture she handed him was a worn five-by-seven in a simple frame. It was a close-up, showing two little girls and a mom, the girls' hair done to perfection, a plane in the background. They must have been on the tarmac.

"This is the trip to the U.S.?" he asked.

She came to sit beside him. "Yes. Noel and I had never been to an airport before, much less on a plane. You'd have thought we were flying to the moon, we were so excited. I had bought—look, see right there? I had bought Noel that necklace with the charm on it, her name, for the trip. You can't see the rest, but we were in blouses, skirts, white lace socks, black patent leathers."

"When people dressed to travel."

"I thought the streets here were made of gold. I really did, the way people in Maidstone talked about America. You have to realize this was a place of maybe four hundred people, without a streetlight or a traffic signal. There were five or six shops on the main street, with tin roofs. Two of them were pink. Mrs. Bailey ran one. Hers was one of the pink ones. Then we came to America."

"And?"

"And we lived on Kennedy Street. Don't get me started. Point is, Noel loved that necklace. Wouldn't do anything without it. And when I was cleaning out her place, it wasn't there. She must have been wearing it when—when—"

"—she died—"

"—she died. But it wasn't with her, her body. It's just gone."

"Could have been stolen. Could have been lost there at the bottom of that house."

"Or whoever killed her could have snatched it off her neck, thinking it was worth a lot more than it is. But that's what has been sending me over the edge all afternoon. Her necklace. I can't find her necklace. Since she died, it's been like my temper, my patience, goes off in weird directions, and today it's this. The damn necklace."

"Maybe it got lost in—in the dirt down there."

"It was silver. I asked the police to do the metal detector search. I asked them to go back and look." Her body turned awkwardly and her hands fluttered.

Before he could stop himself, he reached out to touch her hand, catching himself, then leaning forward, going ahead with it, but then he felt a rush of heat to his face when her shoulder twitched away from him, just half an inch. She looked at him, then down.

"So—so I've pretty much got the receipts in order, the ones close to the date of her disappearance. I just haven't keyed them in yet," she said, sniffling, blowing a strand of hair away from her eyes, getting it back together, giving him cover to pull his hand back. "There are some others that don't have a store name on them, so I didn't really know what to do with those."

Sully turned and saw a stack of receipts on the floor. The laptop was on the coffee table. He started thumbing through the receipts, sweat pooling in his armpits. He pulled his arms away from his sides to keep the sweat from showing in the folds of his shirt, embarrassed in a way he hadn't felt in years. Had he really been reaching out to touch a murder victim's grieving sister?

He looked through a box of sheets and papers she had set out apart from the others and came across the story written in the campus paper, the *Hilltop*, about Noel's disappearance. He'd seen one piece they'd done, but not this.

Noel had made her last class of the week, MKTG 544, Marketing Research and Strategy. It was on the third floor of the School of Business, at 2600 Sixth Street NW. The story noted she carried an A average and quoted a classmate, Alicia Mabrey, who said she sat next to Noel and had seen her walk out of the building and into the courtyard. He entered this on the chronology, then went on with the receipts Lorena had left out, immersing himself in building the timeline.

He had lost track of time when he got up, went into the kitchen.

"Bourbon, by any chance?" he called out.

"Chardonnay's in the door of the fridge. It's all I got."

He found a glass, opened the refrigerator door, noting the paucity of food inside, and saw the wine front and center. All that was left was a slosh at the bottom. He turned to see if she was looking, then turned the bottle straight up, draining it. The digital numbers on the microwave showed it was almost nine.

Dusty was supposed to be working at Stoney's tonight. To go or not to go. She was great, sure, but . . . the gap yawned wider. He didn't want it to be so but it did. Who made him this way? God? Darwin? He wasn't particularly fond of either at the moment. Flicking off the light in the kitchen, he walked to the opening that led to the dining table on his left, and the wider open area of the living room off to his right. Lorena was still there, not looking up, keying in more facts, more figures, all in the belief that it would help him write something that would lead to the arrest and conviction of her sister's killer.

There was a remote buzzing.

"You left it in there," she said.

He hitched himself up and limped back into the darkened kitchen, the stone floor cool beneath his feet.

The number was Eva's cell. He called her back, turning his back to Lorena and walking to the far side of the kitchen.

"Yeah?" he said.

"Meet me at Stoney's," Eva said. "I'll be there in ten."

"What? What is this? Christ, it's—it's nine at night. I'm sort—"

"You're wasting time," she said, and disconnected the call.

thirty-three

Half an hour later, he was slouched back in the booth, a bourbon in front of him. Eva leaned forward and asked, "So how close are you to publishing?"

She meant the story on the missing girls, he was pretty sure of that. She did not know about Reese, and there was no way he could tip her to that. He sipped the whiskey, snuck a look over at the bar, trying to get Dusty's eye, stalling.

"Maybe not for another week. There are some leads I got to run down. It got a little complicated."

"It's about to get a little more."

"Yeah?"

"We have a confession from one of the Reese suspects," she said.

He looked at her. "Bullshit."

"Reginald Jackson. Seventeen and wants to be sentenced as a juvie."

"I don't buy it."

"Says it was a robbery. They bumped into Sarah in the store, she got spooked and ran out back in the alley, they cornered her. She bucked."

"Oh, come on. I could make this up and I was sitting here with you when it happened."

"Deland, the oldest, grabbed her and spun her around, pulling her up against him, getting his hand over her mouth. Highsmith put the knife to her throat to keep her still. But she was shaking her head side to side, trying to get Deland's hand off her mouth. She apparently didn't see the knife. Ripped her head to the right and—"

"—cut—cut her own throat. How much of this fairy tale do you believe, Counselor?"

"The 'cut her own throat' is nonsense, but I do buy the 'she resisted' thing and they got pissed."

Sully was about to say that his information from the coroner's office was that her throat was cut postmortem, but that was not in the public sphere. She already knew that. She was telling him what Jackson's story was, without telling him the specific holes in it. If he let her know that the throat was postmortem, it might burn Jason as his source.

He said, "It takes three dudes to hold down one fifteen-year-old chick?"

"She was trying to scream, so the man says. Deland was choking her to get her quiet."

"And they got out of there without blood on them."

"Says they had some blood to deal with, but not a lot on them. I already told you there wasn't a lot on the ground out there. Most of it was in the dumpster. It's plausible. Says they trashed the clothes, changed, and burned the old ones."

"And went back to playing basketball."

"For cover, to establish an alibi."

"And what does he get out of this version of events?"

"A clean conscience and a juvenile adjudication, if he testifies at trial against his associates."

"Because, magically, he didn't participate."

"He was the youngest accomplice. He could make a fair showing to a jury that he was young, intimidated, didn't realize this was going to be violent, and, when it turned out to be, was under deadly pressure to go along with what the big kids were doing."

"So you guys have already cut the deal."

"Yes."

Sully sat back, trying to hold his temper in check.

"You didn't say this was off the record. Any of it."

"I didn't. You can source it to a 'law enforcement official familiar with the investigation.'"

"When's the presser?"

"Tomorrow. Noon if the chief can get everyone together. Highsmith and Deland will get murder one, assault, robbery, assault with a deadly weapon, and a couple of others."

Sully looked at his watch. It was ten minutes to ten. He could get it in the suburban edition if he quit fucking around.

"Meaning he could skate when?"

She shrugged. "Prisons and parole boards release people, not the U.S. Attorney's Office. But I would say Mr. Jackson would be celebrating his thirtieth birthday back in D.C."

"You got the wrong guys, Eva. They're not on the hook for this."

"That would be remarkable, buying yourself nearly twenty years in lockup for something you didn't do."

"Maybe he thought that deal would be less worse than what would happen to him if he didn't."

"Meaning what, life without parole?"

"Meaning a very short life span, for him or someone he knows."

"He's not on the wrong side of anybody, Sully. He's a featherweight."

"Which doesn't mean somebody doesn't have something on him."

"Are you going to enlighten me? Or are you just talking out of your neck?"

"You can't tell me everything you know, and vice versa. But I'm telling you, Eva, don't get tied in tight on this."

Outside on the street it was dark. He dropped his phone, maybe a little drunk, then stooped down to pick it up, got Tony on the rewrite desk on the phone and dictated a few paragraphs about the impending plea bargain. Tony asked him, stifling a cough, the name of his source and Sully told him that wasn't going to happen. There was a pause, and Tony asked if he was absolutely certain about the leak and Sully said he could add it to the Ten Fucking Commandments.

He hung up and called R.J. at home.

"Holy shit, Sullivan," he bellowed. "Beautiful. This is going to lead the paper."

"Yeah."

"So . . ."

"So yeah."

"So now what about Reese and Pittman?" R.J. said. "What about the other, what are we calling them, mysterious deaths?"

Goddamn. He was right to the point.

"'s the same as it was before."

"That can't be. I know Reese had the affair, and I hate to agree with Melissa about anything. But we've got to have something really solid to go ahead with this right now. Just him having the affair isn't going to do it. Public sympathy—"

"We already have him nailed."

"Dazzle me with how."

"Failure to disclose. Failure to report his knowledge to MPD about a young woman missing and believed dead. He knew damn good and well that she went missing, that the last time anyone saw her was at Halo, and he alone knew she was alive at least eight hours after that. We can establish that he, an officer of the court, knowingly withheld that information from law enforcement to preserve the secret of an adulterous affair. Minimum, judicial misconduct."

R.J. paused. Sully could visualize him stroking his beard.

"You're not bad at this. If she was just missing, well, maybe it was just a moral dilemma. But after her body was discovered last week, it's a game-changer. She was killed—I don't care if they call it a murder investigation or not—and she was killed in that neighborhood, perhaps on the day of their liaison. Christ, he's sounding like a suspect."

"So."

"So I'll talk to Edward. I can get you another day or two. I'm not saying we're there yet. I'm saying we can make a case. I'll have Chris do the presser tomorrow. But you've got to go on this, champ. You've got to go hard."

At home, in the darkness, Dusty next to him in the bed, both of them teetering on the edge of exhaustion, of sleep. Other than it being a long time after midnight, he had no idea of the time. The sex had been something close to violent, and he was trying to let the afterglow lull him all the way to sleep.

"Who is this we're listening to?" she said.

"Tom Waits."

"It sounds like he's gargling."

"Don't blaspheme."

"'Freeways, cars, and trucks.' Is this supposed to be profound? What *else* would you see on the freeway?"

"It's about being in love."

"Well, I'm not in love with him, I can tell you that."

"How was class this week?"

"Kicked my ass. I was cranky, I'm sorry. I didn't realize—I mean, really realize—there was so much math to being an RN."

"Math?"

"Chemistry. Dosages."

"I can barely add."

"No kidding. I've seen your checkbook."

He laughed, softly, in the dark, turning to let her leg drape over his. "That's mostly subtraction."

"My mother always said"—she yawned, closing her eyes, setting into her pillow—"to date men with at least six figures in the bank."

"Momma didn't date me."

"Obviously."

"How is she?"

"Playing tennis three days a week, down there at Boca."

"You feel nice."

"Mmm," her voice drifted lower, sleepier. "You're too amped up about—about this Sarah Reese thing, baby. Feels like I don't know you."

He debated telling her about the gunfire, but that was over before it started. He could never explain and she'd never understand.

"These three guys, the suspects?" He decided to go that route. "They didn't do this. The judge was screwing Noel. These other women, missing, dead . . . something out there is really fucked up. It's not as neat as what the police are saying."

"I still can't believe the Judge Reese thing. What are you going to do?"

The music went off. It was quiet, the occasional passing car, a breeze in the trees outside, the year getting colder.

"I don't know," he said, almost a whisper. "Find out who killed Noel. That seems to be the key to the lock."

"Can't you just let it go? It's eating you up. You're—you're different."

"Can't."

"Can't what?"

"Let it go. It's—I can't explain."

After a while, she yawned and pulled the covers up, the last nesting before sleep. "Can we at least go somewhere when it's over?" She hated murder and the talk of it, he could tell.

"Where to?"

"You've never taken me to New Orleans."

"'Never.' Well, damn. We've only been dating, what, not even a year."

"Still."

"I took you to New York," he said, feeling defensive but not wanting to sound that way. "We ran away to Broadway. Stayed at the Algonquin."

"But New Orleans, though."

"Okay. Alright. You want to spend Christmas in the Quarter?"

"Sure," she said. He felt some of the tension release in her shoulders. "We could do that. We could eat beignets." She was almost asleep, her body heavier on him, her breath slowing. "You could take me to that bar where you used to work. I could check it out. Maybe they'd hire me."

"I'm not sure getting hired at the Chart Room would be a career destination."

"What's wrong with it?" Mumbling, drowsy, dreamy.

He wondered if she'd remember the conversation in the morning.

"Nothing. It's just a dive. And you'd have to be a who dat."

"Never," she said, turning her head away on the pillow, pulling her knees up. "A 'fin to the death."

"Un-hunh."

"Only unbeaten team." She was asleep.

He reached over and touched her nose with the tip of a finger in the dark. "'Christmas in the Quarter.' It sounds like a song about being in love." He wanted it to be true. He really, really wanted it to be true.

thirty-four

The next morning Sully was back at Lorena Bradford's. Standing in the kitchen, he looked on the patio table and saw the paper, the A section, flapping lightly in the breeze, drawing him outside through the sliding glass door. The story on the right of the page, the anchor, had the headline "Confession in Reese Slaying" and a thumb-sized picture of Sarah Reese tucked into the deck head. His name was there. He picked it up and opened it to the jump and saw the story ran nearly half the page. There were the mug shots of the three suspects. Chris and Tony had done serious legwork after he had called in the bombshell.

He wandered back inside. It was nearing noon. He'd left his house early, Dusty still asleep and he sweaty and restless, nervous as a cat. Tooled through the neighborhood, tried Sly on his cell, wound up here. Lorena had been awake and staring at the television when he'd knocked.

Now the television was still on with the sound off, the anchor on the cable channel blabbing about the case, the confession, the unraveling of it all. There was filler footage of Georgia and Princeton Place, of Doyle's Market the night of the murder, the yellow police tape up and the squad cars with their lights flashing.

"Turn it up," Lorena said. She had been upstairs and had come down behind him. He found the remote and pressed the volume button.

". . . but now appears to be on much more solid footing with the confession. Jackson's attorney, Avram Kaufman, said his client would be in protective custody at the D.C. jail until the case is fully resolved. The D.C. Public Defender Service, which is still representing

Highsmith and Deland, did not return calls. But the head of the agency issued a statement saying the two men maintain their innocence."

The camera came back to the studio, the reporter standing outside U.S. District Court in a split screen.

"And, David and Emily, a final irony for you," the reporter said, talking to camera. "The trial of the two men will take place in D.C. Superior Court, directly across the small courtyard behind me from the federal courthouse where Sarah Reese's father presides. His office, on the fourth floor, has a view that overlooks the building where his daughter's alleged killers will be tried."

The camera came fully back to the studio and the anchors segued into another story, about the implications the case might have for Reese's chances at the U.S. Supreme Court.

"Fucking Av," he said.

"You know him?"

He shrugged. "Some."

"Is he good?"

"When he wants to be." Sully pointed the remote at the television and held the volume down until it was mute.

"Not a word about Noel," Lorena said.

"Nope," Sully said. "We have the field to ourselves."

She sat on the couch. "If the police aren't going to be interested, then I'm not sure that just embarrassing David Reese is—"

"They're not going to care until we *make* them," he said, more emphatically than he'd intended. "Reese—Reese—he's got all the advantages. Everybody's so goddamned worried about being fair to him. I'm worried about being fair to Noel, Lana, Michelle, Rebekah—any and all the women up there. You realize I haven't even been through all the files of the missing yet? That there could be more? I'm not about to let him skate on his relationship with Noel. She died and he didn't do a damned thing. Like she never existed."

"Okay," she said. "But it's like we were saying a few minutes ago—if I take it to the police myself, they're not going to do anything. Fucking Detective Jensen."

"No, they're not. They're going to bury it."

"Keeps telling me there's no evidence of violence. Says the department's resources are stretched."

"On Sarah?"

"You think?"

He kneeled down beside her. It killed his knee but he did it. He reached out again, no pussyfooting around this time, took her hand in his. He needed her right on point. "Look. We don't have long. This is edgy, and the longer edgy sits, the more it loses momentum. Every day we take is another day the paper is likely to go, 'Well . . .' and let it sit."

She looked back at him and squeezed his hand a little, less a sign of affection, more a sign of nerves.

"Then I'll work on finishing the chronology this afternoon," she said. "You?"

"I'm going to hit the photographer first, then Reese, then Halo," he said. "That's all that's left. After that, writing."

"Wait, Reese? You're going to see him?"

Sully smiled. "The judge and me," he said, loving the taste of malice on his tongue, "we got unfinished business."

Eric Simmons was fiftyish, a good fifteen years older than Sully had expected, the way John Parker had described him as a scared rabbit. He wore blue jeans, loafers, and an open-collared, sand-colored shirt, untucked, working some sort of flowing art-guy effect. A little potbelly under there. He led Sully down a short, dimly lit corridor, then there was a doorway and Simmons turned into an office on the right.

Simmons gestured toward the couch and took a chair for himself, ignoring the desk.

"So, Sully. This is about Noel?" The first-name familiarity. It sort of made his skin crawl.

"Yes," he said, giving the man his card, pulling out the notebook.

"Excellent. But I can't, ah, tell you much, because I don't know much. And what I know, I've already told the police."

"Surprisingly, they don't tell us everything."

Simmons crossed his legs at the knee, offered a false little smile. "Of course. Something to drink? I forgot to offer. Water? Some tea? I've got—"

Sully held up a hand, no no.

"Fine. So. What is it you think I can help you with?"

Sully started to walk him through the basics of the story, of Noel's last days, and Simmons cut in, quickly. His voice had a soft, slightly effete undertone but he projected an air of confidence, of authority.

"I only met Noel—she was a lovely young woman, very pleasant—the three times she came into the studio. There was the day she came in to introduce herself, to tell me what she was interested in, and to ask about terms. Then she came in the first day of the shoot by herself, and the second day with the other girl. I shot the film but didn't process it. That was how she wanted it."

"You never saw the photographs?"

"No. Well, yes. The police later brought some of them to me and asked if I was the one who shot them. So I saw them then."

"But not initially?"

"No. I shot the film, gave her the unexposed rolls. At her request."

"And when were those sessions?"

"In March of last year. The middle part of the month, as I remember. Is the exact date important? I could have Jennifer—you met her out front—look it up."

"If I need it, I can call back. So it was about a month before she disappeared." He looked at his notes. "You said 'terms.' You meant payment?"

"Yes."

"Mind if I ask?"

"I don't mind, but I won't tell you. Not for publication, anyway. My rates are on a sliding scale and I—I wouldn't want clients to see what I'm charging others. So, not for publication?" Sully nodded. "Four thousand."

Sully blinked. He had seen Noel's checkbook, her credit card statements. She didn't have that kind of money. Not anything like it. And Simmons, well, actually, didn't seem like a four-thousand-dollar photographer. "Did she pay with a credit card? Do you remember?"

"I certainly do remember, because it was very odd. She paid in cash."

"A college student paid you four thousand dollars in cash?"

"All one-hundred-dollar bills. It was the most unusual thing about the session. I don't do a lot of erotica, Mr. Carter, but I do some. Most of my studio's work is advertising, things for shoes, women's fashions. All of it local, if you count Baltimore as local. Now, I do have private clients—I mean to say, men—who like to have photographs of their wives or girlfriends or what have you, in erotica. It's very private, and it's very . . . tasteful, if you will. This isn't *Players* magazine, and there are no crotch shots. The women are not professional models. They're excited but uncomfortable, particularly at the beginning of the session. Noel was a little different. She was not a professional model, but she had all the makings of one."

"What about the other girl, who came the second day? Do you have her name?"

"No. She just mentioned her as a friend."

"Didn't you need her name? For a release, or whatever?"

"There was no release to give. I didn't own the copyright. Remember, I never possessed the film. She asked what type of film I needed and how much. I told her, she got it, came by, and dropped it off the day before the shoot. I shot the pictures and gave her the rolls of film at the end. Whatever she did with it was her business. She could have sold them for a million dollars and I wasn't going to get anything else."

"I'm still stuck on the four grand. You mentioned a sliding scale. Why would you think she would have that kind of money?"

"She said they were for her boyfriend, and that money was no object. That he wanted the best."

"Hunh."

"So I, in the business sense, shot high."

"Hunh." Bullshit meter pegging out in the red now.

"Look, let me clear something up, Mr. Carter. I do not shoot pornography or sexual acts. I was clear with her about that, particularly when she mentioned she wanted to pose with another woman. If you've seen the photographs, they are composed, they're not peekaboo nudie snapshots. She could have sent half of them to lingerie or swimsuit campaigns, which she said she might do. The shots of the pair of them, the women are embracing, as I recall, or entwined, or perhaps kissing. But it was all posed. They did not come into my studio and have sex while I took photographs."

"Did she say, or even hint, who this boyfriend was? Did she mention anybody by the name of David, or just 'D'?"

Simmons spread his hands and gave him that same resigned smile. "I thought the police said she was shooting it for a portfolio, for men's magazines. They didn't mention a boyfriend."

"Ah. Just one more question, Mr. Simmons. You've been very generous with your time. Did a woman named Lana Escobar come in for some of the same type of photographs?"

The man tensed. "I don't know what you're talking about."

"Lana Escobar. Hispanic, early twenties, would have been nearly two years ago. Did she come in for nudes, too?"

"That's the young woman in your story the other day." The smile frozen, hard.

"Yes, actually."

"What are you trying to say?"

"It turns out she had a boyfriend who liked nude pictures, too. I happened to see those photographs. I'm just asking."

"You're—you're implying—I think this interview is over."

"Michelle Williams, by any chance?"

Simmons stood.

"We're done here."

Sully came outside on the sidewalk and turned back up the residential street. He could go after Simmons right now, the sleazoid. Yeah, he'd passed MPD inspection—so what? They weren't even looking hard for Noel when they interviewed Simmons, and they certainly weren't thinking of Lana and Noel as a connection, because they didn't know Lana had posed nude. That the cops hadn't been interested in Simmons probably didn't mean anything other than that he had a clean record and no sex offenses. But Christ, hadn't John told him the guy had been sweaty? Simmons knew he wasn't goddamned innocent of everything. Okay, okay, then how did Noel come to be in Simmons's studio, peeling down? Sully thinking now, mind racing. She or a friend would have known about him, that's how. That's how she would have gotten there. Certainly not from Reese. So, okay, Sully would have to get into Noel's realm, dig into the modeling circuit, the party crowd. Fine. He could start that tonight at Halo.

That left him time for a more urgent task. Leaning against the bike, he pulled out his cell and punched in the numbers for Reese's chambers in District Court.

"Hi, it's Sully Carter, over at the paper," he told the secretary when she picked up. "I need to speak with David this afternoon."

There was a pause, frost developing on the other end.

"That's not going to be possible," she said.

"Ah. Maybe he's at that press conference. How about tomorrow?"

"I'm afraid the judge has no media availability for the foreseeable future."

"I see. Well, look, could you do me a favor, ma'am? Could you ask the judge if he wanted to comment on a story about his extramarital affair with a college student named Noel Pittman, who is now dead? And that the last phone call she made was to him, eight hours after the rest of the world lost touch with her? And that D.C. police are going to find that very curious?"

"I—"

"Wait—wait. Ask him, also—ask him if he wants to comment on the documentation I have that he paid the—the—what is it—here, the Eric Simmons Studio to take sexually explicit photographs of Ms. Pittman and another woman, another dancer at a downtown strip club who worked under the name, I think it was, of 'Bambi'?"

Glacial quiet. Then, "Is that all?"

"That seems to about cover it for today, yes."

"Just a moment, please."

He sat there, leaning against the bike, looking at the weak blue sky overhead. She came back to the phone a few minutes later.

"The judge said he will see you at six p.m. in his chambers."

thirty-five

The U.S. District Court building officially closed at five, but was always open, save for federal holidays, via the guarded entrance off John Marshall Park. Sully walked in at ten minutes till six, after stopping by his house for a shave and slacks, white shirt, and a black sport coat. He kept the coat in his backpack, not pulling it on until he parked the bike on C Street.

The U.S. Marshals greeted him by name, but still made him go through the formality of the metal detector. He went down the hall, his hard-soled shoes quiet on the carpet. He went to the elevator, struck, as always, by the difference between this courthouse and D.C. Superior Court, catty-corner across C Street. This was federal court, a temple of Justice, with the uppercase J and the big-think ideas, red carpet covering the marble floors, massive oil portraits of past justices on the walls, muted lighting, the building symbolically situated between the Capitol and the White House, balancing the twin powers.

Superior Court, next door, was the local bus station of justice, the dead end of urban life—loud, profane, noisy, crowded, ill behaved, umbrellas dripping rain on courtroom floors and switchblades confiscated at the front entrance.

The elevator took him to the fourth floor of the other, more powerful courthouse, and he limped down the hallway and turned again to get to Reese's chambers. The doors were locked, as always, and the receptionist buzzed him in. He said hello and smiled. She ignored him.

He sat down and pretended to look through his notebooks. The phone buzzed, she answered it and said, without looking at him, that he could go in.

Pushing open the huge oak door—what was it with judges and big-ass doors? he'd always wanted to know that—he stepped into Reese's office.

The judge was seated behind his desk, glowering at him. Next to him, on his left, was his private counsel, Joseph V. Russell. Willow thin, a light gray suit, maybe fifty years old, balding, with the slightly gaunt expression of a man who ran marathons for relaxation. To his right was a legal stiff—good God, the man looked like he had to pay to breathe—in a brown suit and a personality to match.

Sully sat down in the chair across from Reese's desk, though no one asked him to, crossed his legs, and did not attempt to shake hands. Power play, he thought, the dual lawyers flanking Reese. He returned service by being rude. He rustled in his seat, getting comfortable, thinking that this was going to last less than ten minutes, and might be less than five.

"Judge, thanks for meeting me this afternoon," he boomed pleasantly. "I'm at work on a story—"

"The judge has advised us as to the nature of your call," Russell cut in. "You are aware of who I am, I believe, but for the record—we are recording this, Mr. Carter—I am Joseph Russell, of counsel to Judge Reese. Seated on the opposite side of the judge is Brian Cannan, of the Justice Department's ethics division. He is here as an observer only, to ensure—"

"That Judge Reese does not dictate a quotation to me, have me read it back to him, and then write my editors a note, on court letterhead, saying that he never said what he said and demanding that I be fired for making it up?" Sully said, nodding to Cannan, who did not blink. "Because that's what happened the last time."

Russell gave him a patronizing smirk. "Mr. Cannan is here to provide an independent, benchmark observation of this meeting and to see if, at the end of it, he will recommend charges against you."

"For?"

"Attempting to blackmail a federal judge."

"And what would I be receiving from this alleged blackmail?"

Russell shrugged his shoulders. "We are not in your business, Mr. Carter, and thus we would have no idea. We are merely taking appropriate precautions."

Sully felt his temperature rise a notch. He hid this by reaching down to pull a recorder from his backpack and put it on the desk, facing Reese. "Well, that's lovely. Thanks for your time, Brian. And, Joey, always a pleasure. Always like to help you run up billable hours. I have a recorder here, so I guess we can play dueling banjos. You'll understand, from my experience with your client, that his word isn't exactly his bond. Did your recorder pick that up?"

Russell made no response. Sully punched the record button, then gave the date, the location, and the names of the people in the room, and set it on Reese's desk, facing the judge, while he looked down at his notes.

"Okay. Judge Reese. Noel Pittman. As I mentioned to your secretary, during the course of our reporting on Ms. Pittman's death, we have come across her diary, which names you as her intimate acquaintance. It sets out the time and date of those liaisons, which was often Saturday mornings at ten fifteen. That corresponds with your daughter's dance lessons at the Big Apple studios. Also, we have seen Ms. Pittman's cellphone, which lists your private office number and your cell. She lists you, by name, on her personal contact list. Also, I have talked to two eyewitnesses who have seen you entering or leaving Ms. Pittman's apartment. One of those sources saw you two embracing at the front entrance, with Ms. Pittman in what is described as bedroom attire. And, also, we are in possession of copies of erotic photographs of Ms. Pittman, taken by an art studio in town, and we have banking records that show you gave her four thousand dollars to pay for the session, plus several hundred more dollars for the film and developing."

For the first time, he looked up. Reese had the stunned look of a seal at a clubbing party. Russell was biting the inside of his gums but keeping a courtroom face. Cannan suddenly looked like he wanted to be somewhere else.

"And what is the point of these allegations, these alleged sightings?" Russell said.

"I believe the point would be that Ms. Pittman left her part-time job at a popular nightclub out on New York Avenue in the early-morning hours of April 25 of last year. She was never seen again. However, the last phone call made from her cellphone—of which police are not yet aware—was at 10:47 the following morning, to Judge Reese's private cellphone. The call lasted seven minutes. They talked. Or maybe she talked to Mrs. Reese, which might have been an even more interesting conversation.

"The point would also seem to be that your client spoke to Ms. Pittman eight hours after the rest of the world thought she'd gone missing. And her decomposed corpse was found a few days ago, in an abandoned house at the end of her block, just across the alley from where Sarah was killed. So the question I have is if your client has, at any point in time, informed the police of this information, either after her disappearance or after her body was found."

The two men did not confer.

Russell said, "We have no comment on these outrageous and defamatory allegations. This is a sinister smear campaign, being unleashed at a time that can only be called grotesque. The judge and his family are grieving the loss of their only child. There was a monumental break in that case in the past few days, which was just announced publicly a few hours ago. The judge has political enemies who are attempting to leak this information in an attempt to stop his ascension to the Supreme Court, no matter his family's suffering. Even in my long experience in Washington, I've never seen anything this base."

Sully wanted to ask if he'd read anything about Monica Lewinsky and a blue dress, but refrained.

"That's all interesting, Mr. Russell, but it wasn't an answer to the question, although I appreciate you speaking so clearly into the microphone. Did Judge Reese meet Noel Pittman at 10:15 on the day she disappeared, as her schedule indicates they were to do, and has he informed the police of his last conversation with her?"

"We are not dignifying it with a response. What are your intentions with this information?"

"To print it."

"You must know you are on very thin legal ice if you do."

"Hunh. I'm researching a story about a federal judge and his ties to a college student who was killed and his lack of disclosure about that relationship. The ice seems pretty thick here. The nude photographs were shot just a few weeks before her disappearance. Did the judge and Ms. Pittman discuss those on that last phone call?"

"What, other than your personal bias, makes you believe Ms. Pittman was murdered? There is no homicide investigation into her death," Russell said. "That young woman's body was examined, postmortem, and the coroner's office did not state her cause of death was homicide. *That* is the sort of irresponsible speculation, Mr. Carter, that puts you and your paper on thin ice."

Sully felt a tingle in his fingers. He had just overstepped. He had gotten ahead of the facts on the table, and not just the bluffing he was doing about Reese's paying for the pictures. That was right, and he had known it as soon as Simmons had said the amount. But this was on tape, and the tape showed him saying she was "killed," which the coroner had not specified. He swore at himself silently.

"Ms. Pittman's corpse turned up a dozen houses down from her apartment in such a decomposed state that no cause of death has so far been determined, whether by means fair or foul. Homicide has not been ruled out. But the freight train is moving down the line, Mr. Russell. Try to address it. I can use smaller words if need be. Again, has Judge Reese disclosed his ties to Ms. Pittman to law enforcement? There is no murder investigation into the death of Ms. Pittman, but the case's status with D.C. police is listed as open. Has the judge aided *that* investigation? Has he told them he spoke to her eight hours after she was last seen or heard from? I can't imagine he has, because if he had they wouldn't keep telling me she was last seen at Halo. They wouldn't keep telling me the nude photographs were shot for a men's magazine, when in fact they were shot for him."

Reese's head, he thought, was going to explode. The man's face was red and his jaw was clenched. He was leaning forward against his desk. Cannan was keeping his head still but cutting his eyes back and forth between the two.

And Joseph Russell, as he was handsomely paid to do, looked as if he were riding a gondola in a spring breeze.

"These are lies, but we have heard your questions, Mr. Carter, and we are not going into your cesspool of innuendo. You may publish these—these *things* if you wish, but you are aware that we will pursue legal action if you do. This is your career on the line, Mr. Carter, not his. Don't think it isn't."

"'Cesspool of innuendo.' I like that, Mr. Russell. That's a very fresh cliché. I'd say we're done." He reached forward and clicked the recorder off.

He put his notebook in his backpack and the three men on the other side of the table leaned back and conferred in whispers. Sully stood to go, picked his recorder up from the table, and walked toward the door. He heard, before he saw, Reese get up from his chair and hustle around the table, rushing to get to him. Sully slowed, ever so slightly, to let the judge beat him to the door.

"Carter," he snapped, pressing the door handle closed to keep him from pulling it open. He leaned forward, using his bulk to press in close.

"I can hear fine, Judge Reese. You don't have to stand three inches from my face to talk to me."

Reese snatched the recorder from Sully's hand and glared at it, making sure it was turned off. "You limp-legged little prick, you will be dead to the world when I'm finished with you," he sneered. "*Dead.* I don't care if you print this piece of shit or not. You think you can fuck with me? You think that what I did to you *last* time was bad? That was a fucking *warning* shot." He ripped opened the door, slapping the recorder back in Sully's palm. "Now get the *fuck* out of my sight."

Sully looked behind him in the office. Cannan had a blank look on his face, but Russell had a contemptuous smile playing out across his lips, arms folded across his chest, enjoying it all.

Sully returned the smile with a nod.

"Judge?" he said, turning back to Reese. "Just a minute ago, when you snatched the recorder out of my hand?" He held the slim digital device aloft and twiddled it between two fingers. Then, swiftly, like a magician with a rabbit and a hat, he reached into the interior chest pocket of his sport coat and produced, with a slight flourish, a second digital recorder. The red recording light was glowing.

"I'm sorry, did you mean to get this one, too? I wasn't sure, and you never said. You gentlemen have a fine evening now."

thirty-six

It was all going to happen now, no way to stop it. Calls to John Parker, spilling the Reese angle, asking if Reese had been in contact with MPD about Noel's disappearance.

"Absolutely not," John said. "This is material to the investigation, you know that. You print this, I guarantee you we'll move on it. Source it through the chief if you want to publish it, but I'm telling you, he never said a damn thing to us about it. And I will personally kick Dick Jensen's ass for not following up with the sister. She ought to be spilling to us, not to you."

Then calls to R.J., to Eddie, narrating the interview, Reese's blowup, the photographer, his conversation with John, whom he described only as a police official. The agreement with R.J. and Eddie was to meet first thing in the morning, reassess, then likely make the official calls to the chief in the afternoon, the last push before publication. Those calls had to be last, to keep it from leaking to other papers, the networks. You call those fuckers, they'd call CNN two minutes later, saying, "Hey, did you know the paper just called us and asked . . ."

By the time he got to Halo, it was close to midnight and the place was thumping. He slapped down twenty bucks for the cover, checked his cycle jacket and helmet at the counter, and went up the steps, Mary J. Blige so loud the handrails vibrated. It was a converted tool and die warehouse, a five-story crumbling shell that an entrepreneur named Jeffrey Gaston had turned into the capital's trendiest nightclub.

Going for the glory of slumming, Gaston put Halo in the brutally ugly, dysfunctional eastern side of the city on New York Avenue two years earlier. There were the beat-to-shit used-car lots, the Harbor Light Center (old drunks in wheelchairs, livers and kidneys gone), the fast-food joints with the bathrooms littered with condoms and needles, the freight railroad tracks across the avenue, and Ivy City, the neighborhood devastated by crack, just down the street.

Inside the fences and barbed wire lining the parking lot, inside the club, it was a different universe.

The second floor was paneled walls of cherrywood and black marble bar counters, and Sully took the wide, circular stairwell to the third floor, which was the source of the Blige. He knew enough about the place to know that he would find Gaston on the fourth, penthouse level.

Once there, he got a gin and tonic from the bar and waited, watching the dancers, the crowd light because it was still early in club time. In half an hour, Gaston finally showed, emerging from black curtains at the far end of the dance floor. He was flanked by a bodyguard and a young woman in a short black dress. They took up a booth at the rear of the room, the bodyguard standing post in front of the table.

Sully gave him five minutes to get settled, then crossed the floor and gave the bodyguard his card. The man looked at it, then leaned forward to shout in his ear, "What's it about?"

"Noel Pittman," Sully shouted back.

When the man gave the card to Gaston and said something in his ear, Gaston looked up at Sully and motioned to the woman beside him to let him out of the booth.

He was light on his feet for a big man, nimble. Close-cropped beard, perfect teeth, black suit, black shirt. It was a look that was good for looking respectable in a city council hearing, good for looking hip at the club. He shook Sully's hand and motioned him to follow.

They went through the black curtain, down a lighted hallway, framed pictures of club life on the walls, and wound up in a workers' break room. Gaston pulled two petit bottles of French spring water from the fridge and sat down at a table.

"What's this about Noel?"

"I'm just—"

"I'm just about tired of hearing about it, is what I am," Gaston cut in, crossing one leg over the other, tapping Sully's card on the table. "Police out here yesterday. Wanting to know when the last time we saw her. Everybody knows when that was. This is some sort of trap, some sort of shit."

Sully twisted the top off the water and swallowed twice.

"Who was out here, a detective named Jensen? Old white guy? Cranky?"

"Asking me and Conrad the same questions the other detectives did last year."

"Like what? And, I'm sorry, who's Conrad?"

"Conrad runs security. The cop, he wanted to see the surveillance tape of her leaving. What was she wearing? Where was she going? Any problems with her."

"It sounds pretty basic."

"Yeah, basic, until they start trying to lay some shit on you."

"You think that's what he's doing?"

"Who knows? Fucking cops."

"So what was the deal that night? What'd you tell him?"

"What's it to you?"

"Nothing. Hey. But to—to you? It's the difference between being suspects and helpful employers."

"Who said we're suspects?"

"You. You just said Jensen was out here yesterday asking you the same questions you'd already been asked. You know why they do that? To see if you say something different this time around. They're looking at you. You want to stay out of a paper like mine? Help me know there ain't shit to look at."

Gaston looked at him, still tapping the card, Sully looking back, poker-faced, playing it straight.

"The deal was there was no deal," he said, finally. "Conrad saw Noel out of the parking lot that night. It's standard. We keep customers away from the girls. Some guys have a few too many, they want to chat 'em up. So the policy is the dancers wait thirty minutes after closing to leave. Conrad or a bartender or somebody walks them to their cars."

"You looked over the security tapes that last night?"

"Made a copy for the cops when they came by last year. Jensen, he didn't even know that. Made him another one."

Oh, yeah, Sully thought, getting the idea even clearer that Jensen was liking Gaston or Conrad or someone at the club as a suspect, asking for a second tape, seeing if they'd give him the same one, sweating them a little bit.

"Jensen ask you anything about David Reese? Like, has Reese been coming out here, he a member of the VIP club, does he show up when Noel's dancing, like that?"

Gaston stopped tapping the card and his face started to open up, almost as if he were going to laugh. "Reese? *The* David Reese? The judge? At Halo?"

Sully nodded, not grinning.

"Ah, shit. Nah. No. David Reese? We don't discuss our clientele, but him?" Then a facial tic, a thought registering. "What, you saying he was kicking it with Noel?"

"Just checking a rumor. You hear wild stuff. You know anything about Noel's modeling career? If she posed nude?"

"Oh, man. You're talking about those black and whites Eric shot. Look. Here's what I'll do. One, make it *clear* in your story that she shot those on her own time, not here at the club, okay? Two, I'll call Conrad. He'll take you to the office, show you the tape. And I'm guessing you'd like to talk to Elissa, which is fine as long as you don't say she works here. You saw her out there dancing tonight."

"Elissa?"

"You probably know her by her stage name. Amber. She's the one posed nude with Noel."

"You shop off the rack?" Sully asked when Conrad walked him to the back room of the security office. The man looked like he could bench-press a Mercedes. Massive chest, arms, and the dude couldn't go more than five-seven.

Conrad gave him a "pah" and kept walking through the offices in the basement. "Not since college. Custom tailoring. I got a guy, you need one."

Once in the office, he unlocked a bookcase, pulled out a videotape, and returned to the desk. There was one small television monitor and a video deck. He popped the tape in and turned on the television. "I hope Gas told you this was short and sweet." He motioned Sully to sit in his chair so that he could see it.

"You don't mind me asking," Sully said, "you were the last one to see her alive. How bad did the cops sweat you on that?"

"Some," said Conrad. "They don't like Puerto Ricans, you ask me." He excused himself to the toilet.

The video was grainy security footage, taken from a second-story camera in the parking lot. Noel was a figure in a white sweatshirt with a hood beneath the security lights—you couldn't really see her face. She paused at the door and Sully saw Conrad appear in the frame, coming outside, walking into the parking lot, she following. She had on running shoes. He could see the car's fog lights flash as she hit the remote alarm button, and then she pulled the hood back from her hair and stepped into the car.

A moment later, she was pulling out of the lot, her turn signal winking toward the left. Conrad gave her a half wave and her arm came out of the driver's-side window, waving back. The car pulled out of the camera's view and Noel Pittman vanished.

Sully backed it up and watched it five or six times. It was the only time he had seen her in motion; he had still never heard her voice.

The door opened and he turned to thank Conrad. Instead, there was a young woman with long brown hair, flat-ironed, stepping just inside the door and looking for him in the semidarkness. She was wearing a black silk robe, but he already knew what she looked like unclothed and in bed.

"Hi, Amber," he said.

He got to his bike in the parking lot, ears still ringing with the noise of the club and the sense of disappointment. You get right to the edge, think you're onto something, and it goddamn belly flops.

Amber said she was one of Noel's best friends, they hung out some, partied some, but they weren't *that* close. She did the shoot because Noel had offered her five hundred dollars from her "boyfriend" and she was les anyway so it's not like it was a big taboo thingy; no, she'd never met the boyfriend or heard his name; Noel was "really pretty and really nice." Eric, the photographer, she said, had not been particularly creepy, though she had thought it was embarrassingly obvious he had an erection during the shoot.

La-de-fucking-da.

Sully straddled the bike. Before he cranked it, he pulled his cell from his pocket.

"It's a little late, don't you think?" Dusty said, her voice tired.

"So, okay, look—I'm finally done for the day. I'm trying, okay? I'll come up and see you. We can catch up. You have no idea how crazy this shit is getting. I got to be back down here early."

"It's a little late for a booty call, Sully."

"Since when?" Trying it as a deadpan one-liner.

Crickets.

"Okay, Christ. Look, I was playing. I just would like—"

"I know, Sully, I hear you, but I've been thinking this isn't the best thing, you know? Like this? You're still locked in on Nadia, and that's understandable but—"

"No, no, I'm not," he said.

"I'm not going to debate this. Last night? We went to sleep talking about New Orleans, Christmas, all that? Then it's three a.m., you were sound asleep and mumbling. It woke me up. I had to nudge you to get you back to sleep. You were soaked with sweat. I went to the closet for a robe, a T-shirt or something, and her pictures were everywhere. That box you have of them."

His turn to be silent, smoldering. "Look," he finally said, "I like us together. I like—"

"And I like you, Sully. Which is one reason why I'm not coming back over there. I don't like sleeping with ghosts. This has to be different, or it has to be better, or it has to stop. I don't think it's good for me. Or for you."

Air.

"I want you to be better," she said. "But I can't help you with this."

thirty-seven

A little after nine the next morning, a hangover banging on the front of his skull, Sully clicked the off button on the recording of Reese's meltdown and the executive conference room of the paper was silent. Edward Winters sat leaning forward in his chair, forearms on the desk in front of him.

After a while, Winters said, "I just can't believe that."

R.J., seated beside Sully, shook his head. "Never heard anything like it. Not in this town, on tape."

"He's unhinged," Eddie said.

"Caged," said R.J. "Bear in a cage."

The morning meeting for the paper hadn't even taken place, and it was clear this was going to dominate the day. Lewis, the attorney, chipped in, "His Supreme Court bid ends the instant we publish this. Probably his judicial career. Also, if you're looking for the definition of clear and actionable damages—"

"I know," Eddie said, waving a hand, "I know."

Melissa cleared her throat. "I hate to be the wet blanket again, Eddie, but to what end do we publish this? Are we insinuating that he had something to do with her disappearance? That he actually killed her? It seems to me that would be the implication of any story we write. I think we have to keep in mind that there's the danger of his history with Sully, and then this one-potato, two-potato trick he just pulled with the recorder. I'm not saying—"

"You're not saying anything!" R.J. thundered. "I don't give a goddamn about the recorder being on or off. What we've established is that Noel Pittman left her job at two thirty in the morning and, for more than a year, that was the last known sighting of her. Now, after her corpse has been recovered, we find out that she placed a call to the chief judge of the U.S. District Court for the District of Columbia eight hours after she was last seen. I don't care if it was for coffee or coitus. What we're *saying* is that the chief jurist of the courthouse at the foot of Constitution Avenue did not bother to inform the police or Pittman's family of that call, or of their relationship. *That* is the point, and that is what will keep him off the Supreme Court, and possibly have him expelled from the bench. Because he *should* be."

It was quiet again, and then Edward spoke.

"Well, here we are again. Sullivan, as much as I admire your work, I do not admire—and we do not print—gotcha journalism. And that's what that stunt with the second recorder amounts to. Given your history with him, it looks like you set him up. And the matter of the pictures and his payment may be a correct hunch, but it's nothing we can prove."

"I did—" Sully said, but Eddie cut him off.

"That said, R.J.'s point carries the day. Once Pittman was missing, Reese had an obligation to go to the police. We can demonstrate, to a clear and convincing standard, that he did not inform them. It may or may not be obstruction of justice, but it clears the bar of public interest. If his daughter's death matters, so does that of Noel Pittman."

He looked at the room, people sitting still, looking back at him.

"Which makes it news," he said. "And I want it for tomorrow. Where are you in the writing?"

"About thirty inches in," Sully lied. "And for the record, I didn't set him up. I was working with a recorder and a backup. It's not even uncommon."

"And you had one on the table and one in your jacket. Don't bullshit me, Sully. Moving on. You're at thirty inches. What's it worth?"

"Am I including the other missing girls, or is this just the judge and the dancer?"

"Mention Escobar, Bolin, and Williams somewhere up high for

neighborhood context, and maybe you can loop back in late for another couple of grafs. But this is about Noel Pittman and David Reese."

"Then I think it's sixtyish."

"Good. You're sure on the police, that they haven't heard of this?"

"It's news to the head of Homicide, who would know. He wants us to have it come from the chief, though. I'll call him in a minute."

"Okay. Now, if Reese releases their tape of your interview with him later today as some sort of preempt, and tries to make it look like you jumped to a conclusion about a murder investigation, I'll have a very short conversation with him and Joe Russell about your second tape."

Lewis coughed and said, "Does that mean you're going to threaten them with releasing Sully's tape?"

"Absolutely not," Eddie snapped. "It means if I hear so much as a peep out of either one of them, I *will* release Sully's tape."

U.S. District Court for the District of Columbia Chief Judge David H. Reese, widely viewed as the Republican favorite for the next Supreme Court opening, had a relationship with a missing Howard University student and spoke with her eight hours after she was last seen, phone records, documents and interviews show, and he has not disclosed that information to police.

Noel Pittman, 25, disappeared after leaving work at the nightclub Halo in the early-morning hours of April 25 of last year. Her decayed corpse was discovered last week in the basement of an abandoned house in the 700 block of Princeton Place NW, a few houses down from where she lived and directly across an alley where the judge's daughter . . .

This was on the computer screen, Eddie sitting at the copy chief's desk, reading over it, his fingers on the keys but only moving the cursor back and forth. Melissa, R.J., Sully, Lewis Beale, and editors from photo and layout were arrayed in a semicircle behind him. It was nearing eight p.m., deadline for the first edition.

"Do we have it from the police, formally, that he didn't tell them?" Edward asked.

"A statement from the chief is coming," Sully said. "They've been stiffing me on it all day. I gave them until eight or said I would go with the chief had no comment, but police sources have confirmed it."

"Then let's soften that to 'apparently' didn't tell the police, until we get the confirmation or the nonstatement. And make that lede two sentences."

He kept reading, eyes not lifting from the screen. "And I want you to show Lewis your documentation and your notes. With all due respect, I'm also going to ask him to call Lorena Bradford to verify the phone information."

"Sure."

A few minutes and quiet remarks to the copyediting staff later, he half spun in his chair away from the computer and looked at the assembled. "It's solid. Hard to believe but equally hard to dispute. Let's keep going through it."

The mini conference broke up.

Sully went back to his desk, a printout of the story in hand, and found, lying on his keyboard, a package that a news aide had left. It was a large envelope from Lorena—the complete chronology she'd worked up. Pushing it aside for now, he got a red pen and went through the story, testing every assertion of fact against his notes, putting a red check over each when he verified it. The room was quiet, and he worked without interruption. Lewis waddled by, terse, hurried, and Sully looked up. He was surprised to see that more than an hour had passed.

"The old lady across the street? Show me the notes. And the sister's number."

Sully gave him the numbers for both, Lewis nodding, writing the numbers on his legal pad, and left.

The newsroom population was thinning out, it was down to the late-night metro editor and copy editors and layout artists. He leaned back in his chair, stretching, nerves jumping. Either his career or David Reese's was going to be over in twenty-four hours. There wasn't much way around it.

To the right of his keyboard, underneath a flurry of papers he'd gone through in fact-checking, was Lorena's manila folder. Yawning, he tore it open and pulled the thick chronology out. "Just in time!" was written in a sticky note attached to the front page in Lorena's swirling hand. She'd dropped it off downstairs earlier, her note said.

When he pulled it out, a smaller sheaf of papers fell out onto the floor. They were held together with a paper clip, and he bent over to pick them up.

"??? Stores???" was written in Lorena's hand on the sticky note on top of them. "Didn't go through—I don't know what these are/where they're from."

He removed the clip and they fluttered out onto the table. None of the receipts had any identifying information, hence Lenora's shorthand. Most appeared to be from an old-fashioned cash register, narrow slips of paper with a serrated edge at top and bottom. The receipts listed prices, with a date and time at the bottom, but no store name or what the purchased items were. There were something like two dozen of them, the amounts small, $.99, $2.25, $1.39, $4.58, and the like.

Dealing them out across the table like playing cards, killing time while waiting for editing questions, he started making piles by date.

It was clear after the first ten or eleven receipts that they were all from April 1998, the month Noel disappeared. There were a couple dated the third, one on the seventh, the eighteenth, the fourth, the twenty-second—he was putting them in a line, left to right . . . and then he stopped. The receipt dropped to the desk like a flaring match.

The date on the receipt was April 25. The day she was last seen.

There were three items on it—$2.49, $3.39, $3.39—but it was the time that glared out at him, radiating.

The time was 4:47 p.m.

Speckles of sweat burst out on his back, the palms of his hand.

Noel hadn't died the night she came home from Halo, and she didn't die shortly after her phone call to Reese that morning.

No, no, she was still alive and shopping that afternoon. Not only that, but she'd come back to her apartment after buying whatever it was in a calm enough state of mind to put her daily receipts in the record-keeping coffee can.

How late did that make it? Five thirty? Six? Eight?

Frantically, he finished assembling the other receipts by date—the twelfth, the seventeenth, the third, the twenty-first, the second—but none came after the twenty-fifth. He counted them all again—twenty-two purchases for small things in twenty-five days, apparently from the same store.

As soon as the thought flickered, the tumblers of his mind, the ones that had been rolling, clicking, never settling down, finally stopped, a combination that clicked.

Pushing back and sideways in his chair, he reached in his back pocket for his wallet and yanked it open. He pulled out a tumble of paperwork, dollar bills, a couple of twenties. Here they were, the tab for Halo . . . gas for the motorcycle . . . drinks with Eva at Stoney's.

And then there was a simple till receipt, for $0.99 and $1.29. Total of $2.46 with tax. He placed it against the final receipts from Noel's. It was an exact match.

Sully sat back against his chair, dazed.

"Peanuts," he said flatly. "Peanuts and a Coke."

thirty-eight

The bike roared out of the garage and he redlined it at the first light, revving, popping the clutch, and *wham,* he was hitting sixty, moving the needle to seventy, blowing through traffic, his mind moving faster than the bike.

David Reese wasn't the last one to see Noel. He'd lied. He hadn't volunteered information. He'd covered his ass. But he wasn't the last one to see her, and he wasn't the only one covering his tracks.

Noel had been to one place over and over again that last month. Sully was certain she'd been to it several times a week for the entire time she'd lived in the neighborhood, someplace she was known as a regular: Doyle's.

It all came screaming at him now. Doyle had said he barely recognized her when Sully had shown him the pictures of the three girls—yet he knew her well enough to recognize her on her front porch with Reese. What if his rage that day hadn't been fury at being slighted by Reese, but jealousy of the man? What if half of the "D's" in the diary were for *Doyle,* not *David,* and Noel, silly, giggling, had written in the double meaning to amuse herself? What if *he* was the boyfriend with the money for the photographer?

No, sweet Jesus, no.

And then it came to him so clearly he nearly dropped the bike: When he'd shown Doyle the pictures of Lana, Noel, and Michelle? What had he said? "*They're the three dead girls.*"

Lana and Noel were dead, yes, but Michelle was missing. Nobody said she was dead.

He slowed the bike with the thought, on a straight shot of Georgia now, the commercial low-rise storefronts and the prewar four-story apartment buildings populated by fortysomething immigrant men driving taxis and their dour women and their children loud as shit on the playgrounds.

His breath came back to him, slowly, one inhalation at a time. By the time he pulled into the neighborhood, the mixed wave of euphoria and revelation was wearing off, and self-doubt and paranoia were settling in.

Doyle had said they were three dead girls? So what? Two of the three women were dead. Doyle might have lopped Michelle in with the rest out of laziness, or by a simple mistake. It wasn't some irrefutable Freudian slip.

And the receipts? So what?

It was important to know Noel was alive later in the day, absolutely. But maybe Doyle didn't have any idea she'd come in the store that day. Maybe he happened not to work that weekend. Maybe he had, and the encounter was so routine that its very familiarity blinded him as to the date of its actual occurrence. And even if he had recalled her coming in that day? Maybe he'd decided to keep his mouth shut for the same reason a lot of witnesses in this town did—to stay out of it, to avoid the possible retribution from suspects. Hadn't he already said that business in the store was half off?

The bottom line was, how could he know? The presses were going to roll in an hour and, suddenly, he had no fucking idea.

God*dammit.*

There was only one thing to do, and he'd known it as soon as he saw the matched receipts. He'd started out of the paper's garage at a hundred miles an hour, and where had the bike taken him? He was already turning onto Rock Creek Church, the blinker on without a conscious thought, the bike slowing in front of Sly's dilapidated house.

You wanted to know what was happening in Park View? You dealt with the devil and you paid the price.

• • •

Sly listened to his spiel, to his hunches, then pushed back on his bar stool, balancing it on the rear two legs.

"So you thinking we ought to go sweat this photographer, Eric."

"At least two of the dead women posed nude. We know he photographed one of them."

"Carter. Eric? Known him since back in the day. Got to be the gayest motherfucker this side of Luther."

"Amber said he had a hard-on during the shoot with Noel."

"Eric probably gets a hard-on buying groceries. Back in third grade? He had a hard-on then, too."

"So I don't hear any brilliant ideas from you."

"You been yapping." Sly set the stool back down on all four legs. "So, if you're done? I been taking this sort of hard, you see what I'm saying here, the judge tipping in my backyard." Only dim lights along the kitchen wall were illuminated, the stereo was off, Donnell was asleep by the couch, and Sly's voice seemed to rise from the shadows.

"So me and Lionel, we been pushing. Beating the pavement. Making it known we want to hear from people, that we *better* hear from people. And so this female who's been in the lockup for a few weeks comes to see me. She's what your paper would call a working girl, right, walking Georgia between Princeton Place and the Show Bar? She comes by to tell me she saw this 'Missing' poster about that girl Michelle, and then she saw the thing you wrote in the paper, about them girls missing or dead or whatever, and she said it gave her this fucked-up feeling, because she saw Michelle a few weeks ago in the back room at Doyle's."

"Michelle was in Doyle's? When?"

"Wait, now. This female, she's all the time going into Doyle's to buy a little something so they let her go pee while she's working. She says when Doyle is there, he's eyeing her up, telling her she can get shit for free for a little favor in the back."

"Did she?"

"Nah. Pussy ain't for bartering. Hers, anyway. But here it is. She's back there squatting one night and she hears grunting, *unh unh unh.*

She walks out the toilet real quiet, the office door ain't all the way closed. She peeps, sees Michelle, titties out, shirt open, kneeling in front of the desk in Doyle's office. She just tipped on out, didn't think nothing about it, just thought Doyle musta been making his offer to a lot of females and Michelle took him up on it."

"Michelle was turning tricks?"

"Girl was a crackhead. Crackheads'll suck an exhaust pipe for ten dollars and a hit. So girlfriend here, she leaves out of Doyle's, gets picked up the next night for, what do you call it, soliciting, and doesn't know anything else until she gets out a couple days ago."

"So what day was this she sees Michelle?"

"About six weeks back."

"She sure?"

"She was in the lockup for forty-something days before the charges got dropped. She remembers it was the night before she got picked up."

"And she reads the newspapers, does she?"

"There ain't a lot to do in lockup."

Sully leaned against the counter and thought for a minute.

"So, okay, Doyle lied about Noel. And he's getting blow jobs or whatever from Michelle. Which means what to us exactly? I mean, I got a story running tomorrow, and it's the judge's ass or mine."

Donnell's eyes flicked open, looking up at Sly, then Sully, as if startled to see them there, then laid his massive head back on the carpet and yawned, long pink tongue flicking out over his teeth. Sully could no longer make out Sly's face in the darkness, just glints of the sides of his glasses and his small, narrow nose, surprisingly delicately boned.

"I told you me and Lionel, we been pushing this hard. Turns out Doyle is a regular pussy hound. Man runs a tab up at the Show Bar, after he shuts his store down. And you know as well as me that Les, the owner? He's working girls up in there. Les, he tells me that Doyle likes sisters, black and brown, don't matter, long as they got some pigmentation. Gets blown off in the men's once or twice a week, maybe more on the side."

"All the women who are missing or dead—they're all hookers or got a drug problem or they live right there on Princeton," Sully said. "You thinking Noel was turning high-end tricks? That the judge was paying for it, and maybe Doyle, too? That, what, *Doyle* is the one out there killing women?"

"You got a better idea?"

"Why Sarah, then? She's not anything like the others."

"She got in the way. She saw something. He decided to branch out."

"But she wasn't sexually assaulted."

"Maybe he couldn't get it up, killed her when he got pissed off. I'm not a sick fuck. I don't know. I don't have to know the *why*. I just have to know the *if*."

"So what is it you propose to do?"

"I don't propose nothing. I'm saying what *we're* going to do, brother—we're *going* to find out. Lionel, he's down there at the Show Bar keeping an eye on Doyle."

"You don't mean we're going to go press him at the club."

"No no no. You don't think right. We're going to check out his house while he's up there getting his johnson polished."

"What? Right now?"

"You got something better to do? Somebody's shooting at you. Probably Doyle, you ask me. Then you come in here and tell me your comfy-ass job is on the line. I'm saying police are pressing people to talk about them three. It's making my people nervous, and it ain't in my best interest when my neighbors are nervous. So, brother. I'm taking care of my business. You? You in or out? I mean, I'm not the one going to get fired tomorrow if I'm wrong."

thirty-nine

Sly went to the back room and came back two minutes later with a large envelope. He opened the flap and held it down at an angle, shaking it. A series of pictures, all eight-by-tens, slid out. It was a series of pictures of houses just up the street. He fanned them out across the counter.

"Now. This here is Doyle's place. All these old row houses on this street? They pretty much the same layout, same front porch, same front room, dining room, kitchen, basement, and bath and bedrooms upstairs. Look here. Window units. Cheap-ass ain't even put in central air."

Sully was going to point out that the top two floors of Sly's house looked like a crack squat, but decided against it.

"You been staking him out?" Sully asked.

"I said I'm taking care of business. Now look. These here are the backyards of the houses on that block. See if you can pick his out."

Sully looked at the pictures Sly had spread out—five, taken from different vantage points of the rear alley. The yards were all tiny, rectangular, sectioned off by stretches of sagging chain-link fences, overgrown grass and flowerpots and concrete parking spots in the yards. The paint on the rear brick walls on every house was peeling or chipped or faded. Some of the houses had drives that sloped sharply downhill from the alley to their basements. There was a recent-model blue BMW in one, a silver Honda just beyond, and a Caddy, sagging at the ass end, in another.

There was no need to guess.

In the middle of the block, there was one house with a yard sealed off from view by a solid wooden fence at least six feet high.

"So you still think the man ain't done nothing?"

"It's a fucking fence, Sly."

"Y'all got problems with your belief system. Why would he have a fence up like that, he ain't up to something?"

"He likes to sun himself naked. He wants the shade. Tired of kids jumping the fence and stealing his barbeque."

Sly rolled his eyes and went to the back room again.

When he came back, he was dressed in a black tracksuit. In each hand, he held a ziplock bag, stuffed thick, and he tossed one underhanded to Sully. Inside was a black watch cap, gloves, plastic booties. Sly set two pencil-thin flashlights on the counter and told him not to pick his up until his gloves were on. He told him to leave the cycle jacket and tossed him a long-sleeve black T-shirt, a turtleneck, and told him to burn everything when they were done.

"Are you fucking kidding me?" Sully said. Sly just looked at him, and Sully, in spite of himself, put the gear on. A few minutes later, Sly's phone buzzed. He looked down at it and said, "Lionel's out front. Let's go."

He opened the basement door, Sully out in front, and then locked it behind them. He took Sully by the arm as he walked past. "You ain't gonna pussy out now, are you?"

Sully responded by taking the steps two at a time to get to street level and there was a Honda Odyssey idling at the curb, the side door sliding open. Lionel was at the wheel.

Sully stepped inside, then Sly.

They pulled out slowly, and Sully could not help himself.

"When did you start pushing a minivan, Dad?"

A full block passed before Sly spoke.

"Nothing is so stupid as driving your own car to do your dirt. We borrowing this from a driveway in Bethesda. The Camaro, see, one of my associates is tooling around Southeast, outside a few clubs, going to a drive-through McDonald's."

"So people will think they saw you."

"I told you that boy was quick, Lionel."

"So who's watching Doyle right now?"

"I tipped one of the girls to pay *special* attention to him," Lionel said, without taking his eyes off the street, "until I get back."

It was only four blocks to Doyle's, Lionel pulling into the alley that ran between Princeton Place and Quincy Street. The alley had a cut-through that went behind the houses on both streets—the backyards faced one another across the alley—and they were in the alley behind Doyle's, the place where the pictures had been taken.

The side door slid open again and it dawned on Sully that it had all gotten out of hand, this story, his life, everything, since he'd come back from Bosnia, from Romania, from Afghanistan, from Gaza, from Nagorno-Karabakh. He had lost the ability to draw lines, to compartmentalize, to keep one part of his life separate from another. What was the morality in the war zone and what was the morality out of it? They were different, the rules were different, but what worked in war often worked on the streets if you just had the nerve. The blues were running into the greens, the yellows into the reds, the whole color wheel was just a blotch, and he did not think the colors would ever go back inside their lines again.

He shoved the thought aside, forcing himself to think of Lorena, of Noel, of Lana, of Michelle and her father. He was going to make this shit right and he was going to do it right now, before sunrise. In front of him, Sly slipped out of the car without a word, as quick and quiet as a leopard, vanishing into the shadows of the alley. Sully followed, a sense of freefall, as if he'd just parachuted out of an airplane, thousands of feet of dead air beneath him, and then suddenly he landed. He was shuffling forward over the rough concrete as fast as he could.

Behind him, Lionel pulled away, a thin plume of exhaust trailing. There was no sound now but that of his footsteps, his breathing. He and Sly were alone, and Sly had already cut the padlock on the wooden gate.

forty

The gate swung open when he pushed it—there were no springs—and it slapped back against the wooden fence. Sly, already inside, turned and glared. Sully pulled the gate shut, making sure the clasp did not click, and then turned and leaned his back against it. There was only one streetlight working in the alley, but it still cast dim shadows. Everything was quiet again.

Sly, letting out a breath of exasperation, gestured toward the house with two fingers and then he was gone, hunched over, moving fast down the concrete slope, where a car would ordinarily be parked, to the peeling garage door, which looked as if it hadn't rolled up since Nixon was in the White House. Sully could see, through a patch of streetlight, Sly move to his right, to the entry door. He was pulling open a pouch at his hip. Sully peered forward and saw Sly make a circle in the glass pane of the window on the door and tug. There was a faint tinkle of glass. A moment later, the door swung outward and open.

Sly was gone, pulling the door closed behind him.

Sully kept his eyes flicking from the windows of one house to the next door, expecting lights in adjacent windows to flick on, sashes to be thrown open, a belligerent voice to yell, "Hey! The fuck you doing?" But nothing stirred. He could not hear any cars passing, either on Princeton or on Park Place, the street running along the edge of the golf course behind them. After a few moments, he began to pick up the sounds of rain dripping from trees, from eaves, hitting the pavement below.

In front of him, in Doyle's weed-choked backyard, were two metal chairs pushed up against the wooden railings of the fence, a pair of wet cushions on the ground beside them. The sloped drive in front of him had a thick oil stain. The streetlight shadows over the edge of the fence made it hard to see the interior borders of the property, and in this darkness he felt safe.

He counted to thirty, then forty-five, then eighty, and then the screen door opened on the tiny back porch. Sly came out into the half-light. He beckoned with a windmilling motion, and Sully kept to the shadows until he stepped onto the porch. From there he took hold of the open door and stepped inside, into the suffocating darkness.

Sly pulled the door shut behind him and turned the bolt. He took out a flashlight and turned it on, keeping the beam on the floor. When he did, Sully could make out the thin nose, the cheekbones, the angular cast to his head, and he could see the flicker in his eyes.

"What?" Sully said. "What?"

"You take the upstairs, I'll do the basement," Sly hissed. "Move."

Sully advanced across the cheap linoleum of the kitchen, past the wooden shelves and pantry, all of it looking shipshape neat and well ordered. He kept to the right in the narrow hallway, then, when near the front door, made a U-turn to his left and was at the base of the stairs. He shone the light up the stairwell. He bit his lower lip and went quickly up the steps, keeping his feet to the outside edges to minimize the creaks.

When he reached the landing, one bedroom was in front of him, a bathroom to his immediate left. The hallway was just to his left, on the other side of the banister, running back toward the front of the house. He flicked the beam down the hallway, illuminating two doors opening off to the right. He knew, from the layout of his own house, there would be a small bedroom first and then the master bedroom, with the windows facing the street.

He walked down the hall and shone the light into the first room. There were three steel filing cabinets, each four drawers high and each looking as heavy as an engine block, set beside a heavy desk. It was designed to be a bedroom but Doyle had converted it into an office.

Sully took three steps farther down the hall, pushed the door open with the flashlight, peeking into the man's bedroom. It was neat, orderly, and almost completely bare. A bed: a mattress on the floor, no box spring. The sheets were pulled up and tucked in neatly. There were no pictures, no paintings, nothing on the peeling walls. An ancient telephone, its cord coiled and looped, sat by the pillows.

He went back into the converted office, the steel desk looking identical to the kind Doyle kept in his office at the store. The top of it was bare—free of paper, of files, of anything. The filing cabinets were not locked. The top two drawers were packed thick with manila folders, headings scrawled in bold black lettering on the raised tabs. Most seemed to apply to the store, others to cars he had owned, others labeled REFRIGERATOR and HAULING and BOAT, then folder after folder marked PAYROLL. There was tax information and three files on roofing problems. It smelled musty, old.

The bottom drawer was packed solid with pornography.

It was, Sully noticed as he bent down to lift a few magazines to peek at the titles farther down, all hard-core stuff, all black and Hispanic women, crude titles devoted to specific parts of the female anatomy.

"Hey."

He jumped halfway to the ceiling. Sly materialized at the door, shining a flashlight in his face.

"Goddammit, would you give—"

"Come on. You got to see this."

Sly led the way to the first floor, making the U-turn at the bottom of the steps turning to the back of the house. When he got to the door that led to the basement, he pulled it open and stepped down to the landing. Below them was a gulf of blackness, pierced only by the narrow beam of his flashlight. He looked at Sully and said, "We're out of here in five minutes—I don't care what you think. Pull the door behind you. And don't fucking trip on anything."

Sully nodded, closing the door, following Sly down the wooden steps, concentrating on the beams of the flashlights. When they both reached the bottom, Sly said, "There's a laundry room at the back, and he blacked out the windows, so the lights don't matter."

He flicked on the switch.

Sully blinked rapidly and closed his eyes for a second in the sudden brightness of the bulbs that dangled overhead.

His first thought was that Doyle had closed off the garage years ago and converted the back part of the basement into living space. The floor was packed dirt with large rectangular planks of wood set over it, covered by cheap brown carpet.

The carpet had been pulled back, though, and one of the planks partially pulled to the side. The smooth, packed dirt beneath it was loose.

"I walked in, nearly tripped over the planks," Sly said. "So I pulled it back to see."

Only then did Sully look at the walls, at the dozens of photographs, at the shelves with their neatly packaged rows of mementos. The pictures and talismans were grouped by each woman.

It was some sort of shrine, an altar. He recognized pictures of Rebekah Bolin, Michelle Williams, Lana Escobar, and other women he did not know. Items of clothing were neatly set out—a T-shirt, bras, panties, shoes. The photographs of Michelle featured a picture of her at the front door of Goodwin's house, taken by some sort of overhead camera in the center. Others had similar pictures. Then there were the death pictures, the women nude, dead, posed as if in erotica.

"Christ, he got half of them to come here," Sully said. "For what? Cleaning? Washing the dishes? But what did he do with them all?"

"You ain't looking," Sly said, tapping his foot.

Sully looked down again. With a toe, he pushed the plank all the way to the side. The dirt beneath it had been freshly disturbed.

"Jesus fucking Christ."

On instinct, the buzzing in his ears now, he went to the laundry room at the back, turned on the light, and there, in the back corner, was a shovel. A pick was next to it. Hurrying now, carrying both, he came back to the main room.

"The hell you are," Sly said.

"You said five minutes. Won't take that if you get off your ass."

The shovel pitched into the earth with ease—it was not settled earth—and he was digging hard, attacking the loosened soil, throwing spades of earth back without regard for the grit or the noise of it or the damp clumps spraying everywhere. Sly sighed and worked the top end of the dirt with the pick.

After a minute, Sly said, "Shit."

He did not remove the pick, but moved the dirt around it with his foot. Sully worked his shovel a foot or so from the pick until it met resistance. Sly pulled up the pick, gingerly. A rotted leg appeared. Sully, dropping to his knees, was digging at the dirt with his gloved hands now, moving it aside, until the corpse's chest and neck and, finally, decomposed face came into view.

The clothes were rotting, most of the skin gone, but there was still hair and fingernails and a blouse. Sully stood upright, looking down at the corpse.

"Michelle," he said.

Sly picked up the shovel and pick, moving them back to the laundry room.

"You got to go," he said. "Get on out the back, walk to your bike—do not fucking run, you hear me, I said walk—and get home. Call somebody. Get an alibi. I got work here."

"Work? What work?" There was an electric air to the room, a static charge that seemed to set everything atilt and lit from within, as if the whole room were wired to explode. "All we got to do is get out of here and call the police. This shit is over."

Sly was already in the doorway of the laundry room, looking back at him.

"Leave, and leave quick," he said. "You not listening. I ain't far behind. But get. Don't you fucking call the cops until you hear from me."

"When is that going to be?" a harsh whisper, his voice feeling strangled.

"After daybreak."

"Fuck that."

"What?"

"Fuck that, Sly. You not telling me to get lost till the sun comes up. We walk out, make an anonymous call, game over. We got all we need. Ballgame."

"Yeah?" The pistol in Sly's right sleeve dropped down into his hand. Sully looked at it and rolled his eyes but did not move forward.

"'s what I thought," Sly hissed. "Now. I'm respecting you, right? I ain't starting no shit with you, right? Gimme a minute and I'll see you on the block."

Sly disappeared into the back, conversation over. Sully took another look around the room, the sickness of it, and turned, ready to be outside, ready to be somewhere else, fuck Sly and fuck this nonsense, it just wasn't worth all this shit. It was not his best moment, but he didn't care anymore, he just wanted out, and he hurried up the steps as fast as his gimp leg would allow, feeling claustrophobic and sick, the smell of death getting to him, the eyeless skull. The stairs creaked beneath his weight. Once in the hall, he turned to the back of the house, making his way by the streetlight from the alley out back.

The hallway light clicked on.

He wheeled around to whisper at Sly to turn the goddamn thing off and Doyle Goodwin stood in the foyer, jacket still on, closing the front door behind him.

forty-one

It was still misting rain. That was the first thing that shot through Sully's mind.

Doyle was looking at him, his hair dotted with raindrops, the jacket damp. He must have walked home from the Show Bar, his evening stroll past the houses where he buried his victims, back home to the nest. His hands were in his jacket pockets and his right hand moved this way and that. Sully, keeping his eyes locked on Doyle's, knew he was getting a grip on his gun, clicking off the safety. The movement, a thumb moving from right to left, made him remember that he'd left his own gun in his cycle jacket at Sly's.

He backed up involuntarily. *Never back up never back up. You want a dog to chase you? Run.* But he didn't have any choice now, he had to give ground to gain time. The kitchen, he was backing into the middle of the kitchen, furiously trying to recall the layout and what cover or weapons he might find. The back door was perhaps twenty feet away, a fatal distance.

"Didn't know you had a thing for sisters and hookers, Doyle," he said, stalling, oh sweet Jesus, stalling.

"I tried to help you," Doyle said, shaking his head. "I *tried.* I gave you the judge. And you just wouldn't take it and go." A high-pitched giggle.

He's drunk. Drunk off his ass. Stall him, stall him till you get to the door.

"You got a real bad problem, Doyle."

"No," Doyle said, bringing the gun out and up now, smiling, drunk out of his mind. "*You* got a problem. *My* problem ends with you."

"How come you don't got the pictures of Sarah up yet?" Sully said, gesturing toward the basement, desperate to retrack Doyle's mind. "You did her to get back at Reese, yeah? You saw Noel every day. You wanted to fuck her so bad you could taste it. And she ignored your ass and gave it up to the judge. Left you with fat, ugly hookers."

"Sarah?" Doyle laughed, a mirthless rattle in the chest, still walking forward, passing the basement door, cutting him off there. "*Sarah?* What makes you think—?"

A shadow burst out of the basement, a blur that slammed into Doyle and catapulted him into the wall. Doyle dropped his gun. It fired on impact with the floor, blowing a hole in the wall. Sully leapt forward to get the gun and Sly pinned Doyle, whipped his Glock out and against Doyle's temple, hammering it against the wall, and then there was an explosion of noise and blood and brains and shattered skull.

Doyle's body slid down the wall, mouth open, eyes open, half his head gone, his blood and gore painting the wall, until he reached a splayed sitting position. Then he slumped forward.

Sully's ears rang. The blood was still oozing outward on the wooden floor. It was coming over to the kitchen linoleum now.

A moment passed. Sly looked down at the body, then lightly kicked Doyle's thigh. "I ought to get a gotdamn reward."

Sully leaned down and put his hands on his knees, trying to get his breath. "I wasn't thinking about that exactly."

"No?" Sly was still looking down at Doyle.

"What—what I was thinking about was more about how he came in the—"

"Wasn't nothing to worry about. Lionel buzzed me he was coming up the sidewalk."

"And you let me walk upstairs?"

"You were halfway up there already. It worked out better, catching him in the hallway like that."

"Better for who?"

Sly didn't answer, but bent down and picked up Doyle's gun with his gloved fingers, then reached into a pocket and pulled out his cell, punching in numbers.

Winking at Sully, speaking to Lionel, he said, as relaxed as if going for a Sunday drive, "Come on. Bring the stuff. Them gas cans, too."

forty-two

By dawn, the blaze was billowing out the first-floor windows, glass breaking with the heat, orange flames licking up the front of the house. Firefighters were shouting that the roof was caving in at the back. Fire engines, set up in the rear alley and out front on Princeton, were as much watering down the houses on either side as they were training the hoses on Doyle's, trying to keep the flames from jumping from one roof to the next, Sully figured. That happened, the entire block would be an inferno.

He was standing on the sidewalk behind the police barricade, showered, in a fresh change of clothes. All the old clothes—shirt, pants, shoes, socks, underwear, everything—were in a dumpster in an alley halfway out to the Beltway.

The David Reese story was on the front page, dominating the early news shows, but it was quickly being engulfed by the fire and its darker revelations, the thick black cloud of smoke going straight up and then spiraling over the golf course, filtering toward downtown and the federal city.

It was visible from the Capitol building as a dark finger on the horizon, a foreboding image, and the networks and cable channels were keeping their cameras trained on it from their rooftop sets near the Capitol. Cameras could take in the host talking with the Capitol dome in the background, and then just pan to the spiraling smoke.

At the scene, uniformed officers were holding the crowd at the barricades, most of them residents who'd been evacuated from adjacent houses. Four television trucks sat at the curb, their antennae sprouting up like tiny metal hairs on the asphalt head of the city. Traffic on Warder was at a standstill, people getting out of their cars, walking up to be able to look around the corner and see the enflamed building. Boys in big, loose T-shirts, riding their bikes in circles, whooping.

A hose sent a huge stream of water toward Doyle's, the torrent bursting into spray and steam upon contact with the roof, shooting through the windows, the hiss of it meeting flame and ember, cascades of water running off the porch. The yard was drenched, the overflow pouring off the postage-stamp yard, over the low stone wall to the sidewalk, where it splattered and ran into the street.

Sully was steadily dictating to Tony, the man still on from the overnight shift, updating the story on the fly for the paper's nascent Web site.

"'The interior of Goodwin's home appeared to be austere and grim, with some sort of death chamber'—call it a '*macabre*,' Tony, '*macabre*,' death chamber—'in the basement. A hurried view of the premises this morning, just as the fire was breaking out, showed an upstairs bedroom with almost no furnishings other than a mattress on the floor and a tidily kept office.

"'The basement was decorated with grisly displays—pictures, mementos, items of clothing—of several dead women, their photographs in both life and death. The packed-dirt floor appeared to be a burial pit, partially obscured by floorboards and carpet. Recently turned earth showed the remains of what appeared to be human skeletal remains.'"

"Jesus."

"I know, right?"

"How the hell did you get in there?"

"Luck and nerve."

"What does that mean?"

"It means I was over here early and, Christ, there was fire coming out of the front window. Knew it was his place, ran up. Door was open. Went in to look for him."

"And found this."

"And found this."

"Was he in there?"

Sully paused, thinking.

"Not that I saw."

"And you're sure? I mean, you are fucking-A sure about the basement? The corpse?"

"I don't know how many times I can say it."

"Okay. I'm still going to couch it as it 'appeared' to be a body, 'appeared' to be this and that down there. Now. They're beating on me for an update. Gimme something on the scene outside."

"A couple hundred people, I'd say, top and bottom of the street. Two fire engines out here now. Looks to be just the one house going up. Tall, tall plume of smoke. Very black. Is Photo over here yet? And hey—so what is Chris getting from the cops about Doyle's location?"

"They think maybe he's inside."

"Yeah, well, he's a crispy critter if so. I'm sweating and I'm at the back of the barricade. I'll call you in a few when I know something else."

"Keep that phone in your hand."

Sully clicked off the cell and sat down, ignoring the damp pavement.

After a while, the flames began to die down, and then some more, and another fire engine came and put a third hose on the blaze, and soon the last of the flames were gone and a huge cloud of smoke was rising, ash filtering out into the air, gobs of roof caving in, the occasional sound of bottles exploding inside.

Warder Avenue was cleared and traffic began to move. Most of the crowd broke up. The street smelled bad, like burnt insulation, like waterlogged carpet.

Sully kept calling in updates, the story blowing up, R.J., Eddie, both calling him, asking him if he was absolutely sure about what he saw, if he was alright, that this was breaking all over the networks now, citing the paper as the sole source as to the interior of the house.

"Unbelievable," Eddie said, his voice thin down the line. "Just unbelievable. He just sat there, hiding in plain sight."

Sully called R.J. and asked him what the Reese camp was saying about the story. R.J. said, "They're holed up. Not even a denial."

Midmorning, Sully finally answered John Parker's calls and told him that what he had seen was in the paper and he didn't have anything to add. Parker said they would need a formal statement and Sully, as politely as possible, referred him to the paper's attorneys.

He stood at the top of the 700 block, less than fifty yards from Noel's apartment, maybe thirty from where Lana Escobar was found, six houses down from Rebekah Bolin's resting place.

It struck him that, for a navy man, Doyle didn't like to travel much.

A little after nine that night, and long after dark, paramedics in heavy fire gear finally came out of the house with what looked to be a body beneath a white sheet. It was loaded into an ambulance and it pulled away, lights flashing but no siren.

A few minutes later, a couple of patrol cars came up Warder, *whoop-whoop*ing to clear the traffic, and uniformed officers opened the barricade to let them and a small convoy of black SUVs pull inside. Once they were inside, the yellow tape and the rubber orange traffic cones were put back in place behind them. The mayor materialized out of one of the SUVs, and Sully spotted the chief waddling around in the middle of the block.

By then, there were more reporters than gawkers, dozens of them, from television stations and networks and cable channels, from newspapers, from magazines—everybody who had a bureau in Washington had a crew up here, the serial killer in the nation's capital. Metro was all over this in force, Chris staking out turf, two or three other young reporters asking and interviewing bystanders and making calls, Sully still out there just to call in the big picture or telling detail or whatever. He was standing off to himself, not in the mood to bullshit with the rest of them, his thoughts running in loops.

By ten twenty, with the eleven p.m. news looming, a police sergeant Sully didn't recognize told television crews to set up at the top end of the street for a presser, just inside the barricade. This set off a brief and unpleasant scrum. Print reporters howled until they were allowed to cross the barricade, too, standing just behind the cameras. A small forest of microphone stands blossomed on the pavement, floodlights beaming on the small patch of blacktop. A techie stood in front, holding a white rectangle of paper for a white balance, then stood behind the microphones for focusing.

Sully saw Chris interviewing people and then immediately calling it in.

For himself, he'd called in only a couple of bits of color in the past few hours, both from neighbors. One man, who lived three doors down from Doyle, said he'd been in bed with his back window open, said there were gunshots, plural, and then the fire boomed into sudden life. The other, a man in his sixties who lived directly across the street, said he was lying on the couch watching television when he heard a *bap*, one shot, looked over, and noticed that fire was already licking at the drapes inside Doyle's. Not two shots, he said. He was sure of it.

Sully was sure to call in the conflicting reports to the desk.

At five minutes after eleven, the chief, the mayor, the fire chief, the U.S. Attorney for the District, and a small group of racially diverse suits from Main Justice and the FBI stepped out of SUVs and patrol cars down the street, stood together, waiting for one more, and then approached the reporters together.

The group stopped about five yards from the microphones. The chief walked ahead and took the microphone; the rest formed a supporting line behind him.

"Good evening," the chief began. "I'm joined this evening by Mayor Barnes; U.S. Attorney Stanton Holmes; Chief Bolden of D.C. Fire; Agent Montgomery of the Federal Bureau of Investigation, U.S. Marshal Medford of the Judicial Security Division of the Marshals Service; and Paul Cavna, deputy director of the Justice Department."

The chief paused and looked back and forth across the lights arrayed in front of him, as if he were somberly taking in an audience, though Sully knew, from standing in front of such lights at such short distance himself, that you couldn't see a damned thing but glare.

"This morning, the city's fire department responded, at roughly 2:20 a.m., to several 911 calls of a fire in the 600 block of Princeton Place Northwest. This was preceded, by a few minutes, of calls reporting a possible gunshot or gunshots at or near the same location. The house in question was 673, the remains of which are behind me. Officers were unable to enter for several hours because of the blaze.

"The homeowner, Doyle Goodwin, who was, ah, he was a well-known and long-established member of this community, and owner of the market that bears his name just up the street there at Georgia. The remains of Mr. Goodwin were found in the front hallway. His body was very badly burned, let me say, but there was a gunshot wound in his right temple, passing through the skull."

There was a ripple of noise that ran through the reporters, a vague sigh, the lot of them scribbling while they held out their recorders, or perhaps the exhaled air came from the seventy or so onlookers, the hard-cores, who were stacked behind them.

"Mr. Goodwin . . . Mr. Goodwin lived alone. A pistol, with one shot fired, was near his right hand. Although the investigation is continuing, preliminary reports lean to suicide. There was no note found, but it may have been lost in the fire.

"The fire, Chief Bolden tells me—you're going to hear more from him in a minute, I'm not the expert—was clearly set. Accelerant found all over the first floor of the house, going up the stairs. It's our scenario—this is early, I want to emphasize, this may change—that Mr. Goodwin set the fire and then shot himself."

Here, he looked up. The man hated his job right now, Sully thought, and he didn't blame him.

"However, that is not all. Found in Mr. Goodwin's left hand was a necklace, a silver sort of charm necklace bearing the name 'Noel.' It has since been identified, by a family relative, as the cherished keepsake of Noel Pittman, whose body—"

—a louder ripple from the onlookers, a stifled cry—

"—buried in the basement of a dilapidated home behind Mr. Goodwin's store. Mr. Goodwin had been interviewed about that homicide, as well as that of Sarah Reese, but as a possible witness. He showed no signs of distress in those interviews. He was not, ah, a suspect of a material crime."

He sighed then, and let the final shoe go, played it out and put an end to it all.

"Finally, in the basement, which was only partially burned—very water damaged, but not badly burned—was some sort of—of burial ground, as you may have seen reported. I cannot go into details at this time, but I can say that there were what I would call mementos from several women who have been listed as missing or dying under mysterious circumstances. Our work into that is just beginning, but I can say that we have found at least one set of human remains in the basement, as yet unidentified, and we also found two items belonging to Sarah Emily Reese and an industrial type of serrated knife, which may be the murder—"

Whole shouts now, yells, gasps.

"—murder weapon in that homicide, which, as you know, took place just outside of Mr. Goodwin's store. The forensics tests will take a couple of days for final verification, but we believe that blood on that knife is likely to be a match to Sarah's for several reasons, not all of which am I at liberty to go into."

Silence now, total and astonished silence.

"There had been a confession in that case, as most of you know, and we will sort this out in the coming days, but at—at this moment we would expect the three suspects in that case to be released and most of their serious charges dropped. Obviously, we are just starting an investigation into Mr. Goodwin, and that will be an investigation that takes some time.

"I want to let the others speak to this very sad, very disturbing case, and I want to stress that our information is preliminary, but let me take at least a few questions now."

The dam burst. Shouts, yells, repeated questions, one clamoring over another, a final one floating in at the end of the others, and thus gaining clarity.

"—was there, right in front of you—how was he able to elude you for this long?"

"Probably because we weren't looking at him."

“Why weren’t you looking at him?” The shouted follow-up.

“Probably because one of the primary suspects, Reginald Jackson, confessed.”

“Why would Jackson confess if he didn’t do it?”

“I have no insight as to that.”

Full barking now, the media dogs were loose.

“Was Jackson coerced into that confession? Was that confession videotaped?”

“Why would Goodwin kill Sarah?”

“Will charges be filed against Judge Reese for failing to disclose his ties to Noel? Does that classify as obstruction of justice?”

“How many other bodies in that basement?”

“Will you resign?”

They came tumbling, end over end, one over the other, most not even expected to be answered, thrown out as an accusation, as an insult, as an indictment of police incompetence, stupidity, failure.

The chief held out both hands, palms down, looking like a man warming his hands by a fire.

“We’re not going to be able to answer all these tonight. Judge Reese, that’s a different issue. We haven’t had a chance to talk to him. We’ve only read the story in the newspaper today, but yes, that’s something we’ll want to talk to him about. Gasoline, I can tell you that. Gasoline was the accelerant. And no one in our custody was beaten or maltreated. I can tell you we were as surprised as anyone both by the things we found downstairs and by the fact we found them at all. Mr. Goodwin had been a helpful and forthcoming witness in our investigation in both cases.

“We have no idea as to motive. It may be we find that in the coming days, although the fire has pretty much destroyed Mr. Goodwin’s house and any evidence that might have been in it. I would guess that might be a reason for setting it, but I don’t know that. We had thought of him as helpful. We thought of him, until we walked in that house earlier today, as a victim in his own right of these murders and their consequences. He was, instead, it appears, the perpetrator, the man who killed both Sarah Reese and Noel Pittman, and several others.”

forty-three

Sully called in a couple of final grafs to Tony, the celebratory lap, the last touches. Tony had left, gone home, and come back again. He was taking feeds from who knows how many reporters. He keyed it in, asked some basic follow-ups, and then stopped.

"Just shipped it," he said, finally. "Done. Story's gone."

"I'm clear?"

"You're clear. One-A. Above the fold. Jesus, man. Two days in a row. Reese and now this."

R.J. was on the phone two minutes later, before Sully could even get to the bike.

"Boy. You boy, you *boy*. Just watched it on television. You were right. Brilliant. You told me you had a feeling about those women up there. You did. It was—I'm sitting on the couch next to El, I'm saying, 'It's Ruth calling his shot to center, this kid.'"

Sully let the feeling soak into him, the exhaustion, the end of the adrenaline spike.

"Thanks, amigo." He didn't know much else to say. "Reese? We ever hear anything on Reese?"

"You mean, other than he's dead to the Supremes, and possibly off the bench? You didn't see the punditry today. The Senate is making noises there'll be hearings."

"I meant corrections, denials."

"Not a peep."

Sully blew out his lips. "Well. Okay."

"So," R.J. said, "you know we're going to want you on this full-time for a while, the big picture about Goodwin, the women up there, the whole shebang. God only knows how many women he actually killed."

"It's going to be more than we know about right now."

"Yeah. Oh, yeah. And we'll want you on it."

"Can you let Chris do the wrap-up on the three suspects? I would imagine they'll get released tomorrow. There'll be a ton of stuff on that."

"You feeling bad about making him look like a punk?"

"Maybe a little. Speaking of punks, I haven't heard from Melissa today."

"Ahaha. Neither have I. She'll eat shit on this one, but she's not going anywhere. I'd smoke the peace pipe with her, I was you."

"Maybe."

Sully got to the bike, cranking it into life, unlocking the helmet, straddling it. He saw the glittering sign of the Show Bar two blocks down. Why not? he thought. Plop down in Doyle's old haunt, sit where he sat, look at what his twisted mind had looked at night after night.

"I'll see you tomorrow, R.J. I'm going to have a drink. Don't look for me before noon."

When he stopped the bike and got to the red front door of the strip club, he gave the man in a black suit ten dollars for the cover. The man ushered him inside, the music throbbing, the purple and red lights revolving. He started to put Sully at a table near the front until Sully motioned toward a booth at the back of the club, and the man took him there.

He got a gin and tonic and watched the show. After a while, Sly walked in. Sully had not spotted Lionel, but someone must have seen him and called the boss.

Sly walked to the booth, sat across from Sully. The waitress came and Sly took a Hennessy.

The dancer finished her routine. Scattered applause, maybe a dozen bills stuffed in the white garter adorning her right leg. She came around the room in a short white silk robe, propping a leg on each customer's chair to say hello, to let the robe fall open and allow them another view and to tuck more bills into the garter. Sully obliged with a five. Sly did not look at her and she left.

Sully watched the new woman onstage for a minute. He leaned toward Sly, semishouting to be heard over the music. "The necklace? In his hand?"

Sly kept his eyes on the dancer, sipped his cognac.

"Nice, hunh? Couldn't take a chance it getting lost in the fire."

"Where was it?"

"On a shelf down there, the basement. He had a whole lot of Noel shit."

"Hunh. Didn't see it. Didn't see anything from Sarah."

"You didn't look around in that back room. That was his—his what? His workshop. That's what it was. His workshop."

Sly put his drink down, popped a crick in his neck. He seemed upbeat, almost ebullient. Sully had never seen him like this before. It dawned on him that perhaps Sly was slightly drunk himself.

Now Sly leaned back over, shouting in his ear. "Coldhearted mother, got to give him that."

"Who? Doyle? How you mean?"

"How I mean? How you think I mean? I mean all that shit. Noel? Bitch that fine, dumping her ass in the basement, by his own store? Michelle, in his own house? Who does that? He probably did the Mexican girl just for practice. And the white girl, goddamn."

"Sarah," Sully said.

"What a white-girl name."

"Don't see a lot of white chicks named Keisha."

"You not getting racist over there," Sly said.

"It's just an observation about your observation."

"Yeah, well, my man fucking chokes *Sarah* and then cuts *Sarah's* throat after *Sarah's* goddamned dead. That's some sick shit, you wanna ask me. Why would a nigger do that?"

"Am I supposed to answer?"

The waitress came back and they both took another round. They watched the dancer onstage for a while without speaking. She put Sully in mind of Noel, a dancer herself, who was dead and buried at the hand of Doyle. Lorena, he thought. Today had to just be hell on her. It was too late to call now.

"Noel must have died the same way," Sully said, blinking back a sudden wave of nausea, an intense vision of her last moments of life, what she would have seen, heard, felt, sweeping over him. It had happened just a few hundred feet away.

"How you mean?"

"The knife. The throat."

"Hey, the fuck, you not going to be sick over there."

"No," he said, opening his eyes, his forehead clammy. "Just tired. And this damn railroad gin."

Sly nodded. "Girl's got skills," he said, looking at the stage, but the evening felt spent. After the girl finished and another came on, Sly rapped his glass twice on the table during the middle of the song, something by Rick James. He nodded to Sully, slid out of the booth, walked between the tables and out of the place, that slow lope, unhurried.

The liquor and the lack of food and the exhaustion settled into him now. He watched the spinning Donna Summer disco ball overhead. He felt like he weighed a million pounds. Standing up, getting out, it just felt impossible.

Three songs down and another dancer up, a thick light-skinned woman, not really his type. As he looked up at her stepping out of her short black satin cover-up and then spraying the mirror with Windex, it bounced into his embalmed brain that Sly said Sarah Reese's throat had been cut after she was dead.

Jason had told him that at the morgue. He had never used it. It had never gone public.

He blinked.

No. No no no no no no.

By 8:55 the next morning, he was outside the U.S. District Court clerk's office, rumpled, the same jeans and wrinkled shirt from the day before, reeking of cigarette smoke and spilled gin. His mouth tasted like the floor of an adult-movie theater. He had not slept.

In the courthouse hallway, he waited for the clerk's office to open. Sitting on a leather-upholstered bench, he chewed on the cuticle of his left ring finger.

At 9:01 someone opened the door and he bolted upright and walked to the public-access computer terminals.

"David Reese," he punched into the computer's case program, putting the name into the box for "Presiding Judge" and limiting the search to cases within the past three years. He clicked on the drop-down button to have the results displayed in alphabetical order by defendant. The array of cases came up a few seconds later.

The lawyer's name flagged it first.

Kaufman, Avram.

His spine curled inward and he slumped as if the air were being let out of him.

The case had gone into Reese's court for trial April 3, 1998, a year and a half earlier. The defendant's name was Nikki Jacqueline Phillips. Sly Hastings's sister, or half sister, to be precise, as Sly had told him back when this started. She was managing his rental properties for him. Nikki worked at D.C. Housing Authority, the pleadings said. Of course. How else would she have learned how to manage her half brother's low-rent places?

Nikki had been up on charges of kickbacks from a contractor on a city contract, something like $238,000. There had been a motion to dismiss, and Reese rejected it. She'd been convicted on four of five charges. Reese sentenced her at the top of the guidelines, even more than the prosecution had asked for, on August 18.

Six weeks before his daughter was murdered.

Sully, too late now, remembering, *I got that he was one of those Southern crackers from the accent, the time I heard him in court.*

Staring at the screen, legs pumping under the desk.

Sly's sister, his most precious asset in laundering his money, had gotten busted. He had looked for ways to get her out and free and back to work ("Nikki, she's been distracted") and that would have led him to any number of sources—and what do you know, the presiding judge's daughter was taking classes in Sly's backyard.

His legs stopped pumping.

Sly wouldn't have had to go downtown to get to the judge. Just get to him at his most vulnerable, when he was dropping off his daughter, then going to see his mistress. Just sit with Lionel, watching him come drop off Sarah on a Saturday morning . . . and, lo and behold, up the sidewalk he went to Noel's apartment, the one place where the judge would be certain not to have a trailing security detail. What a gift this was to a man like Sly.

He could see it, clear as day, the judge coming out of Noel's. Sly and Lionel getting out of the Camaro, falling in step beside him, one on either side, *Say, Judge Reese, we need to talk about this misunderstanding with my sister . . . Nobody'd want pictures of you in there with Noel getting around, right, sure, nobody wants anything to happen to a pretty thing like her . . .*

But if this was the mild first step offered, it had not been taken. Reese had not dismissed the case.

That led to step two, and it opened so beautifully that Sully shook his head in equal parts admiration and disgust. Of course Sly would have known about Doyle. How could the warlord of the neighborhood not have? Doyle was perfect for Sly's darker purposes—a patsy with a penchant for prostitutes and strangling them, right in his backyard. He made a perfect fall guy for any hit Sly needed to carry out.

So Sly or Lionel (or both) killed Noel, dumping her in the basement of the house behind Doyle's Market, matching the man's MO. Her disappearance was a mystery to everyone except its intended audience—David Reese. It hadn't worked, though. The judge, thinking he was Texas-tough, flexed back at sentencing, hitting Nikki with the max, still not knowing the depths of Sly Hastings.

And so the killshot, the message back to Reese: Sly's street soldiers, them three, follow Sarah into the store, spook her out the back. Sly waiting, Lionel waiting, one or both.

And then the cover story, Sly playing him like a violin.

Who told him the three suspects weren't guilty, spurring him to look into the idea of a serial killer? Who delivered Lana Escobar's stepfather? Sly had. Sully, properly fed, had put a story in the paper about the possibility of a serial killer. That story, the community meeting, the cops looking at it all again—it had not only opened an investigation, but it had also flushed Doyle. That had resulted in Sly's lucky break, an unexpected bonus: Doyle outing the judge to Sully for his own reasons, panicking, trying to divert the sudden attention.

And then it had all been downhill. Who took him to Mommy, who told him what she'd been told to say, with a little theater thrown in? Who delivered the story about the nameless hooker miraculously seeing Michelle and Doyle in the back office? Who put Noel's necklace in Doyle's hand? Where did the knife from Sarah's murder come from?

Bring the stuff. Them gas cans, too.

He closed his eyes against another wave of nausea, the bile in his gut churning, and suddenly he was back at lunch with Eva, back at Stoney's on the first of October. She had told him. She had told him as clear as day. *He gets rid of people who get in the way of him running things, and then he skates on it.*

And what was Sully, an accomplice to the murder of Doyle Goodwin, ever going to do about it?

"Goddamn," Sully said, closing his eyes, rubbing them, and the court clerk looked up from behind the counter. "Just godfuckingdamn."

The clerk rapped the counter, frowning.

"Language," she said.

epilogue

Mom's Place was more of a three-walled shed at the back end of a parking lot than it was a florist's, but it was adjacent to the cemetery and the prices were reasonable. Across the open front of the shed, there were heavy plastic sheets that unfurled to keep out the wind and cold, and most of them were down when Sully pulled in. It was late November. The wind was up and rain was threatening. He bought a bouquet of bright gerber daisies, yellow and red and orange and white, wrapped in clear red plastic.

"These for next door?" Skinny kid, tall, bored behind the register.

"Yeah."

"Trim them?"

"Why not."

"Spray for the deer?"

"While you're at it."

The bike took him back through the cemetery, the flowers between the fuel tank and his hips, and he let it idle past the graves and the stones and the JACKSONS and the STEVENS and the CHANGS and the MARTINS.

Noel Pittman's grave had only a flat marker. It took him a few minutes to find.

PITTMAN, NOEL ANGELIQUE
Sept. 30, 1972–April 25, 1998
Loved and Missed

There were two small metal vases set into circular rings on either side of the slab. He pulled a vase out of a ring on the right side and took it over to a spigot set by the white wooden-railed fence that set off the roadway from the grounds. The water was cold, clear. He shook his hands to dry them.

The car topped the rise when he was halfway back to the grave. It slowed and stopped. Sully pulled the flowers from their plastic wrapping and set them in the little vase, and then set it back in its holder. He adjusted the flowers so that they didn't list to one side.

"They're beautiful," Lorena called out.

He half turned and saw her. She was two steps out of the car, alone on the landscape, just the two of them, and the bouquet she was holding, a spray of red and white roses with carnations and baby's breath tucked in the greenery, spread out from a light green wrapping. It was huge, something from a proper florist.

He slumped on his good leg as she came over to him. "You're making me look bad," he said, knowing her just well enough to put an ironic spin on it.

"Well, I didn't know you were coming."

"Ditto."

She took his flowers from the vase, and mixed his in with hers, divided them into two smaller batches, and placed them in the vases on each side of the marker. She stepped back and they considered the effect. Neither of them said anything. The silence stretched out.

"You come out here a lot?" he said into the breeze, finally

"Two or three times a week. You?"

"The holiday, you know, I guess."

She nodded. They stood, silent again, looking at the marker and the flowers. The sky was gunmetal gray, the breeze in the limbs making a soft rustling noise, the traffic too far away to be heard.

"I don't think I ever said thank you," she said.

Thanks? Thanks for what? Jesus, the things people said.

"What will you do now?" he said, ignoring it. "Now that this, well, this part of it, anyway, is over."

"I was thinking of getting away for a while," she said. "Go back home maybe, for a week or two over Christmas. See some family. Reconnect with the old country. I don't know."

"Negril? It's beautiful," he said. "Those cliffs, the volcanic things. Stayed there one time at a place where you could jump right off the edge into the ocean."

"The Xtabi," she said. "Where they filmed—"

"*Papillon*," he said.

She looked up at him and smiled. It was the first time he had ever seen her do so without some sort of irony or skepticism or anger, and he was surprised at how pretty she was, at how radiant.

"Didn't know you were a movie fan," she said.

"We didn't really get a chance to talk." He smiled.

She was gone a few minutes later, the car backing out and disappearing over the rise, a tap on the brake lights and then he was alone again.

He was looking down at the marker, letting his thoughts blow around to whatever they settled on. Trees at the edge of the cemetery, the pines and a few hardwoods, the oaks and maples, a small stand surrounding a narrow creek if not more properly called a ditch, three-story apartment blocks and a crappy grocery store with a parking lot on the other side, low-rise, low-income, discount-market suburban America.

"I think this is it, Noel," he said, finally. "I don't imagine I'll be back. I didn't fix anything for you. I didn't get the right guy. I tried. I'm sorry."

He walked back to the bike, the wind ruffling his hair.

Late in the afternoon, Stoney's was almost empty, a lazy Sunday, the evening settling in, the lights spilling out onto the patio. There was a murmur of voices, the television above the bar showing the West Coast game, the Raiders and Broncos, the sound on low.

Sully sat with Eva in their regular booth, a half-finished grilled cheese in front of him. Eva was playing with her salad. She was drinking white wine, maybe her third glass, her manner a little looser. Sully kept stealing looks at the bar, to where Dmitri was cleaning glasses with a towel and watching the game. The Broncos converted a third and four, just past midfield.

After a while, Eva said, "Dmitri said she quit. You can stop looking."

Sully dropped his gaze and looked over at her, tilting his head, a jab he hadn't seen coming. "What do you know about it?"

"Enough." Steady, not even tipsy.

"And what's enough, lady?"

"You're not, Sully—you're not the only one who knows secrets."

He paused, waiting to see if she was going to add something, about Dusty, which is what she was talking about, or about Sly, which is possibly what she meant. Their eyes held. She didn't add anything, but he could not determine if the silence implied an innocence of knowledge or a tactical omission.

"Isn't it convenient Doyle killed himself?" she said.

"Not for him."

"For everybody else."

He saw the sudden flicker in her eye, nothing more, some fleck of the pupil that flashed and was gone. The door is open. I think but I don't know. Tell me. Tell me what you know. He held her eyes but did not give any acknowledgment something had passed between them. No, he thought. I'll take care of it my way.

"You ever get tired of all this?" he asked, finally, breaking the gaze, gesturing in the air with his glass, a roll of the wrist.

"This?"

"Yeah, this. All this shit. The assholes and the shooters and the half-assed cops and the coke and the ganja and the general lack of intelligence or productive thought and, every goddamned day, more hustles, more stiffs, more vics, more rapes, more robberies."

"Well," she said.

"We operate in the goddamned margins."

"I don't know about that," she said. "I think it means something. It almost goes to the eternal."

"Jesus H."

"No, listen. Sometimes I don't think my decedents are even really all that dead. Sometimes it seems like they're right there in the next room, or they're going to come around the corner and their mom or dad or their cousin or girlfriend or whoever will go, 'Oh, hey, sorry, there he is now.' Like it was all a bad dream, the time they got the call, the police."

"Hunh," he said.

"I can hear them talk at night sometimes, you know? They talk and talk but it's not like anything you can understand, it's like a conversation in the next room. Mumbles and phrases, nothing distinct, and then I fall asleep."

She paused. Sully was looking at his drink.

"Hey, you. Any of this make sense? You know what I mean?"

Sully Carter looked out of the front entrance of the saloon, the twin doors flung open, a little of the last light of day falling inside onto the tile floor, making a skewed rectangle. Leaves blew up on the street and one fluttered upward, in a lazy looping circle, and then it came sailing downward, sliding just inside the door. It stopped in the rectangle of light. It was brown, brittle, lifeless, and the image of Nadia's grave four thousand miles away blossomed before him, her body entombed in a casket on a wooded hillside, deep in the earth, the freezing silence of winter descending. He thought of her body again, warm in the bed beside him, the white sheets, her tanned brown skin, the scent of her body, her breasts against his chest, her leg draped over his, Nadia, warm, breathing, sleeping, safe, his.

"Yeah," he said. "Yeah, I do."

acknowledgments

The fin de siècle Washington, D.C., in this book is a representation of the time and place itself, but it is not intended to be an exact duplicate. I have taken the occasional liberty with geography and timelines and events.

Most notably, there was a serial killer at work in and along Princeton Place in the late 1990s, and those crimes were slow to attract police attention. However, this novel uses those events as an inspiration, not as a factual guide, and there is no tie between any of the persons involved and the fictional characters herein. For more on the Princeton Place murders, please see www.neelytucker.com.

In helping establish certain police details, I am indebted to MPD detective Danny Whalen, who was instrumental in solving those killings. Former assistant U.S. attorney June Jeffries prosecuted homicide and sex crimes for a quarter century in the District and patiently answered many queries about the intricacies of that line of work. Connie Ogle and Michael Cavna read the manuscript and cleaned up details.

But mostly, this book would not exist without the efforts of five wonderful women.

I am very lucky to be married to the first, Carol Josephine Tucker, who believed in this project when it was a gauzy sort of idea, and who created the time and space for me to develop it into the thing now in your hands. (Also, editing. She excels at politely telling you that your brilliant late-night inspiration, that stunning literary passage not equaled in our time, does, in fact, suck.)

The second is one of the free world's great literary agents, Elyse Cheney, who signed on before the first page was written. She worked through drafts, editing with a sense of patience and perspective, before representing this book as well as it can be done.

Lynn Medford, my very most wonderful boss at the *Post,* supported this project in ways large and small. She sneezes better than anybody.

Allison Lorentzen, my editor at Viking, turned this from manuscript to finished book, making sure everything was in its final place, adding good edits, grace notes, and enthusiasm.

And fifth and finally is Elizabeth Tucker, my mother, who read me books when I was a child, took me to the library over and over again, and, intentionally or not, instilled in me the sense that stories are how we make sense of the world.

I am blessed among men.

Neely Tucker's latest Sully Carter novel is available from Viking.

Read on for the first chapter of

ONE

SULLY CARTER HAD a pleasant little bourbon buzz going. It was a fine afternoon in the first spring of the twenty-first century. He'd been out on a fast boat in the Washington Channel, taking in the sunshine and the brisk spring breeze and the view of the dead body being pulled from the water. It was all pretty cool and mellow until he decided to go over to Frenchman's Bend and see if that's where the guy got popped.

A little after two in the afternoon, maybe four hours and change before deadline. Stillness. The wind tickling his ears, the sound of water slapping. Closed his eyes and the world was a warm yellow light behind his eyelids. Opening them again, it was almost . . . peaceful. He was walking past the first trees of the Bend, the buds tight along the branches, the faint scent of brackish water in his face, when he saw two enforcers for the drug crew that ran the place coming out of the apartment block to his right.

They let him pass, the little fuckers, let him walk deeper into the park, out toward the open grassy knob that stuck out into the channel like a thumb, and now they were sliding in behind him, cutting off his retreat. He did not have a clear view of either. The shorter figure came in behind him off his right, a too-big hoodie draped over his head. The other, taller, faster, but not in any real hurry, peeled off behind him toward the brick-wall boundary with Fort McNair, coming in off his left.

He could not hear them but didn't expect to, what with the wind in his face. Their appearance wasn't unexpected—it was the Bend, after all—but there was going to be some shit. There was going to be some shit now. Slowing his gimp-legged walk, dangling the motorcycle helmet from his right hand, the cycle jacket unzipped and open, doing his best white-man-without-a-clue impersonation. Under his breath, he swore at himself for getting involved in this two-bit homicide because now it was going to screw the entire day. He felt, somewhere behind his eyes, the bourbon beginning to burn off, his senses coming alive, calculating the moves of the men behind him without acknowledging their existence.

This was how your day went south without even trying. :

He'd been having lunch with Dave Roberts and his crew from WCJT, having a gentleman's drink or three at the Cantina Marina, on the waterfront. Dave got a call from the station about tourist boats shrieking to 911 that they'd seen a body floating in the waves. Good people from Iowa come to take a tour of your nation's capital, starting out from the marina in Southwest D.C., just a few hundred yards from the cherry blossoms at the Tidal Basin, then heading down to Mount Vernon, George Washington's place, for a picnic lunch. Then bam, they get a view of how the other half lives. The body was floating just off the tip of Hains Point, at the confluence of the Potomac and the Anacostia, not even three-quarters of a mile from the marina.

The station rented a boat on the fly; Sully bummed a ride because, hell, it sounded like fun. A quick story for the paper and away they went, roaring out into the channel, all boys, giggling that this was a three-hour tour *a three-hour tour,* the camera man swaying, trying to get steady B-roll.

Two police department launches were already out there, the station's boat skittering beyond them so that the camera guy could shoot back toward the city as a backdrop. The body was floating like a cork in a bathtub, tangled up with a clutch of driftwood. The police techs got a net under it and then the winch on the launch's crane creaked. The net pulled the body up and up until it was in the air, water pouring, long thick hair, dreadlocks falling away from the skull, the corpse in jeans and a jacket of some sort and one shoe. It lay there like a dead cod pulled off the bottom.

"What do you know, we just made the six o'clock," Dave said.

The camera guy spread his feet and the camera whirred, getting the focus tight, pulling the body into clarity. The police boats had a lot of guys in sunglasses and Windbreakers with DC MPD on the back. Dave talking to the camera guy, "You got the Monument in the background?"

"The money shot," the man said, nodding.

Cops crowded around the corpse and after a few minutes the huddle broke up. Lt. John Parker, the chief of D.C. Homicide, emerged, walking to the rail, hands on his hips, feet at the width of his shoulders, sunglasses, and a blue-and-black Windbreaker over his suit, glaring at them like they were walking on his lawn.

"Hey John," Dave called out, cupping his hands into a megaphone. "Any ID on floater man?"

"That thing off?" John yelled back, rolling a hand toward the camera, shades still down, that hard-ass cop look he had.

Dave sighed and nodded and the cameraman flicked the camera off and set it by his feet. The boats idled closer, pulling alongside, the sun splashing on John's bald head, his sunglasses.

"All off the record," John said, "and I mean, I don't want to hear 'police sources say,' 'a source familiar with the investigation,' no shit like that. All y'all hear?"

Everybody on the boat on the forward rail, leaning to hear him, nodded: Dave, the former Redskins linebacker turned local news personality; Sully, the alleged hotshot for one of the nation's great newspapers, nodding, yeah, yeah, whatever.

"No I.D., no name," John said.

"Courageous , taking that sort of bombshell off the record," Dave said.

"Was he still recognizable?" Sully chipped in.

"Mostly," John said.

"What does that mean?"

"He still had a face."

"Jesus," said Dave.

"Fish, shrimp, crabs get after them when they been in a couple of days," John said, "so I'm guessing our guy was a recent entry."

"Cause of death?" This was Sully.

"I'm just a homicide cop, and I just got my body five minutes ago, but I'm going to go out on a limb here and say the extra hole in his head, entry at his left temple, exit on his right, contributed."

"That's actually two extra holes," Sully said.

"Thank you, Pocahontas," John said.

"The head shot is on or off the record?"

"Did I stutter?"

"Theories?"

"Drugs, guns, pussy, turf," John said. "Take your pick. Brothers get popped like clockwork around here and you asking me, without so much as an ID, a motive?"

John was somewhere between irritated and angry, so when Dave said they were going to need to back the boat off and shoot some more B-roll, Sully. just shrugged. He'd ask John more later, after the autopsy, in private, when he'd cooled off. The boats pushed back and the camera guy went back to filming the police boats at a distance.

Sully killed time by studying the D.C. waterline, about four hundred yards to the north, already having a pretty good hunch where this particular corpse would have come from, and no doubt John Parker did, too—Frenchman's Bend, which bellied out into the water like a limp dick, like a mini-Florida, about a half mile back up the channel. It was a bullshit city park, scrubby grass and beat-to-shit trees, sitting right before the pencil-thin strand of Southwest D.C. gave way to the brick walls and manicured lawns of Fort McNair, the small U.S. Army base that ran to the end of the peninsula.

From his vantage point, the fort's long row of precisely spaced waterfront houses seemed so close that you could almost tell if the drapes were pulled. The jonquils and tulips and pansies and begonias were coming up around the porches. The flowers were planted at each house in the same pattern. The exacting nature of this arrangement, replicated at house after house, made the fort appear monotonous if not robotic. And yet it was those startling bursts of red and yellow and pink and white that made the protruding knob of the Bend so identifiable and desolate by comparison: brown dirt and weeds too dumb to die and scraps of paper and brightly colored plastic bags, trash flitting across the scrub. No wonder there was a seven-foot brick wall running between the fort and the neighborhood.

The Bend, meanwhile, wasn't on any tourist map and was scarcely acknowledged by the city itself. It had been the District's most notorious antebellum slave market, its chattel packed into long-gone wooden pens, slaves brought from the farms lining the Potomac or the Anacostia, put on a platform, and sold off onto ships bound for cotton plantations down south. It had opened long before Washington was the capital but stayed in business for decades, the shame of the city, slaves force-marched through the streets in neck shackles.

Its stigma was so great that the land had never been built upon, not in the late nineteenth century when Southwest was a working-class address of the Irish and Germans, not later when it became a warren of blacks and Jews, not even in the post–World War II razing and building boom in that quadrant of the city.

For the past thirty years, it had been a yellowish scab, a drug park run by one crew or another, and nobody really seemed to give a good goddamn. If Sully hadn't been raised in Louisiana, an entire state of a yellowish scab still haunted by slavery, he might have thought the Bend was poisoned or cursed or defiled, a city block of malignant soil so infected that it seeped into the souls of the living.

Now, twenty minutes after Dave had dropped him back at the dock, Sully was walking across this sorry expanse of real estate, seeing if there was anything that passed for a connection to the body in the water. The giddy high of the bourbon and fucking around with Dave's crew was fading into a headache and a slow burn. John Parker was right. This was going to turn out to be another drug shooting in a city that had averaged almost a homicide every day of every week of every month, all year round. For John, that likely meant another unsolved killing. For Sully, it translated as a fuckall story that was going to take too long and add up to not much.

He stopped a few feet from the water. He slid the backpack off his left shoulder, pulled the notebook out of the backpack, and then reached around inside it, looking for a pen. When he found one, he set the helmet and the backpack down, flipped open the notebook, and started writing down the basics of the park. No relevant details as to floater man jumped out at him, but he was after scenery, not specifics. The main atmospheric—the big picture that gave the place its sense of foreboding, even in the daylight—was the dearth of anything anyone would want. Across the channel at Hains Point, East Potomac Park looked like an emerald idyll, bike paths and the golf course and manicured roads. Over here, on the wrong side of the water, it was all packed dirt and broken glass and the hard hustle.

"Not buying," he said loudly, still writing, not looking up.

The footsteps behind him paused, then resumed and stopped again. He kept writing, idle observations about the desolation of the place and the meanness it gave off, like the scent of blood in a coroner's office. He had been here once or twice at night on crime scenes and thought it depressing and mean. The fresh spring disinfectant of daylight and a good breeze didn't do much for it.

"Working on a story," he said, still writing, but turning around, "about this guy who wound up in the channel last night? Shot in the head."

He looked up. Didn't recognize either of them. Foot soldiers. It wasn't like the Hall brothers, the identical twins who ran this turf, would stoop to checking out the loco paleface wandering into the Bend in the middle of the afternoon.

The one on his left, he dubbed him Short Stuff, the hoodie still pulled over his head. That tall drink of water on the right, he'd go with Lanky Dreads as a nickname, at least for now. They both had their hands in their pockets and regarded him with the dull, flat glares that a nobody like him warranted.

"Probably military," Sully continued, making it up as he went, selling it, gesturing off to his right, "from the fort? But it turns out you can't get in there. So I stopped off here to look around."

He'd never been to the fort in his life and had no idea of the entrance requirements, and he was guessing the same applied to these two half-wits, so it wasn't like they were going to be reciting U.S. military protocol to him.

"Man dead in the channel?" This was Short Stuff, his voice deeper than Sully would have thought, and he moved his guess on the man's age from eighteen to twenty.

Sully nodded, yeah yeah, sure.

"White man?"

"Nah."

"You police?"

A shake of the head. "Reporter."

Lanky Dreads, the tall one on his right, shifted his weight to his back foot, eyeing him, Sully recognizing the long gaze on the scars. Then Lanky Dreads said, "The fuck's with your face?" his voice raspy, like a grate, like somebody sandblasted his vocal cords when he was three. Short Stuff laughed. It sounded like a bark.

"It's a shrapnel tattoo," Sully said.

"It looks like shit."

"Good thing I got it for free."

The same dude, flicking a wrist forward at him. "Whyn't you walk right?"

"Same shrapnel."

"It hurt a lot?"

"Until I passed out."

"You military?" This was Lanky Dreads again, but Short Stuff flicked a glance over at his partner, irritated, not hiding it.

"Nope," Sully said, cutting his eyes between them, trying to figure out who was in charge. "Reporter, like I said. I was in Bosnia. The paper? Sent me over there. They had a war going on. I got blown up."

"They get the guy?"

"What guy?"

"That fucked you up."

"It was a grenade. There wasn't any guy to get."

"So why you down here?"

"Curious," said Short Stuff, flicking that glance at his partner again, "cut that shit out."

Lanky Dreads blinked, three, four, five-six-seven times, like he was processing the interruption, but he did not take his gaze from Sully. "Brothers get capped on the block all the time," he said, defensive, like he was justifying the line of inquiry. "Ain't no reporters show up."

Sully shifted his weight, time getting short. You could only talk to dickheads like this for so long before it got ugly, and the clock was about to strike half past. "I already done said. This dude floating out there in the channel? Had six holes in his head instead of the usual five. Seven, you want to count the exit wound. Tourist boat spotted him riding the waves, they freaked, so now it's all over television. Police? They figure he's military, went in the water off the fort over there. Turns out you got to have a pass to get in. Which I don't got. Like I said."

"Whyn't you think he didn't fall off a yacht?" *Yat.*

"'Cause that's not what MPD thinks."

Short Stuff snorted like he was about to hawk up a wad. "Like they know shit."

"John Parker," Sully said, cutting his gaze back to Shorty. "When I say MPD? I'm meaning John Parker."

He threw the name out there—the head of D.C. Homicide—to show he wasn't a fuckhead, right, and to see if they knew the name, to get a gauge of what level of the crew he was dealing with. Short Stuff clocked his head a quarter turn.

"Hey, Parker? *John* Parker? Hey, fuck him, fuck you," he said. "You know where you at, fool?"

"The Bend."

"Then you ought to fucking know better."

"So you saying you didn't see nobody down here last night, picking up a couple dime bags? Gunshots? Nothing?"

The two didn't speak or look at one another. But Lanky Dreads blinked again—three, four times, bap bap, just like that—and it gave Sully the idea that maybe Lanky didn't have the heart for what had gone down. That was all the confirmation he needed.

"MPD been down here?" Sully said, putting the top back on the pen, flipping the notebook shut. Short Stuff and Lanky were ten feet away, standing maybe three feet apart, between him and the rest of the park.

"Parker's your bitch," Short Stuff said. "Ask him." *Axt.*

Sully nodded, a half smile, not putting much into it. "Well. Yeah. So." He picked up the helmet and backpack, moving forward, right between them because going around would have been giving ground and if you flinched, hunched over, slowed, showed any sign of deference, they'd beat your ass into the dirt for being that weak. It was the same everywhere you went. Bosnia, Somalia, South Africa, Lebanon, the Bend. Dudes, half-cocked.

He got within two steps of them and Lanky said, "That your Ducati at the curb?" Sully got the smell of sweat, of flesh, of ganja, of closed rooms and broken mirrors and moldy carpet, the smell and feel of the projects.

"The 916. Yeah."

"Bring that out to the Cove. Run you for pinks."

Sully worked up a cough, laughing, the you-gotta-be-kidding-me thing, turning his shoulders to edge through, making sure he didn't bump either one of them. "For *pinks?* Nah, nah, you ride what, I'm guessing here, a 'Busa?" he said. "And it's an eleven-second bike in the quarter, some shit like that?"

"Ten-eight."

He was past them now, walking backward, keeping eye contact, keeping it light. "Doubt that. But the Duc ain't a straight-line bike. I'd be looking at your ass the last two hundred."

"Reporter man?" This from Short Stuff.

Sully kept walking backward, not slowing down but not going any faster than he had to, either, and now he switched his gaze to acknowledge who was talking. Short Stuff had shucked his piece down into his hand, which was now out of his jacket pocket, flat against his leg.

"Stop walking."

"I'm on deadline."

"I say stop walking."

Sully, still moving, looked at his watch, looked up and smiled. "I got an hour and fifteen. And I got to—"

Short Stuff flipped the pistol forward and brought it level, pointed sideways, gangster chic, aiming at Sully's chest.

Sully stopped, still smiling, but raising his eyebrows, giving the man the respect he wanted. He brought his hands up a hey-you-got-me motion. "Okay. What? What are we talking about here?"

"Don't be bringing that broke-ass bike back down here, 'less you want to float yourself. You feel me?"

"Yeah. I do. Yeah. Okay? I hear you. But you got to know MPD's gonna come down here in a couple hours, start sweating you, the Hall brothers, everybody? You know that, right? That throwing the dude in the channel didn't fool anybody with a double-digit IQ?"

Short Stuff brought his chin up. "Thought you said they made the floater for military. From the fort. Over there."

Sully, giving him that same shrug, moving backward again. "Me, myself? I don't trust MPD for shit."